DAUGHTERS BEYOND COMMAND

Véronique Olmi

DAUGHTERS BEYOND COMMAND

Translated from the French
by Alison Anderson

Europa
editions

Europa Editions
27 Union Square West, Suite 302
New York, NY 10003
www.europaeditions.com
info@europaeditions.com

First publication 2022 by Europa Editions

Translation by Alison Anderson
Original title: *Les évasions particulières*

Library of Congress Cataloging in Publication Data is available
ISBN 978-1-60945-790-7

Olmi, Véronique
Daughters Beyond Command

Art direction by Emanuele Ragnisco
instagram.com/emanueleragnisco

Cover design and image by Ginevra Rapisardi

Original cover photo: Pexels

Prepress by Grafica Punto Print – Rome

Printed in the USA

CONTENTS

For Bonnie

DAUGHTERS BEYOND COMMAND

Come gather 'round people
Wherever you roam
And admit that the waters
Around you have grown
And accept it that soon
You'll be drenched to the bone
If your time to you is worth savin'
And you better start swimmin'
Or you'll sink like a stone
For the times they are a-changin'
—BOB DYLAN

I
All Together They Were Someone

Hélène was arriving from another world. She was on her way home, with her suitcase and her new red slicker, with its matching rain hat; she was different, she stood out. She liked wearing the slicker, the scrunchy sound the fabric made when she sat down, the smell of it, slightly chemical and sour, its bright red color. It protected her from the rain when she was living at her uncle's in Neuilly, and from the mistral wind when she went home to her father's in Aix-en-Provence. It was 1970, end of summer, she'd been going back and forth now for eight years, between luxury in Neuilly and simplicity in Aix, and she didn't question the situation, she just lived with it. She adapted. She was eleven years old.

During the week, the arrivals hall at Marignane airport was deserted. Her father came to get her, and this man who had never been on a plane waited apprehensively, then saw her from a distance in her red slicker, often the only child in the sudden flow of adults, most of them businessmen. Around her neck was a sign with her name on it, "Hélène Malivieri," but unlike when she was younger, she no longer had to hold hands with one of the stewardesses, who all looked like Françoise Dorléac and went up to her father with their look of emancipation and piquant sensuality. He would show them his ID, which he'd already gotten out, and kiss his daughter with restraint. He longed to take her in his arms. He didn't. She was returning from a world he felt excluded from, and in this arrivals hall, this vast space with its luxury advertising depicting enraptured couples touting perfumes and countries he had no interest in, he would not allow himself any displays of tenderness. He was anxious. Slightly self-conscious. His daughter, in this place conceived for affluent people—would they really hand her over to him personally, to him and no one else? He'd been offended the one time when the stewardess didn't ask him for his papers, his ID card proving he was her father.

"You would let my daughter go off with a complete stranger?"

"But Monsieur, she threw her arms around you!"

"So?"

His aggressive stance toward this stewardess capable of entrusting his daughter to a stranger was one of the rare times Hélène saw her father lose his temper with a woman, but it was not that surprising he'd betrayed his anxiety to this stewardess, for the moment she let go of Hélène's hand, she abruptly erased weeks of separation. The two men Hélène lived with in turns had nothing in common other than the fact they had each married a Richert daughter. Bruno, Hélène's father, was a teacher in a private school, the youngest in a family of two girls and five boys, who, like him, set aside part of their salary every month to absorb the enormous debts of their father, François Malivieri; after the war he'd invented and marketed folding trailers and, unfortunately, they did not unfold. David, Hélène's uncle, had started importing a major camera brand from Japan, and was the son of the Swiss banker Franz Tavel. He was a man of means, with a brilliant career. The father of two boys, he loved Hélène like a daughter, the one he'd never had, and ever since she'd turned three and could travel unaccompanied, he'd been asking her to come and stay during school vacations and the three summer months, sometimes more, when he decided he missed her too much and made her skip the last days of school, "which are pointless anyway." Every month, he sent Bruno a check, financial assistance that Bruno accepted with painful humility, and part of which he made over to his bankrupt father.

In the Simca 1000 taking them from the airport, Bruno didn't ask Hélène how things had gone *there.* She had just got back from her rich relatives; he lived in La Petite Chartreuse, at the edge of the city center, and while the family didn't want for anything, it did seem like there was a lot that they made do without. Life in their apartment was simple, almost austere: the walls bare of paintings smelled of wallpaper glue, and there was so little furniture that their voices echoed, as if the family had just moved in or were getting ready to leave again.

On the way home, with her red hat on her lap, Hélène looked through the window at these landscapes she had missed—the raw pine forests under the all-consuming blue of the sky; she let this landscape paper over the one she had just left. She would find her place again among her siblings, between Sabine the eldest and Mariette the youngest: her place in the middle, which supported her, as if she were lying between her two sisters in a narrow bed, protected by their closeness.

Once Hélène was home, Sabine opened her suitcase. No sooner had she carried it to their room than her sister was inspecting and touching everything Hélène had brought back: new clothes that no one had worn before her, and which had been picked out and purchased to suit her, and not to be worn by one younger sister after the other, for years. You couldn't see the hems on the dresses; they hadn't been altered over time. The sleeves were neither too short nor hastily rolled up, and, as she unfolded the new garments, Sabine could understand the expression, *it fits perfectly.* Neatly folded, the collars buttoned and the sleeves folded behind, with the little cuffs laid flat, they were like obedient little animals waiting to be let out into the great outdoors.

"Gosh, this is pretty . . . can you wear it every day?"

"Well, sure."

"You wear it to town?"

"To town?"

"I mean, in Paris."

"Yes. In Paris, in Neuilly, in Normandy, too."

"You go horseback riding in these clothes?"

"I go horseback riding in trousers, she didn't buy me any new trousers."

"Can I try this dress on?"

Sabine put on the dress, it was too small for her. She turned this way and that, taking tiny steps as she looked at herself in the mirror on the wardrobe, smiling as if the dress *fit perfectly*, appreciating the look of the new fabric, with colors as pure as a summer morning. At fourteen, she had a solid body, generous curves, and a face that had too much character for her liking. She admired Audrey Hepburn's slim figure, her lively, defiant personality. She envied girls who seemed to have a natural style, girls who looked good in anything, not just in their clothing, but in their lives as well, a life they had chosen and could wear gracefully. Hélène watched Sabine, afraid the seams might burst, but she didn't say anything. She had missed her so much that at the Galeries Lafayette her eyes had filled with tears when she saw two sisters amusing themselves trying on a pair of gloves. Hearing them laugh made her sad, and her solitude gave her a confused feeling of insignificance. Her aunt Michelle often took her to the big department stores—endless days spent as if they were in a giant jewelry box overflowing with light, escalators, and artificial fragrances. Standing at their counters, the saleswomen resembled the mannequins in the shop windows, their eyes heavily made up, their expressions frozen in radiant politeness. Once, Hélène saw one of those mannequins on the floor, with its naked body severed into pieces, and she wondered if the saleswomen, too, if they fell over, would maintain their delighted, amiable expressions.

When Sabine lay down on her bed, the dress split under the arms.

"While you were away, Mariette was sick again, Maman was crying all the time."

"Do you think it's serious?"

"Mariette or Maman?"

"The dress doesn't fit you . . ."

"Of course it doesn't. Do you think I can come with you one day?"

"Come where?"

"Paris."

"I'd like that. Is she still getting sick at night?"

"Yes, it's always when Maman and Papa are asleep, it's a good thing she's in their room, Maman hears her right away. Mariette starts coughing and she can't breathe, it scares the hell out of me, but I don't dare go and see."

"I'm here now."

"Yes, you're here. We'll be going back to school soon."

There were the vacation days with the Tavels, and the school days with the Malivieris. One place for leisure—and boredom, too—the room without her sister, the days in the department stores, the rule never to speak at the dinner table, and all those adults, her uncle, her aunt, their friends, and their sons, two teenagers who lived their lives elsewhere; and even if the dresses did fit her, the world around Hélène was uncertain. And so, she went out, to the neighbors', even though she didn't like them very much; she made friends, mostly ephemeral ones, childhood crushes. When she was younger, she'd spent a lot of time with Dolorès, who'd been the Tavels' maid at the time, and whose children had stayed behind in Spain. Dolorès wore black, and in her windowless room she taught Hélène how to knit. She also took her along to do the shopping at the end of the day, a quick trip to the grocer, the baker, and she held Hélène's hand with unquestionable authority. Dolorès had gone away, and Hélène was older, no longer entrusted to the servants. From the very beginning she'd had a trusted friend at the Tavels' who asked for nothing and understood everything. Caprice was a shorthaired dachshund who worshiped Hélène with unstinting devotion. You only had to say Hélène's name for him to begin whimpering; a panicked joy set him to trembling and whining. Hélène loved it when they told her how much he'd missed her, the constancy of his attachment to her. She often spoke to him in his dog language, lifting his ears and barking gently, modulating each sound so he would understand what she meant, and it seemed to her that the less he understood, the more attentive he became. Her barking was no good and eventually she stopped it altogether, and told him in human language that she was feeling down, fed up being stuck here with all these adults; and her spirits fell even more when she got a letter from her family, who'd gone away on vacation, camping in Ramatuelle, and they all seemed to make their letters as big as possible to fill an entire page with formulaic messages and cheer she didn't share. She left Caprice behind as soon as vacation was over. They said goodbye several days before her departure. And they spent their lives leaving each other.

The joy she felt being back with her family was somewhat forced; she was always afraid, on seeing them again, that she wouldn't be in step anymore. She had to adapt quickly and without any apparent effort, as if she'd simply gone downstairs to play outside and had come straight back. She couldn't see the connection between her aunt and her mother, couldn't situate them in the same family with the same name, these two women who were so diametrically opposed. Michelle, the eldest of the seven children, had been allowed to pursue her studies, and she'd obtained a librarian's diploma. (As for the eldest boy, he'd gone to medical school.) But once they'd produced a daughter and, above all, a son, their parents figured they'd done their bit, they were now properly represented, and the children who came afterwards grew up as best they could, in the shadows, learning to fend for themselves. Agnès was the youngest, she didn't go to university, and at eighteen she married a man whose profession as a teacher lowered the glorious status of head of the family to that of a boy without ambition. Michelle, on marrying David Tavel, had to learn the codes of the French *bourgeoisie*: the couple said *vous* to each other, just as the sons said *vous* to their parents. They were served at dinner, they sat up straight, treated the maid politely, even though they teased her and thought she lacked a sense of humor when she took it badly. At Bruno and Agnès's house, if they weren't having guests, they ate in the kitchen—Formica furniture, plastic tablecloth, dishes washed by hand, taking turns. Most of the time, Agnès didn't join them at the table but remained standing, she said it was more practical that way and she enjoyed watching them eat what she'd made for them. The shortage of money made their bonds fragile, as if everything might disappear from one day to the next, and by dint of constantly doing without and being careful, the parents were like two children fidgeting at the side of the road and never finding a moment to cross. *We couldn't get far.* As for Hélène, she already had a foot in the door to elsewhere, and when her mother introduced her children, she would smile and say as naturally as could be, "This is Sabine, my eldest, Mariette, the youngest, and this is the Tavel girl." And the reply would be, "Oh, yes, the Parisienne!"

*

The evening Hélène arrived, dinner always seemed strange to her; she found her place at the table. It was a bit of a squeeze in the kitchen, but at last the entire family was together again, and Bruno gazed at his daughters with touching satisfaction.

"I want to go with Hélène to Paris next time," said Sabine.

Agnès was serving the artichokes and her gaze lingered above the pressure cooker, the steam burning her arm. She swore under her breath. Bruno said, "Why?"

"She gets bored by herself. Don't you get bored, Hélène?"

"Tavel didn't invite you."

Agnès said it with a touch of spite, unusual for her. She was a kind mother, who invested all her energy in running her family, and it was as if she'd taken on the job to prove to someone how competent she was.

"I've been dreaming of going to Paris, Maman, you know that!"

"What's so interesting about Paris? Don't you get enough watching *At the Theater this Evening?*"

No, watching *At the Theater this Evening* was not enough, even if it had also nurtured her interest in Paris. On the black and white screen, Sabine had watched plays by Molière and André Roussin with equal fascination, more than twenty a year, evenings when the entire family showed up on time and spoke quietly. Her longing for Paris, where she'd been a few times for family gatherings, was a longing for a different life, an opportunity for transformation, exactly what kind she didn't know, but it seemed possible that something extraordinary could happen there, and that she might prove capable of experiencing it.

"Not at All Saints', the break at All Saints' is too short. And Christmas, after all . . . Maybe Easter, we'll see . . . Later on, we'll see . . ."

Go and live in Paris. Agnès could see why. She thought about everything she'd dreamed of studying and hadn't studied, about the countries she'd dreamed of visiting and had never been to, simply because a girl doesn't risk her virginity in the dangerous world of men, and the youngest girl in a Catholic family has to find herself a nice husband, and have nice children with him, and happiness will come all by itself. She never took her final exams, and she'd only ever dreamed of becoming. Ballerina. Interpreter. Pediatrician.

"I'll ask Michelle."

She said it without looking at Bruno, her gaze focused on the sink, where she was beginning to wash the pans. He lit a cigarette and said to Sabine, "If you go to Paris with Hélène, it'd give me a chance to re-paper your room."

Hélène knew she'd be going back to Paris at All Saints', for the "too-short" break, and while she spent Christmas Eve with her parents, she always left the following day, heading first to Marignane airport, then on to the dog waiting impatiently behind the car windows, to her presents at the foot of the tree, which she opened on her own since the party was over. But at Easter, maybe Sabine could come with her . . . would they travel together? Would she teach her the difference between a Boeing and a Caravelle? In Neuilly, would they take a bath in the huge tub Maria filled to the brim, while in La Petite Chartreuse they would be putting "a trickle of water" for three in the washtub they placed in the shower stall? She would show Sabine something incredible: when you lie down in a full bathtub, your legs float up all by themselves. She'd also warn her about a few things: if you don't sit up straight at the table, Michelle will poke you in the spine with her fingernail; it doesn't really hurt but it's annoying. She'd also tell her not to put her cheese on her bread ("Are you making a sandwich?"). And she'd teach her how to peel a peach with a knife and fork, never to cut her lettuce, not to say "horse riding" but "go horseback riding," not to say "eat" but to say "lunch" or "dinner." But above all she would introduce her to Baloo, her Shetland mare that for some reason had a boy's name and wasn't able to foal but had one phantom pregnancy after another, and then she could ask Sabine if she knew what that meant.

Every night, Sabine dreamed of Paris. She couldn't wait to go to bed to continue the exciting story she was telling herself, a story like a really dramatic soap opera, until eventually she fell asleep, still imagining. She was the narrator, and the sole protagonist, and what she invented for herself sometimes moved her to tears. She had encounters, survived danger, attracted and fascinated imaginary creatures—walk-on parts next to her intoxicating life. Everything took place in Paris and, most nights, in a theater. She had always wondered where the spectators at the Théâtre Marigny went after the final curtain, along with the invariably mentioned set designer Roger Harth and costume designer Donald Cardwell. You could see them get up and put on their coats amid an indecipherable hubbub. She wanted to follow them. To find out how they got home, what Paris was like at night. There were evenings when she didn't follow them down the boulevards, or into the brasseries, some evenings she would spend auditioning on stage at the Théâtre Marigny, performing the inevitable scenes from bourgeois plays where everyone cheated on their spouse in a good-humored way, entering or leaving the stage solely in order to complicate the situation. She was chosen. She performed in Paris then went on tour with the company, it was thrilling, a little bit adventurous, a life that was different from any other, the life of an artist with moments of success, love affairs, hard-won battles. And why not? Anything could happen. She knew she wouldn't always be in her room in La Petite Chartreuse, with Mariette's night-time cough resounding through the wall, and when the neighbors banged with their broom handle, she absorbed the cruelty of the world and promised herself never to forget. Just as she would never forget her mother, holding her younger sister close for nights on end, standing by the hot water faucet in the bathroom, because the steam helped her daughter breathe, and, by morning, the boiler would be empty of hot water.

Sabine had just started the third year of collège, and she'd decided to give herself a head start, to think and act as if her adolescent years were already behind her. She had to break free from her family and from the collège; she had to prepare herself for the life that was waiting for her. She strove to be more confident, to observe the world and defend her own opinions, but she couldn't find anyone to share them with. Her girlfriends only cared about their first period, going shopping at the Prisunic, talking about the Sunday night movie and the Thursday afternoon party. A life made up of inevitable worries, and secrets they did not know how to express, so they borrowed the expressions of others, decisive words that reassured them. Sometimes she bought a magazine or a newspaper, *Le Nouvel Observateur* or *Le Monde*, and read them timidly, overwhelmed by the thought that she was surely meant to read every page, something she never managed to do. She signed up at the local library and discovered worlds she didn't always understand, but as her reading progressed, her life mingled with that of the protagonists and became more inspired: these were extraordinary lives, wings spread wide to beat against the wind, as if every one of them deserved to be praised.

The more she pictured herself elsewhere, later in life, the more she began to live in a multi-layered time, a sort of life with several dimensions, vanishing lines, and extensions. The cloister of the Collège des Prêcheurs, the gray stone stairway leading to the classrooms, the schoolyard with its disgusting toilets: she no longer saw them. Math classes with Mademoiselle Beyer, who fiddled with her chalk and said, "You may think I'm harping," and in fact she was harping . . . but about what? Sabine didn't understand a thing, it was confusing and pointless. Then there was the music teacher, Mademoiselle Chef, who terrified the younger students—that quivering sound emerging from their plastic flutes, followed by their crazed delight when the girls realized that Mademoiselle Chef was only a stupid woman at the mercy of their collective power. And what about the English teacher: the entire class would stand up, trumpeting in chorus *Good morning, Mrs. Thomas!* before sitting down, chairs squeaking, for an hour of resigned, droning repetition. These months and years spent among girls, without even a single professor or supervisor or any other element of the male sex, the girls in one school, the boys in another, like incompatible wildlife. And yet, since May '68, the principal had stopped writing girls' names on the blackboard in the supervisors' room, the ones she would see on the weekend in Aix with a boy, girls who would immediately be tracked down in the courtyard thanks to the nametags on their uniforms. Some of them hid, others collapsed in tears. The ones who dared to confront opprobrium and curiosity were rare. Only recently had they been given the right to elect class delegates. And to hold their heads a bit higher. But their eyes lowered. The world was still narrow-minded, thick with the dusty film of ignorance. What was the point of it all? Where was joy? And above all, what space were they entitled to live in? Where to find wonder in their lives? The pupils began their first year in fear, looking for protection from an older sister; four years later, they left school astonished they had taken it all so seriously, astonished at how much they had suffered in that hostile, old-fashioned world.

Bruno was driving with the windows down, his left arm on the door, and the smell of mown grass mingled with the odors of the Simca, the dusty seat covers, and the *Gauloise brune* cigarette he was slowly smoking. He was on his way back from the Aiguilles wine co-op, where he bought his wine in boxes before bottling it himself, and he could still smell the odor of the cheap co-op wine, the wet floor, the cork and the straw, which the strong presence of the surrounding vineyards and pine trees failed to conceal. The sky was getting dark, insects were hurtling against the windshield, evening was rising like a thick mist, and suddenly he felt sad, as if he'd been hiding this sadness from himself and it suddenly came over him by surprise. So, he began to hum a rather stupid song, *The Three Bells,* his daughters liked it, but it felt strange singing without them, as if he were telling a story into the void. He wondered if he had the right to stop Sabine from going to Paris with Hélène. What was it that drew her there? The city itself, or the Tavels? He didn't feel like re-papering their room, he was lousy when it came to putting up wallpaper, lousy at all sorts of home improvement jobs, something Agnès took as a personal affront. Her husband was not a handyman. No. He was not a handy husband. And he only produced daughters. There was something lacking in him, a virile element missing, as if it were impossible for him to assert himself. Three girls and no children, said his father, when he asked Bruno what would become of the *Malivieri* name after he was gone. A hypocritical jibe, because Bruno's brothers had boys, they had children. His father forgot, or pretended to forget, that there was something else. Something Bruno banished from his memory the moment it surfaced.

He saw her from a distance. Gave a start, as if this harsh, unexpected image had landed on his windshield. He instinctively thought of his daughters, as he did whenever there was danger. He pulled the car over to the side, the secondary road was narrow and unlit. He switched on his hazard lights and ran toward the girl. She was on the ground, next to her bicycle, and conscious. She answered when he asked her name, she was called Rose, and she said her leg hurt and her shoulder too, she couldn't move them anymore, and she burst into tears. He told her he was going to see if she was bleeding, she buried her head in his shoulder, she was cold, her teeth were chattering, biting the inside of her cheeks. Apparently, she wasn't bleeding. Bruno knew you were supposed to place injured people in a recovery position, but he went on holding Rose close to him, like a baby, protecting her from the approaching chill of the night. He carried her over to the shoulder of the road while he put the bike in the trunk of the car. The child's body was shaking convulsively, like a battered animal, and she vomited in the grass for a long time. The headlights of the Simca cast a glare on her, an insistent flashlight searching for something. Bruno could hear the traffic in the distance, the motors of the clanking trucks as they turned before the intersection and came no further this way, the secondary road was deserted and he felt abandoned in a dead world, a world made empty by the accident. He lifted the little girl up again and settled her on the back seat, saying comforting words to her, of the sort he would have said to his daughters, but he didn't love this injured child, he was afraid of her, and he was in a hurry to entrust her to others. He drove slowly, talked to her to reassure himself, the hospital wasn't far, they'd be there soon, he kept saying it, we'll be there soon . . .

When they got to the emergency room, he saw she had fallen asleep. In a panic he ran to reception, and everything went very quickly. Nurses rushed out with a gurney, and one of them handed the little girl's bag to him. "We're taking your daughter to the operating room," and they disappeared behind the swinging doors, no one faulted him for having brought her, no one paid him any attention, but nevertheless he felt as if he had done something wrong, he was almost astonished they weren't accusing him. In the bag, he found the name and telephone number of Rose's mother, he got change at the reception and called her. Ten minutes later, Laurence arrived at the emergency room. She hadn't even taken the time to put on her shoes, she was wearing slippers, her hair unkempt, her cardigan buttoned wrong over her dress, Bruno knew immediately that this was her, a mother looking for her child. She was waiting for a reassuring word, the confirmation that everything would be all right, he was embarrassed that she was giving him this power, all he had done was rescue a child lying on the ground. He smiled at her with a forced sense of calm, then looked away, avoiding conversation. He didn't see how he could make her feel better, and he was trying to hide his own fear, his anger, too, when he thought of the bastard who'd knocked the little girl over and driven off. They waited in silence, seated to one side of the swinging doors that led into a world that told them *NO ADMISSION*; they were living through a confused, oppressive time, a time no one ever wants to live through, and yet it tells you that this is life. It is possible that you will not be spared.

Laurence pleaded with the girl at reception for some news, and not long afterwards, or maybe it was hours later, an intern came to reassure them. Rose was doing well, her leg was broken, they'd fitted her with pins and plaster, she would be in the recovery room soon. His words erased their worst fears. Laurence took her face in her hands: this good news was as powerful a shock as the news of the accident had been. Bruno felt the burden of it all suddenly fall away, and he was left with the slightly cowardly feeling that the benign nature of it all had done him a huge favor.

They went out to smoke a cigarette. Laurence was smiling through her tears, her fingers trembled, she was beautiful, a distraught mother whose tears illuminated her dark eyes. She is like a Madonna: Bruno allowed himself the thought, both accurate and upsetting; it was almost unreal to be sharing the intensity of that moment as complete strangers. Before long, Laurence said she had to make a phone call. He stayed alone in the keening night, the insistent song of crickets lending a poignant surface to the darkness; something was lying in wait, in this invisible world. He closed his eyes and held his face up to the cool, humid air, his back to the hospital. He slowly felt his body begin to relax, while his skin let in life again, let in air and the sounds of life. He took Rose's bike out of the trunk and leaned it against the parapet, looking around in spite of himself to see whether Laurence had come back out, and he decided not to go and say goodbye. He was eager now to see his wife and his daughters, to be back in his stable, serene world. Taking the injured child in his car had been a mistake, he knew that, and the thought that it could have gone horribly wrong pierced his guts with a searing pain. Death had been lurking. Once again. He told himself he must pray, that prayer would calm him down.

Sabine and Hélène were lying in their beds, whispering confessions in the dark. Their parents' room, where Mariette slept, was separated from their own by a plasterboard wall as thin as cardboard. What they were saying was private, because, when they were alone, they dared to speak about *there*. What was so different about that other family, that uncle and aunt who belonged more to Hélène than to her sisters? What did she have to say about them? What did it mean, exactly, *having money*? Woe to the rich. They often heard their parents quote this phrase from the Gospel with a sigh that conveyed discord and envy, and it seemed that being rich was a curse that was full of blessings. Sabine knew that *having money* meant you were *comfortable*, that living free of the burden of so many worries meant you became more carefree and relaxed. She was amazed when Hélène described the sort of freedom she was given at the Tavels:

"You'll see, they leave you alone there, Michelle never worries about anything. You go out, you tell her you're going to see friends, neighbors, you want to walk the dog, and she says fine, see you later."

"She doesn't worry?"

"Not much."

"You go out in Paris all by yourself?"

"No, not in Paris. I stay in Neuilly. I can't take the metro by myself."

"With me you'll be able to."

"I feel like dancing."

"Now?"

Hélène got up and began to dance in the middle of the little room, between the beds and the board they used as a desk. Her white nightgown was a moving patch of light from a cloud-trapped moon. Over and over, she said, "We'll take the metro the two of us, the metro underground, and the metro in the sky, the Paris sky, Paris, Paris sky . . ."

"Get back in bed, Hélène, you're going to wake Mariette."

She sat on the edge of the bed, her breathing audible, gripped by joy that bubbled like a little splash of water beneath a flame. She was tall and slender for her age, so unlike Sabine in that respect, who was big and earthy, and, at the age of eleven, Hélène was already described as "flat as a pancake" and "beanpole." Her face was pale, her lashes very fine, almost translucent, above her green eyes; her own impression was that she must be as drab as a faded drawing. Above all she couldn't figure out "who she took after." Agnès told her she looked like one of her great-aunts, but since she'd never seen her, she didn't know whether this was a compliment or a reproach. It was above all terribly old.

"It must be nice to take the metro above ground," said Sabine.

"I already have, with Vincent."

"Is he nice, Vincent?"

"He's my favorite cousin. You know, when the metro is above the water, it's like on a bridge, and sometimes I get scared it will fall . . . of course it never does."

"Do you go to the theater very often?"

"All the time."

"Don't tell me."

"Why not?"

"Because. Don't tell me. I can imagine it all."

"So, what can I tell you?"

"Dunno."

"My pony has phantom pregnancies."

"Ah."

"But it's not like she's a phantom. Are you listening?"

"Yes, but get in bed, don't stay with your bare feet on the tile floor, you'll catch cold."

"What *is* a phantom pregnancy?"

"It's when you think you're expecting a baby but you're not, it's like a ghost in your belly."

"Like when I feel like I have to wee, but in fact it's my imagination?"

"Yes."

"How do you find out?"

"Because you never give birth."

"But how do other people know? The ones who say she's having a phantom pregnancy?"

"Oh, hush now Hélène, you're wearing me out. Are you crying?"

"No, I have a cold."

"No, you don't!"

"I'm crying for my pony."

"That's ridiculous, she's not crying."

"How do you know?"

"She's an animal. Animals are like babies, they don't feel pain."

"Why not?"

"They just don't. It's scientific, I suppose."

"Ah . . . that's strange."

"No stranger than a phantom pregnancy. Come on, go to sleep now."

There was a moment of silence, where each sister thought about what had just been said, and imagination mingled with ignorance, so much ignorance that it seemed that being an adult must be another state altogether, where nothing remained of what they once were, a molting that would release their former skin in silence and oblivion, and they would go on living like that, suddenly aware of everything, knowing the codes, the laws, making important decisions without hesitating, meeting other people, other informed adults with whom they would share this world that greeted their flawless participation. They felt fragile in their cotton nightgowns, their single beds, the thin walls of these apartments piled one on top of the other, where you could hear the neighbors switching on the light, the dogs' claws clacking on the tiled floors, the plumbing, the toilet flushing, as well as the rhythm of beds shaking with bodies, women crying out and men crying out, the violence and shame of something they knew nothing about. Night-time was the place of this exposed intimacy, but, in the morning, people met in the stairwell and greeted one another politely, as if nothing had happened, as if the people who lived during the night had stayed in their rooms, and those who showed their faces in broad daylight were their tidy, civilized doubles.

Hélène was crying softly, refraining from blowing her nose, noiselessly letting the snot flow through her fingers. Baloo could feel pain. She knew she could. In the morning, when Hélène went to get her in her box stall or out on the meadow, the pony would whinny when she saw her coming, and then she rubbed her head for a long time against Hélène's belly. This was joy. Hélène imagined that if she walked past her stall without going in, the opposite thing would happen. It would be pain. "Scientific." She didn't know that word. Gradually, she stopped crying, saw her pony's huge belly, anyone would think it was full of babies, but in fact it was nothing but guts, flowers, grass, and brambles. And then she fell asleep, after lying in wait, like every night, for the moment she would slip from waking to sleep, but she missed it, she slid without transition from emotion to oblivion. Sabine knew exactly when her little sister dozed off, she pinpointed from her breathing the moment she'd stop asking questions and stop pretending to have a cold. Sabine resumed her Parisian reverie. The faraway city was her second address, her evening rendezvous. And she didn't just want to be in the metro above the river, she didn't just want to be sitting in a red velvet armchair. She wanted to walk through Paris alone, without a sister, an aunt, a cousin, or a dog. She wanted to get up and be on her way.

And then, in Aix-en-Provence there was that flurry of public condemnation, over some scandal. For a little provincial town, reclusive and bourgeois, it was a stain that was impossible to hide.

One evening, while her sisters were still playing outside the building and she'd gone back up to do her homework, Sabine heard her parents in the kitchen. They were whispering, agitated. Agnès was holding her face in her hands, she seemed tired and vaguely disorientated.

"Why are you crying?" Bruno asked.

"I'm not crying . . . I'm just upset, that's all . . ."

"You wept already when she died . . ."

"I told you, I'm not crying! It's just that it . . . I'm disgusted by the fact they're daring to show it in Aix, when the boy's parents live right nearby. Aren't you?"

It was as if they both wanted to stop something, ward off some danger, and they couldn't.

"Bruno, that poster, here, it's shocking. It's a scandal, yes, that's what it is, it's—"

"Sabine, sweetheart, what are you doing here?"

Even though he tried to make his question sound only faintly surprised, Bruno's voice was trembling, and Sabine had come into the kitchen on tip toe, out of respect for the awkward atmosphere.

"Why aren't you downstairs with your sisters? Who's looking after Mariette?"

"Hélène."

"Have you been here long?"

"Yes, ages."

And so, they had to explain. Since she wanted to know. Since she asked, What's the scandal? And the question made both of them so awkward that for a moment she thought one of them must be involved in some way. They didn't know how to go about it and kept trying to get the other to speak: Go ahead, you tell her, No, you, go ahead, and she could see how young they were. "They're going to live a long time still," and this thought seemed to suggest that they would live forever, and so she was merciless and demanded that they hide nothing from her, otherwise she'd find out on her own, and that did the trick: neither one of them wanted the matter to be divulged to their daughter with words they hadn't chosen, or without all the care that was necessary. It was as if they were wrapping a hand grenade in tissue paper. The story was taboo, about a "divorced woman," said her father, as if that in itself was enough to make her a bad woman. A divorced woman and a mother, on top of it. The words didn't go together. This woman had committed suicide, in Marseille; she turned on the gas and then she died. Sabine thought she must be someone her parents knew, and that the scandal would end there, a-divorced-mother-with-children-who-committed-suicide-in-Marseille, and she asked if they were going to the funeral. They looked at her as if she'd suddenly been stricken with some abnormality.

"She was buried a long time ago. She killed herself in 1969."

"Have you seen the posters around Aix for that film with Annie Girardot? A red rose on top of a police mug shot? Didn't you see it?"

"No. What is it?"

Her mother was looking tenderly at her hands, her palms facing the kitchen ceiling, and in one breath she said:

"*To Die of Love.*"

"To die of love?"

"Yes, that's what they've called the story. This woman, Gabrielle Russier, was a teacher in Marseille and, at her age . . . she was thirty-two . . . at her age she . . . slept with one of her pupils, yes, he was sixteen. She was sent to prison for it. Of course. And the boy's parents teach here at the University in Aix. And the posters for the film are all over town . . ."

"I see."

She said it so they would stop talking. But she didn't see at all, surely because they themselves didn't understand the source of their sorrow, or why they felt so upset. The affair had profoundly impacted their beliefs, disturbed the integrity and fairness of their life plan, a plan they would have liked to believe was unique and universal. There was no place in their Christian morality for the messiness of feelings, but not far from where they lived a woman their age had been suffering so much she'd forgotten her own children, had opened the door to the oven and stuck her head inside. How could they not be deeply shaken?

They forbade Sabine from going to see the film and she didn't disobey them. Nor did she share the story with Hélène or any of her friends. She just sat on her own with this explosion that had blown so many holes into things. Love like a river overflowing its banks. Love that wasn't just conjugal, sanctioned by the priest, authorized by law. This was at the very beginning of 1971, the month of January. Two months later in *Le Nouvel Observateur* she came upon a short statement by Gabrielle Russier's former pupil. He said: "It wasn't passion at all. It was love. Passion isn't lucid. And this was lucid," and his words merely added to her failure to understand. She would have liked it better if *To Die of Love* were a disease carried by two careless, selfish people, far removed from everything she knew. But she read in the article that they were educated, politically engaged, disobedient, and good-looking. She read the story her parents hadn't told her, where there were expressions such as *unlawful intercourse with a minor, psychiatric hospital, Les Baumettes prison*, and even *President Pompidou* and the poems by *Paul Éluard* that the president had recited, so bizarrely, in Gabrielle Russier's defense. It was a wild dance, and everyone seemed to have examined the love affair inside out, the entire country turning their attention to love, making it into a question of morals. After she read the article, Sabine went and hid so she could cry. Cry for her desire to love, and the shame she felt, that perhaps love had been dirtied by feelings, by couples, by sexuality. Love was a scandal. And she wanted it to happen to her.

They were about to discover a different Provence, and they entered the domain with the respectful enchantment of people who had no right to be there. And yet the gates had been opened for them, they were being welcomed. The long drive to the house, down a dirt lane as fine as sand, bordered with cypress trees that smelled of incense and vintage green boxwood, the solemn beauty of the place—everything troubled Bruno and Agnès, and they accepted Laurence's invitation with the gratitude of the timid. They couldn't stop thanking her, their voices fragile.

"I'm the one who's grateful," she said. "All my life I'll be grateful to you, all my life."

It was Agnès who had found Laurence, even though she didn't know her, one Saturday morning at the market. She heard a rather untidy woman (she said *eccentric*) talking loudly to a friend about the accident her daughter Rose had had. And because Agnès found her eccentric and incredibly beautiful, in her outfit that didn't exactly suit her age, something a hippie might wear, she eavesdropped on the conversation and then she said, "It's my husband, I think, it must be my husband who took your daughter to the hospital." And she couldn't get over the fact she'd dared to interrupt them, she'd had to hold Mariette close to do it, as if to establish her authority. Laurence made a noisy exclamation, and hugged her with the spontaneity of people who rarely feel awkward, and said she'd tried to locate her husband, she'd wanted to thank him, but he hadn't filled out any papers at the hospital, she was so happy to find out at last who he was, the man who'd saved her daughter. And then she looked at this woman who was so proud of her husband, and who was like an exhausted child.

"You must come for tea. You and your husband. And your little girl, of course."

"I have three daughters."

"Already? How old are you?"

"Thirty-four."

"And already three children. And no boys?"

"No."

"Do you want any?"

Agnès went a little pale. Then replied fervently, "I certainly don't."

They sat out on the terrace; the country house behind them was a dark hole, protected from the sun by large blue shutters, while they were in the shade under the linden tree with its low-lying branches, which obliged them, when they were standing, to stoop a little, as if they were trying to find each other in the dark. It was early spring, that most tender of seasons in the south, free of the overwhelming drowsiness of summer. The large pool was empty, and it troubled Hélène to see the bottom, full of dead leaves and broken toys. She was terrified of swimming pools, and, without its water, this one seemed even more impenetrable. A few months earlier, a girl from her collège had drowned at the local swimming pool, right in the middle of her swimming lesson. Hélène couldn't stop thinking about it, day and night, all the time, even though she never spoke of it. She herself had nearly drowned when she was very little, in the English Channel, on vacation with David and Michelle, and since then, she couldn't put her head underwater without feeling precisely what death must be. She hadn't merely come close to it. She had experienced it, internalized it. David had rescued her, but the girl from the collège, they'd got her out of the water but not out of death. They'd set her down on the hard cold edge of the swimming pool, but she was already somewhere else. Or nowhere. And Hélène wondered why they never talked about her, how it was possible that a girl could come into the changing room alive and out of the swimming pool dead, without that being the sole topic of conversation. She later learned that whether she'd been in the water or out of it, the girl would have died that morning anyway, at the same time, wherever she happened to be. She was born with a hole in her heart and *it was bound to happen.* Hélène didn't know her and yet this girl became her companion, her sorrow, her unrescued double.

Sabine and Rose took Mariette for a walk in the garden, and Hélène joined them, to banish these thoughts that were spoiling everything. Rose walked with a crutch, and Sabine and Hélène were intimidated by her; she had an air of mystery about her, conferred by her nocturnal accident and their father's rescue. They felt they were the daughters of a hero, and the tiny superiority this gave them helped to balance the social game. They'd noticed how Rose admired their father; he seemed distant, merely smiling at her without referring to that night, a smile that said, Let's leave it at that. They also knew that Rose must find him handsome, because he was, their girlfriends said as much, as did the neighbors, and their friends, who would point out that he looked like some actor, but they could never remember which one. The girls imagined an American actor, bound to be taller and more heroic than a French one, and they were proud of this paternal beauty.

"Have you been able to go back to Cézanne?"

Sabine was only slightly younger than Rose, and next year she would be starting her first year at the lycée Cézanne, behind the hills. It still wasn't coed, but they'd heard they could go out with the boys who were in the advanced placement math sections, their classes were held in the same building, and there were so few girls in those classes that most of the boys must be free, but they'd also heard that they didn't mingle, even during break time, they were always clustered together and you could only see their backs. The prospect wasn't very attractive, but maybe if one of them turned around, he would show them a luminous face, free of all his theorems. Someone would have to, eventually, one of the boys would have to turn around someday and show his face. The boys who went to the Thursday afternoon parties were so young, it was as if they were all cousins—clumsy, harmless boys. They would practice on the girls who gave their consent, Sabine thought they were pathetic, she could see how unhappy they were, how they kept watching each other. Which one would succeed in picking up a girl? Or two girls. Or three. And however often they closed the shutters and danced slow dances in the semi-darkness, their clumsiness was as visible as in broad daylight.

Rose wasn't pretty and Sabine and Hélène thought her name didn't suit her. But she was kind, in a calm, confident way, and this intrigued them. A fifteen-year-old girl with no hang-ups. She offered to show them the room that her mother had arranged for her on the ground floor. They went inside the house, which smelled of citronella and overripe figs. Dust floated in the light that slanted through the closed shutters and fell on the red floor tiles. There was an upright piano, a large buffet, and a wooden table where flower vases held wilted flowers, and cups offered their dregs to the buzzing flies. Water was dripping into a stone sink, marking slow, distracted time. Everything seemed to be living an autonomous, disordered life. A ginger cat lay on the table: Mariette went up to it, Sabine took her hand, "Don't caress it too long, Mariette, you're allergic," and they stroked the cat together, he gave them a weary look then leapt down from the table and disappeared, knocking down the newspaper he'd been lying on. The newspaper had a black background, where the drawing of a man with a puffy face, full of wrinkles, gazed out at the reader with an expression as evasive as his features. The headline of *Charlie Hebdo* said: *Who Got Them Pregnant, the 343 Sluts Who Signed the Abortion Manifesto?* Sabine hastily put the newspaper back. She didn't recognize the Minister of the Interior, Michel Debré, but she'd read the Manifesto in *Le Nouvel Observateur*, a long plea, and she didn't understand the insult. *Sluts.* It added violence to abortion, a burning topic that put her ill at ease; she didn't dare talk about it. Mariette had gone over to the cat again, and was bending down by his food bowl, so Sabine followed her. Her sister was so small, it was as if she weren't growing, her huge eyes filled her tiny face as if they were obeying a separate growth curve, and she looked out at the world with constant, determined curiosity.

"I've already told you not to go up to animals while they're eating."

"I'm not touching him."

"Even so. Don't put your face anywhere near him."

"He likes me."

"He doesn't know you."

"Well, are you coming?"

Hélène was calling them from Rose's room, she felt like her sisters were far away, as if they would have to go through more than one dark room to find her.

"What were you doing?"

Sabine was surprised by how aggressive Hélène sounded. Straight off, she took Mariette on her lap. The child pulled away, wriggling, and sat like the others on Rose's big bed, which was covered with crushed pillows. She tried to imitate the way they were sitting and put her chin in her hands, couldn't keep the pose, and fell onto her back to gaze at the ceiling. Hélène asked again:

"Hey, what were you doing?"

"Nothing! We were petting the cat, all right?"

"The cat, yes, the cat!" said Mariette.

"I don't have any sisters," said Rose, proudly.

The sisters felt miserable. They had given Rose the wrong idea; she wouldn't understand. They weren't fighting, they were calling out to each other. It took only a second for them to start missing one another, and that second was like a tiny drop of water that contained everything. The difference in their ages did set them apart to a degree, but Agnès had told them that, over time, the difference would fade, "Three years is nothing, it counts a lot when you're young, but not when you're grown up," and Hélène saw the "three years" fade like a number written in the sand, it was sad and pathetic. *I'm being followed by a moonshadow*, sang Cat Stevens. That was exactly how she felt. You were followed by a moonshadow, practically nothing. You died at the bottom of the local swimming pool. You died at the bottom of the sea. You died on your bike on a road in Provence. You died from a hole in your heart or from carelessness. In a moonshadow.

Their mother was calling them, it was time to go, where were they? And her call was again filled with thanks, "Such a beautiful garden, really, thank you so much." "Come whenever you like," said Laurence, and when the girls came to join their mother, she marveled, "It's incredible, you look like four sisters!" Agnès smiled, she was flattered, Hélène and Sabine both noticed, how their mother seemed flattered. Agnès said she'd had Sabine when she was twenty. That figure, however small it might be, would not fade over time. That figure indicated that their mother had not lived through her youth, because she hadn't had one.

*

All five were eager to get home now, to run a bath for three in the little tub, to eat in the kitchen, put Mariette to bed and watch the Sunday evening movie eating Mars bars, which Agnès cut into bits, dividing two bars into four pieces, because one bar each would have been too expensive. They would share the story of the film—embarrassed by the kissing scenes, moved by the beauty of the actresses, who had sad, complicated things happen to them; and in those stories each one of them saw some of her own desires and confusion. As they watched the film, they sensed that their places would change, that sooner or later they would replace each other, that time would redistribute their roles. Perhaps that was why they enjoyed these moments when they were just family, because the situation was fragile and ephemeral, and all together they were someone.

At Easter vacation, Hélène and Sabine left for Paris on the Mistral train from Marseille. Michelle had sent money for train tickets, not enough for the plane. In tears, Agnès stood making their sandwiches. This was bound to happen. It wasn't enough for her sister to take one of her children, now she wanted two. She'd always had everything her way. Allowed to study, because she was the eldest. (She never worked, and her librarian's diploma had served absolutely no purpose.) Allowed to give her opinion about everything, because she was rich and lived in Paris. And since childhood Agnès had been the one who got given advice, and a bit of help, and nothing was expected of her. Every month, after he deposited the Tavel check at the bank and transferred the money to his father, Bruno gave her some cash so she could buy meat: shoulder of beef for the stew, and filet when they had guests on Sunday. The Tavel money filled them all with protein; it smelled of black butter and cooked flesh.

Sabine put her worn, poorly cut clothing in her suitcase. She'd saved from the hours she spent babysitting, and in Paris she was going to buy her first pair of jeans and her first mascara. Her father thought makeup was indecent, he didn't like artifice, which turned a decent girl into a vulgar one, the sort of girl whom men, obviously, would not respect. A fast girl. She figured she could wear the mascara in secret, and her father would get used to the jeans. She was fourteen, she had every right, but her parents saw everything new as a potential danger, and she got the impression that even the questions she asked them were improper, as if the ferocity of the world flared up in everything she didn't understand. She would have liked to talk to her mother in such a way that not a single word would embarrass her, but every remark seemed to be a questioning of her very existence, even an accusation. Agnès's everyday life was so committed, so rigorously adhered to, that it was hard to get anywhere near her private domain. Last winter, she had agreed to let Sabine do the basement run for the coal, and it was like a renunciation to her. How many times had Sabine seen her in winter, lugging those buckets up from the basement to the sixth floor, then filling the stove? Agnès's life could be summed up by that verb, to fill. Fill the stove, fill the fridge, fill the tub, fill their stomachs, fill the emptiness; ward off every danger. Would it have been simpler if she'd had only one child? Sabine had heard her advising one of her sisters-in-law, who was pregnant for the sixth time, to use her moped more frequently and hop vigorously when she was dancing. How were you supposed to take this? What was the difference between a desired miscarriage and a deliberate abortion? Reading the manifesto in *Le Nouvel Observateur*, which *Charlie Hebdo* had renamed the "Manifesto of the 343 Sluts," Sabine had been so distraught that she had hidden that issue, with its headline like a warning, colored words against a black background. A death notice, scribbled over with life. Signed by Catherine Deneuve, Simone de Beauvoir, Françoise Sagan, Marguerite Duras, Gisele Halimi, and so many other famous women she hadn't heard of, and so many unknown women who, apparently, were paying a heavy price for their signature. The manifesto said that women did not have the freedom of their own bodies. Like slaves. That women were forced into reproduction. Like cattle. And the manifesto compared Catholics to fascists. The harshness of this accusation added to the shock value, as it listed the figures for women who'd had abortions and those who'd died from them. Everything was about the womb, that was all that mattered, a woman's womb. To whom it belonged. To whom it answered, and what women had the right to do with it. And the word *scandal* was in the manifesto, too. It was virulent, dangerous. And so close. When Sabine had her first period, Agnès said to her, "You're a woman now, be careful." She thought she had to be careful not to stain the sheets or her skirts. And then she understood that something else was meant. She could have a child. She had just been thrust into the place of every danger. But she didn't know how she was supposed to protect herself, or even how to tell when it was coming. Adults didn't talk about these things. Nor did parents. Or teachers. Or any of their books. Something had just ended and something else, powerful and evil, was about to take its place. That was all.

Hélène and Sabine stayed only one night in Paris. And it wasn't even Paris, it was Neuilly. One night, and Sabine wept with disappointment, while her sister slept cuddled up against her dog, each of them in a bed with so many pillows that Sabine tossed half of them overboard. It was a room like the ones you saw in movies, with indirect lighting, paintings on the walls, curtains and double curtains, and a huge walk-in closet where the light came on when you opened the door. It contained shelves full of neat piles of sweaters and shirts, then hangers in close ranks like a headless crowd—with jackets, coats, dresses, suits; and on the doors there were ties, belts, scarves; on the ground a display of shoes with shoetrees and immaculate brushes—and at the sight of so much plenty Sabine asked, "Whose are these?" Her tone implying, What the fuck is all this? And Hélène understood that, this time, her sister would not be in the mood to try on a dress that wasn't hers and look at herself in the mirror, gently twirling.

Sabine knew the apartment, she'd been there several times, before or after one of the family reunions, but she'd never had a meal served to her by Maria, who appeared the moment Michelle rang a little brass bell; she'd never put away her toothbrush in a bathroom that was just for children, nor had she ever seen, in the bathroom reserved for the parents, a bathtub that was level with the floor, nor had she ever seen the safe, the laundry room, or the room for the automata collection;

she'd never opened the closet with lighting, or the picture window onto the terrace, all the roundabout discoveries and surprises in this place that smelled of leather, ambergris, and beeswax. But above all she'd never seen the way her uncle behaved on seeing Hélène again. This man—whom at home they referred to by his last name alone, *Tavel*, as if he were a brand name—this rich, powerful man, this company head: how he needed her little sister. She'd never understood what it was that Hélène had that she didn't, nor what her own shortcomings might be. What was it about her that was not as pleasing? Did her Mediterranean physique clash with this bourgeois apartment? Or was it her lucidity—someone who could see into all the workings of the mechanism, the power of money, how it could dazzle you? Did Tavel love Hélène simply because he'd never had a daughter? But then, Hélène or another girl, it would have made no difference. It would have been like an arranged marriage, like her grandparents. A love from another era. But when Hélène and Tavel were together again, Sabine understood they really loved one another. The moment she saw the two of them, the lines by Racine came to her: "They are in love! . . . Where did they meet? Since when? How did it arise?" There was something powerful and forbidden about that love, just like in a tragedy. It was a betrayal of the Malivieri clan, and Sabine was astonished that her sister could flaunt her bonds of dependence so naturally. She watched as Tavel showed Hélène a prayer wheel he'd brought back from a Japanese temple. He made it spin and they both smiled, as if they had discovered some new species of animal and were enchanted by its appearance. She watched as Maria set the table under Michelle's weary authority. She looked at the framed photographs of her cousins who had not yet come home. Happy times on horseback, in cars, on boats. It was like a huge advertising campaign. It filled her with rage. There had to be something behind this publicity for the life she was being shown, both here and at home, in the silver frames of photographs, or poor people's kitchens, behind the slogans like *Moulinex Sets a Woman Free*, the injunctions to promote progress, comfort, and the frenzied pursuit of happiness, luxury, and family life, there was something else. Which could be neither bought or sold. She had to find it; she'd have to manage with whatever it was. She didn't want to leave for the seaside the next day. Paris was so close. On the drive through the city from the Gare de Lyon, she'd looked out at the charcoal gray sky and the first lights on the Place de la Concorde, the Champs-Élysées, the Place de l'Étoile. It was time for the theaters to open. For the bars and night clubs. For tragedy. And the open city was waiting for people to enter with it into the night. But Sabine had been no more than a tourist, sitting in a Mercedes as it hurried toward Neuilly.

The house in Villers was set on a cliff overlooking the sea. There was a sharp crystal beauty to the sky as it stretched toward the horizon to blend into its colors. The relentless shifts of luminosity brought on an indescribable nostalgia, regret for another life. It was hardly perceptible, but it was always there, whenever you looked closely at the colors of the sky on the sea.

Hélène rode her pony every day. In the meadow, on the beach, and in Villers, too: Vincent harnessed Baloo to the cart and they went together to do the shopping. Everyone stared at them, they didn't care, money freed them from the regard of others, and they didn't need anyone else. Vincent treated Hélène with the amiable complicity of an older brother; he was a spontaneous boy, liked making jokes and playing pranks, and he was generous toward his cousin. But whenever Hélène left to go back to Aix, they would forget each other and never felt the need to write or ask for news. Their relationship was in the moment, it would pick up where they'd left off, and vanish again with no regrets. Sabine thought that in their cart they looked like the illustration of Phaethon driving Helios's chariot in her *Illustrated Greek Mythology*. And secretly she hoped for a fall—something minor, with no consequences other than to bring them back on earth among other mortals. She felt as if she were farther away from her sister at that moment than when they were actually apart.

When she came back from her day spent riding, Hélène smelled of old leather and sweat, something acrid, not very pleasant. She was tired—happily tired, rid of all ordinary preoccupations, and she was no longer either a girl or a boy, either a Malivieri or a Tavel, she was just herself. Grooming Baloo, changing his straw, cleaning the saddle and the bit immersed her in the concrete aspects of a life where she could act on her own, without anyone else watching her or expecting something. When she was galloping on the beach, she sensed how it could all come to an end; privilege was fragile, she was going to grow up, would David give her a pony twice the size, a real horse? Would it all continue when she was an adult? David had left for Tokyo, Joseph had stayed in Neuilly, there were only four of them in Villers, their little community dominated by a single boy, who tried awkwardly to fill the space his father had left vacant. But Vincent's authority was tentative at best, and Michelle did not hesitate to tell him to sit up straight at the dinner table—a way of showing him that domination is imposed surreptitiously, and while she adored Joseph, the eldest, her feelings for Vincent were colored with the irritation caused by those who, one way or another, never fail to disappoint. Conversations invariably revolved around horses: horse shows, trophies won, which were the good stallions, the best trotters; and life was organized in consequence, a competition where everyone had to prove their worth and, without fail, take home a prize. The goal was victory.

Sabine was afraid of horses and did not spend much of her day with Hélène, but early in the morning they would walk together along the beach, chatting breezily, aware of how, at the Tavels', they were not treated in the same way. Sabine was told not to say *vous* to Michelle the way Hélène did, and far from inviting greater familiarity, saying *tu*, on the contrary, established distance. Everyone else—husband and wife, sons and parents—said *vous*, and she was not part of that circle. The two sisters also spoke at night, out of habit, in the attic room; they could hear the sea, though not see it, and the light of the phosphorescent moon fell on their beds. There was a flinty tension that prevented them from relaxing, and this tension was reinforced by the hierarchy that reigned among them all. They did what they could to enjoy each other's presence, but each sister felt she was being watched by the other one, and they weren't at ease.

Sabine sought refuge in reading. She'd brought along some books borrowed from the local library in Aix. She'd got a shock when she saw Gabrielle Russier's *Prison Letters* on display; the book's presence there meant that not everyone reacted the way her parents had. The letters disappointed her, she'd expected something else, more details about the doomed love story, but the preface was longer than the actual correspondence, and Gabrielle Russier wrote that her story had made "everyone chew things over," and it was time to "demystify it." From her prison cell, she worried about her children's childcare, who was feeding the cat, what about the cleaning woman, or the key left at the concierge's. There was less about love than about how to get out of a huge mess; her anxiety was constant. Reading *Gone with the Wind* was far more enchanting, but growing up must surely mean preferring prison letters to sentimental novels. Sabine thought she would have to choose which side she wanted to be on, find her path and not stray from it. She knew so little. Life was there before her, vibrant, enigmatic. There were things to discover that were both extraordinary and implicitly forbidden, and everything exciting went hand in hand with remorse. The pleasure she felt masturbating at night while Hélène was asleep was both a deliverance and an insult. To whom she didn't know. Her sister? Herself? Everyone who slept under the same roof and who would be offended by her transgression? The Church, she knew, viewed masturbation as a mortal sin, and if each time she died a little, it was of shame. She thought she must be the only one who was obsessed with sensuality, who felt the repeated need to masturbate in order to calm more than her body: her mind. But one day, when Michelle sent her to the stables to get Hélène, she heard something she immediately recognized as sighs of pleasure. Two people making love. The sound excited her, as if hearing it was an immediate, forceful way of being involved; it spoke directly to some part of her that was uncontrollable and consenting. The sound their bodies made. Their movements could be heard. As much as their voices. She went closer, her heart pounding, a pain in her lower belly, and she could sense that, through her arousal, she was participating in their duet. She saw them. It was two men. She froze with confusion. It was as if they were fighting, and if she hadn't heard their moaning to start with, that's what she would have thought, two boys fighting. But they desired each other. A desire so great it hurt. They wanted one another the way you want what's good for you, with all your strength, another life joining with your own. She hadn't recognized Vincent at first, when she saw his cap on the ground next to his Elvis T-shirt. Was this fierce man—she could see his member, her first male organ—the same boy she'd had breakfast with that very morning, that boy who said *vous* to his mother? She fled. For a long time, she would be ashamed she had seen him, watched them.

She sat on the dune, looking out at the sea, the tide was far out, you could see the kelp now, the dead fish, the tide had sculpted the sand into infinitesimal repetitive ridges. It was a temporary, threatening landscape. Sabine breathed in the salt wind as it gusted and whirled, blasts of invigorating salt air. She felt good now. She'd learned something more about life. Of course, she'd known it existed, a lot of writers were homosexual—Verlaine, Rimbaud, André Gide, even the actor James Dean, and Nureyev, the dancer; but most of those men were dead, and it had always seemed to her that living people were never homosexual. But last year, a classmate she was spending the afternoon with told her she liked making love with girls, and she'd suggested doing it with Sabine. Sabine had been shocked and upset and answered, vehemently, "I like men." And hearing herself say it had been like a jolt, as if this assertion, I like men (although thus far she had only ever flirted with them), meant she now had to put into practice, without delay, this assertion that would define her from that moment on. To be honest, she didn't know much about any of it, male or female homosexuality. She'd heard her parents talking compassionately about unhappy homosexuals, and she wondered if they would have felt so sorry for them if those people had been happy. Last month she'd heard Ménie Grégoire on the RTL radio station talking about *that painful problem.* She said no one knew why people became homosexual, but that all human beings could make mistakes. And then one of the guests started speaking (Sabine didn't know whether it was the priest or the psychoanalyst) and maintained that not all homosexuals suffered from their situation, that some of them even propagandized; she learned the word: propaganda. And then the guy said that it was perfectly possible to check it and become normal again. And someone in the audience shouted "Freedom," but Agnès came in the room just then to put away some laundry, and Sabine, confused, immediately switched off the radio, as if she were being disobedient. But to whom, she didn't know.

Sitting above the absent sea, she felt like running. And laughing. Crying, too. Like the Russians, in books by Dostoyevsky. Laughing and crying. Understanding nothing about oneself or others. Letting yourself be overcome by emotion, overwhelmed with sentimentalism and ideals. To live, you had to make noise. Seek your pleasure. Laugh. Cry. Be loud, incoherent, extravagant. She could see people fishing, holiday makers with their shrimp nets. They were tiny. They were happy. Their voices came to her from a distance, faint cries of joy that were swept into the wind, like locks of hair let loose. She was happy, too. Why, she didn't know. It had been so astonishing, seeing Vincent making love to a man. There'd be a fuss, a hell of a row. Did Hélène know? Had she decided not to mention it to Sabine, to protect him, to defend her second family? Did she share the Tavels' secrets? And what about the fine patriarch, so proud of his sons? All of them, screwed to the pedestal of their legacy—how could they accept this? Suddenly she understood that in the stables she had been a witness to what was known as *an indecent assault*, and that maybe Vincent, that daddy's boy, that dunce who said *vous* to his parents, might have a police record. Unless there, too, money protected him from danger? Money didn't just buy horses, servants, and pretty houses on cliffs. It didn't just allow you to get out of military service and work in Daddy's factory without being an actual worker. It also allowed you to have a body, and for your body to be free.

Sabine never asked to stay with the Tavels again, and Agnès was relieved. She didn't know that her daughter dreamed of setting off on her own, emancipated, and she took her silence for a preference: Sabine would rather live here with her in Aix than in Neuilly with her sister. But she felt renewed bitterness toward Hélène; after all, she had never said she didn't want to go there, never raised the slightest objection, and she was bound to make comparisons between her mother and her aunt, the way Agnès's own parents had, comparisons where Agnès was no more than a discreet daughter turned worthy wife and mother, whereas Michelle, by marrying a rich man who practiced a man's profession (providing for his family), had shown more ambition. Hélène sometimes displayed habits that came from elsewhere—the way she peeled her fruit, or looked absently for the fish knife. And there was the time she'd said *vous* to her: "Maman, don't *you* know where my cardigan is . . . forgive me! Forgive me . . ."

"Why are you saying *vous* to me?"

"Out of habit . . ."

"Are you in the habit of saying *vous* to me?"

"No."

"Well?"

For the first time they looked at each other with a sorrow they would not acknowledge.

Should Hélène not have enjoyed going *there*? Should she

have come home unhappy? Should she have never worn her red slicker, or the new clothes and shoes? And what about the pony? And the dog? Hélène's slicker didn't fit anymore, and she was getting too tall to ride Baloo—Before long you'll be able to brake with your feet, Vincent had said. Her body kept on growing, she felt she was bursting out of her own seams, only her breasts stayed small, as insipid as her gaze, which she didn't like, the green of her eyes like pale water in sunlight. Inside, she was still the little girl David had saved from drowning, and as ever there was that shadow, that threat: it can all come to an end, suddenly, it will all come to an end, inevitably, it's only a matter of time. And so, imperceptibly, as the months passed, everything became muddled and difficult. Keeping up in class. Remembering her lessons or simply writing correctly. She began racking up punishments, detention, notes for her parents to sign. Everyone said she was distracted. The minute there was a pillar somewhere, it was for Hélène. She would bump into it and say sorry. It was funny. Ridiculous. One morning she forgot to button her shirt and went out with her torso uncovered, and, by the time she finally realized, it filled her with such shame she became convinced that all the people she'd seen that morning would remember it all their life, that she would carry her nakedness around with her forever. She tried to be vigilant, to control herself, but she had bursts of temper that surprised even her. When it was over, she felt confused and exhausted. After catechism, she would go to confession, and to an invisible priest she said, I shouted at my little sister I wasn't kind I talked back to the teacher, and the priest behind his lattice gave her prayers as penance, which was something of a change from the hours of detention. In the long, cold church, while she was purging her sins, she missed her pony. She would have liked to hear the sound of those calm hooves, see her coming down the aisle toward her, guileless little pony, and since now she could *brake with her feet*, she would simply have walked with her, with Caprice as her watchful friend, proudly trotting alongside. She liked walking, feeling the sudden boldness of the wind, walking for a long time and feeling so small, almost invisible in a vast space. But Agnès was always afraid of losing her, and even during their Sunday picnics, she wasn't allowed to wander off. Agnès was a mother hen who constantly wanted her chicks under her wing; if they grew up, they would tear her wings, break her heart. Had Hélène caused her more heartache than her sisters? She couldn't remember her first stay at the Tavels', the first time she'd taken the plane with her name tag around her neck. She recalled one trip she'd taken when she was little, so proud, all of three years old, sitting in her seat, handing her ticket to the stewardess, who congratulated her on getting it right. Now she knew the stewardess had been putting on an act, because she herself had led the unaccompanied minor to her seat. The actual first visit to the Tavels' was forgotten—how she'd settled in, how they'd shown her to her bed, her place at the table, unless it all happened gradually, she came a first time, and they asked her back because it had gone well. Everything about her was just what they expected. And so, they came to an agreement, perhaps it was implicit, too, and everything evolved slowly, there was nothing sordid about their *arrangement.* Everyone had something to gain from it. Simply, as time passed, a breach had come between Hélène and her parents; adaptation upon her return required quickly taking stock of her loved ones. She saw her father, who made up with kindness and altruism for everything he could not lavish on his family financially. She saw her mother, hard-working and attentive, doggedly managing her household, and the rare moments she seemed to cast off her condition as housewife, when she really seemed to be her true self, were when they visited Laurence on Saturday afternoons at her *bastide.* Bruno would drop the four of them off then drive on to give his literacy classes in the old city in Aix, or in

Cité Beisson where the immigrants lived. At the entrance to the property, they left some of their worries and propriety behind, as if they had stowed their little bag of gloom in a checkroom, then they would walk up the avenue of cypress trees as if into a fairytale. When she saw her friend coming, surrounded by her daughters, Laurence invariably said, "They look like four sisters." Sabine had dubbed the place "the Embassy," because it was a haven of safety amid peril, amid real or imagined vexations. The girls went off together, and Agnès and Laurence stayed outside in all weathers, sitting under the linden tree, which acted as a parasol or an umbrella, and, when the mistral was blowing, they raised their voices and their words were scattered on the wind. What can they be talking about? wondered Sabine and Hélène, and while they were relieved their mother was no longer watching them, they were a little jealous.

Laurence was a free woman—untidy, joyful, and assertive. She didn't live with her husband. She wasn't divorced, just *separated*, and the difference was huge, because otherwise Bruno would never have allowed his wife to be her friend. Marriage vows are sacred, he explained to his daughters, they can never be broken, marriage is indissoluble, like metal in water, it is in-dis-so-lu-ble, it never ceases to exist, even after a divorce, because a marriage cannot be annulled, so divorce is simply impossible. It had been a relief to them to learn that their parents would never get divorced, that that particular misfortune *could not* happen, but in that indissolubility lurked a powerful energy that made marriage seem somehow doomed. Celebration took on an air of servitude, watched over by a god whose purpose was to make sure the contract was respected. Seen from such an angle, marriage suddenly seemed rigid and, above all, terribly risky. Matrimony was supposed to be happy, otherwise . . . But if you ended up an unwed mother, or practicing "free love," you would cut yourself off from the world of the living, or at least from your family, which to them amounted to the same thing. Laurence bewildered them, and they secretly hoped she would never divorce her faraway husband, who had left her the *bastide* and sent child support every month for Rose, while Laurence wrote articles for *Le Provençal,* trivial news items she filled with passion, as if every murder, burglary, or assault somehow concerned all men.

Sabine could spend hours in Rose's room, whispering, sitting cross-legged on her bed. The room was stuffy and always darkened, and there was a pervasive heavy smell of patchouli. Hélène thought that their murmured conversations went well with the rather dingy, soporific atmosphere. She would go off with Mariette to walk in the garden, where they would look out for lizards, catch grasshoppers that fidgeted in their closed hands, and Mariette would bring imaginary characters to life: there were blue children in the trees, and pigs in the thickets, and you had to talk to all of them, but quietly, making sounds in your throat, murmured trills. She was so diminutive, like an elf, she invented a world and Hélène went along with it. It was restful to enter that world, to believe in all sorts of things. Fascinated, they watched the gardener at work. Marius was a sort of gentle giant, a man of few words (perhaps he was mute), constantly nodding his head. Despite his apparent kindness, they were a little afraid of him. Sometimes, Mariette fell asleep in the grass, and so Hélène lay down beside her, gazing up at the trees, the clouds among the dancing leaves, the rapid flight of birds whose names she did not know. She gazed at this life in the sky, and wondered where the dead went, with their sadness, their holes in their hearts, could they breathe better up there, had they joined the dead who'd gone before them, was there a gathering of all the departed? She heard the rake scraping over the gravel, the clack of the pruning shears, the spray of water, as if the gardener were the conscientious guardian of the world of the living. She loved the smell of damp earth, and of the scorched grass, which tickled her throat; she rubbed mint and thyme between her fingers, and, mingled with her sweat, they smelled nasty, a mixture of bitter sugar and sweat. This was life. Everything mixing. Contradicting. Dissolving. Unlike marriage and the laws of marriage, unlike families and the laws of families. Sometimes, she closed her eyes and fell asleep, too, holding Mariette's hand to be sure not to lose her and to always remember this plump, innocent softness. She thought, Little sister, it suits you so well: little tiny little sister.

Then there was that afternoon Mariette wanted to stay "with the girls on the dirty bed," and Hélène went for a walk in the garden alone, then ventured further, beyond the well-kept lawn and the tidy flowerbeds. It wasn't as welcoming. Yellow bushes, low crumbling walls, the roots of plane trees reaching out of the ground like dead arms, and the smells were already different, dry, slightly fetid, old. You could see what the house had been built on, and what it had been like before the labor of men, the deep mark of their desire to live there. She saw the cabin where the gardener lived, and because she was a little afraid, she went closer. The door was open and the interior was so dark that it was like a burrow, and it took her a moment to make out the room. It was narrow, with a single high window. A table, a dresser, two chairs, long strips of flypaper spotted with insects, and a fireplace so small it could have been a simple hole dug in the stone. As for the gardener, she saw only his back, and, initially, she didn't understand what he was doing. He didn't turn around to her, and if she said hello her voice was so timid that maybe he didn't hear. He was making careful, repetitive gestures. Crouching down before a tiny fire with the tongs, he was taking something very small from what looked like a shoebox, by his feet, and placing it in the fire. The flames were low and slender, they put her in mind of sickly, wriggling tongues, being patiently fed by the gardener. She sat down on the chair, because her legs were trembling and she wanted to watch. She couldn't detect any smell from what was burning. And, slowly, Marius turned around to her, holding out the tongs, to show her, then he turned back, and, putting the object into the flames, he said, "They destroy everything." It was the first time she'd heard his voice. Now that she had seen, it was as if her senses had come alive, she could hear the faint squeaking in the shoebox and smell the burned flesh. How many were there, she wondered, in a litter of mice. Marius made the same movement over and over, reaching down, burning, and starting over, and she saw the pink, translucent skin, the ugly baby mice like huge commas of curled flesh. She stood up, out of politeness, not to vomit in the cabin but further away, in the garden.

That evening, she asked Sabine if she was sure that babies and animals didn't feel pain, and although she now knew what the word "scientific" meant, she wanted a bit more of an explanation. But Sabine didn't feel like talking to her that evening, she was reading with the flashlight she switched off as soon as she heard her parents' footsteps in the corridor, and only then she asked her, irritated, to think for just five minutes about whether babies and animals were conscious, or what? "Just ask yourself for five minutes whether babies and animals have emotions, all right?" "What are you reading?" asked Hélène, and Sabine turned over in her bed and sighed, "A weird magazine." To end the discussion, she said that they operated on babies without anesthesia because scientists—them again—were absolutely sure they didn't suffer, so Hélène could sleep in peace and leave her to her reading. But Hélène didn't sleep in peace. She slept with a lump of anxiety in her throat. Sabine was growing away from her, it was as if she were living in the Pampas with a little machete in her hand, and she was trying to make her way, slashing through the tall grasses; the geography teacher had shown them a documentary, Hélène couldn't help but picture her sister in that distant landscape, lost and militant, a selfish person who thought only of her own survival.

The children's room became the teenagers' room, with secret lighting, inhabited by awkward questions and forbidden emotions, but beyond all the things that put them ill at ease (all this new, sketchy knowledge) was the intuition that maybe they weren't obliged to live the way they were being asked to live. As a carbon copy of their parents. After their final exams, they would go on to university, would learn a profession they might actually be able to practice, even if they had children. Bruno regularly said that women who worked were taking a man's place, that the finest job for a woman was . . . and before he could finish his sentence, Agnès and his daughters would shout in unison, "A wife and mother!" then burst out laughing, nervously, somewhat exasperated.

Agnès was better off at home than with some boss at a factory or a supermarket, of course, and what sort of profession could she have had? She no longer had the body of a ballerina, and it was too late to study languages or medicine. All her plans had become old childhood dreams, and she would never know what she might have been good at, what her place in a world without motherhood might have been. Her daughters were growing up, "They no longer fit in my arms," she said, and she had to look up to speak to Sabine, who was so tall now. Mariette went to nursery school every morning now, and wanted to go in the afternoon, too, but Agnès kept her with her, it was better for her to take her nap at home. As for Hélène, it seemed like she spent all her time going down to the basement to get her suitcase, that mysterious suitcase that Sabine went on opening every time her sister came home, as if performing some sort of customs check. Going to see Laurence, yes, there she found some peace and quiet, at last, there in the Embassy, Sabine had found the right word for it, as she often did, it must be all those books she read, and which she hid from her most of the time. She figured that when Mariette started primary school, she would borrow books and read. When she told Bruno this, he advised her to join a reading group where she'd meet "young women her own age" and that left her feeling incredibly low. Meeting "young women her own age"—the flock of rejects. You could be sure that "the young women her age" would talk about their children, and their children's problems, that they would talk about their husbands, and their husbands' salaries, proud of their social status—and, after all, was Laurence any different, claiming as she did to live as an independent, emancipated woman? But who was paying her rent? Who was paying for her daughter's education? Definitely not the articles she tossed off now and again for *Le Provençal.* Hers was a luxury emancipation, the Bohemian life of people with means, and if the *bastide* was an embassy, it wasn't for the reasons Bruno imagined. His wife wasn't having tea with a friend while his daughters were picking flowers. His wife could at last openly express a dissenting opinion. Laurence would bring up a topic they didn't agree on—religion, education, and what she called "female emancipation"—and they would embark on heated verbal sparring matches the likes of which Agnès had never known, clashes from which she emerged disturbed but happy. Her own virulence surprised her. Was it because she was frustrated, as Laurence said? But frustrated about what? She liked making love with her husband, and he was "very good at it if you really want to know." This confession had left her troubled, because she wondered whether Laurence might want to try for herself, to find out. Her husband. That handsome, upstanding, loyal man. Who liked to sing, drink, smoke, and make love. A sensual Catholic, and there were safety barriers all around his sensuality, which in some respects made their lives easier. They didn't have the time or the energy for suspicion. They had to trust each other and that, they did. They'd been kids when they met at David and Michelle's wedding, and they'd followed the protocol to a T: a chaste year for their engagement, preparing for the marriage with a friendly, distracted priest, who alternated pastoral metaphors with injunctions to obedience. Nothing tangible or very enlightening. As a child, Agnès had realized that she was being told a lie: it wasn't the storks who brought babies, but, honestly, that it turned out to be such a secretive, dirty thing—what was anyone supposed to do, what was this repulsive thing they were taking on? What she'd thought was: you have to drink your husband's urine. That was surely what you had to do to have a baby. As an adult she knew, obviously, that something else would happen, but she didn't know exactly what. She learned everything all on her own. She learned to make love with a man who, on their wedding night, was as innocent a virgin as she was. Who had never been to a brothel, either in the army, or in town, because he had "kept himself for her," the woman he would marry. They were two kids, full of desire and taboos. Two adults who were deeply religious, for whom Christ and the Virgin were solid role models; they'd never believed in the vengeful God some had tried to sell them during their youth, they believed in the goodness of their Maker. They respected the Ten Commandments and dreamed of a world that would respect them, too, by abolishing violence and eradicating evil, they dreamed of a more egalitarian life, where the poor would not be as poor nor the rich as rich, and there would be clemency and forgiveness, too. But they didn't always understand what the Church expected of them, and sometimes they disobeyed: they took Communion on Sunday even when they'd made love the night before with no intention of procreating. They didn't always keep the fast during Lent, or confess before every Communion. That way, they allowed themselves cumbersome freedoms, and, in the end, whatever they did, it was a sin. Sin was everywhere. From the bedroom to the films you watched, the books and newspapers you read, the number of children you had and the education you gave them. There was never anyone to reassure them, to say a single merciful word to them, to grant them a little indulgence in life. It was never enough. It was never right. And their daughters were growing up surrounded by influences they could not control. They wanted them to know something radically different from what they had known, which was the indifference of their own parents, the impression as they were growing up that with so many siblings, they were mere numbers in the family, although they were amused by the fact that both of them were "number seven" in their families, and the youngest, as well. They wanted their love to be a weapon to take on the world, and they tried to find their bearings in order to be good parents. The events of May '68 had frightened them. The students, the feminists: surely, they would jeer at the likes of Bruno and Agnès, find them old-fashioned and ridiculous. But there had been a joy to the movement which intrigued them, despite its radical, uncompromising nature. The slogans, demands, cobblestones hurled, fists raised: Bruno had condemned it all, but Agnès, sometimes, could understand. The desire to see the bigger picture, to see for oneself. She could feel the blood in her veins, she could feel the muffled rhythm rising in her breast, this invitation to throw off all the taboos that had always structured the heavy routine of her existence.

II
Dreams of Anything Else

It was an evening in May, night softly falling, a half-moon drifting timidly in the brown sky. Bruno was at a meeting at Sainte-Catherine, Hélène was sleeping over at a friend's, Mariette was in bed, and Agnès and Sabine enjoyed the luxury of expediting the evening meal. It hadn't taken long to prepare, nor were there many dishes to wash, so it was like a foretaste of vacation, a cozy, girlish complicity. They settled in front of the television hoping to be entertained, and they were ready for a story. But from the very first images, they were sorry they'd started watching the news together. The reportage was a descent into a world where no one would like to be. The music was mournful, the images bleak, an empty building in a housing project with deserted stairways, a place that might have been urgently evacuated or, on the contrary, abandoned long ago. A tragic voice warned them: "Our investigation found that a veritable network had been operating in Grenoble for several months. Let's take a closer look at the facts, as they have come to light." They were afraid of what might come next. They didn't look at each other. "The police have uncovered a very well-organized abortion center." The camera zoomed in on a poster, to focus on the words FREE ACCESSIBLE ABORTION, and, filling the entire screen, the words remained printed on their retinas. Agnès and Sabine felt as if they were being pointed at. Targeted. All those girls being led to the altar by their mothers, the twosome of resourcefulness, anxiety and humiliation. Now a woman was speaking: "At

Choisir[1] we have decided to take action on two fronts: the legal action with which you are familiar, namely a draft bill, initiatives among the deputies in government, but also illegal action. We have been carrying out abortions in an exemplary manner." Agnès switched off the TV, with feverish authority. Sabine had recognized the lawyer, Halimi; she recalled the trial in Bobigny six months earlier, in November, their French teacher had devoted an hour of class to it. Was it allowed? She'd mentioned the presence of Simone de Beauvoir at the trial, and provided figures, the numbers of those who'd died, been mutilated, left sterile for life, or imprisoned. The students had listened in tense silence. After the First World War, in 1920, state policy had been to boost the birth rate and ban any contraceptive measures. Did they, the students, understand that this trial, thanks to Gisèle Halimi, was not therefore simply the trial of an under-age girl who'd been raped before undergoing an abortion, but also that of a law that was over fifty years old, which assimilated abortion to a crime warranting prosecution? The students didn't really understand, they sat there silent, almost hostile. And then one girl cited the exact cost of an abortion: over four thousand francs,[2] and everyone wondered how she knew. One girl said you could hear the fetus's heartbeat, that it was a crime, and another countered that it was poverty that was on trial, the bodies of women who were poor. Everything was difficult, vaguely nauseating, what was being said, and what was being kept quiet, too.

Sitting in front of the silent television, in the gloom of the

[1] Or, *Choisir la cause des femmes* (Choose the Cause of Women), a movement founded in 1971 by Gisèle Halimi and Simone de Beauvoir to decriminalize abortion in France.

[2] Nearly 4,500 euros in today's money.

unlit living room, Agnès said in a hushed voice: "You would tell me, wouldn't you, if something happened to you?"

"Would you go to prison for me?"

"I'm your mother."

They heard Mariette crying. Agnès leapt up, as she always did. Then hesitated a moment and said, not looking at Sabine: "Above all, I don't want you to feel ashamed."

And she hurried to give her youngest daughter some Ventolin, which had replaced the vapor of hot water.

Sabine went out, she didn't slam the door, but she felt like ransacking the apartment. How dare her mother ask her not to be ashamed, when everything existed precisely to ensure that shame was like her second skin? She ran through the housing project, it was ugly here, too, so they must also carry out illegal abortions here, organized massacres, and looting. She ran, and didn't know where to go. She stopped once she was past the buildings, by the road, under a plane tree that was standing to attention in the night like a wayward sentry. "Above all I don't want you to feel ashamed!" And what else, while you're at it? Ah, yes, feminists wanted a happy sex life, a revolution in birth control, all that stuff was like their "exemplary abortions"—what a joke. Who was going to prescribe the pill for her? Who would she get permission from? Her father, or her mother? Under the official pretext that she wanted "to make her periods more regular!" And which parent would she ask to foot the bill? to agree to be on file in the pharmacy's counterfoil book? She felt the anger welling as she enumerated all the obstacles governing her life. She felt trapped, under surveillance, too, as if she were accountable to men in high places who didn't know her.

She was all alone by the side of the road, and she felt uneasy, she wasn't used to being outside at night. She had just turned seventeen and her parents never let her go out at night, only in the afternoon—as if they hadn't worked it out that you can make love in the afternoon. And yet that was what she was doing, she'd been living this new life, a shared sex life, for several months now. Jean-Louis, her boyfriend, was good in bed, the way others are good at math or soccer. He played twelve-string guitar, and, she told her girlfriends, "He's got a great fingering technique." This made them laugh, made them want to take him from her, they just had to wait a little, relationships never lasted long, wait a few months and they'd split up, the fear of becoming a couple, of getting stuck in that old pattern, that was good for their parents. It wasn't so much the act itself that gave Sabine pleasure, but what they called "foreplay," but she didn't dare tell anyone because in the books they said just the opposite, the girl went crazy the moment she felt a man's penis inside her, maybe that was another stage, something that would come when she got older. For the time being, there was no question of love, just logistics: hygiene, the price of a condom, where to hide it, how to put it on and where to dispose of it, where the parents would be at a given time, doors that didn't lock, stains on sheets, and all the ruses to hide the fact that *yes, something was indeed happening to her.* Her sex life was bound by strict contingencies: don't make any noise, don't act like you're fast (don't show you like it too much, don't ask for more) and an implicit contract: you could need your partner, but don't ever get attached to him. And obviously, you had to demystify it all when you talked about it in the schoolyard. The twelve-string guitarist had a thick North African accent, he called Sabine "my sweetness" in that accent, and for a laugh, her girlfriends did the same, when they saw her coming, they shouted, "my sweeeetnessss!" as if they were imitating a goat. The point was to make light of everything, brush off any disappointment, and bury your dreams of anything else deep in the ground.

Sabine slowly walked home. She was sorry Hélène wasn't there, they could have talked for a while. Her sister was growing up, too, and she knew things that Sabine didn't. She talked to her about river pollution, about peasants who died from touching plants they'd been looking after, it was nightmarish and confusing. Sometimes, she caught her reading the newspaper she herself had bought but, embarrassed, Hélène would put it down, carefully, making no comment.

Agnès was waiting for her. She went down the stairs to meet her as soon as she heard the front door.

"Your father is here. I didn't tell him you went out. I was worried sick. Where were you?"

She led her into the kitchen. The light was yellow, dingy. It looked to Sabine as if her mother was smiling, but it was surely a trick of the light. Now she put a little box on the table, as if slamming down a playing card.

"One pill every evening at bedtime, starting the first day of your period."

"What's this? How did you get it?"

"I'm of age, after all."

"Does Papa know?"

"You're not allowed to tell him. If he knew you were taking this! At your age."

"But Maman . . . it's forbidden . . ."

"Well, the Pope can say what he likes, I'm taking the pill, but I'm faithful to your father. Go to bed."

Lying in bed, Sabine touched the blister pack blindly with her fingertips. So, this was it. It was so small. A concentrated dose of hormones, and the misery was over. Could her mother be charged for what she had just done? Sabine didn't have a doctor's prescription. Did she have the right to one? Would she have to ask her for a blister pack every month? Did this mean that she, Sabine, was depriving her mother of her own dose? Would the twelve-string guitarist believe her when she said, I'm on the pill? Would it give her a bad reputation? She got up. The fine sliver of half-moon lay in the sky as if baffled at how it got there. She looked at the buildings across the way, beyond the tall pine tree. There were lights in some of the windows, little squares of solitude. Sometimes, a light would go out and it was impossible to guess where the person had gone, whether walking around in artificial light had helped them a little. Sabine thought she would sign up for a drama class, here in Aix-en-Provence, since Paris was so far away. She felt like her life had just changed. Her life had just handed her an invitation. And she said, Yes, I'm on my way.

He was handsome, dressed the way Hélène liked him, no longer the hurried CEO but a man of leisure, with his sailor's cap sitting proudly on his head, his moth-eaten sweater, his old canvas trousers, there was a childish joy about him, he was happy, as if he were giving them the ocean, the wind, the burning sun, and even this slight seasickness, the panic when the boat heeled, "Drink some whiskey!" he said, and Hélène drank from the bottle, like a guy, it was disgusting but it really did make her feel better; Michelle drank, too, her hair escaping from her scarf, she had to shout to make herself heard, her voice caught between the wind and the boat's engine, she was complaining because there was no one to serve her and she was overwhelmed, pointlessly busy. David laughed; his wife was incapable of doing anything properly without a servant. He looked on her like a father who's realized he's raised his daughter all wrong and turned her into a spoiled brat. Whenever they went somewhere like this the three of them, Hélène became an only child, and she knew very well she was helping to improve the situation: if she weren't there her aunt and uncle would have trouble putting up with each other.

David asked her to take the helm, to stay with him and let Michelle prepare the meal, "let her get on with her housewife business on her own." Hélène had made her way to him at the rear of the boat, holding on to everything she saw—the table, the seats, the railing; she was careful not to put her bare feet on any ropes or cables or boat hooks as, hunched and clumsy, she made her way aft, and in spite of her desire to do a good job, her desire for David to see her as a proper little sailor, she felt clueless. She would never be someone he could rely on for long crossings, and maybe he'd eventually get fed up with her awkwardness, which, for the moment, simply amused him. They were on their way to Jersey, and he asked her how good her English was. She hesitated to lie, she would have so liked for him to be proud of her, but the minute they reached the island he would unmask her, so she confessed that she wasn't very good at languages. She didn't mention her failings in other subjects, how difficult she found it to study, to get used to the school system.

"Your mother said you got a very good score for the school certification exam."

"Yes, but the school certificate is easy."

"Look further into the distance, stare at a point on the horizon . . . steer a little to the left . . . gently, no abrupt gestures, stare at that point . . . straighten up . . . straighten up a little more . . . not too much . . ."

The wheel seemed to quiver in her hands, she focused, and before long the sustained concentration on that spot in the distance made her fall into a sort of trance, nothing could distract her attention, it was as if she were being sucked into the metallic glaze of the sea, and she felt as if she were at the heart of the world. A threatened heart. Her geography teacher had told them about the *Torrey Canyon* disaster, 120,000 tons of oil spilled onto the coast of Brittany and the island of Guernsey . . . so close to Jersey. How long would the water be poisoned? How could you see the death of the ocean depths? Here, the sky was pure and the ocean was in harmony with it, two magnificent mirrors, superimposed. She wondered if it was possible for the sky to gaze at her; did she really exist in this seascape?

David settled on one of the seats, to show her he trusted her, but despite his encouragement she was afraid of disappointing him. Of not steering properly. Not speaking English very well. Maybe she'd be seasick, start to feel faint. He raised his thumb to congratulate her, so she relaxed and began to enjoy what was around her, the privilege of what she was experiencing.

"Watch out for the buoys! Steer a little to the left!"

She gave a start and jerked on the wheel, the boat heeled and she could hear things sliding in the cabin, and Michelle shouting. David laughed and came over to her, resumed his place at the wheel and told her she just needed practice.

Their arrival at the port of Saint Helier was a nightmare. David was shouting orders with an urgent authority that left her in a total panic, and the harder she tried, the more her efforts came to naught. Holding out the boathook, she clumsily pushed away from the fenders of the boats that were moored, but she didn't manage to catch the ring on their mooring buoy. She tried over and over, her arms aching, her body broken in two, and, in the end, the boat hook slipped from her hands and fell into the water. "What a clumsy birdbrain!" said Michelle, while a young guy dove off a sailboat a bit further along to tie up their boat for them. Tanned and relaxed, he was like something straight out of a commercial for *Hollywood Chewing Gum*; he shouted a few words in English, and once the boat was moored, he set off again, executing a perfect backstroke. Hélène was bright red, shame suffusing her face, while the world around them was so calm. Motionless boats under the sun, the lapping of water against the aluminum hulls, the fortress towering above the island: the place was a haven of indolence and well-being. But she—Michelle had said as much—was a birdbrain. A ninny. A silly goose. Words with no obvious intent to hurt; polite insults. Birdbrain. Ninny. Silly goose. Words her aunt was using more and more often, and she wondered what had brought about the change, how they had gone from affectionate closeness to exasperation. Michelle called her a birdbrain when she played poorly at Scrabble, when she didn't know how to make hospital corners on her bed, when she put the stem glasses in the wrong order, when she failed to put a horse's bridle on in one go. Michelle made fun of her, then suddenly turned warm-hearted again and told her for the umpteenth time, "stories of when you were little." Like when Hélène, in a daze, reached for a strange woman's hand in a department store, or the time she'd taken a surgeon, a family friend, for a deliveryman, because he was holding a bouquet of flowers—and then gave him a tip; or when, to impress Michelle, she ran across the Champs-Élysées just as the light for the cars turned green; or when she'd criticized her aunt for wearing makeup and "spoiling God's work"—all those remarks that made little Hélène so charming, so naïve, and, most of the time, completely out of touch. The more she heard about the adventures of that little girl who was three or four or five years old, and rarely older, the more she wondered whether growing up wasn't a disadvantage. The awkward age, the sudden growth spurt with pimples and mood swings: that was what characterized a thirteen-year-old girl. That was what she had in her suitcase until Michelle got around to filling it with new clothes and good manners. That was what she brought with her from her provincial backwater. And sometimes, too, a little local color. Her aunt asked her to sing *La Chanson de Toulon* for her friends, "with the accent." Hélène didn't have the slightest Provençal accent, but she knew how to imitate it, and she also knew that, to keep Michelle's friends happy, she would have to exaggerate as she sang by adding a very loud, bouncing "eh" at the end of practically every word, weighing it down as if she were sucking on some sticky molasses, while adopting the clueless air of the actor Fernandel staring at Christ on the cross. Michelle's friends laughed and congratulated her, and sometimes asked for an encore.

But that wasn't the worst of it; the worst had been that morning in Villers when, in the maid's room, Michelle found half her tea set, a Chinese vase, two Art Deco lamps, silver flatware and a few crystal glasses. The tiny room was in the basement, adjacent to the garage. Michelle had forced the maid to spread her loot out on the bed; all the disparate objects resembled a flea market. The girl had packed her bags and no one had taken her to the station, she left in a hurry, just thanking Madame for not pressing charges. So that day, they'd had to come up with their own lunch, and at the end of the meal they'd each cleared away their plates, then Hélène had swept. Michelle was having coffee with a girlfriend, both of them glanced at Hélène, and her aunt whispered apologetically: "She's used to . . ." and her friend had replied, her tone gently pitying, "She's a good girl." Hélène went on sweeping.

She took a shower in the marina's facilities then met David at the bar. He had washed and changed, too: Lacoste polo shirt, a neat crease to his trousers, and now he was sitting in one of the club armchairs with a cigar in one hand and a glass of whiskey in the other, surrounded by satisfied men. He introduced her as his daughter, then told her he'd come and join Michelle and her later, they should go ahead and start on the shopping without him.

She left him to his virile affinities, those men who had the same cards to the same clubs, a caste unto themselves, cut off from the rest of the world, a world which was there to serve them, one way or another. They were not parvenus, they were rulers, far from the vulgarity of the nouveau riche, they were to the manor born, sons and grandsons of men who had a talent for managing their fortunes. Theirs was a domination without arrogance, taken for granted. Hélène was flattered that David had introduced her as his daughter, but then superimposed upon the image of her powerful uncle was that of her own father, an image of patient altruism and humility. To Hélène, it was as if she had a heart for each one of them, the left side and the right side, a steady, constant rhythm. But she didn't know which one she was betraying by loving them both.

The afternoon was spent in a vaguely ridiculous fashion, going around the shops instead of walking around the island, seeing nothing but shopping streets, buying pearls, Shetland sweaters, and toffees, a frivolous way of sticking with what they knew best: spending money. That evening, they had supper on board the boat, the hurricane lamp swinging gently above the table, the light dancing on their plastic plates, and this gave the meal an unexpected, almost rustic simplicity. They could hear the voices of the yachtsmen on the other boats, the sound of their dishes, their footsteps on the dock, and Michelle said, "You see, Hélène, there's something just as cozy and friendly about sailing as going camping." It was probably true, and yet, inexplicably, the comment hurt. After dinner, she sat at the bow to watch the night close over the sea. Vanished horizon, the lanterns on the boats, the lights on the island, the quivering stars: there was something sad about all this beauty. David came noiselessly, discreet as a cat, and sat beside her, and, his voice low, he said, "It's beautiful, isn't it?"

"Yes."

Both of them were very moved, and aware of their shared emotion. This moment belonged to them. Something was sealed. Whatever might happen to them later in life, without ever evoking it, they would always have this moment. Maybe they had come here for no other reason than to live it. And leave again.

On returning from a crossing, they were in the habit of having dinner served to them during the televised evening news, as if to gently re-immerse themselves into the real world they seemed to have left behind for so long. They felt vaguely disoriented, but were pleased to get back to their usual comfort, their ordinary obligations. Hélène recalled something her mother once said, "You have to go out, that way you're glad to get home." She was reunited with Caprice, who whimpered with happiness, frenetically licking her face; she thought how funny it would be if humans could be reunited in the same way, could manifest with similarly shameless sincerity their joy at seeing one another again. And yet, confronted with such immoderate affection, she sometimes thought the dog had the wrong recipient. Had he really chosen her? Could he sense qualities in her that no one else had noticed?

Joseph had just arrived in Villers—the eldest son, the cousin she had no affinities with, was slightly afraid of. He was self-assured and very handsome, she was intimidated by his aura, his aloof irony and his "*sex appeal*" (she misheard and wrote, "sex-apple-peel"). He had a reputation as a Don Juan, and worked at his father's firm in the advertising department. He was rumored to be an incompetent dilettante; he'd obtained a Mickey Mouse baccalaureate in 1968. Michelle and David didn't speak to him as a son, but rather as the sort of friend you admire, grateful for their presence. Hélène felt very marginal in their immediate circle; to be called "the Tavel girl" was only an expression, their name would never figure on her ID card. They really expected something from Joseph. He was the future of the family, the pride they took in the name. His parents invested all their hopes in him, the way they invested money in stocks and shares.

That evening on the news, there was much talk of the exceptionally hot weather that day, Tuesday, August 14, 1973; people were shown sunbathing in noisy, cheerful groups. Then, with no transition, the anchorman said: "Besançon was taken by surprise this morning. Shortly before 6 A.M., three months to the day since the workers first occupied the factory, riot squad police entered the premises and forcibly evacuated the company's entire personnel of fifty or more workers . . ." When they heard the word "Besançon" David and Joseph sat up and leaned toward the television set, as if on high alert. Hélène could see how their shared hostility brought them closer. Television cameras and microphones had traveled all the way to the Doubs region at the break of day, and, in the gray morning air, sleepy workers were shown leaving the factory, answering the journalists' questions, their thick accents weighing on their words. One young blond woman was asked, "How does it feel to be leaving the factory?" but she didn't reply. She ran her hand through her hair, tried to say something, and couldn't. Another worker answered for her: "It's sickening."

"How long had you been holding out in there?"

And as if she'd suddenly regained her wits, the woman said, "Almost four months."

She couldn't seem to believe what was happening and slowly walked away with the helmeted policeman who had come to rouse her from her sleep, shoving her in the back. David and Joseph remained watchful and silent. But when another worker denounced the "intolerable power granted to employers," that led to something else altogether. They were instantly filled with anger. Their words turned virulent, committed, they were father and son, equally incensed, they were more "Tavel" than ever before, a powerful family defending themselves. Hélène looked at them, the way they dared to protest against the televised evening news, as if what was being reported concerned them personally. Michelle said, "This country will never change," and David said, "I'm going back to Paris tomorrow." Language of the utmost urgency.

Not even finishing his meal, he called his associate, or was it his accountant, or his lawyer, it was hard to tell, tense telephone calls, where each time he said, "I'll be back in Paris tomorrow," and then he called his father in Geneva. He pulled on the telephone cord and went over to the picture window, looking out at the red sun dropping into the sea, and he said, "Papa, it's me," and his voice—maybe because Switzerland was far away, maybe because his father was elderly—was high-pitched, like that of a kid who can't make up his mind. The telephone cord, Hélène saw, was quivering slightly, like a leash when a dog tugs a little. The atmosphere was electric. It was as if the Lip[3] strike concerned David directly, and yet he didn't sell watches at all. Franz Tavel, his father, was friends with a man who was high up in the Swiss multinational that was taking over the Besançon factory, one of those directors who, to reassure the stockholders, had decided to lay off workers and restructure the company around spare parts. Hélène looked at David, his brow against the picture window, his gaze focused on the sun, which had almost disappeared, as he listened

[3] The Lip factory produced watches; the factory was self-managed and workers went out on strike when the Board attempted to restructure the factory.

closely to his father's loud voice, which they could all hear. Michelle explained it all to Hélène, in a hushed voice: the workers had locked up the administrator, stolen documents, and watches, too, to sell them themselves and make as much money as they could. She had grimaced when she said it; she was disgusted, and she stood by David, he would protect her, because she was afraid. The anchorman had also reported that there had already been demonstrations and walk-outs that morning all over the country: the workers at Kelton, another watchmaker in the region; government employees at the Social Security, at the post office, at the national railroad. Make as much money as they could . . .

That night, lying in her bed, Caprice curled at her feet, Hélène thought about Sabine. She missed her terribly. She wouldn't dare to go buy *Le Monde* at the bar-tabac in Villers tomorrow: that "left-wing" newspaper was not allowed in the Tavel home. Sabine had surely heard the news, maybe she'd even seen it on television, even though she was in the Landes with the family of the little boy she babysat for during the year; now it was a full month of childcare. Hélène would have liked to ask her sister if she knew what to expect, once they left their childhood behind. She pictured riot police in helmets at the door to their bedroom, about to shove them in the back toward the adult world. "How long had you been holding out in there?"

The next day when she awoke the house was quiet. David and Joseph had already left for Paris without saying goodbye. It was low tide, the beach was deserted, the sky was as straight as a die, a very pale blue. It felt like September. Michelle informed her she had just signed her up at the Tennis Club, her first private lesson was at two that afternoon. Hélène thought of her mother, her constant advice, unchanged over the years; and so, instinctively, out of habit, she obeyed. She said thank you.

It's all because of the war in Vietnam, didn't you know? That war you see on television, Hélène, and the photo of that little girl those imperialist Americans burned with napalm, you remember? 'We have to fight communism,' Papa said, 'but burning children, and showing that little girl naked, no, no, no, and when I think about her parents, oh my God.' Don't you remember? And I thought you were so interested in ecology, haven't you heard of agent orange, the stuff the American army uses? I can't believe you don't know about it!"

"Why?"

"Because there's nothing left, there, in Vietnam, no more forests, no more agriculture, and they contaminated the Vietnamese and the GIs with dioxin, it's horrible. Cancer, malformations, can you imagine . . . Well, no, maybe you can't imagine, maybe it's better that way . . ."

"Why are you talking to me like this, as if I were an idiot?"

"Let me explain, don't get annoyed. What I want to tell you is that, way before the photograph of the little girl who was burned, everyone was furious about the war, well . . . when I say everyone . . . mainly students, but everywhere, in America, Australia, Scandinavia, in Rome, Berlin, London, and even Tokyo, didn't Tavel tell you about it? He works in Asia, doesn't he, and he never told you? Ah . . . It looks like he doesn't tell you much . . ."

Hélène hated it when Sabine mocked her love for David, as if it were a ludicrous sentiment that made everyone laugh. At the time, she could never find the words to defend herself, and, by the time the right repartee finally occurred to her, the discussion was long over. Sabine was full of a newly-acquired self-confidence: "What do you think it was all about, May '68? Maybe you only remember that Maman was stocking up on sugar and we couldn't buy gas anywhere. But the world is waking up, Hélène! I found out, I've been talking with some really cool people in the Landes, people older than me, and now I understand it all."

I'm a birdbrain, thought Hélène, and she could feel the anger welling inside her, turning against her, already she was pinching her thighs through her dress, and clenching her teeth fit to chip the enamel.

"What do you do in Paris all day long, huh? You walk the dog and have the maid serve you? Is that it?"

"Shut up! Just shut up!"

Hélène's voice was so loud that Sabine gave a start, she hadn't seen it coming, so much raw pain. She was actually impressed.

"For a start, we don't say 'the maid,' we say 'the household employee.' We don't call him 'the dog,' his name is 'Caprice,' and besides, I know a lot of things, oh yes I do!"

"Such as?"

"Like . . . like . . ."

"Go on, tell me! Politics? Do you know anything about politics? Do you, Hélène? You live with people who think they rule the world, but the world is turning and turning, and the faster it spins, the sooner it will send them flying, simple as that!"

"I don't live with them. I live here, too, this is my room here."

"Oh, don't go putting on your sulky face, huh, that doesn't work with me. You asked me why employers are afraid of the workers at Lip, but that's like asking me why straw is afraid of fire! Nowadays workers—on their own, for their own survival—

can produce what, yesterday, they had to produce in order for the stockholders to get rich, don't you see? And as a result, other workers have been showing their solidarity toward them. Do you see how they're all connected, these strikes all over France? The connection, Hélène, is the proletariat, it's freedom. Do you hear me? Free-dom!"

There was so much spite in Hélène's gaze that Sabine was disconcerted, and as if for the first time she saw tiny gold specks in her sister's green eyes.

"Don't go putting on that poor hurt little sister act, Hélène. I know you're angry all the time, so angry you're scratching yourself all over. I've seen you when you leave the bath, your thighs are covered in scratches, and your butt, too. It would do you good, you know."

"What would?"

"To decide whose side you're on."

She had no answer for that. Hélène went out of the apartment and sat outside by the entrance, on a bench covered in graffiti and bird shit. She was overwhelmed with a burning sorrow; she thought of the gardener's tongs holding the baby mice. She didn't want to be seen anymore as the privileged, ignorant sister. She was not a pawn. A piece to take and move around the board. "You walk the dog and have the maid serve you?" If you only knew, Sabine, all the things I do, you're the one who would never understand. Sometimes, I put on a little white skirt to play tennis, and sometimes I go to the Channel Islands on a yacht, only we never put up the sails because that would take too much effort, and we make a crossing for no reason, just to drink a whiskey in the marina, and buy toffee, and pearls, real pearls like in that film with Audrey Hepburn you like so much. From time to time, I even get to be "the daughter of the house." Maybe you don't know what that is. You go up to each guest, holding a little tray of petits fours, and you smile. Sometimes I sweep up, too, but that's not something you could understand, either. I wanted to know why David was afraid of the strike at Lip. I worry about him, and I miss him because I love him, and even if he sent the cops in against his workers, I'd still love him.

She could sense that Sabine had come to sit on the bench next to her. She was aware of her smell, the shape of her body, this new thing she had of sighing all the time. She'd brought her tape recorder with her, and was holding it on her lap. This was a clear sign she wanted reconciliation. Hélène wasn't sure she felt like making peace. Sabine spoke to her more calmly, as if she'd regained a touch of respect for her:

"All I wanted to tell you, Hélène, is that for years students all over the world have been demonstrating and getting killed for demonstrating, and others keep going, and that girl who was occupying her factory, the one you told me about, she reminds me of another female worker who went on strike, too, and she didn't want to go back to work, she was weeping and screaming that she'd never set foot in that place ever again, that it was like a prison, a shit house, and they were all disgusting, their arms were all black, and she knew she'd be screwed if she went back to work, the boss would've won, and it would all have been for nothing, she'd go on making batteries on the assembly line for a shit salary. But in the end, she did the same as everyone. She was crying, but she went back to her shit factory. I saw it on TV. But that's all changing now, believe me. And don't you think that's great? To think that things are on the move?"

Hélène blew her nose in her fingers. Her tears seemed to magnify the buildings across the way; a deformed, floating world. She said, "Are you a communist?"

Sabine burst out laughing, flattered.

"No. I don't have time."

"You don't have time?"

"I don't have time for politics, I want to go on the stage."

"Ah, yes, that's right . . ."

"Let me play something for you."

She switched on the tape recorder, she'd chosen the right time and the right song, she'd planned it all ahead of time. It started with a little harmonica and a guitar, and then a guy with a weary voice began singing in English; the tape was worn and Hélène couldn't really understand the words. She pictured the singer, he must be handsome, his voice was sensual, a little scornful. Sabine told her his name was Bob Dylan and that his song said, more or less, that the world was changing, you had to keep your eyes open, and the parents had better watch out, their sons and their daughters were beyond their command. It was a political song.

"Do you like it?"

"I like it a lot."

It had begun to rain, a fine drizzle that gave a sweet smell to the asphalt. Sabine tucked the tape recorder under her shirt, then said, astonished: "Maman gave me the pill. I'm taking the pill."

"You're not a virgin anymore?"

"No."

"I was sure. I could tell."

"How?"

"I don't know. You can just tell."

There was no one outside, people in the south flee the rain, and everyone had gone in. They gazed at their surroundings, which made up their world, and they didn't know whether they were happy or unhappy, whether they wanted to leave their parents or go back to being the little girls who used to play on the tiny plot of grass and take baby Mariette for walks, as proudly as two little mothers. They felt as if they were growing up in secret, that they were always a little marginal compared to everyone else.

"I'm beginning drama classes when we go back to school,

the parents have said yes—well, Papa didn't really like the idea, but Maman won him over."

"It sounds like she's on your side . . ."

"She's afraid I'll leave."

"I can't imagine being like her someday, like her or our teachers or Michelle, I can't imagine that one day we'll be old, all the time, all the time old."

"We won't be like our parents, we won't stay in their shadow for long, believe me."

"But we're bound to take after them in some way, aren't we?"

"Sometimes I think that if it weren't for us, they'd be bored to death."

"You've become so mean. You make fun of me, but I like to walk the dog. I love him as much as I love you, I love him like a brother, well, a sister, I don't know how to say it. But it's too bad you don't understand."

"But I do understand . . ."

"No, you don't."

"Listen, I understand that you adore that dog, and horses, and all the stuff that goes with it, but, in the meantime, you don't see what's really going on, how the world is changing and you're completely clueless."

"But animals are the world, too! You always told me they don't suffer, didn't you? Well, you're wrong. You got it completely wrong."

"I don't believe it!"

"Believe what?"

"You're like Brigitte Bardot now? You believe animals suffer?"

"Yes, and I think she's right. I think it's horrible what goes on in slaughterhouses. She's been talking about it for a long time, and no one will listen, I wasn't even born and already she was talking about it, and nothing has changed, nothing at all!"

"Enough, I saw the program, too."

"What program? It was in 1962, are you kidding me?"

"It was this spring, the program where she says she won't make any more movies, so she can devote herself to animal rights, poor thing!"

Hélène's stern expression told Sabine they were almost there: the three years' difference in their age was disappearing. The rain was falling harder now, steady and warm, but they took no notice. Sabine liked the way the conversation was going. This summer, her discussions with other young people had left her with a real appreciation for that feeling of getting carried away. Hélène's vehemence meant her little sister knew how to stick up for herself.

"Don't get me wrong," Sabine continued, "I really like Brigitte Bardot as an actress, and I think it's disgusting the way they see her as nothing more than a sex object or a sex symbol. Simone de Beauvoir thinks she's the very image of female emancipation!"

"I don't give a shit! And don't you start with your feminist slogans when I'm talking to you about animals in slaughter-houses getting their throats slit! Don't you realize, nothing has changed in France since the Middle Ages? Nothing! At the riding school one of the instructors explained it to me. In the program, Bardot says that it's not like that everywhere, in other countries it's not like that, and we could do what they do, we could anesthetize the animals, or knock them out before cutting their throats instead of letting them take so long to die, sometimes it lasts five minutes. Can you imagine? Five minutes, suffering, while their blood pours out?"

"It's a pity you don't feel as passionate about the cause of the human race."

"If you really think an animal or a baby doesn't experience suffering, try this very simple thing: look them in the eyes."

Hélène fell silent: their mother was standing before them with her umbrella, looking worried.

"You're going to catch your death sitting here in the rain, go inside right now!"

Her gaze seemed to be begging them. Sabine made her sit down, the bench was soaked, the bird shit sliding, spreading. She took the tape recorder from under her shirt, while Hélène protected it with the umbrella. Bob Dylan's drawling, prophetic voice mingled with the rain, *Come gather 'round people, wherever you roam*, and Agnès listened carefully to the song she didn't understand.

"It's nice," she said when it was over, "it makes you want to dance, slowly."

She reached for her umbrella and stood up. They climbed up the five flights in silence, the song lingering in their heads, they were out of breath when they reached the apartment. Bruno was giving a private lesson to a neighbor's son; he looked up, his gaze tense.

"Where were they?"

"Downstairs," said Agnès.

He looked at her, troubled, and murmured: "You look so young. It's true what Laurence says, you could all be sisters."

"I'm not their sister, Bruno, I'm their mother."

They could hear the irritation in her voice, like when she complained that the apartment was in a mess and that she "was always going around picking up after them." She seemed to be weary of everything. That night, for the first time, she joined them at the dinner table and didn't get up, didn't wash the dishes, didn't even pass the serving bowls. She'd acquired an authority her daughters had never seen in her, because they'd only ever seen her as a woman who was always there—watchful, indispensable, and there to serve them.

The following week, Bruno brought home a record player and a single by Gilbert Bécaud to inaugurate it. It was a rare event to have something brand new in the house, and they played the song *La solitude ça n'existe pas* over and over; it became the theme song of that autumn of 1973, back to school time for the three sisters. Sabine would be preparing to take her baccalaureate exam, Hélène was starting the first year of lycée, and Mariette was in primary school. Buying school supplies was, like every year, a source of terrible anxiety to Agnès. The lists would tremble in her hands when she went into the Makaire bookstore, and no matter how often she did the math, and watched out for Tavel's checks, and fed them on pasta and rice, September was always a dreadful month, and she could not understand why Bruno would go out and buy a record player. She was angry with him for yielding to her desire, because she'd told him she'd like to listen to music when the girls were at school, she was angry with him for earning so little, she was angry with him for reimbursing the debts of his pathetic father, she was angry with him for choosing that particular single, *There's no one but me at home anymore/ And yet I'm not afraid/ The radio and TV are here by my side/ To tell me the time and the weather*: it was creepy, Bécaud had other songs, love songs, funny, poetic songs, too (Bruno often sang them to her, holding his ear the way Bécaud himself did), but he'd chosen that one, because he was so distracted and so eager to do things right. Now, not only would they have trouble making ends meet this month, but there was also the fact that Mariette had started proper school, and to Agnès this dispossession meant that it was all over, that none of her children would ever fall asleep in her arms again, none of her daughters would ever be her silent love and consolation again. She had watched in wonder as her babies grew, and now she was simply watching them leave, and every morning after she dropped Mariette off at school and stopped off to buy a baguette, she would go home, astonished to find herself the guardian of an empty temple.

Yes, the school supplies ruined her budget. School was free for people who weren't keeping track, but for others it meant dread and humiliation. Most of the books, thankfully, could be bought second hand at the Lycée Mignet, but it meant hours waiting in the large schoolyard where the girls and boys were at last allowed to be together before returning to their respective establishments, Cézanne for the girls, Mignet for the boys, their books in their arms, and their phone number written on the last page of their French lit anthology, with the times their parents were absent and unlikely to pick up the phone. It was worth standing and fidgeting for hours in the dust of the dead leaves beneath the tall plane trees, because this was where emancipation began, one transaction following another. Something simmered, and it had nothing to do with a desire to pass the baccalaureate exams, it was about sex, how to get it, who with and in what circumstances, the atmosphere in the waiting lines was not unlike conscription, the anticipation of possible futures laid bare. On the girls' T-shirts a logo proclaimed *Make Love Not War*, which immediately set the tone. The war in Vietnam had its good points: Jacques Brel could sing, grimacing, *Je fais glou glou, je fais miam miam,/ Je defile criant, "Paix au Viêt Nam!"*[4] But the irony of some could not stop the combat of others, their lust for life that was born with the congealed blood of wars—their fathers' wars, and the wars in the countries they saw being bombed, on television, that box that brought to peaceful living rooms all the chaos of the world. Rebellion had gotten under people's skin to arouse desire, was its sap: it beat in their bodies to the vital rhythm of an artery to the heart.

[4] *Glug glug, I go, Yum yum, I say/ I join the march shouting, Peace in Vietnam!*

Sabine and Hélène now saw each other at the Lycée Cézanne, the way they used to see each other at the Collège des Prêcheurs a few years earlier, but Sabine no longer introduced her "little sister" to her girlfriends with the bored, weary expression she'd had back in the days when she wore the green smock of the third year of collège, and Hélène the humiliating pink one of the little newcomer. At Cézanne, no one wore smocks anymore: this was their first emancipation. The second consisted in meeting boys on the hill behind the gym to make love in the open air and talk about it afterwards. Well? How was it? How far did you go? And curiosity rivaled disdain, as if the hill behind the lycée was the place for lovemaking at a discount. If you couldn't find better, you fucked outdoors, and that seemed every bit as pathetic as it did emancipated.

"My sister, Hélène, the great defender of animal rights!" Sabine said now when she introduced her, with a touch of admiring irony, but the others didn't care, "animal rights" meant nothing to most of them, and they would turn and walk away, with their bell-bottom jeans, their noisy wooden clogs, and their binders pressed against their ample bosoms.

They're like fillies in a paddock, Hélène had said, and Sabine shrugged, she couldn't really picture it, but enclosed, yes, that they were, and they were on the hill, too, and more than they knew, because after all, what were they destined for?

She'd been accumulating appointments with the lycée's guidance counselor, Monsieur Arnaud, who seemed to hold her future in his hands, but was a mere kid of twenty-four himself, who didn't know much more than she did, leafing through his sheets of paper in a big notebook marked "JOB OPENINGS AFTER BACCALAUREATE: LANGUAGE AND LITERATURE SECTION."

"I'd like to go into the theater, but my parents want me to learn a trade first."

"They're right."

"So, I need some studies that won't take long, then."

"What are you interested in?"

"The theater, I just told you."

"Nursing is good, and it's short: two and a half years of training."

"No, I don't like being around sick people, I like Racine and Simone de Beauvoir."

"Librarian. That doesn't take long either."

"Oh, no thanks—and end up like my Aunt Michelle?!"

"Teacher, then."

"I'll come back another time. I'll give it some thought, and I'll come back."

"Fine. I'll give it some thought, too."

"See you next week."

"Yes, next week. Beautician, would that tempt you? Oh no, of course not, you like Simone de Beauvoir."

"My baccalaureate is in literature, after all!"

"You ought to know that any baccalaureate, if it's not in science, or math . . ."

Life was this tiny little proposition, this crust of bread held out beyond the fence, and most adults refused to see that the earth had trembled, and all the young fillies would not simply go back to grazing on some green grass while waiting to be impregnated. Teachers who were newcomers were prepared to engage, some of them met with their students outside school, at home in their living rooms. Sabine thought about Gabrielle and Christian, *To Die of Love*, she was proud now that it had happened in Aix, her town was not a provincial town like the others, here love was dangerous, and they were demonstrating along the Cours Mirabeau, the university was full of unrest, of ideals, and she had begun her drama classes. Madame Paillard seemed a hundred years old to Sabine. She was forty at the most. You couldn't tell if her hair was her own, or whether it was white or blond, or whether she was prematurely bald, or had only been able to afford an appalling wig. She seemed fragile but she wasn't. With her vibrant voice of a former *tragédienne*, her sagging, translucent skin, her too-high heels and her shawl, she resembled a convalescent heron. Her authority was indisputable. She didn't have a single friend among the students. She taught her class in a tiny room at the back of a little courtyard; only the stage was lit, and the students sat on the floor on a worn, dubious carpet and were always in a disturbing semi-obscurity. Who was sitting behind you? Whose legs were brushing against you? Whose bare feet were touching your lower back? Sabine followed the class with her head thrown back, to give herself an air, and make it look as if her hair was much longer than it actually was; she felt like lying down, having someone lie on top of her, but the half hour of relaxation they began the class with was not at all sexually exciting. It was much more than that. The students were on their backs, their arms along their sides; the carpet smelled of old cardboard, but Madame Paillard told them to imagine they were lying on hot sand. *And your body is heavy*, her body was heavy, flowing into the heat, she felt every patch of skin, every vibration, her breathing was in harmony with this spacious, almost airy letting go, she realized that the twelve-string guitarist hadn't taught her much, her body had not displayed all its talent, that much was sure. This was a magnificent discovery, but it left her sad at the same time. She continued to see the musician all the same, while allowing herself to flirt with the boys in her drama class, fewer in number than the girls, who shared them with good grace, a polyandry of convenience driven by a hippy philosophy. With the dullest, most uncertain, and most astonished among them, Sabine had absolutely palpitating adventures; she was gifted with a solid imagination, for life was never up to scratch, and she had to help it along a little.

She was learning texts by Cocteau, Giraudoux, Sartre, Camus, and Anouilh; she recited them with earnest conviction and a great deal of exalted suffering. Antigone was her favorite character—her stubborn rebelliousness, her opposition to power, her courage: she did not play her well, but she put all her heart in it. Madame Paillard was not very demanding, just hearing the text seemed to be enough to make her happy. She never had them tackle tragedies by Racine or Corneille, nor plays by Chekhov or Molière, either because she thought her students were not up to it, or because she herself had only ever performed contemporary authors and liked re-visiting them. Sabine never knew what her career had been like, she didn't talk about it, never came out with any of those endless exhausting anecdotes about touring, triumphs, getting drunk, cheating on each other, or other hazy scandals that typically pepper the conversation of actors.

That year, 1974, there were two unexpected deaths. The first happened one evening, interrupting the Tuesday night movie: a brief newsflash announcing the death of the President of the Republic, Georges Pompidou. It was April 2. Agnès and Bruno were mournful and astonished: how had they not seen this coming, yet Pompidou had shown all the signs—he'd put on weight, his face was puffy, they'd wanted to believe it was repeated bouts of flu, and hemorrhoids to explain the trouble he had walking. Agnès and Bruno had believed it all, like children adults hide the truth from, and all of France had done likewise. It made them sad because they'd liked the man, this son of teachers, who'd protected them from socialism and those rabble-rousing students who'd tried to "destroy the nation in 1968." With Pompidou, in spite of the first oil crisis, France seemed prosperous; it had been a long, sweet evening by the fireside, interrupted from time to time by storms outside, but the president had been firmly rooted in his country and had the discretion of the uncorrupted. He launched a program for the construction of thirteen nuclear power plants. Thanks to him, France would become the most nuclearized power on earth, and their future was assured: in the end there was a solution for everything. Even if Agnès and Bruno's everyday life was hard, or maybe because it was hard, they wanted to trust, they had no other choice; they stood at the edge of destitution with the faith of the fragile, and their reason urged them to believe in progress.

The second death that year, shortly after Pompidou's, was just as sudden and unpredictable. But it didn't interrupt anything for all that. The news came the afternoon Mariette was baptizing her favorite doll Mehdi (named after the actor in *Sébastien et la Mary-Morgane*, a TV series Mariette referred to pompously as "the series of my youth."). Agnès organized a little party, just as she had done for her older daughters' dolls, with bowlfuls of colored candy, and grenadine syrup drunk through a straw, in addition to a little French toast to make it even more cheerful. There were no sugared almonds, no priest, either, but there was salt and water and Agnès recited the ritual words with no fear of blasphemy. Sabine was lucky to be babysitting at the downstairs neighbors', Hélène was unlucky to have been chosen as Mehdi's godmother, and had to put in a token appearance for her little sister and her friends, who were somewhat surprised by this ceremony that they didn't celebrate at home. Agnès knew that Mariette was a mystic; she made her recite her prayers every evening, a Hail Mary, then the Lord's Prayer, and since her First Communion the previous year she'd been reciting them with exaggerated fervor, her fists clenched so tight that her knuckles went white, and she would squeeze her eyes shut until her lids creased. She talked about Jesus as if she knew him personally, and described his miracles as if they were being told for the first time. But that afternoon, the atmosphere felt false, they couldn't distinguish the playacting from what was real, the joke from what was holy. Hélène had every intention, once the holy sacraments had been given to the celluloid doll, of disappearing into her bedroom to study and listen to the Hit Parade on Radio Monte Carlo.

So, it was during Mehdi's baptism, in the little apartment overflowing with bouncing children, just as Hélène was wiping a little girl's dress stained with French toast, that she heard her mother say she'd had a letter that morning from Michelle.

It's extraordinary how some words reach us before they've been said, and extraordinary how we immediately reject them. Before Hélène could tell her mother to remain silent, she heard her say what she didn't want to hear. Your dog died. It was a sudden tumble, an explosion. Stop rubbing that little girl's dress, you're going to ruin the material. Agnès didn't want to know, not about her daughter's grief, not over a dog, life has enough other troubles in store, she knew that only too well, and she sincerely thought it was her duty to distract Hélène, to turn her away from a passing sorrow. She asked her to play musical chairs with the children, she'd manage the chairs if Hélène would turn the music on and off, put on Gilbert Bécaud's single, *La Solitude n'existe pas.* But Hélène chose Dalida's *Gigi l'Amoroso* instead, and she shouldn't have. The rhythm of the song, the guitars and piano and mandolins, were perfect for musical chairs, but contrasted so sharply with her sorrow that, instead of dispelling it, they made it worse. *Let me tell you / before I let you go / the story of a village near Naples / where there were four*—Hélène lifted the needle from the record and five little girls rushed for a chair at the same time. One was left standing: she'd lost, and went to sit on the sofa, as if she were punished. Agnès removed a chair. Hélène started up the music. Predictably, she was unable to find the exact place where she'd stopped it. Caprice's eyes, the patience of his questioning gaze, always a touch worried, eager to obey, to do things right . . . *Giorgio on guitar / Sandro on the mandolin / And me I was dancing / Tapping my tambourine* . . . The gaze was fading, slowly disappearing, no more watchfulness, no more expression, no light. A sudden darkness. Did they bury you? Did they cry for you? *Then came Gigi / Gigi l'Amoroso / All that you knew about love / Your velvet gaze as soft as a caress* . . . I'll come see you, don't worry . . . I don't want you to worry . . . *Gigi l'Amoroso / Always the best / Sometimes heartless / But full of tenderness / What a party / When he was singing / Zuna luna caprese . . .*

"What are you doing, Hélène? The girls are exhausted! Stop the record!"

You know I always come back, wait for me, and I'll come . . .

"Stop it, I said!"

Dalida wasn't singing anymore, but talking: *Gigi Giuseppe, but everyone called him Gigi Full of Love . . .*

And when I come, I'll bring some driftwood, and stones from the seaside . . .

"Hélène, do you hear me?"

. . . and the women went wild over him, every last one—Agnès abruptly switched off the music, and something poignant lingered in the silence.

Hélène put the record back in its sleeve, the chairs in their place, she put everything away, and swept up, and wiped the surfaces, and even scrubbed the tiles in the kitchen, she was cleaning inside the fridge when Bruno and Sabine came home that evening, and all Mariette's friends had left and she hadn't even realized. She had *Gigi l'Amoroso* stuck in her head, now she couldn't stop the song, nobody could lift the needle from the record, there were no sulky little girls on the sofa, just one little girl hiding deep in her gut, weeping with a sorrow to which she had no right.

She wanted to know what Michelle's letter said, did she give any details, what happened, exactly? No details, and Hélène was left with a deep abyss between herself and the world, this new color of mourning which wasn't black but transparent, as if she were living in a plastic bag and couldn't breathe, life masked by the opaque mass of her sorrow, night and day this urge to let herself go, and this new feeling of absence, which left her with no purchase on life, no reassurance, the dizziness of thinking only of what had happened but never speaking of it, ashamed at how strong her love had been, the love for a dog, and she was sure he hadn't died like a dog, because there was something deeply human about him. And yet he hadn't even been buried. They'd just left him in the garbage can. She found out three months later that he had died of sorrow. A death in keeping with his soul. The day before, someone had given Michelle a new dachshund, and Hélène could imagine how she had neglected Caprice to welcome the newcomer. He'd shown no aggression, no jealousy, he hadn't tried to defend his territory, or seek anyone's tenderness. He lay down and died during the night, his little dog's head on the edge of his basket, it flopped over when he stopped breathing, without disturbing anyone. He was Hélène's first and last dog, her first experience of grief and her deepest, too, an irreplaceable loss that left two indelible marks on her heart: the knowledge of suffering, and of the indifference of mankind.

Mariette, drink up now, you haven't drunk a thing the entire meal! Mariette, finish your glass!"

The little girl folded her arms over her chest, shrugged her shoulders, and kept them lifted, pursing her lips and puffing out her cheeks.

"Mariette!" Agnès shouted again. "Don't you dare try holding your breath again, drink that glass of water!"

Mariette tensed up even more, tears touching her eyelashes. Bruno tickled her under her arm, she let go and ran screaming to her room. She had knocked her chair over, and he picked it up as carefully as if she were still sitting on it. They could hear her in her room, crying her eyes out. Sabine stood up to go to her.

"I'll go before she *really* suffocates."

Agnès looked at Hélène.

"Well? You have nothing to say?"

"No."

"Are you serious?"

"No."

"What is that book?"

"It's not because of the book."

"Give me the book, Hélène," said Bruno, in support of his wife.

"I bought it with my money."

"Hélène, give your mother the book!"

"What, you're going to censor what we read now? Send me to the Gulag?"

Bruno got up and lit a cigarette. Reading Solzhenitsyn had made a great impression on him, and his daughters regularly referred to the author. He was hurt by her stupid provocation.

"Hélène, if it's not because of the book that your sister refuses to drink, what is it, will you tell me?"

"It's because of that guy you don't like, the one who's running for election, the one you make fun of all the time."

"Le Pen? Mitterrand?"

"No, not them, she means the ecological, the guy in a sweater who says they have to ride bicycles in Paris because it's polluted."

"Ecologist. The word is ecologist, Maman, not 'ecological.'"

"Dumont? He's a bird of ill omen, that guy, worse than Nostradamus."

"Precisely, because before long there won't be any more birds."

"And you want me to believe that's not in your stupid book!"

"Anyway, he's right, I saw them two years ago, all the kids on bikes blocking Paris! They said that if we keep on driving cars, in ten years we'll be dead! Yes, dead and then . . . well, that's it!"

The fact she dared speak about Paris stunned her as much as it did her parents. Their anger subsided. They were confused. Sabine came back from Mariette's room.

"She says all the water is poisoned, that she'll never drink again, or go swimming, or take a bath, and she's afraid her tears will get in her mouth. Anyway, I put her to bed and tried to calm her down, reading that dumb *Cinderella*."

Sabine and Hélène burst out laughing. Bruno looked at them, disgusted and astonished at the same time.

"You think it's funny? Your mother is fed up, you know, she doesn't think it's funny at all."

"Why is it always me? You're fed up with it, too, Bruno."

"Right! I'll take her glass of water to her and you, Hélène, no more telling her those horrible stories, I forbid it."

He left the kitchen, and they heard him muttering to himself, "As if I were reading *The Gulag Archipelago* to her for a bedtime story." As soon as he was gone, the atmosphere changed. Hélène felt that speaking the way she had that evening had allowed her to assume her rightful place. And it was time to assert herself: "Listen, Maman, that guy Papa can't stand, the ecologist, it's not my fault, Mariette saw him on TV. He took a glass of water and said, 'I stand here before you drinking a glass of precious water,' and before drinking it he explained that everything is polluted—the rivers, the seas, it's all a cemetery, and it scared her. It's normal."

"Is that true?" asked Sabine.

"Of course, it's true."

"Girls, you're young, you'll see, there will always be old people trying to make you believe you're going to live in a horrible world and that everything was better before. Don't believe them."

"Did you see, there's a girl who's running for election," said Sabine.

"Arlette Laguiller? It's complete nonsense," said Hélène, "she'll never get elected! 'Well yes, I'm a woman, but I'm daring to run all the same . . . '"

"Why are you doing that? Why are you making fun of her?"

"I'm not making fun, I'm imitating her! Isn't that what you learn in drama class?"

"Is it because she sticks up for the working class that you're imitating her?"

"Yes, that must be it, of course. You can be so stupid sometimes, I can't believe it."

"I forbid you from talking about politics," said Agnès. "You start giving your opinions and you always end up shouting at each other. And you're vulgar, on top of it."

"I'm doing the dishes," said Hélène.

Hélène felt more like breaking the dishes than washing them, felt like telling her mother that all the products she used to clean her kitchen—"from floor to ceiling," like the ads said—were dangerous, full of pesticides. She was poisoning herself every day that she believed—helped along by all the Mr. Cleans and White Knights, strong men dashing to the rescue—that she could "get tough on dirt and grime and grease" on the surfaces around her. Hélène looked at her hands in the scummy foaming water and thought about the fish in rivers, and cats in houses, and unobtrusive dogs, and her pony, too, how she was infertile, and she thought about that terrible book she'd come upon even though it was published over ten years ago, *Silent Spring*, by Rachel Carson. She read it at night, just a few pages at a time, not too much. She read, then put the book back down abruptly, as if coming up for air, getting her head above water to breathe. That was what she had found again, reading this book: that instant she had known and that she never spoke about. That instant between life and death that she'd experienced when she nearly drowned. She'd been there. She knew. Is that why she understood, why she *felt*, what was happening in nature? They were everywhere, the "elixirs of death," as Carson called them. In the distant lakes of mountains, in the great forests, on the leaves and in the bark of trees, in worms and the soil, ants and larvae, in the belly of birds and the eggs of birds, in flowers and bees, in rivers and in the oceans the rivers flow into, in houses and gardens, in swamps, fields, and every wildlife habitat—burrows, nests, scrubland, stands of trees and undergrowth, in people's bodies, in mothers' milk, in the tissues of unborn children. The invisible poison. DDT. Aldrin. Dieldrin. Parathion. Heptachlor. Poisons with names from a foreign country. A language you don't speak. That you'll never learn. Because, as her mother said, you mustn't believe people who talk about the future as if it is bound to be a disaster. You had to believe in growth and progress. You mustn't read books that describe the death of birds and squirrels: paralysis, convulsion, asphyxiation. You mustn't think about blind foxes, disoriented bees, sheep gone mad. Larks. Robins. Pheasants. Blackbirds. Warblers. Linnets. Thrushes. Wrens. Pixies. About the birdsong you'll never hear again. About their last flights. Their names that will be forgotten. Migration, finished. Seasons without a compass. Autumns without a journey. Their forgotten Africas.

No, you had to be reassured, and you had to reassure your children. Read them bedtime stories, fairy tales, confound their fright with whims, answer their questions with charming childish words. You had to suppress everyone's fear, preserve your illusions, your need for calm and security.

"Peace and security." That was the presidential slogan on the poster, where a man in a suit and tie was smiling, his gaze clear and confident. By his side, an adolescent girl, her hair neatly tied back, was turning her loving face to him. Valery Giscard d'Estaing was posing with his daughter. Bruno and Agnès had voted for him and were relieved when he took office on May 19, 1974. For this former Finance Minister—a liberal from the petty nobility who made a good marriage, was the father of four children—they felt a happy respect. He had defeated the leftists, and they wanted to trust him; they were prepared to believe everything. He was both a man of authority and "simple," he said as much himself. The day of his inauguration, which they had both watched on television with the timid hopefulness of decent people, he had walked down the Champs-Élysées, people couldn't get over it, the President of the Republic walking and greeting the cheering people who are standing behind the police barriers waving flags and applauding. Sometimes he stopped to shake a few hands, and reporters asked him to speak, so he spoke: "The crowd is so friendly and joyful." His two daughters were in the crowd, they also cried out as he went by, he stopped to embrace them, and continued to the Élysée Palace on foot. It was incredible how he was walking, it was as if he had come from far away, as if he had spent a long time making his way through the crowd to reach his goal, to lead France, to be the head of the country and guide it. "For me, the consecration, taking office, has been arriving at the Élysée Palace this morning on foot." He was so young, the youngest president ever of the Fifth Republic, you might almost think this breach of protocol was spontaneous: he was young, he had to keep himself from running, and he walked. After his appearance on the Champs-Élysées, his daughters straddled their bikes, then, followed by a horde of photographers and admirers, set off to catch up with him. They were an active family, they walked and pedaled, the weather was fine, on their side. "I got the feeling, this morning, that the people of Paris, the people of France, were aware of what it means to elect a new president of the Republic." Giscard said this, and everyone realized they would have to get used to this voice, this king's voice, his exaggerated pronunciation, words like a hail of bullets from his pursed lips.

Bruno and Agnès did not keep their trust for very long. On July 5, the age of majority was lowered to eighteen and they were appalled. They had gotten married as minors and they could understand that this reform would be beneficial to young people who weren't happy at home, but their daughters had everything. Sabine had celebrated her eighteenth birthday in March and successfully obtained her baccalaureate in June. From the Landes, where she was babysitting, she now had the right to phone them and say she wasn't coming home. That she'd just gotten married. Started a new job. In the Landes, or even further away. She could buy her own ticket to board an airplane, or drive to her chosen destination. Above all, she could decide to do all of that without even informing them. But it didn't happen that way.

Sabine had not learned much from Madame Paillard, other than a taste for multiple partners and a cruel realization: what she'd hoped to find in love did not exist among young people her age. It was a narcissistic, indecisive élan that brought boys and girls together; your partners were merely the witness to your powers of seduction; you needed them, but they didn't really interest you, encumbered as you were by your own self. Sabine had a heavy, Mediterranean figure, "wide hips just made for having babies." She wanted none of it. They told her she had a pretty voice: she couldn't hear it. They saw a person in her she didn't know, and she was surprised by the existence of this Sabine who wasn't her, who was maybe better than her. She wished she looked like Audrey Hepburn, or Romy Schneider in *César and Rosalie*, or her young French teacher who was so brilliant, or even Gisèle Halimi, calm and formidable. They had an impressive presence; they didn't need to turn on the charm. They were free. Sabine felt as if there were someone behind her, and it was not her parents, or her family and friends. It was something more than that. It was the world that had been there before her, with its laws, its morality, and its religion, everything that had been invented and constructed before her time. And destroyed, too. Because maybe Hélène was right, and some sort of destruction was on its way. Everyone assumed that the fleeting nature of their lives would save them, that they wouldn't witness the cataclysm, so they put it off to a time that had no reality, to the years that began with 2000. An abstraction. She knew that the first step she took outside her family circle would wreck the life they had together, the three sisters and their parents, that time would be erased and never come back, and each one of them would come away from those years feeling nostalgic for a time when dreams were not ruined upon contact with reality. To go and live in Paris remained her ideal, and her only aim. She had to earn money, and soon. She didn't want to take any of the short courses the guidance counselor had proposed with so much resignation. She was eighteen, and she was in a hurry. She would work as a waitress and study acting at the same time, that's what girls her age did in other countries, in America, for example, where not everything was rotten. She would go to auditions, casting calls, maybe she'd find an agent, have photographs taken, put together a portfolio, be on every front at the same time. Her radical choice galvanized her. To give her all. At last.

She waited for Hélène to return at the end of August, and as soon as her sister arrived, she invited her for a drink on the Cours Mirabeau.

"Did you have fun with the capitalists?"

"I passed my French Riding Federation exam. Level 3."

"On your neurotic pony?"

"On a horse, what did you expect?"

"The one they gave you?"

"No. The horse they gave me, Everest, I've known him since I was three, he's old and no one rides him anymore. I rescued him from a rotten life and from the butcher's."

She took out a small spiral notebook and put it on the table, then slid it across to her sister wishing her manner could seem more mysterious. Sabine said: "Any luck?"

"You tell me."

She opened the notebook: Hélène had written down the names and telephone numbers of potential places to stay in exchange for hours spent doing housework, or babysitting in the evening, or looking after old people; even low-rent maid's rooms (seventh floor with no elevator, toilet on the landing). All summer, Hélène had been asking friends and acquaintances, along with Parisians vacationing in Villers, and regulars at the Bois de Boulogne riding school; she'd inquired and spread the word.

"I'll call from Rose's place," said Sabine, looking at the list, "her mother isn't back from Majorca yet, it'll be easier."

"So, you're really going to leave, then?"

"If I find somewhere to stay, yes."

"There'll be a huge scene."

"From now on, a lot of things will cause a scene. Unless you and Mariette decide to spend the rest of your life with our parents."

"Actually, Vincent is leaving Neuilly, he's getting engaged. He's getting married next summer."

"Vincent?"

"His fiancée is very pretty and really nice, I've known her for years, her father made his fortune in canned peas."

"Sounds really enticing."

"She's sweet. Why are you laughing?"

"I'm not laughing, I just think it's . . . Well, anyway, if everyone is happy with it."

"Will you invite me?"

"Where?"

"To your place, when you're in Paris, will you invite me?"

"To come for tea in my maid's room? Of course, I will."

"Oh, goody!"

"Plus, it'll make an exotic change for you, to go slumming a little."

Since Hélène didn't answer, adrift in her attempt to find a retort equal to the barb, Sabine put the little notebook in her pocket and said, "I'll enjoy it, too."

Sabine left one week later. In the morning, very early. She'd seen a want ad in *Libération*, and found a girl who was driving to Paris in her Deux Chevaux and wanted to share expenses. As she left the town, so peaceful under an absent sky, no traffic in the streets, not a single café open on the Cours Mirabeau, it made her feel as if she were leaving a place that had already ceased to exist.

Sabine had guessed right: Hélène had had fun "with the capitalists." She spent her time between her pony and the horses, the ones she rode and the one she had saved, Everest, already sitting perched high on his back at the age of three. (The photograph that recorded the moment showed a tiny girl with her hand delicately placed on the neck of a massive horse, a butterfly on top of a mountain.) She'd been driving, too, a lot, without a license. For two years, David had been teaching her to drive, but they never went very far. That summer, he wanted her to try his latest passion, a two-seater Maserati convertible, so low-slung that when you were driving you saw the road go by like a rasp ready to scrape your skin if you leaned out too far. "I don't know how to drive!" Hélène screamed, as she started the engine, and the mere touch of her toe on the accelerator made the car leap forward. David replied, "Go!" and, of course, she obeyed. The car was nervous, unstable, the gear stick and the wooden steering wheel vibrated in her clenched fists. They left the house as evening was setting in, the little country roads around Villers were deserted, and only the cows watched them go by, with blasé indifference. After shouting, "I'm going to die!" Hélène pressed harder on the gas pedal. But with David she would not die, she was living a life where risk was a challenge, never a danger.

They were happy in that car, although David would tire of

it very quickly; they felt as if they were the same age. They were doing something other people didn't do, and it had nothing to do with money, it was a naïve, shared pleasure. Unlike Michelle, David was not nostalgic for the childhood of the girl they had, in a way, adopted when she was three years old. That girl had fulfilled her mission: she had amused them, and loved them, asking David for a cuddle every evening to postpone bedtime, going with him to all his horse shows and cheering him on, and they still talked about how she'd sat for an entire day on the hood of the car in the pouring rain, shouting, even though he couldn't hear her, "Come on, David! Clear that triple bar!" and applauding when he scored a clear round. A docile, affectionate, and often funny little girl. What more could you ask for? Fortunately, David also loved the adolescent she had become. They didn't agree on everything, but that was something they liked, too. Easy rhetoric, squabbles, and diverging opinions gave a certain sparkle to their relationship. Sometimes David provoked Hélène, showed her what he'd brought back from the hunt, and he would have been disappointed if she hadn't turned away from him, reproaching his cruelty.

"Next time you'll come with me. You'll see, hunting is full of old gents with weapons!"

"Don't expect me to take part in your slaughter!"

"Giscard has invited me to join the presidential hunt, I'll bring you some feathers!"

"Then don't forget the tar!"

She tickled him when they went for dinner at Les Vapeurs in Trouville and, recalling Brusati's film *Bread and Chocolate*, she said, "Are you familiar with the working conditions of the waiters in this sort of restaurant? Did you know that most of them are exploited?"

"Eat your sole, my dear child, and don't go pissing off the ruling class."

"Most of them are underpaid immigrants, and they live together in—"

"*Garçon!* Pour the young lady a glass of wine, she needs to relax!"

It went no further. Hélène didn't want to call into question the privileges she herself enjoyed, or remind David where she came from, playing the resident pauper. She'd gotten used to this compartmentalized life, but she couldn't get used to seeing the two couples together, the Tavels and the Malivieris. It happened, occasionally, at a wedding, or the grandparents' golden anniversary, or a funeral. When they met, David systematically offered Bruno a position in his company, an offer which implied that Bruno could make a better living if he really wanted to. Bruno would smile and nod his head, and look all around for somewhere to settle his gaze, to no avail. There were people around them, and, more often than not, a cousin or an uncle would voice their support for David's generous, unexpected offer. Confronted with his brother-in-law's embarrassed silence, David patted him on the shoulder and said, "I'm sorry if I've upset you," then offered him a cigar. Hélène could see how awkward her father felt. How he tried to establish a rapport with David and couldn't, and no matter what he did or said, he would never have the last word. Sometimes he would leave these family reunions in a jacket David no longer wore and had given to him. Everyone would compliment him on it, he was even more handsome when he was well-dressed, he was downright elegant. And Bruno would reply, "It's one of Tavel's jackets," for years he said it, whenever someone complimented him, "It's one of Tavel's jackets," as if he intended to give it back someday.

At these family reunions, Hélène found herself with her cousins, bored to death. Even if they belonged to the same family, they had nothing in common, viewed their relatives' lives as less appealing than their own, and were relieved when the time came to depart with their own tribe, with whom they shared a language and codes; and after the requisite mutual criticism, they were also mutually forgotten. At the next gathering, they would be astonished to see that their cousins had changed so much, but that their parents were no older than before, old age being the only state they'd ever seen them in. Depending on the time of year (vacation or not), Hélène would go home with the Malivieris or the Tavels. Her sisters waved to her through the window of the Simca, her mother reminded her to be good and to say thank you; Bruno would say, "I'm leaving her in your hands," and, confused and shy, he would place his palm on her head, as if she were already no longer there. Hélène would climb into the Mercedes, and Caprice curled up on her lap, unintentionally scratching her bare thighs. While he drove, David put on a cassette of Yves Montand singing Prévert, *The Autumn Leaves*, or *Barbara*, and the drive to Paris was lulled by poetry that sang of vanished memories, the disappearance of loved ones, and the stupidity of war. Hélène would place her forehead against the window, night was falling over the fields, the mown wheat, the electric pylons of Île-de-France, and when the car slowed she knew the heavy traffic meant they were getting close to Paris, and she would wonder whether Sabine and Mariette were almost home, too; the distances were hardly the same, but she knew that in the Simca her father would be singing Gilbert Bécaud songs, and Les Compagnons de la Chanson, in his fine voice, as conscientiously as a choirmaster. In the car no one would move. They were listening to him at last. And maybe even admiring him.

Agnès knew what Sabine's departure meant: everything they had brought her up and programmed her to be would now go up in smoke. As a mother, she was being dispossessed not only of her eldest daughter, but also of the eighteen years spent with her: the joy, the worries, the fatigue and the strength, everything that child had given her by being born. Her place in this world. But that was finished. Her daughter was no longer there. Mariette slept in Sabine's bed now, and the absence of a child left a deep hole in the conjugal bedroom. She'd always known that the end of childhood would come someday. But not so soon. Sabine was leaving at the age of eighteen just as she herself had done, but it wasn't to go from a father to a husband. Bruno wouldn't be leading her to the altar to give her to another man, to bear his name and his children. Sabine was leaving "to live her life," as she put it. Live her life . . . was it possible to even hear this expression without feeling a sort of guilty jealousy—and what exactly did it mean?

Six months earlier, Agnès had tried to talk to Bruno: she didn't want to upset him, but she'd found a part-time job in a clothing boutique on the rue des Tanneurs. Bruno sat down and did the math: someone to take care of Mariette after school, the cost of the cafeteria and transportation from La Petite Chartreuse to the center of town: that alone would take every penny Agnès earned. She understood that if she put her foot out the door, she would cost money. Staying at home was the surest way to save, so the world reached her only as the faint rumor of other people's days. She wasn't yet forty, but she felt twice that age. She was watching her daughters grow up, and her husband grow old, and, in the meantime, other women left their houses, a multitude of women, and had a life outside the family home. There was even, now, a government minister who was a woman, a magistrate, a very beautiful woman with the poised demeanor of a *bourgeoise*, who was putting forward a draft bill for the Chirac government to decriminalize abortion. Her name was Simone Veil, a Jewish name that not everyone pronounced the same way. There were heated debates against her draft bill; there were arguments and insults on the part of the men—politicians, lawyers, journalists, and writers, who denounced the "nightmarish ovarians," the "monstrous clitorises" of these "under-fucked, unfuckable women." They went looking for the real woman and couldn't find her anymore. They'd been robbed. Agnès was shocked that such important, high-ranking men could speak in such a vulgar manner and thus prevent her from being fully on their side. In the streets of Aix, glued on poles, stapled on plane trees, there were pictures of bloody embryos lying in garbage cans. *Let them live!* Agnès was against abortion and she prayed for all these massacred babies. But she hated the photographs. She tried to imagine the person who had dared, camera slung over their shoulder, to rummage through a garbage can, position the embryo and take several pictures, hoping one of them would be the right one, the one they could reproduce thousands of times.

On November 26, 1974, Simone Veil submitted her draft bill to the National Assembly. Agnès listened to this woman whose views she did not share, and who spoke for an hour, on her feet, looking out at hundreds and hundreds of men, most of whom hated her. Agnès envied her self-confidence, the impression she gave of being in her place. From time to time, Agnès's mind wandered and she thought about Sabine, who was supposed to call them that evening, from the apartment of the old gentleman with whom she was lodging. Then she went back to listening to the polite, indefatigable minister. How much time had it taken her to write such a lengthy speech? Agnès didn't believe Sabine when she told her she was going to live in Paris, at the home of Robert Cousin, a retired surgeon. She hadn't grasped the meaning of her words. Her daughter was going to live with a surgeon? Simone Veil spoke about the women who took charter flights to get abortions abroad, she spoke about the tragedy, the shame, and the solitude, an even pitch to her voice, and her calm manner was like a shield raised between herself and the sharp-eyed deputies. To make herself heard, did a woman have to maintain such an impassive attitude? Must a woman, above all, never shout? Sabine had explained to her that Gérald, the surgeon's son, wanted nothing more than a presence at night in his father's home, and all Sabine had to do was come home every night, and they would give her a place to live. This had reassured Bruno, as if an elderly gentleman was a pledge of an ordered life, and to sleep at his house would imply an absence of sexuality. As if Bruno was forgetting that his daughter wanted to become an actress, and how terrible that was. But maybe he didn't believe it. And was waiting for her to come home again. Agnès knew you don't leave your parents just to come home. Simone Veil was still talking, Agnès couldn't understand what she was fighting for, but listening to her was like being urged to show respect: "What matters is to change the image the French have of what constitutes an ideal number of children per couple." An ideal number of children . . . She remembered Charles de Gaulle exhorting French women to produce twelve million beautiful babies. That was right after the war, and the idea was to replace coffins with crowded cradles, the cycle of birth to repair the cycle of death. An ideal number of children . . . Agnès switched off the television. Something inside her had just reawakened, something she hadn't felt since adolescence. A desire to live so powerful that it made her feel sick.

It kept her awake at night. It took her days to even to dare speak of it to Laurence. And even longer to Bruno. She knew he wouldn't understand, that he would think it was a joke or a whim, and his response would be attentive but intractable. She had anticipated her husband's various reactions. But not his fear. So, she didn't love him anymore? She didn't love her children, or her home, or anything he gave her, everything he had fought so hard for, so proudly, yes, what was he supposed to do with his pride? What would make him want to get out of bed in the morning?

"But . . . I just told you . . . Mariette. You'll have to be here for her in the morning . . ."

"Are you serious? You want to make me into some weak female? It's not enough for you already that I'm doing the job of a girl, huh—according to your beloved brother-in-law?"

"He's your brother-in-law, too."

"You know what? I don't want to even discuss this anymore. That's it. End of story."

And so, he did indeed not speak of it anymore. Of it or of anything else, and Sabine's departure was followed by a silence that would be the last thing that they went on sharing. Meals were cut short. Evenings in front of the television, gone. The parents no longer touched, no more tender gestures, no more private conversations or intimacy. They seemed to go around with permanently downcast eyes. Hélène read the bedtime stories to Mariette at night now, rediscovering the closeness they had known when they used to lie together in the garden at Laurence's place and fall asleep beneath the trees rustling with wind. The little sister said her prayers less ostentatiously now, more sincerely. She had secret conversations with herself, questions she unburdened and others which arose and troubled the simplicity of her life. When Hélène left for Neuilly, she went through a time of loneliness which, she knew, would soon be her daily fare. Big sisters leave. Little ones stay with their parents, and they understand, long before the others do, the meaning of the word *loss*.

One night, the disagreement between Agnès and Bruno came out into the open. The two sisters stood there in their nightgowns, listening to their parents say the words of a man and a woman who thought they'd had a happy life together and are suddenly confronted with the rancor of the betrayed. Their voices trembled like two muted, warring instruments. At first, Hélène had trouble understanding what they were saying, then she had trouble believing it. Mariette was crying, and she put her back to bed, told her to breathe calmly, so as not to bring on an asthma attack.

"Is Maman going away?"

"No, Maman isn't going away."

"Are you telling the truth?"

"Yes. She's just going to take an exam in Paris, and then she'll be back."

"I hate it."

"Hate what?"

"Paris."

Neither her husband nor her daughters could understand where Agnès came up with the idea of becoming a mail carrier, now that women had just been allowed to apply, by taking the exam in Paris. She couldn't explain it to them, but one thing she did know: things couldn't go on like this. It was a modest profession, not held in high esteem, but it was what she wanted to do. She laughed when Bruno said that, ten years earlier, he would have invoked his rights as a husband and forbidden it, and she drove the point home: she was going to open a bank account in her own name. He felt as pathetic as his own father. To Laurence, all she said was, "I need to get out and see people." And then she confessed how the urge had come about, while listening to Simone Veil speak at the National Assembly; it might seem funny, but it was true.

"I was watching Simone Veil, I didn't agree with her, naturally, sometimes I even thought it was incredibly boring, and maybe because I was bored, I got a little spaced-out, anyway, I don't know . . . her words were like a punch in the gut. It's weird, isn't it? The first time you and I met, at the market, you asked me if I wanted to have a boy. And I said no. You remember? But I already have a little boy. I was a young bride and I was seven months pregnant when I saw some blood in my underpants. It was my first child, I was alone, Bruno wasn't there. I went to the hospital. The doctor just laughed at me, she said to her students, 'These silly women always make a fuss over nothing, that's something you have to know.' I was ashamed so I obeyed her, I went home. I was in pain all night long, like when you have your period, I didn't dare complain anymore, to make a fuss like a silly woman. I didn't know that I was having contractions. That morning the sheets were soaked in blood. I went back to the hospital. They told me that the placenta had gotten infected. Bruno came, the doctors asked him if he wanted to save the mother or the child. According to our religion, he should have chosen the child, but he said, "The mother." They gave me shots to induce the birth, so I gave birth. It was a boy. He lived for a few minutes. They didn't show him to me. He didn't cry. I never saw him or heard him. Bruno . . . Bruno held him in his arms . . . And then the doctors took him away and I don't know what they did with him. I think they cremated him, I think that's what they do . . . In our family booklet,[5] we registered our first child in the 'Deaths' section. I've never told anyone. I want so badly to get out of the house, Laurence, I absolutely have to do something to make a living . . ."

[5] In France, every married couple is given a "livret de famille," which will contain all the essential certificates of a lifetime: marriage, births of children, deaths, divorce. Similar systems exist in Japan, Germany, and other countries. Separate certificates can of course also be issued.

At the Lycée Cézanne, Hélène met Éléonore, one of the math whizzes from the advanced placement classes who surprised everyone with her pretty face and, above all, by not using it to her advantage. There were rumors that she was a lesbian, the word they used was "dyke," as an insult, but Hélène misheard "like" and thought she was as unique as she was fascinating. Éléonore stood by the gates to the lycée handing out leaflets against vivisection, with photographs so terrifying you either had to look away, or, if you did have the courage to look at them, you could hardly grasp what you were seeing. Dogs cut in pieces, scalped macaques with holes bored in their skulls, birds dying of thirst, cats torn apart, mice with their bellies cut open and their eyes gouged out . . . And these bloody corpses were not as hard to look at as the ones where you saw the actual gazes of prostrate living creatures, with strange devices screwed onto their open skulls, and needles planted in their crossed limbs, or enormous tumors in their throat or their armpits, forced to stand on their hind legs. Their resignation was devastating. They all seemed to be asking: Why?

"Vivisection is legalized torture! Vivisection is a crime! Sign the petition!"

By the gates to the lycée, a majority of students would look at Éléonore, then avoid her; she went on in the same tone, with the same conviction, deaf to comments from all sides about her beauty, or that she'd do better to offer them something else if she wanted them to come closer. The first time, Hélène did like the others and gave her a wide berth. To avoid her. But when she spotted her in the corridors or the schoolyard, she wanted to speak to her, and didn't know how to go about it. She couldn't exactly walk up and ask her for a leaflet or a petition to sign the way you ask for a cigarette. And besides, there were all those insinuations about her homosexuality, she didn't want to look like she was flirting with that girl, that strange chimera who allied her own beauty with the ugliness of vivisection.

"Aren't you being kind of stupid?" Sabine asked her on the phone. "What do you care what they think about you at the lycée? No one gives a shit about you, don't you realize? No one gives a shit what So-and-so does, sure they gossip about So-and-so, but the only thing that really makes anyone tick at the lycée is indifference."

So, Hélène found the courage to go up to Éléonore, to break through the circle of math students clustered under the covered area on a day of driving rain that echoed loudly and released the smell of asphalt into the courtyard, a vaguely nauseating smell. She simply said, "Hello," and Éléonore immediately gave her a petition to sign along with a photo of a mutilated mammal floating in a liquid so viscous that it was no longer possible to identify the species. Then she asked Hélène if she wanted to join the French League Against Vivisection, or support them financially, or would she rather start by coming to one of their meetings? Hélène was about to politely say yes, then she thought of what Sabine would say: what the hell did she care what others thought? She signed the petition without reading it, and said that she didn't want to support them, she just wanted to know whether the animals suffered. Éléonore looked at her with stupefaction and jotted down her address on the back of the gory photograph.

"Come to my place at six this evening, we'll talk about it."

Not waiting for Hélène's reply, she turned back to the group of math students. Hélène put the photograph in her bag, feeling slightly disgusted, as if the unidentifiable animal might start bleeding or empty its guts onto her binders.

Éléonore lived in a tiny studio cluttered with books, lecture notes, photocopies, and all sorts of notebooks; the room was like a messy cubbyhole in a university library, a place without poetry. She was a down-to-earth girl, a student in the advanced math class and therefore overwhelmed with studying and exams, she had no time to waste, and, that evening, she didn't beat around the bush:

"So, it's really very simple: the nervous system of mammals and birds is very similar to ours. The human cerebral cortex is more developed than theirs, of course, but that's a part of the brain which is more focused on thought processes than on emotions or sensations; like all impulses, they are located in the diencephalon, and the diencephalon in mammals and birds is highly developed. So: why should their pain be any less significant than ours?"

"I . . . I don't know."

"It wasn't a question."

"Oh."

"When animals suffer, they express it just as well as we do: they writhe, moan, grimace, cry, sweat; their hearts beat faster, their blood pressure drops. Like us, they feel acute fear and terror, because, like us, they're in pain and they're afraid of dying. But they also feel pleasure and well-being. However . . ."

"Yes?"

"Our parents were very hungry during the war and ever since, as you must have noticed, they've been obsessed with eating meat, as much meat as possible."

Hélène thought of David's checks, the famous protein the checks allowed them to buy at the butcher's.

"Nowadays, they mass-produce animals for human consumption on assembly lines. Moreover, it was when he saw intensive animal farming practices that Henry Ford got the idea of assembly lines for his cars, do you follow? Along with their technology the Americans sold us all the paraphernalia that goes with it—herbicides, pesticides, and fertilizers included. Because, in all this business, the only thing that matters is profit. You didn't look at the leaflet I gave you this morning, did you? You want to know, yes, but not too much all the same, right? Easy does it . . . Well, if you'd read the leaflet, you would know that medical testing on animals does not really reflect the way things are with humans. Sometimes it's even just the opposite. So instead of blinding them, electrocuting them, disemboweling them, depriving them of oxygen, drugging them, filling them with alcohol, drowning them, and slicing into their glands and their organs, why don't they just do their experiments on the basis of cell culture, tissue and organ culture? Isn't that what cellular biology is all about, after all?"

Hélène was caught between the urge to ask her to stop talking and a desire to be brave. This girl was too extreme, it was better not to question anything she said, better not to say anything that might fuel her vehemence.

"What right do we have to decide that we can rule over animals and subjugate them? Why are we the dominant ones and they are dominated? Is it because we don't belong to the same species?"

Confronted with Hélène's embarrassed silence, her attitude that was both skeptical and apologetic, Éléonore changed tack: "I sleep with women. Does that bother you?"

"No . . ."

"You're not prejudiced against my sexuality? So, there's no reason to be prejudiced against animals. Why should we liberate women, homosexuals, or Blacks, and not animals? We have to protect the interests of all creatures. You still following?"

The doorbell rang, and the studio was so small that Éléonore had only to reach out her arm to open the door. A girl stood on the threshold, her hands full of shopping bags. Éléonore kissed her on the mouth then took the bags from her. It was the first time Hélène had ever seen one girl kiss another, and she was surprised at how natural it seemed. In a confused way she thought that it ought to have been more complicated. In what way, she didn't know. She was relieved that someone had come to interrupt Éléonore's diatribe.

"Allow me to introduce Hélène. Am I right—Hélène?"

"Yes."

"Hélène, this is Sylvie."

Sylvie smiled at her and quickly went off again after kissing Éléonore one more time. Hélène had looked away.

"I'm working so hard I don't even have time to go shopping. Do you smoke?"

Hélène shook her head. Éléonore lit a cigarette, tossed her head back, closed her eyes, and sat down at last.

"Do you see the book by Peter Singer, there, on the bookshelf, on the bottom to the right?"

Hélène looked for the book with the anxiety of someone taking a test. She was afraid she wouldn't find it, that she would seem totally clueless, it was like when she was on David's boat, birdbrain, ninny, silly goose. Finally, she found the book: *Animal Liberation*.

"Read the first few chapters and come back in two weeks. Same time."

Éléonore took another long drag on her cigarette, her eyes still closed, and told her to just slam the door behind her.

Hélène left Éléonore's place feeling as if she'd discovered another world, another way of speaking, of living, and of thinking, and she was troubled by the fact that this other world was as real as her parents', that Éléonore was no less important than they were on this earth. She thought she'd read the first chapters of Peter Singer's book very quickly, with the determined application of a student. But she read Singer and regretted her loss of innocence. What was she supposed to do with this unbearable book? She hesitated between leaving it on Éléonore's doormat, or avoiding her if she ran into her at school—let her think she hadn't read it yet, so she wouldn't have to talk about it. But she went to her appointment, two weeks after the first visit, and told her up front she didn't know what she was supposed to make of the book. In the end, what was the point of knowing?

"The point of knowing is knowing, that's all. Knowing where you are."

Éléonore's calm manner, as if she were not at all surprised, as if she had planned the whole thing, upset Hélène: "Know where I am? I'm at home, curled up in my bed, crying with rage. That's where I am."

"False. You came out of your room, because you're here."

"But what good does it do me to know that this crazy professor Harlow raised monkeys in order to turn them into psychopaths? Huh? I can't do anything about it!"

And since Éléonore didn't say anything, she felt obliged to go on arguing, her anger welling up like an urge to vomit: "I didn't open the doors to those rooms made of steel where he'd isolated the monkeys from birth, and I'll never do it, *because I'm not there*. Okay, maybe I'm here, but above all I'm in my nightmares, Éléonore, and every night I'm afraid to go to sleep. The experiments with the monkeys he turned into psychopaths—I read it once and imagined it dozens of times! Those robotic mother monkeys manufactured to drive the babies mad, the way their little teeth chattered when they were thrown on the floor, and they . . . they . . . Oh, my god!"

"And they always go back, straight into the arms of those mothers who are going to stab them with steel spikes, and they'll all end up in shreds. You're right, Hélène, the real question is, what's the purpose of it? There is none. Just like the rest of the experiments served no purpose, with real mother monkeys programmed to tear their offspring to pieces. None of it has any meaning or purpose."

They fell silent. All of a sudden, a sense of harmony and sincere understanding filled the messy, unpoetic studio. In a hushed voice, Hélène said, "My dog died of a broken heart."

And she was surprised she'd shared it, this need she had to speak about Caprice to this girl she hardly knew, who was no longer just an over-brusque militant, but a girl her own age, from her school, someone close. She added, "I know animals suffer. I came to see you so you could tell me about their ability to endure, their defenses, their brain . . . you must know all these things. I didn't need to read these stories about dogs whose bodies were heated until they died, or with their vocal cords torn out . . . I didn't need to know so much. It made me feel sick, and full of guilt. When I had nothing to do with it."

Éléonore reached for a cigarette, removed the filter, took out a sheet of rolling paper. Her gestures were slow and poised. With surprising kindness, she said, "Then you shouldn't have read so much. Shouldn't have read anything at all. It's that simple. Forget it and move on. I'm rolling a joint, do you want some? Have one or two drags and you'll feel better afterwards."

"No, I won't feel better afterwards."

"You'll feel better now. And now is important too."

That night, Hélène had smoked her first joint; she went home very late, exhausted, and full of a resolve that she would hold on to: since she had to be somewhere, she would be where the animals were.

III
A Procession of Silences

The theater was gripped by fear, the spectators trapped in unexpected anxiety. They had come to see the play everyone was talking about, which a few privileged people had already seen in Poland or in Nancy, and, intellectually, they had been warned. They didn't know it would be like this. They didn't know it would be primitive, repetitive, with nothing to think about. Little old people, gray and silent, came out on stage. Black suits and white shirts, men and women walking around a classroom, one behind the other. Going around in circles. They sat down at the pupils' desks, which were as gray as they were, as old as they were, and, on the desks, there were dusty, closed books. The playwright was on stage, accompanying them with his presence. He was tall, he leaned toward their procession, his eyes hollowed out, his hands, like those of an orchestra conductor, silently waving, exhausted, too. Sometimes the old pupils tried to speak, to answer a question from the teacher. Painfully, they sat up straight, to raise a finger and speak, but their voices were muffled and their language incomprehensible. They spoke in a lost language. And then it started all over again. They stood up and walked in single file, overwhelmed, demeaned. Music from bygone eras—mournful waltzes, military marches—accompanied these rag-and-bone men, faded clowns, little soldiers, an old man with a miniature bicycle, a sleep-walking prostitute . . . It went on and on. Chaos. Fatigue. Obedience. And if the spectators were hypnotized by this submissive procession, it was because each one of those old people was carrying a wax doll. And this mannequin they held tight against their chest, or on their shoulders, swaying to the rhythm of their movements, was none other than that very same old person. It was their own childhood they were holding, their murdered childhood. The anxiety floating through the theater: you could have reached out and touched it, and fear adopted the dimensions of terror. The old people and their murdered childhoods collided, hid behind windows that were too small, rocked silent cradles, spoke in a lunatic dialect, everything seemed both well-ordered and disjointed. Were they dead? Were they alive? It wasn't the fragility of memory that was at issue, but the inevitability of the future. Death and nothing else. The play went on for a long time. Haunting. A long, revolutionary malaise.

Sitting in the eighth row, Sabine felt the accusation strike her right in the heart: we are all guilty of murdering our childhood. And on stage, the décor was no longer a classroom, it was a bedroom, and that bedroom was her own, the one in La Petite Chartreuse. She recognized the landscape of her youth, her sleepless nights picturing herself elsewhere, and being there. The shadows of her childhood were superimposed upon the wandering souls of the characters on stage; she knew she had left her childhood behind, at the door to her parents' home, and that door would never open again.

All through the play, through that terrified amazement, she had sensed the presence of the young man sitting next to her, something emanating from him, and, at times, she had found herself breathing to the rhythm of his emotion. Something shared, invisible and burning. When the play came to an end, there was no immediate applause. There was a long pause before the audience dared to break the spell of what had just happened. Then the clapping, once it started, came with a flood of energy, and everyone stood to cheer, the shouts of bravo, the whistles, expressing an overwhelmed gratitude. Sabine saw the face of the young man next to her, and he was not as she had imagined, not handsome as she had fantasized during the play. He was tall, with a pale, emaciated face, and an unquiet intelligence to his slanting blue eyes.

"That was . . . it was . . . incredible, wasn't it?"

He nodded, gravely, not openly.

"Had you already seen it?"

"No. And you?"

"This was the first time."

They left the Palais de Chaillot together and walked along the banks of the Seine; behind them the Eiffel Tower, placid and rooted, watched over them. It was exceptionally warm for the month of October, a weather for festivals, theater, and encounters. They talked about *Dead Class*, how stunned they were by this production from Eastern Europe, a theater that had its origins in the cellars of bombed-out Kraków. Sabine was overwhelmed with sensations—the play, this man, it was as if her life were exploding, and Paris, that evening, was all hers, Paris acknowledged her legitimacy. The man's name was Mathieu, he was an English teacher at the Lycée Jules-Ferry, and he had come to see Kantor's play on the advice of a friend. When they came to the Champs-Élysées metro station, he gave her his phone number, he lived near the Porte d'Orléans, she was on the rue Raymond-Losserand, so they were virtually neighbors, something that happened so rarely in Paris. Sabine gave him Robert Cousin's phone number, stammering that, for the moment, she lived at his place, but that it was temporary. They were each taking a different line, and they walked away without looking back. But long after they had parted, Sabine could still feel Mathieu's presence, sensed that he was thinking about her, and that for once something was beginning.

She recalled her arrival in Paris three years earlier, the sixteen-hour drive in a Deux Chevaux, without ever taking the autoroute, and Robert's face when he opened the door to her, it was past midnight, his worn, wary face, that of an old man who lives alone, easy prey. She came into the apartment with its smells of mothballs and roses, and at the end of a long, dim corridor, there was her room. She didn't feel as if she were beginning a new life, but perpetuating an imprisonment. When she opened the window to light a cigarette, she took in the luminous humidity of the city, rooted in history and so vast and open, a city she'd be playing heads or tails with. She worked as hard as a pupil who has to make up lessons she's missed, and from morning to night she was studious and conscientious. She would leaf through her thick red book, *Paris by Arrondissement, Index of Streets, One-ways, Metro, RER, Buses, and Various Information*, in hopes that certain quartiers would become familiar. She made the Saints-Innocents fountain her designated meeting place, she ate dinner Chez Chartier, she bought her books from the *bouquinistes* along the quais, beginning with the best known and most obvious, and gradually ferreting out more subtle points of reference, places where she could rest from so much opinionated assertiveness. She wanted to have her own habits and good ideas, seek out her own favorite places and, already, a few memories. She had not imagined how much she would miss her family, the easy flow of a life where she had her place and everything was stable. She had not imagined how hard it would be to plan her days, her evenings, all on her own. No one to ask her in the morning if she'd slept well; no one to ask her in the evening how her day had gone. Her parents' concern for her well-being was all-encompassing, they could not visualize where she lived, the apartment or the street she was phoning from; her landscape could not be shared, and she realized that those years that had seemed endless were nothing.

Her immeasurably slow childhood was over, period. There was no going back.

To support herself and pay for her room, she had worked as a check-out clerk at Félix Potin, a sales girl at Tati, and now she was cleaning house, twelve hours a week, for people she never saw but about whom she knew so much—picking up after them, cleaning their bathrooms and their toilets. It was indecent work, and it reinforced her mistrust of those she referred to indiscriminately as "the rich."

She had tamed her solitary nature, forced herself to chat with shopkeepers and neighbors, to speak to strangers at the cinema, or at sidewalk cafés, ever on the lookout for the first lead that might come her way, the first hand held out to her. With the sole aim of leaving her mark on Paris, she'd flirted with boys she didn't really fancy—a fling, a face, a name soon forgotten. She'd had girlfriends, easily replaceable, they were kind and most of the time from the provinces like herself, but they seemed to have come to Paris with no curiosity, and made do with very little. The life she had always dreamed of was beyond reach, as if her plans had been nothing but fantasy. She wondered if it was possible to lose what was deepest inside you—your dreams, your whims, your strength; could she have gotten it all wrong? But after drifting through drama classes whose only talent was their reputation, and once she'd hesitated between returning frequently to Aix or getting used to her autonomy, once she'd accepted that Robert wasn't her jailer but a charming host; once she'd dared to get lost during her exploring; once she'd idled and wandered aimlessly and dreamed again, Paris united with her. And that evening, when she saw *Dead Class*, she had shared the emotion of an entire audience and walked through the streets, with someone, simply chatting. She had arrived at last.

She was studying drama with Jean-Laurent Cochet. At last, they were getting into the great works, and the technique it took to perform them; to speak was to understand. Breathing was more important than emotion, as were the rhythm of articulation and the control required by alexandrines, and Cochet, whom the students called the *Maître*, was a terrific teacher. But tough. Scathing. Partial. And a misogynist. Out of the question for girls to wear trousers. To be caught smoking. Out of the question to like any other theater than his own, any other way of performing. He often made fun of Jean-Louis Barrault, could not forgive him for opening the Théâtre de l'Odéon to the students in '68, who all wanted to be the next Jean-Paul Belmondo. He could not understand why Barrault had let them occupy that temple of the nation; such a desacralization. He could go on for hours about Arletty, Greta Garbo, and Jean Cocteau, whom he had known and loved so deeply, about Gérard Depardieu, who had met his wife Élisabeth in his class, and he referred to this as his most extraordinary encounter—as if that magnificent ruffian were both his opposite and his double. Cochet had been born before the war, had acted with the Comédie-Française, and behind the bourgeois gentleman with his mannerisms of a notary, there was a wounded man, a moralist who preferred men. His teaching was necessary and brilliant, but the time had come to cast it aside. Now that she had seen Kantor's play, Sabine knew that Cochet's class was dead. She hadn't seen Mathieu again since the performance, a week earlier; they had spoken once over the phone, it was a nascent relation that strengthened her, and with Jean-Laurent Cochet she did what she hadn't dared to do with her parents: she made her exit. In front of all her friends, serious students who took the slightest remark from the *Maître* as a sign of elevation or censure, students who were praised to the skies or condemned with a droll, quick-fire cruelty: they were all waiting to be chosen to go on stage. Sabine wanted to confront Cochet in front of them, so they would all remember. It was very simple. Maybe too simple. Before class she lit a *Gauloise blonde* and stood out on the sidewalk smoking, and of course she was wearing trousers. When the *Maître* arrived, with his little dog in his arms, he saw no one else. He liked her enough to understand from the look she gave him that he was being targeted personally. He didn't say anything, he went into the classroom while everyone followed and sat down in silence. Then he spoke loudly, with his head voice, shrill and weary:

"Malivieri, you can go home. Go on, beat it. Go back to your province!"

Sabine stood up. Some of the students who'd seen her smoking, in her trousers, had been expecting a punishment, but not that she would be expelled. No one dared react. The room was charged with a craven emotion. Sabine sought to keep her gestures steady: pick up her bag, walk calmly toward the door, act determined.

"Hurry up, we have work to do! Go on, scram! Go home!"

At the door, gathering her strength and remembering her goal, she turned around and shouted, "Your theater is dead! You will never be Chéreau, Mnouchkine, or Brook, you will never be Vitez—"

The *Maître* gave a sign, and two boys stood up to escort her out, *manu militari*. She couldn't have wished for more.

"Tadeusz Kantor has killed you! You're nothing now! Just a petty bourgeois, spouting your Sacha Guitry!"

The two boys shoved her out onto the sidewalk, and the door slammed. The little dog could be heard barking, faintly.

Sabine had been ejected into a clear October morning, a luminosity that gave the daylight the brilliance of an invitation; everything was vast enough to take her in.

A few months earlier, on Monday, March 10, 1977, on her way out of the Collège des Prêcheurs, Mariette picked up a pamphlet that was being handed out, stuffed it in her pocket without reading it, and went home with her father, who left at the same time from the nearby Sainte-Catherine School. Her sisters were living in Paris—Sabine at the old surgeon's, and Hélène, since last year, at the Tavels'—and she had become an only child, cocooned with worry and suspicion: would she go away, too? Was there a curse that meant all three sisters would leave Aix and their parents behind and go and live in Paris? What was it that was missing, here? What thrill was it they needed so badly? Bruno had created something for them that he had never known, a childhood where they were loved and protected, and he had thought that would be enough. He'd been wrong. Nowadays he behaved around Mariette like a man whose spirits are low but who forces himself to be cheerful, a worried father who grants freedoms that make him feel guilty—as if by avoiding his responsibilities, he was gently nudging his youngest toward the edge of the precipice. But Mariette didn't ask for much; she was a well-behaved child; gifted, she'd skipped one year of primary school which meant that now, in the first year of *collège*, she was the youngest again, back in her usual place. Her diminutive figure seemed to reflect this, she was barely four foot three, and they'd started calling her *Mouse.* Most of the time, her head was down, and her big brown eyes looked up from below; she wasn't hiding anything, she was observing.

The tract she hadn't read called on students to *skip school to show your support for the detainees of the MLAC,* the Movement for the Liberation of Abortion and Contraception, and when the following Thursday at 9 A.M. she arrived in the vicinity of the collège, which was next to the Church of the Madeleine and the courthouse, she had the sudden overwhelming impression that she'd come to a foreign place. From the streets all around, outside the collège and where the market stalls usually were, and on the square outside the courthouse, there were buses full of riot police, ready to contain a huge crowd. Two thousand people. Beneath a banner proclaiming *JUSTICE IS FUCKED THE WITCHES ARE IN THE STREET,* a crowd of mostly young women and a few men were relentlessly chanting the same words: *let us live, we won't let go, let us live, we won't take no.* Another city had emerged within the city, as if Mariette, without realizing it, had traveled in the night and woken up elsewhere. Her schoolbag on her back, she was so captivated by the crowd that she didn't even think about missing class, was simply carried by the movement, the teeming life, warm and compact like the inside of a body. She realized that these thousands of women had come from all over—Marseille, Grenoble, Toulon, Lille . . . and Paris. So, she began looking for her sisters. Sabine must be here, among these joyful, rebellious girls. And Hélène must be here too, because she missed her so much. And so, she questioned the women, one after the other, as much as she could: had they come from Paris? And if by chance one of them had, she said their names, Sabine and Hélène, her voice trembling, hard to hear. She was angry at herself for being in such a panic, her sisters came home regularly, there was no reason to get excited, as if she had only just then lost them in the crowd. But the possibility they might be here filled her with a joy that was close to confusion. *Paris,* that was her sisters, so if *Paris* was here, they must be, too. Her school bag knocked against the demonstrators, some of them kindly pointed this out to her, but she kept it on, even though it was so heavy, the books made her back and shoulders ache. She wanted to shout her sisters' names, but she knew she never could, that the emotion of shouting their names would break her, and serve no purpose, the clamor all around her left no room for a single voice. She was near the Passage Agard, where groups of determined women kept arriving, tirelessly, arm in arm as if headed for the barricades. She avoided them awkwardly, felt an elbow jab her face, the humiliating pain of it: she was disposable, of no interest. She climbed up on a concrete block to take a better look, but then fell backwards; a girl who was singing with a group to a guitar caught her by her school bag.

"Hey! Stay with us, baby!"

"I'm looking for my sisters."

"We're all sisters, aren't we? What do your sisters look like?"

"They've come from Paris."

Not hearing her naive remark, the girl went back to the musicians. Mariette listened to some people arguing and understood they were still talking about the Veil Act. For two years, she'd heard little else. On television, on the radio, after mass, and at dinner, the adults among themselves, inevitably arguing or agreeing that "la mère Veil" (Mariette heard "la merveille") was no better than Hitler and his ovens. She went up to a stall that said *RECEPTION*, decorated with two flags she recognized, those of Provence and Languedoc, and she asked the women at the stand whether the girls who'd come from Paris were all together in the same place, but the crowd had just started singing the *Internationale* and the women raised their fists and sang, too. The singing rose from the entire square, from the people who were sitting, those who'd been arguing, handing out leaflets, shouting slogans: now they were all singing in one slow, obstinate voice. Everyone was looking toward the courthouse, and Mariette did too, and recognized some girls from her collège, older ones from the last year. She would have liked to join them but they were far away, a few who were already on the steps were trying to get in. Mariette balanced on tip toes, people kept bumping into her, she was no higher than their backs, their bellies, this constant shoving, she tried to make her way out, saying sorry, but the *Internationale* kept on, ever louder, and no one heard her or saw her. She sneezed. And then she understood she had to get out of there as quickly as she could, but the crowd was like a single person you could not split in two, a giant with its limbs rooted in place. She sneezed again. They really had to let her through. But she was invisible, as light as the pollen from the plane trees. She coughed, a dry, hoarse cough, and her heart started beating wildly, she had to get out of this huge rippling wave *now*. She bit a girl's hand, and the girl gave a start and stepped aside, shouting; she bit another one, and there too the girl stepped back, and yet another, between two coughing fits, for all she was worth, she bit every hand that was level with her lips—hands with rings, dirty hands, indifferent, colored with henna, holding tracts, bags, she bit them as if slicing through thread, making her way from bite to bite, and when at last she was out of the crowd, she was out of breath. She wiggled her shoulders to shake off her school bag, dropped it to the ground, opened it, trembling, reached for the inhaler, breathed in the Ventolin and sat on the sidewalk, hunched forward, her eyes closed, trying to calm down. The crowd was whistling and applauding now, but it all came to her from far away, as if she were underwater, a confused resonance from a world where she was not. A loudspeaker was chanting, *MLAC MLAC MLAC So-li-da-ri-ty!* and the crowd replied, *MLAC MLAC MLAC So-li-da-ri-ty!* It throbbed like a furious curse, *MLAC MLAC MLAC!* but Mariette heard *CLACK CLACK CLACK!* and forced herself to think only of her breath, to make the rhythm smooth, deep breathing, the way Hélène had taught her, and it was coming, along with the tired feeling. She was breathing better, it was warm, shallow, but regular, and she'd stopped coughing. She slowly raised her head. A woman was crouching in front of her.

"What are you doing down here, Mouse?"

She recognized Laurence and collapsed into her arms.

Lying in Rose's big bed, in the half-light from the louvered shutters, Mariette wasn't sleeping. She heard Laurence's voice, and her father's, as they spoke close together, trying to keep their voices low, but they were amplified by anger. She was sorry she couldn't hold the old ginger cat close to her, her allergies were a source of constant frustration. So, she held a plush toy she knew well, a teddy bear Rose had dressed with a tie that used to belong to her father. The teddy bear smelled of forgotten fruit slowly drying, and the room still had that scent of slightly stale patchouli. If she closed her eyes Mariette could see Rose, Sabine, and Hélène, she heard their whispered secrets, their declarations, the assertive voices of girls who don't know whether their concerns are a sign of maturity, or a failing. She liked to focus on the details, close her eyes and enter a place in the past—the dining room at her grandparents', the playground at nursery school during recess, and then she found things she thought she'd forgotten, they came to her. It was unreal, yet true. Simpler than with faces. When she tried to evoke her sister's faces, she realized she couldn't remember them very well, maybe because they had changed so quickly. When they came home from Paris, they looked different, they said "*Petite mère*" when they spoke to Agnès, and they said, "Are you all right, Papa?" in loud tones as if their father had gone deaf. Or suddenly grown so old. They wore makeup, and hoop earrings, and Sabine would tap her cigarette and say, "Do you mind if I smoke?" then, not waiting for an answer, she lit the cigarette, screwing up her eyes. Mariette might find it hard to recall the details of their faces, but she remembered everything her sisters told her, and wrote it all down in a notebook she called "The Happiness Notebook," among a thousand little things that gave her pleasure, most often unexpectedly. Tonight, she would write down her joy on finding Laurence at the demonstration. She would describe how soft Rose's sagging bed was, and how she liked holding the bear's tie in her hand, rubbing it between her fingers, and how it made her want to suck her thumb, and how she went ahead and did it anyway, without feeling any shame. But she wouldn't copy down what she heard the moment she stopped focusing on her thoughts.

"I don't want her to see you anymore, is that clear, I don't want her to see you ever again!"

"But it's not up to you to decide, Bruno, that too is very clear. Agnès is my friend, you can't prevent it. What planet are you on? What century?"

"It's been a long time, I suppose?"

"What has?"

"Since you joined that movement?"

"The MLAC was founded in 1973, I've been waiting for this trial for two years and I was supposed to cover it for the newspaper, but then I saw Mariette and brought her home."

She had saved his daughter, yes. She had taken her home and called the school so they would let him know. Agnès was on her rounds, and couldn't be reached. The world upside down.

"Would you like a coffee?"

Bruno didn't answer.

"Right. I'll make you a coffee."

He was tormented by the question he felt he had to ask. If she said yes, as he feared, he would have to take a radical decision, he could not go against his conscience. He remembered the first time he'd seen her, the night of the accident: that image, a Madonna. If he'd only known . . .

"But you have your Veil Act, don't you? What more do you want?"

"We want, and when I say 'we,' I should say, 'they,'—girls who are still under age, immigrants, the poor—we want abortion to be fully reimbursed, and available using the Karman procedure, which non-professionals can perform—"[6]

"You've been doing it! You've been doing it, I knew it!"

She disgusted him, it was as if she had blood on her hands, the skin of the hundreds of babies sucked out by a vacuum aspirator and tossed in the garbage—that was their famous Karman procedure! He saw Mariette standing in the door.

"Get ready. We're going home."

"I am ready."

And as proof of her good faith, she slowly turned around: her school bag was on her back. He would never have imagined that one day they would part like this. They'd been happy here, at the Embassy. But now, yes, war had been declared, and he would tell his wife to choose. Her or me. Laurence kissed Mariette, holding the little girl's face in her hands, a tender kiss that meant, "None of this has anything to do with you." For the very first time, she didn't go with them to the gate. The beloved landscape was disappearing, the linden tree with its low-hanging boughs, the insistent smell of cypress, the soft earth scattering beneath her footsteps, the stones with their lizards, Sabine and Hélène on either side of their mother, "You

[6] The Veil Act in 1975 decriminalized abortion but did not help to make it readily available. Hence the continued use of the "self-help" menstrual extraction or D&C methods, and the necessity for some women to travel abroad. French social security health care would begin to cover the costs of abortion in 1982.

look like four sisters!" We are being erased, thought Mariette, and she turned around, the better to remember it all: the peeling blue shutters, the rusty bell on the wall, its long fraying rope, the clogs by the door . . .

"I'm a good man, you know."

She held her face up to her father. He was staring straight ahead, focused, upset, and when he opened the gate, it groaned, and that beloved sound, all of a sudden, became something terrible.

When they got to the apartment, she went straight to bed; after an attack it was inevitable. Soon after, the front door slammed. She didn't have the strength to get up and listen to her parents arguing. She was too tired to stand yet again behind the door. They were in the kitchen, talking quietly, wearily, they didn't feel like having this discussion, this inevitable argument. Agnès gave nervous little laughs that Bruno took for disdain. As a man, was he upstanding or pitiful? And what about his wife, constantly tired, with her schedule the opposite of his, her short vacations, her aching body, what exactly did she want?

"The problem," she said, doggedly stirring the sugar in her cup, "is that you think everything we're doing, everything that's happening, is about you. But our lives are our lives, Bruno, our lives are lived on their own. You can't stop that."

"Did you know your best friend has been performing clandestine abortions?"

"I've known for two years, ever since they charged the six women who are now on trial."

"And she wasn't charged, was she, how lucky was that. Or else she's well protected."

"She doesn't do it anymore. Since the Veil Act, she's simply been supporting the movement."

"Does she organize trips to England?"

"To England, yes."

"And you're okay with that?"

"No."

He was fed up with all this contraception and abortion business the women were obsessed with. Why didn't they want to defer to nature anymore? Having children wasn't a curse.

"They assist births, too, and they've organized day care, you know, at the Thomson factory, many of them are from a very modest background and—"

"I don't know which is worse. The fact you hid what Laurence is doing from me, or that you can go on being her friend."

He was sitting across from her, and, suddenly, she reached out and took his hands. Put her forehead on their clasped fingers. He could hardly make out what she was saying, her words fell on the plastic tablecloth.

"Haven't you ever wondered why I didn't get pregnant again? I've been on the pill for years."

She raised her head slowly.

"Or maybe you knew?"

He screwed up his eyes, as if he were suddenly blinded, half awake.

"And you must have known, too, that it was thanks to Laurence?"

Bruno said nothing.

"So, you were right."

"When?"

"When you said this is all women's business."

She walked slowly out of the kitchen, reached for her jacket and her bag, opened the door and said, both calm and threatening, "Don't you ever meddle with my friendships again."

And she closed the door so gently you might think she'd never been there.

Hélène had never imagined this could happen to her someday, that she would find herself in such a grotesque situation. Maybe it was because she'd been brought up to believe you mustn't waste food, that you have to clean your plate, and think about those who are going hungry. She was ringing at all the neighbors' doorbells, with a dead, defrosted animal in her arms: the long pink flank of a deer; the belly of a wild boar, bright red and marbled with fat; a hare with only one eye open, and four ortolans she didn't dare look at when she held them out, they were so rare; and yet none of David's neighbors were interested. She really wanted the ortolans to be taken off her hands first. She couldn't help but think of that TV program one New Year's Eve where a famous chef, sitting by the fire about to enjoy a candlelit dinner, had explained to her viewers not how to cook an ortolan, but how to eat it. She had begun with her napkin, the napkin was vital to eat the tiny birds, a big cloth napkin custom-made for modesty, because, explained the chef, stroking her throat to illustrate what was about to happen, you had to hide to eat an ortolan, the bird is very greasy, your mouth would end up full of grease and it would all dribble around your lips and down your throat, and the advantage of hiding like this (here she closed her eyes and her voice trembled), the advantage of hiding behind a napkin was that you could concentrate better, really taste it, *make the most of* the bird. After this long preamble about the importance of the napkin and the route the grease would take, she'd held the ortolan by the legs with two fingers and then it looked more like a mouse, a tiny gray mouse, only its dangling head with its unmoving, cooked beak might remind you that it had once been a bird. Hélène didn't watch the rest of the program. She never found out if the woman had stained her blouse.

"Good evening, I'm sorry to bother you, I'm David's niece, David Tavel your neighbor, well, you see, we have a problem with the freezer . . . Oh, that's fine, thank you, excuse me, goodbye."

"Good evening, I'm sorry to be calling on you so late, forgive me, I live at the Tavels', our freezer is broken, oh, I'm sorry, sorry, good night."

No one wanted their wild game. It wasn't a big building, and, before long, Hélène was back at the Tavels' with her assortment of meat that was about to go off.

"Well?" asked Arthur, lying on the sofa, "any luck with your door to door?"

"No. It will all go to waste."

"What did you expect! A vegetarian trying to offload wild game, that's suspicious. Honestly, you went about it all wrong, you shouldn't have tried to give them the meat, you should've tried to sell it, to make a profit, the people who live around here are businessmen."

She nestled against him, he made more room and they stayed like that, hugging on the sofa, trying not to slide off, glad of the need to hold each other so close.

"Will he be angry with you?"

"David? I don't know . . . I don't think so. What matters most to him isn't eating the game, it's the hunting. Spending the whole day with his rich friends, you see . . . their manly country sport . . ."

"And your aunt?"

"She doesn't care."

"So, it's no big deal?"

"I feel so stupid. I don't understand how I managed to blow the fuse in the kitchen, I know the alarm system for the apartment inside out, that's all I think about when I come in: switch off the alarm."

"You want me to take the meat down to the garbage?"

"Maria will be back from Spain tomorrow, she'll get rid of it."

Hélène buried her face in Arthur's shoulder and gave a disheartened laugh, it was all so absurd, cruel too, and she didn't want to involve Arthur, he mustn't be the one to throw the dead animals away. She'd understood long ago what everyone's role was, and the kitchen was Maria's domain, particularly when it came to the most unpleasant chores. As for Arthur, he wasn't a very practical sort, like her, he was completely absorbed by his studies, living to the rhythm of their schedule of classes, study periods, exams. He was a young medical student from a good family, as fresh as a child just out of the bath, as spontaneous as he was generous. It was easy to see the child he'd once been, what his face had been like when he was eight or nine, his pink cheeks and surprised gaze, devoid of any afterthoughts or ulterior motives, a good student and a good companion. Hélène had met him through friends, right at the start of the school year, as if he'd been placed there for her arrival in Paris, and it hadn't surprised her to be with him so soon, there was nothing complicated about it, neither the attraction they felt nor his confession, it had all happened very quickly, but intimacy required stolen time. Arthur shared a room at the university dorm, so Hélène watched out for moments when Michelle and David were away, and she dreaded Maria's inquisitiveness. They made love like two teenagers, discreetly and in hiding, when it was possible, and there were no surprises to the smooth progression of their complicity. To others they seemed ageless, as if they'd grown up together and shared an affinity they'd always had, and people thought nothing would ever happen to them, nothing that might ever call that affinity into question.

Hélène had left Aix two years after Sabine; as soon as she had her baccalaureate degree, she followed in her sister's footsteps. For her chosen endeavor she needed peace and quiet, and comfort, needed to be away from her mother and the hesitancy of her feelings, her inability to treat Hélène like her own, fully-fledged daughter. Above all, she needed her own room, material ease, and the right to dispose of her time as she saw fit. When she came home at any hour of the day or night, she could open the cupboards and the fridge and find them always full, and never have to think about the cost. Money made the constant, invisible renewal of privilege possible, and, cushioned by ease, Hélène had been hard at work for over a year, studying biology at the Université Pierre et Marie Curie. Despite her baccalaureate in literature, and the enormous gaps in her math skills, she'd plunged headfirst into that unknown world, a foreign language, immersed herself with a constancy and exertion that resembled a never-ending conquest. She wanted to be a zoologist, to get closer to the mystery of the animal world. Thanks to Darwin and the evolution of species, the image of an unchanging world was countered by the theory of a living world where everything was in constant flux. The creation of the world was out of God's hands. Her studies were the re-education of her own mental structures, of her brain, initially so impervious to science—and why, after all, should any of it be easy? She liked working hard, as if her efforts were the price to pay for living in the duplex in Neuilly. David had opened a bank account for her, where he deposited an incredible amount, and she didn't need to look for odd jobs to pay for her transit pass or her school supplies;

she was a bourgeoise, the niece-slash-daughter of a bourgeois family, make no mistake. Her studies were a challenge. Math, physics, chemistry, histology, cellular biology: everything was calculated, and theorems were the key to a world made of numbers and formulas, of solutions to the problems she repeated tirelessly and as often as necessary, to etch them firmly in her mind.

"Do you remember, Sabine, when we were little and you made me recite my multiplication tables?"

"I remember, I called it 'a case of the red ants,' you fidgeted so much when you were reciting, it was as if you'd sat on a nest of vermin."

"Stop saying 'vermin!' Anyway, I said them so often that they eventually lodged inside my childish skull. Well, theorems are exactly the same, I have to know them just as automatically, have to remember instinctively, quickly, without error. I'm constantly confronted with theorems."

"You wear me out, I cannot believe how much you wear me out, here, help me rehearse my text."

"More *Vanya*? I'm tired of playing the old man."

"And don't prompt me if I take ages."

They never met in Neuilly, Sabine would have felt she was betraying her loved ones, and Hélène would have felt exposed. She knew David wasn't sending checks to her parents anymore, as if having his niece at home meant he'd won the match. Moreover, Agnès explicitly told Hélène not to tell the Tavels that she had a job, a poor person's job which, through a strange rebound effect, might lower Michelle's social status and elicit humiliating remarks. And so, Paris and Aix became two little plots of land drifting apart, taking the children with them and an entire procession of silences. Hélène figured her parents had only one daughter to support now, and two paychecks, however modest, and that, in spite of everything, things were getting better, but all she had to do was spend time at home to realize that the only thing that was progressing was bitterness. She was witnessing the slow breakdown of family unity, as if each member, by taking a simple step to one side, had undermined trust; any news they shared was cautious and incomplete, never expressing what was really going on, and, imperceptibly, they became distanced from the heart of things. Hélène thought about this, and then stopped thinking about it, turned toward her new life, and the anger she'd felt as a child was transformed into rebellion: she could no longer ignore the sort of world she lived in, the martyrdom that humankind was inflicting upon other animals; she could no longer ignore the reality, however depressing it might be. There was pride in her desire to know and to confront, pride that she "dared to go there," to join the circle of those who refused to live blindly.

After she'd been thrown out of Cochet's class, Sabine walked for a while, overcome with excitement, then she went into a bar to make a phone call, and she didn't notice the man standing by the counter. She was completely absorbed by what she had just experienced, this brutal emancipation, and she needed to tell Hélène. The man at the bar felt her presence before he saw her. When she shoved the door so hard it banged against the wall, he felt the draft of air from outside as if it were forcing him to wake up. He heard her sharp, precise footsteps, her troubled voice, "Can I make a call?" and saw only her hand when she hurried to put the coins on the counter. She smelled of wind. A smell of autumn trees. And faint sweat. He was wearing his dark suit, and he'd come for his second coffee, the 9:45 coffee, like every morning. He didn't know why, but when this girl passed behind him and practically brushed against him to reach for the telephone on the counter, he adjusted his tie, picked up his newspaper, and noticed that the pages were trembling. "It's Sabine . . . Hélène's sister, yes . . . she's not there? No, no don't bother, I'll call again later. Goodbye, Maria." She had a deep voice for her age, lilting slightly with emotion. He turned to her and, forgetting his manners, he stared at her, captivated. She glanced at him, thought he was old and ugly, and moved further away, ordering a strong coffee. She wished she could reach Mathieu, but he was in class, so she remained alone with her reaction to what she had just done at Cochet's class. The man, burdened by his rush of feelings, gave the café owner a stupid smile. He was overwhelmed with questions, with orders and counter-orders, he had to speak to this girl, he wasn't her type, he'd appear ridiculous, she had problems, maybe this was just the right moment, he had to leave her alone, he was about to miss the opportunity of a lifetime, he'd be late at the agency, he had to go, his appointment must already be there, yes of course, what was he thinking, he paid for his coffee and headed toward the door, opened it and looked back at her one last time. She'd put her elbows on the table, and was holding a scarf rolled up against her mouth, looking outside, but he wanted her to show him her face, her gaze, yes, she had to look at him, at least once, and then he'd go.

"May I?"

He stood before her, holding the back of the empty chair opposite her and, concluding that her failure to react implied consent, he sat down.

"Good morning . . ."

He thought she shrugged her shoulders slightly, and that those shoulders were carrying too heavy a burden.

"Good morning, Mademoiselle . . ."

She turned her face toward him. She had haughty, youthful brown eyes, and he asked, "Is everything all right? Can I help you with anything?"

She'd always dreamed that a young man would speak to her like that, a young man would see her and fall for her on the spot, but this man was wearing a suit and tie, he had gel in his hair, and nothing about his face or his allure could find favor with her, she stared at him, bitterly disappointed, why this guy and not Mathieu? Did Mathieu fancy her? Had he fallen for her? Would he, someday?

"If I can do anything for you . . ."

He put his business card on the table.

"Call me if . . . if you need . . . I don't know . . . anything . . . nothing, too . . ."

She glanced at the card, then stared at him with all the disdain she could muster. He hurriedly crossed out the phone number of the agency and wrote down his private number, giving a faint laugh, "I'm not here to sell you insurance!" His absent-mindedness seemed to amuse him.

A heavily made-up girl came into the bar and hurried over to them.

"Forgive me, Paul, your appointment. He's getting impatient."

He looked at her as if he were trying to understand who she was, until it became clear.

"I'm coming, Brigitte, I'm coming."

And since she didn't move: "Make him wait."

But Brigitte was still standing there, hostile, sure of herself, and he reluctantly got to his feet. Sabine was already looking outside and didn't hear him say goodbye. She was thinking of the hour that had just gone by. Her boldness and courage. You're nothing! Just a petty bourgeois spouting your Sacha Guitry! How could she have said that? Naturally Jean-Laurent—she could call him by his first name now, the way his former students did—Jean-Laurent had not kicked her out solely because of the cigarette and the jeans. There was another grievance between them. Last year she'd begged him to include her in the production of *Amphitryon 38* he'd put on at the Théâtre Édouard-VII with Jean Desailly and Simone Valère. He'd given walk-on parts to a few students, without their asking. She would have done anything to be included among them, and for free, if necessary, just to attend rehearsals, and share a dressing room, and go on stage, to receive a little of the light projected on the leads, and take a bow next to them before the curtain fell with all its thick velvet elegance, to hear the applause, like on television, like on *At the Theater This Evening.* To inhabit her childhood dream. But the *Maître* had simply raised his brows, refusing to let her take part.

*

She walked out of the bar, leaving Paul's business card on the table. She left the Batignolles quartier behind: this was where she'd taken her Cochet classes—her acting apprenticeship, her discovery of technique and poetry. She walked aimlessly, or so she thought, until she realized she was headed toward the Place Clichy, toward the Lycée Jules-Ferry where Mathieu taught, she smiled thinking of the nerve of that little insurance man, and told herself he was right, you must always try your luck. And so, she went up and down the streets and boulevards, wagering on joy or rejection, but never mind if Mathieu thought she was being intrusive, never mind if she found out he was already with someone, never mind if he didn't fancy her, never mind the humiliation. She waited outside the lycée, on the sidewalk across the street, which was narrow and crowded, but she knew she'd see him, she couldn't miss him.

He didn't seem surprised to find her there. At Chaillot, he'd had a hunch that she'd be the one to make the first move, and he kissed her furtively on the lips, as if it were something they did regularly. It was the first time they'd seen each other again, and Sabine felt projected outside herself by a driving energy, maddening but thrilling, too.

At his place, he undressed her slowly, as if cautiously opening a present he'd wanted for a long time; he was sure of himself and of her, as well—he'd known from the way she walked that her lovemaking must be generous, her sensuality guileless. He smelled of warm cake, something familiar and very sweet, and they made love with the slow, awkward hesitancy of the first time, this new geography of the body to explore, they gave themselves with humility and boldness too, aware that it was only a beginning and would be followed by immodesty, passion, and if all went well, dizzying dependency.

Afterwards, twirling his hair between two fingers like a child, he told her he was in favor of free love, and that she mustn't be jealous or ask questions. Once again, reality was veering away from Sabine's dreams—absolute love, exclusive and incandescent—but she told herself that if she went about it the way she had when speaking to him at Chaillot, then waited outside his school, she'd bring him around, so he'd be hers, and hers alone. And her patience was her new battle.

Sabine's other battle, as the months went by, was still, as ever, the stage. Love and the stage shared the same urgency and the same significance: to live life in an intensity of hours and feelings. Upon rediscovering Maupassant's *A Life*, which she'd first read when she was fifteen, then more or less forgotten, she realized that the bedroom of Jeanne the dreamer, who was so sensitive and naïve, was not that different from her own bedroom in La Petite Chartreuse, and, before long, she began working on the text, transforming it into a monologue. Since then, she'd become obsessed, identifying herself with Jeanne, and she found something she'd always wanted: to be restlessly and endlessly fascinated. There was something of Simone de Beauvoir in this novel, which dared to speak of the subordination of women, of pleasure but also of conjugal, domestic rape; of happy or betrayed motherhood, of social hypocrisy, and the influence of the church, like a necrosis in the hearts of the living. Six months after leaving Cochet's course, she was on stage every night, in people's homes, in tower blocks in Bobigny, performing the monologue from *A Life*, in Kantor's glittering wake. She put on her makeup and got changed in her dressing room at the Maison de la Culture, then went and rang at the door of a strange apartment. The Maison de la Culture in Bobigny was the producer; the theater director met with residents who were eager to open their homes to the performance and invite their neighbors and friends. The director prepared the event, drew an outline of every setting, and Sabine came in discreetly, so that the guests didn't even know she'd arrived; she'd put down her coat and her gear in the kitchen and Éric, her partner, would join her with the lights and the musical instruments, djembe and harmonica. She would stand in front of the switched-off television and perform six feet away from her audience, trying not to see what was on the wall opposite her—family photographs, framed needlework, wall clocks: this décor of private lives. The play began with a shared silence, unexpected and reserved, then Sabine would say, very softly so that they would listen attentively:

"Oh . . . I wish I could see the sea . . ."

And everyone could feel how greatly they missed the sea, how much being away from it was like living on the mere surface of days, where there was neither truth nor poetry.

In the beginning, there were not many spectators—twenty when all went well, not even ten depending on the weather, soccer matches, the news . . . Six months later, up to eighty people would cram into a living room, stand in the corridor, and share apple pie and sparkling wine with Sabine and Éric. Every performance inevitably ended with the hospitality of apple pie and sparkling wine, as if everything had to be the same, from the opening silence of the play to the pie on their plates. Staying with the audience after the performance was part of the package, a commitment that was as political as it was artistic, but, in the early days, Sabine made a real effort to speak with the spectators; this was another representation of herself, a role after her role. Sometimes there were children present. One evening, one of them pinched her arm then immediately tried to escape. "Why'd you pinch me?" "To see if you're real." She often thought back on these words, sometimes tenderly, sometimes anxiously. As the weeks went by, critics started coming, curious to discover this new art form;

they came from Paris by car and left again after the pie and the fake champagne. Some seemed refreshed by the novelty of it, others were transported to the living rooms of their childhood—and that time, those places, where they had left their parents' youth, far more than their own, all seemed happy, even though they rarely had been.

It was when she came back from Bobigny one evening that Sabine found the message Robert had taken for her, a certain Paul had left his telephone number, she could call him whenever she wanted, at any time, he would answer. She called right away, out of curiosity and also because, after a performance, before she began to feel tired, there were hours where she was still brimming with energy, she was burdened with an excess of vitality, but since the time she called Mathieu and a girl had picked up, she'd stopped calling him late at night. "Mathieu's in the shower, do you want to leave a message? Is this Sabine? You're in the theater, right, you're an actress?" This happy, casual tone was like a dull knife planted in her heart. As clumsy as it was painful.

That night, Paul answered her call as if it were perfectly natural to talk at two o'clock in the morning, even with a perfect stranger, and with that cautious voice of his he explained that the morning they'd met on the boulevard des Batignolles he'd gone back to the bar, had dialed the number she'd called thirty minutes earlier, her sister had answered and he'd told her he needed to speak to Sabine, the name she'd given when she called. Her sister asked if it had to do with the theater, he lied and said yes, and she'd given him the old surgeon's number.

"Are you angry? I hope I haven't frightened you."

"Only one thing frightens me: going out on stage. I don't care about the rest."

"Ah, so you're an actress."

"And you're an insurance agent, aren't you?"

"Yes."

"And do you like it?"

"Well yes, I do."

She got into the habit of calling him after her performances, he was a good listener, almost neutral, and that encouraged her to open up. It was with him that she shared her reactions when she read reviews of the monologue in the press. She'd immediately thought of her father. She knew he was just waiting for her to give up this whim of working in the theater, that he was sorry she was still going around with her maiden name, that she wasn't married, as if she were rebelling against the proper, necessary stages of life. But now her name, *Malivieri*, was in the newspaper. Would he be pleased? Paul recommended she show him the articles, read them together with him. And so, when she went to Aix the first weekend in July to celebrate her mother's birthday, she took with her the articles that had appeared in *L'Officiel des Spectacles*, *Le Parisien* and, better still, *Le Figaro*, with a column full of praise by Pierre Marcabru, a formidable critic.

Mariette had set up a folding cot in what she still called "her sisters' room." When they arrived that Saturday, Sabine and Hélène put their suitcases on the plank-desk, as it was impossible to do anything in the tiny room other than sit on the beds. To ward off the July heat, they kept the shutters closed until evening, and the half-light was always a sign that, outdoors, sunlight ruled.

"We'll be cozy, the three of us," said Mariette, sitting on the folding bed until the top of it snapped closed and banged her arm.

"Hey, Mouse," said Sabine, "stop bouncing on the bed, it's not sturdy."

"I'm not bouncing, I'm sitting."

"You're bouncing on your butt."

"Leave her alone," said Hélène, "she's happy."

"Fold it back up and come sit next to me, we'll unfold it at bedtime."

As if to make a point, Mariette lay on her back, with her hands behind her head, determined to be comfortable on the makeshift bed which, already impatient, she had set up three days before her sisters arrived.

"Ah," she sighed, "I feel so good."

Sabine switched on the radio, "So we can talk all we want and not be overheard." Julien Clerc was quietly singing *Ma Préférence* in the background; it always made them feel a little sad, those words of love addressed to others.

"What do you want to know?" asked Mariette, staring at the ceiling.

"Tell us how things are with the parents," said Hélène.

"They're making a huge effort."

"Well, that's good at least."

"But it doesn't seem to be working all that well."

"Who's invited to Maman's birthday?"

Mariette jumped off the folding cot, which instantly sprang up, to go and sit next to Hélène, and she whispered, "Maman invited Laurence!"

"Look how she says it," said Sabine, "we shouldn't call her the mouse, she's the gossip!"

"And Papa? What did he say about Maman inviting Laurence?"

"I don't know, I couldn't hear very well."

"You're not a very good spy, are you."

"Well, they do speak very quietly."

"Oh, who cares anyway, they're like two kids, that's all there is to it."

"Right, we better go in, they'll start wondering what we're up to."

"Well, we're settling in!" said Mariette, stating the obvious.

Hélène looked at her, feeling oddly as if in this tiny little person there was a world that was both naïve and stubborn. She remembered how she'd been at that age, coming back from Neuilly with her suitcase full of new clothes, and her parents' embarrassed silence, the way they never wanted to know, how did it go *there.* Between Mariette and her sisters, the years would gradually fade, just as their mother had said; soon they would simply be the same generation, from the same family. And yet they hadn't shared all that much. Mariette was eleven, Sabine twice as old, and Hélène was about to turn nineteen. Mariette had inherited two individuals who were increasingly ill-matched: a mother who didn't open up much, working toward her independence as if it was less an emancipation than a rather forced struggle. By becoming a mail carrier, it was as if she had opted for a certain level of poverty: most of her coworkers were from a rural background, uprooted individuals who, by working for a public institution, sought to escape what their parents had known—backbreaking work for a salary that would never cover their debts and, when time came to retire, they'd be left without their animals, hard up and in ill health. Agnès didn't speak about her job much, didn't complain about her schedule or about being tired; it was as if she had filled a position that was doomed to be hers, and there was no reason to elaborate. Bruno was no longer so proud and handsome—as if his wife had taken the wind out of his sails, and the tenderness he'd once lavished so generously had become a secret thing he couldn't keep hold of. He had bursts of emotion when he said "my daughters," the way he might say "my lost loves," and when he looked at them, you'd have thought he was gazing not at living creatures but at an old photograph, so poignant you could weep.

The girls were surprised when they came out of the room and saw that the table had been laid in the living room, as if they were guests. They would have preferred to eat in the kitchen, where each one had her place, and they asked politely where they were supposed to sit. There was a moment of hesitation.

"Wherever you want," said Agnès, then she asked Sabine to sit next to her.

"You have a dishwasher now?"

"Yes, we bought it on credit."

"Oh, that's great."

A roast had pride of place on the table, the meat for special occasions.

"I don't eat meat, you know that," said Hélène.

"But it's not horsemeat, it's beef, I got it at the butcher's."

"I'm a vegetarian, remember?"

"So, what do you eat?"

"Don't worry about me."

"You drink wine I hope?"

"What's that got to do with it? Yes, I drink wine."

"What a pretty tablecloth, is it new?"

"Yes. No. I don't remember."

Sabine asked, over-eager, "Who's coming to your birthday party, *petite mère*?"

"Friends, neighbors . . ."

"Anyone from work?"

"Yes, I invited two girls I work with. There are a lot of single women in my job, did you know that?"

"No," said Bruno, "you never talk about it."

"Well, I'm telling you now. Since they started letting women apply in 1975, there have been a lot of them." She glanced at Sabine and Hélène. "What's more, a lot of them come from Paris."

"Why Paris?" asked Mariette, warily.

"Because you have to have done all sorts of jobs inside the Post Office before they let you buy your round . . . In other words, you have to have a permanent contract before you can ask to be transferred, and so most postal employees get their start with the odd jobs in Paris."

"So why didn't you?" asked Hélène.

Agnès blushed slightly. Bruno nodded his head as if to encourage her to go on speaking, then he looked away. To break the silence, Mariette declared, "Laurence helped Maman, Laurence knows everyone!"

"It's true. Thanks to Laurence . . . and to you, my three girls, I started working here where I live right away. When you're the mother of what they call 'a large family' . . ."

She was relieved the truth was out, that someone had pulled

strings. Hélène pointed out that the previous year Agnès hadn't wanted to celebrate her fortieth birthday, but this year she was throwing a real party, which didn't make sense, to say the least.

"So, you're over your midlife crisis already!" said Sabine, and Agnès laughed wholeheartedly.

Bruno was surprised to hear his wife laugh, and he smiled, a long, forced smile, unrelenting. Sabine kept the conversation going and asked her father whether he'd read the book by Illich, *Deschooling Society.*

"I'm not about to read any notebooks or letters by that Bolshevik, thank you very much."

"Papa, I'm not talking about Lenin! I'm talking about *Ivan* Illich, the philosopher!"

Bruno swallowed. He'd never heard of the book or the man who'd written it. And yet he acted as if he had: "Why'd you bring him up?"

"I thought about you when I was reading it. He says children learn outside school, and that school is bad for their education."

"Ah . . . and why is that, if you don't mind?"

"Because! It's obvious: school, the way it's set up nowadays, is there to serve capitalism and the state, so individuals will be programmed."

"You're not going to start talking about politics?" said Agnès. "Please, no politics at the dinner table!"

"Maman," whispered Hélène, "this isn't politics, it's philosophy. Illich says that overabundance is destroying the environment and we can't go on like this. It's analysis, not an aim."

Agnès stood up to change the plates, clattering them together, out of nervousness and to drown out their conversation, but Sabine was on a roll, and Hélène knew she'd had too much to drink: "What's the difference between the Church and school, huh, Papa? Will you tell me that? School is a religion. We learn to think alike and toe the line."

"Is that why you dropped your studies?" asked Bruno. "To free yourself from the school that taught you to read and write?"

"Why don't you tell us about your job," Agnès interrupted. "Apparently they're talking about you in the newspaper."

Hélène could see how hurt her father was, and she couldn't understand why he never talked about the literacy classes he'd been giving for years, and the private lessons he so rarely asked to be paid for. Why didn't he stick up for himself better than this? Sabine showed him the reviews of her play.

"Well? How does it feel to see your name in the paper, Papa?"

"I'm proud. I'm proud of you."

There was no enthusiasm in his voice. Just a little reticence. Agnès read them over his shoulder, the articles about Sabine *Malivieri*, and the name changed its meaning, as if it were outside them, and strangers had carelessly gone off with it. They'd surely have to get used to it. To remarks from the neighbors and family, too. Their daughter in the newspaper. Proof in black and white that she'd been right to go away. And they saw a power in their eldest daughter that left them ill at ease. These articles distanced her from them a little, against their will. Sabine suddenly sensed it had been wrong to show them the reviews, which said, "Sabine Malivieri is bringing the theater to people from a modest background . . ." Agnès said she looked very pretty in the photographs, her costume suited her, had it been custom-made? Hélène remembered Sabine trying on her dress, splitting it at the seams under the arms. *It fits perfectly.*

"No, I found it at the flea market."

"The flea market? The theater didn't pay for you to have a new costume?"

"They paid for the costume I bought at the flea market."

"Ah . . ."

Sabine collected all the newspaper clippings, even though she had brought two copies. She understood that her parents didn't want them, that they'd never show them to anyone.

"Hélène got 20 on her exam, the best grade!" Mariette announced suddenly.

"On the written, not the oral," Hélène corrected her.

"Yes! At the oral, you were useless!"

"What do you mean, useless?" said Agnès.

"We weren't supposed to have any combinatorial problems, the professor had told us we wouldn't and then . . . well, I got one."

"She didn't get zero because the examiner he, uh—" Mariette's expression turned coy, and she said again, "He, uh—"

"He what?" said Bruno.

"When he saw I'd got a 20 on the written, he thought that if I was stuck on the oral, it was because I was paralyzed with fear, so he told me to go and get some fresh air, I went out, I went over the combinatorics and when I came back . . . he questioned me on the same stuff again!"

"And this time," Mariette concluded, "she knew everything! I'm so proud of my sister!"

They laughed a little, as if she'd said something witty, then they left it at that. No one really understood what Hélène was studying, and no one wanted to ask her any questions about Neuilly and her life *there.* They ate their dessert in silence; occasionally someone commented on how delicious it was.

Once the dishwasher had been loaded, the three girls and their mother stayed in the kitchen for a moment, as if at last the time to relax had come, long overdue. Sabine lit a cigarette, screwing up her eyes, and Mariette imitated the face she made. Sabine asked her how her Happiness Notebook was coming along, if she'd filled many pages since last time.

"A few," said Mariette. "Would you like me to read you some?"

"No. You have to keep your secrets to yourself. It's better that way, you know."

"Oh, no, it's better to tell the truth."

"They have nothing to do with each other," said Hélène, "secrets and truth."

"Tell me, *petite mère*, did you follow the rape trial?"

Sabine had finally asked the only valid question, thought Hélène.

"I followed it . . . the way everyone did, more or less. The way you did."

"Yes, but were you there? Outside the courthouse, were you there? There were tons of people, we saw it on TV."

"I would've liked to, but I was at work."

Sabine and Hélène looked at her as if she could still tell them more than the newspapers, the radio, or the TV had. The trial had taken place in Aix last May. She must have some inside information.

"Well, I saw the two girls," said Mariette, "and even Gisèle Halimi, I saw her, in person! There were people shouting at her, trying to hit her, and the cop didn't want to let her into the courthouse, he wanted her to wait in line like the others. There were so many people, and the market, too!"

"Now that she's at Les Prêcheurs, Mariette doesn't miss a single demonstration," said Agnès.

"But Maman, I don't do it on purpose, it's just I can't even get into the collège! The feminists always demonstrate right in the same place."

"Can't you take the rue Mignet? No, you have to go through the square. Don't try and fool me, Mariette, go play in your room, I don't want to talk about this business in front of you."

"Why not?" asked Hélène. "It's good for her to know, isn't it? You and Papa worry all the time, and you don't want her to know what happened?"

"There are details she doesn't need to know at the age of eleven, that's all."

"But I know perfectly well what happened," said Mariette, "the two girls were raped because they're dykes. And that's not allowed. It's illegal, even."

"The word is 'lesbian,'" said Hélène.

"Yes, lesbians, and outside the courthouse, there were boys calling them whores, and spitting on them, and—"

"Right, enough!" said Agnès.

Mariette lowered her eyes.

"But it's true . . ."

Bruno had just come in the kitchen. He lit a cigarette, and it was as if the familiar gesture re-established his authority: "Mariette and I already talked about the trial."

Agnès tensed up.

"You didn't tell me."

"I'd rather she heard about it from an adult than from some schoolyard gossip, or the crowd that was there . . ."

Mariette quietly got up and went into her room. Sabine and Hélène understood it was something she was used to. She knew how the arguments started, the atmosphere that fostered them. Agnès asked Bruno what sort of details he'd given her, exactly. He was annoyed that she asked. He'd simply explained to Mariette that the girls had been camping wild by a rocky inlet and that it was very dangerous. Two girls on their own shouldn't camp in the wild.

"And?"

"And that's all! I just told her to be careful! What else do you want me to say?"

"Well . . ." said Sabine, "you could have told her that the three rapists were initially tried in the magistrate's court—as if they'd run a red light or stolen an LP—and that thanks to Halimi, for the very first time, a rape case was being tried in the criminal court."

Bruno stubbed out his cigarette, half smoked, and from the fierceness he put into it, they could sense his anger.

"You don't come here often, you two, do you? And when you show up, it's as if . . . Every time it makes me think of the school inspectors. God knows I love you both . . . well, yes . . . But between you and the inspectors, it's all the same."

They fell silent. The noise from the dishwasher suddenly seemed to fill the room.

"I'm going to take a nap," said Hélène, "I shouldn't drink during the day."

She went out slowly, as if nodding off already. Sabine hesitated to follow, but her pride refused to leave it at that. She said: "There were other things you could've told her about the trial besides 'you shouldn't go camping in rocky inlets!'"

"Good Lord, between the school in the service of the ruling classes, and a father who gets it all wrong . . . !" said Bruno.

"You're very sure of yourself, Sabine, but when you have

your own children, you'll see. You won't be so sure of everything anymore."

Agnès had said it very quietly, then she looked at her husband with real compassion. She knew he had done what he could, and she wouldn't have wanted him to give Mariette the details of that horrible business. She too was happy when her older daughters came home for a few days. But when they went away again, she felt more liberated. It was as if, all her life, she'd been governed by the judgment of others. Her parents'. Her children's. How to behave. How not to behave. In the afternoon, when she came back from her round, she listened to Françoise Dolto on Radio France Inter. The psychoanalyst replied to her listeners' letters—most of them women—and Agnès would think about her advice until the program the following day. She wondered if she'd been doing the right thing by her daughters. She told Mariette about the little brother who died, because she agreed with the psychoanalyst: you had to tell children the truth, telling the truth removed the layers of sadness that women from the same family handed down like an old suit from one generation to the next. But she made Mariette swear to keep their secret and not tell her sisters. Not confessing it to the older girls was a way of limiting her sorrow, not reawakening it altogether. And now she wondered if she hadn't gotten it wrong, yet again. As soon as she did do something right, she immediately went out and faltered. She seemed to mess up everything she did, and, like her daughters, she too would've liked to go straight out of the kitchen and take a nap. One that would last a very long time.

That evening, when Rose came into the living room, Sabine and Hélène didn't recognize her. They recalled a rather unattractive adolescent who liked to make fun of others; their mother called her a "little devil." They only realized it was Rose because she was with Laurence. She had retained her aplomb, and was totally uninhibited, but she had become so pretty that for a moment they wondered whether she hadn't had cosmetic surgery. There was a new harmony to her face, as if everything had eventually fallen into place, and the young woman had shaped herself into this ultimate perfection. Her blue eyes seemed to have grown larger, and darker, too, an almost violet color you wanted to stare at for a long time. She wore her beauty lightly, joyfully, and her laughter rang out at every opportunity, like a tic, or a defensive reflex. Sabine and Hélène hadn't seen her in four years, and, since then, she had gone to live with her father in London to perfect her English; she'd met a banker from the City who was as handsome as he was rich, judging by the photographs she showed them elatedly. His name was William, she called him Will, they'd been married for two years and lived in Kensington.

"You got married when you were twenty-two . . ."

"Very original of me, wouldn't you say?"

Sabine and Hélène were so surprised they didn't know how to react. Was this the English sense of humor? Or did Rose really think it was original to be married at twenty-two? She wasn't working. She arranged bouquets.

"What you mean, bouquets?"

"I garden, I do flower arranging, it's my hobby, my passion . . ."

Mariette had come up to the three of them, and she stated logically that Rose had stayed true to her name, living among flowers.

"It's a good thing your name isn't Charlotte, you'd be making cakes all day long," said Sabine.

There was a brief silence, then Rose burst out laughing: "Or France! I'd have had to come home!"

Then, as if reverting to sincerity, she lowered her voice, adopting the conspiratorial air she used to have when she was fifteen: "My *mummy* wasn't too pleased, as you can imagine. She thought she'd see me grow up on the barricades, shouting feminist slogans and burning my bras!"

She sensed she'd gone too far. She knew how much the Malivieri family liked her mother, and maybe that was what had driven her to make fun of her openly, the jealousy of an only child who doesn't share easily. The girls didn't know how to go about regaining their erstwhile closeness, and, after ten minutes of hilarious laughter and biting humor, they were relieved when their father motioned to them to come into the kitchen. It was time to put the candles on the cake, to close the shutters, and prepare the surprise that wasn't a surprise. The meal at lunchtime had left a bitter impression, and they all wanted to forget what had been said. Sabine put her arms around her father's neck and gave him a kiss. Touched, he said, "My, my, these daughters of mine!"

He ruffled Mariette's hair and embraced them both, a brief hug which came as a relief. Then he went over to Hélène, who had started lighting the candles.

"Forty-one years old, that makes a lot of candles now, huh?"

He ran his hand furtively over her back; Hélène knew he

wouldn't be more demonstrative than that. When the four of them went into the living room, holding the cake aloft and singing in unison, they were aware of the image they projected, and they were proud and happy. They wished someone would take their picture, so they could frame it, and have it to represent them for many years to come.

When Agnès had blown out the candles and the ritual was over, Bruno felt so relaxed that he had no trouble approaching his wife's guests. He went over to one of her coworkers and asked her name. She was a woman with short dark hair who reminded him of Arlette Laguiller,[7] with the self-confident air of someone who can't be fooled, but there was a flicker of hesitation in her gaze.

"Françoise Boussard, I work with Agnès."

"Yes . . . she's told me about you."

"You're a teacher, right?"

"Yes . . . well . . . my eldest daughter would tell you I'm working for the stability of international capitalism."

"What?"

"Nothing. Have you been working with my wife for long?"

"Roughly a year. I got here in '77. I was in Paris before that. I lived for eight months in a hostel run by the Post Office. It wasn't bad at all, but I had a hell of a time trying to find a place to live after that. Paris is expensive."

Bruno looked at Agnès and Sabine, who were talking to Laurence. It was bound to be one of their never-ending discussions about rape or abortion, all that stuff they never tired of.

"I was really pleased when they transferred me here. It meant I could live with my daughters again."

"But . . . what drew you to this profession?"

[7] A left-wing politician.

"There was no more work at the paper factory where I'd been. I started there at the age of fifteen as a technician, for yogurt jars, it was my job to check on the progress of the paper, but . . ."

Bruno was put off by how talkative Françoise Boussard had turned out to be. He wanted to go over to the group of women, Hélène was with them now, and obviously all three were listening to Laurence as if she were the Messiah.

" . . . the problem was that the factory modernized, and they bought a winding machine, so then they began letting people go, and then—"

"Excuse me, I'll be right back."

He left her there with her story that he could not make heads or tails of, and, with a bottle of Asti Spumante, made his way over to the girls. Laurence had them laughing, imitating a man with a Provençal accent: "But what is going on here? You make love to a woman and you see what she does? She hauls you into court? What a load of bullshit!"

"A gendarme?"

"Yes!"

"Unbelievable!"

"Ladies," said Bruno, forcing the gallantry, "may I offer you something to drink?"

"Papa," said Sabine, "did you know that Gilbert Collard, the rapists' lawyer, actually dared to talk about class justice? All because the three guys were half-witted thugs?"

"I was sure you were talking about the trial, I could have staked my life on it. A little glass?"

And confronted with their accusing silence, he asserted, "Yes, I knew that, and he said that the trial showed that the Parisian bourgeoisie had to come to teach the South a lesson."

They looked at him, their surprise full of admiration. He poured the Asti into their glasses, holding the bottle by the bottom, then he said simply, raising his glass, "Today we are celebrating my wife's birthday! And I'd really like to invite her to dance. Does anyone mind?"

The question was aimed directly at Laurence. She raised her glass and flashed him a smile that meant, good move. Hélène put on a Nat King Cole record, and when *Mona Lisa* resounded in the little living room, Bruno took Agnès by the hand to dance to the song, embracing slowly, the way they used to when they were engaged. The guests applauded and began dancing, too; there were more women than men, and they put their arms around each other, laughing. Bruno held Agnès tight, he was sick of losing her, sick of the way she'd rather spend her time with girls who used to manufacture yogurt jars, or bourgeois ladies obsessed with feminism, than with him. It bothered Agnès a little, the way he'd chosen her there, in front of everyone, the way a man chooses a woman he wants. The music took her back to their precious innocent days, when they'd placed an honest faith, and all the goodwill they were capable of, into their commitment to their upcoming marriage. They were still shy around each other then, and excited, too. They could not imagine their first baby would die, or the financial difficulties they would have, or the bitterness and incomprehension that would come between them. Agnès put her head on Bruno's shoulder and thought that maybe this forty-first birthday marked the beginning of her youth. She'd done everything she was supposed to do, and in the right order. Now she was immensely weary. Nat King Cole sent her back to the days where she wore her hem below the knee and went to confession every week. She was pretty and didn't know it. And suddenly she felt a great tenderness for the young woman she once was. Bruno placed his palm on her head as she nestled against him; he lifted the strands of hair that were damp with sweat and kissed the salty skin where a vein was throbbing, gently, tirelessly. All around them were the sounds of a faraway world, a world without truth. Neighbors, friends, children: for the duration of this slow dance, they'd become unreal, making room for them at last.

In the morning, Hélène drove Sabine to the Saint-Charles Station in Marseille. It was Sunday, and she'd borrowed their father's car, a Renault 5 bought on credit to replace the old Simca 1000. The morning was rising, already heavy with heat haze. In the distance, the Montagne Sainte-Victoire drew their gaze with eternal pride, forming a fortress of shadow and light between earth and sky. The two sisters had been driving in unaccustomed silence for a long while, until, at last, they dared to look at each other, and their expressions told them they were thinking the same thing.

"God those apartments are awful," said Hélène with a laugh. "Do architects really think poor people never make love?"

"And yet they go on putting up such damned flimsy apartment buildings!"

"We should be happy for their sake."

"Oh, shut up, let's not even talk about it, it's so cringe-inducing. Good thing Mariette was asleep."

"It was that *Mona Lisa* that did it, why'd you put it on?"

"What was I supposed to do? Put on The Singing Nun or the Compagnons de la Chanson? Seriously."

"But they did try to be discreet."

"They *were* discreet. Just right next door."

To keep from thinking about it, Hélène focused on her driving; the roads were virtually deserted, a few pedestrians slowly making their way to the market, the city was numb, still drowsy. Sabine looked at the familiar landscapes and saw herself everywhere, every street she'd crossed, every little square, with her family, with friends, lovers, so many love affairs imagined for so few experienced. There was the café where she'd told Dieter to meet her, a German who didn't speak a word of French and with whom, after a single kiss, she'd pictured an intense relationship between Berlin and Aix; their relationship would be sealed by a powerful attraction and an uncommon intimacy, and everyone would admire them. Dieter left Aix two weeks after they met and never answered any of her letters. She saw again the effeminate boy she'd met at a party at her philosophy teacher's; he made her think of Tadzio in *Death in Venice*. It had been love at first sight, like being caught in a raging downpour. She'd spent the evening in love with him and incapable of speaking to him. When he got up to leave, she rushed over to say goodbye, even though she'd never even said hello. With a tired hand he'd pushed back his blond curls, slowly approaching his face for her to kiss him, and his breath was so terrible she'd groaned with disappointment. She saw again the boys from Madame Paillard's drama class—their fine long hair, the leather bracelets around their wrists, their hands on the frame of their mopeds parked in the courtyard. The smell of gasoline. The cool evenings. The desire to flirt, to get a gentle taste of each other, to smell the soap on roughly shaven cheeks, to love the still-hesitant voices of young men who did not want to resemble their fathers, the sudden way they had of tossing their heads back to flick their hair behind them, a feminine gesture that could only belong to their generation. She saw them again, those handsome, clumsy boys with whom she'd shared hidden moments of first pleasure. And those other boys, more numerous, whom she'd loved and who'd never known it, lovers she'd wept over, and who hadn't cared. And Jean-Louis, her first lover . . . She'd heard he was working in a bank on the

Cours Mirabeau. She pictured his long guitarist's hands leafing through bank statements, one finger dampened with a sponge to count the wads of banknotes. Did he think about her now and again? Had he seen her name in *Le Figaro?* Did people, in general, remember each other? She wondered if she could name all the people she'd been connected to since earliest childhood, the ones who'd come into her life by chance and who'd left a trace she'd thought was lost. Sometimes, in the simple light of an evening with its smell of cool air, she could feel time blurring, and emotions she'd thought were gone for good came to her, her life became a smooth continuity and suddenly she was every age—childhood, adolescence . . . She thought she would share this with Paul on the phone that evening, and tell him, too, that she'd followed his advice, she'd read the reviews of *A Life* to her father. A wasted effort. She wondered if Mathieu was making the most of her absence, if he met other girls specifically when she wasn't there, or whether it was all the same to him as when she was in Paris, only a few streets away.

Now they were on the highway, and as they left Aix behind it became the size of a simple provincial town, regularly invaded by famous lawyers and journalists who stayed at the Grand Hôtel du Roi René, opposite the Lycée Mignet, where the students had no idea how hard it had been, only a few years earlier, for girls and boys to have to live apart. Mathieu, who had introduced himself as her boyfriend, and whom she had to stop herself from calling the love of her life, had run into Robert in the corridor one night, she'd forgotten to warn him that the old surgeon got up at night to eat. Robert had said, "Good evening mademoiselle," and continued on his way. He was a gentleman. And he surely didn't mention the presence of a young man under his roof to his son Gérald. Sabine's love for Mathieu was intense and impatient. She told herself that, some day, he would translate English plays for her, maybe he would even write one, she would act in them, put them on in Paris, she would be the first to perform them, the eternal reference. She loved him for who he was—intelligent, a touch misanthropic and antisocial, sensual and libertarian, and she loved him for everything he was without knowing it, what he would become thanks to their love, which only she knew. When it became too painful to think of him in someone else's arms, she would remember Sartre and Beauvoir, and, as if through a mirror effect, her own relationship expanded. She wanted to free herself from her upbringing, to move with the times (although she wondered how it was possible not to move with the times), and thanks to Mathieu, and to what she called "his demands," she sometimes succeeded. She loved him, and suffered for it. It was love like a cause to champion, and champion it she did.

After dropping her sister off at the station, Hélène was glad of her solitude. She drove with the windows rolled down, but the air that came from outside was scorching and smelled strongly of tar; everything seemed about to go up in flames—the surrounding pine forests, the farms whose land had been divided by the A51, the cars that would collide and burst into flames, because everything seemed conducive to accidents; an atmosphere of unreality wafted on the dry heat, and she felt as if she were crashing through an invisible wall, searing and hostile. She switched on the car radio, where a commercial was vaunting a special offer on calfskin sofas, a couple was gloating, the woman naïve and excited, the man more responsible because he was paying, trying to dampen his wife's consumerist enthusiasm, but given the exceptional nature of the special offer, he had to give a shout and rush straight to the furniture store. Hélène was getting annoyed with all the frenzy, the horrible jingles on Radio Monte Carlo, when suddenly she was overwhelmed by an emotion as powerful as it was unexpected. Bécaud came on, singing *Et Maintenant*, and she found herself weeping uncontrollably, not even knowing why, it came at once, instinctively, as if she had stumbled into it. *You left me the entire earth, but without you it's so small.* Bécaud wasn't Bécaud, Bécaud was her father, no one else, singing in the car before car radios were there to do it for him, and he didn't know how Hélène missed him even when he was there, he'd never understood that Tavel couldn't ever replace him, had never replaced him. Because he was irreplaceable. Because he was handsome and old-fashioned, he was broke and sincere, altruistic and extremist, but above all because he was loving, and at a time when everything around him told him he was out of touch, out of the running, he continued to feel, unswayed, his insatiable need for love and family. Sometimes Hélène felt like shouting at him, "You're my father! It's you!" But she was afraid he'd think it was hysteria, or worse still, a reproach. And on this highway, where passing truck drivers leered at the thighs of a sobbing girl collapsed on the steering wheel, she wondered what she was going to do. How could sixteen years of airports and monthly checks be no more than a simple anecdote?

She arrived at Éléonore's numb from weeping; the green of her eyes, she thought, must be more faded than ever, as if her sorrow had a direct effect on their color. She still felt as insignificant as ever, too, but she'd eventually learned to live with her evanescent appearance. Arthur sometimes teased her, crossing his eyes and pretending to hold a microphone, imitating the voice of Joe Dassin as he sang to her, *You're like a watercolor by Marie Laurencin*. But I can't stand Marie Laurencin! she cried. All that pink, all those scarves . . . it's so housewifey! But still. She liked the reference to the watercolor.

Éléonore lived in a residential apartment building, the Saint-Jérôme, a place with neatly mown lawns, where the inhabitants had flowers on their balcony, and parking spots in their name. It made you want, in order to fit in, to speak quietly and be fit and healthy.

Éléonore had preserved her determined manner, and that beauty she set so little store by, but she'd mellowed, and something weary and sensual flickered in her gaze. She was on a scholarship, about to take her post-graduate degree in mathematics at the university in Marseille, and she was living with Amélie, a physicist ten years her senior who seemed to spend her life at conferences and conventions in all four corners of the globe. Hélène had never met her. In a photograph placed lopsided on the fridge, Amélie and Éléonore were posing in front of Machu Picchu, with their packs on their backs and their hands on their hips, visibly exhausted and dazzled by the sun, but grimacing happily, and the unaffected nature of the pose reflected the simplicity of their union. It was patently clear.

"Mademoiselle Malivieri! How are you?"

Hélène appreciated the fact that Éléonore greeted her with irony, as if she hadn't noticed her red eyes or distraught expression. But as soon as they were seated, Éléonore cut the filter from a cigarette and reached for the pack of rolling paper. Hélène joyfully agreed to share a joint. They smoked in silence, it was something they could do, see each other only two or three times a year and yet immerse themselves in a wordless complicity. Hélène felt the tension subside. She didn't want to think about the fact she would have to drive soon, take the car back to her father; she wanted to share this weed that released her from the corset of anxiety she'd been wearing since the day before, when she'd arrived in Aix. And then, inevitably, she began to laugh. Éléonore was familiar with her reaction to cannabis: "And yet I made it very very very light, given your delicate nature."

"I'm a simple girl, Léo, it doesn't take much."

"I'm growing it on my balcony now, it's less bother."

"Honestly . . ." said Hélène, with a chuckle.

"What?"

"Everything's illegal here—your relationship, your balcony, your fight against vivisection." And her laughter increased. She said again, "Your balcony is illegal."

"When you think about it, lesbians get even less consideration than animals," said Éléonore.

"What are you talking about?"

"It's true! They've finally acknowledged that animals have feelings, even if it's only valid for domestic animals."

Hélène threw herself back against the sofa and laughed at the ceiling. Being at Éléonore's reminded her of times at the Embassy, at Laurence's, a place with no superfluous politeness. The shutters were closed, and the smell of coffee mingled with that of the weed in the half-light, and Hélène wondered if the neighbors knew about Éléonore's cannabis crop. Or the illegitimate relationship she was in with Amélie. She said, "I heard my parents making love."

"You're lucky, I only ever heard them making war."

"Yeah . . . I suppose I'm lucky."

She sat up again and looked around the apartment, so different from the studio where Éléonore had been living when she first met her. There was proof here of another life, Amélie had left her mark, their things seemed to be all jumbled together—books, records, and she wondered if they swapped their clothes, lent each other a pair of shoes or a handbag . . . Suddenly she gave a start, horrified by a framed photograph Éléonore had hung on the wall.

"How can you, Léo? Hang that thing in your living room? Don't you see how off-putting it is?"

"No more off-putting than a naked crucified man. And the result is the same: to be reminded of evil."

Hélène stared at the photograph for a long time, then she said, "It looks like a sculpture by Giacometti. As if he were caught in bronze, the fuel has immobilized him, like bronze, don't you think?"

"I hadn't thought of it that way, but . . . yes."

"He was flying home, to Scotland. It's a gannet."

She saw again the boxes filled with all the birds they couldn't save, thousands and thousands of marine birds that ended up at the dump. Several tons of them.

"It was last March, during the nesting period. We had to put a lot of them down, they were in too much distress before they died. They would try to clean themselves and that poisoned them, burning their digestive tract, poisoning their liver . . . The cormorants we treated and fed with a tube became terrified of water because their feathers no longer protected them. We rubbed oil over their feathers but it did no good. They were afraid and they were cold. They looked for dry places, giving these terrible cries. I was ashamed. I looked at them and thought, over and over, 'Forgive me, forgive me, forgive me . . .'"

Hélène had never spoken so openly about her experience at the clinic for oil-covered birds that had been set up in Brest after the wreck of the *Amoco Cadiz*. She had kept it to herself, those days confronted with animal suffering. Two hundred and twenty-seven thousand tons of oil spilled into the sea and along the coasts. Éléonore turned the picture of the bird against the wall.

"There, is that better?"

Hélène shrugged. She was sad, the positive effect of the joint had evaporated, and she already felt her usual dull headache. The faint light in the apartment weighed on her, the smell of coffee was acrid, as if it had been mixed with greasy dishwater. Her eyes ached from all her tears. She ran her palms over her hair to smooth it, over and over, a gesture of consolation. She forced herself to think about ordinary things and said, "When are you leaving for Italy?"

"Next week. And you, vacation?"

"I'm going to the Auvergne with Arthur and then it will be study, study, study. I want to be good and ready when I start my second year."

Éléonore looked at her without saying anything, as if gazing at a picture, a concentrated time that took her elsewhere, far away, inside herself. Inside memories. Hélène asked her a bit too abruptly, "Will you tell me about it?"

"About what?"

"Your trip."

"Of course, I will. We'll be sailing along the Italian coast on a schooner, all of us scientists, with flippers and a snorkel. It should be fun, don't you think?"

"I suppose that when you give the results of your findings to the journalists, it won't be as much fun."

"Let alone when we meet the politicians. They're not exactly passionate about having their coasts monitored. Disruption of the food chain due to pollution accumulated among marine wildlife . . . Not really their highest priority. In any case, I'm glad to be taking part, to be quantifying the data, analyzing the disaster."

Hélène wished she could ask Éléonore to take her along, but she knew she couldn't: Arthur was so eager to have this time together with his parents in the Auvergne.

"I don't think we have a full team yet," said Éléonore, as if she'd read her mind.

It took Hélène a few seconds to realize it was an invitation. It would have been perfectly justifiable for a young student to gain experience in the field with professional scientists. She looked at Éléonore and it was as if time had stopped in her gaze and was no longer moving forward.

"I'd be in the way, and besides, I'm ashamed to say it, Léo, but I'm afraid to put my head under water. I cannot put my head under water. It's always been like that. Ever since I was little, in fact."

The upstairs neighbor suddenly began screeching a Patti Smith song, *Gloria*, on the guitar. Completely ruining it. As if he were pounding the walls with an ax. Éléonore said, "Next he'll play *Let It Be*, and after that, *La Ballade des Gens Heureux*. Don't ask me why."

Hélène stood up, slightly dazed.

"I have to get the car back to my father. And then we're having a family lunch."

The air around Éléonore was vibrating. Hélène didn't know if it was because of the dim light, or whether it was the beginning of a migraine. If that were the case, she'd have to get home as quickly as possible, take an aspirin, and go to bed. She'd be spared the Sunday lunch, the embarrassment of seeing her parents after she'd heard them making love that night.

They kissed each other on the cheek, with a loud smack, kisses of camaraderie that echoed down the hall.

Being outside was like putting her head in an oven: the air was even drier and more compact. The chirring of cicadas was unbearable, and to Hélène it seemed as if they were speaking to her personally, to her migraine. She thought of Jean-Henri Fabre, who had complained of the cicadas' "hoarse symphonies." The entomologist was right: there was something fierce and aggressive about their chorus. As if announcing a battle. She sat in the car, an airless block of heat. As she rolled down her window, she saw Éléonore. She'd opened the shutters and was waving goodbye from her balcony. She sent her a smile, but her friend couldn't see it. Then she waved in turn, like a little girl on a merry-go-round, or a woman at a train window, a very ancient gesture to say, we are parting. And we are sorry about this defeat.

Mariette was going away for a few days. Agnès had packed her suitcase according to the list, and she'd sewn name tags on her towels and clothes, which she counted and counted again with a feverishness that betrayed her guilty conscience. Her daughter wasn't being sent to summer camp because her mother was working, but because she was going away with her husband. Three days alone with him. This hadn't happened in twenty-three years, and there was something openly sensual and selfish about the escapade, inappropriate in a couple who were parents. Bruno had suggested they go on a retreat to Branguier with Les Foyers Notre-Dame, a movement of Christian couples where a priest and team members worked with married couples in order to "build a conjugal life in keeping with the sacrament of marriage." But Agnès had refused. What she wanted was to go somewhere alone with him. He'd been relieved. He too wanted to be with her "like lovers," and he wondered how they had managed to go for so long without taking a few days off for themselves.

M.M. Those were Mariette's initials. Jumping on her bed, she tested how it sounded, *M. M. Hum. Hum. Mad. Mad . . . about Me! Me! Me!* She'd never gone anywhere without her family. Had never discovered anything without sharing it with them. She'd hesitated to take her Happiness Notebook with her, then she asked her mother to buy her a new one for fear someone might read what she'd written about her life before summer camp. She was going away for eight days, to Saint-Martin-Vésubie, in the Mercantour National Park. The rather complicated name lent a mysterious beauty to a place she'd never seen. It would be a Catholic summer camp, girls only, so much the better. Without boys, girls would make less of a fuss. Most of them already knew each other; some would be from the same private school, some would have been Jeannettes together, so Bruno had warned her. She had wanted to join the scout movement herself, when she was nine, she'd heard that the Jeannettes made a promise, a vow, and that word had literally transported her. She imagined herself standing there in her uniform, her entire family waiting for her to take her vow, which she would recite flawlessly, her hand on her heart, her gaze looking off into the distance. Her father had read her the exact text: "I promise to do my best to be faithful to God, to France, to my parents, to the Scout Law, and to do a favor for someone every day."

"Why France?"

"What do you think! To be like Joan of Arc."

So, the Jeannettes were little Joans of Arc, and this had moved her to tears, as if she might have been the daughter of that saint—they'd given Mariette a picture of Joan at catechism: St. Joan in her white dress, standing before the stake, two clouds of smoke forming angel wings at her back. She loved the way she held her face toward the sky as the smoke began to suffocate her, *slowly burning*, like Mariette herself during an attack, and she liked to think that she understood some of her suffering. She wanted to join the Jeannettes and *do her best yes best best best!* And complete each stage that would take her from the blue flower to the white, the white to the golden, the magnificent *fleur de lys* that would change color from one promotion to the next, one stage to the next, one prayer to the next. But the priest had refused to let her join the scouts: sports played far too great a role for a "little asthmatic girl." Her passion for Joan of Arc and her horde of miniature Jeannettes died there on the spot, and she redoubled her love for Jesus, who was, in any case, much higher up in the pecking order.

Her asthma posed less of a problem for summer camp than for becoming a scout, even though enrollment had been followed by a list of requirements and recommendations: after she'd taken her treatment and followed a progressive program of warm-up exercises, she'd be able to engage in sports like the other girls. Horseback riding wouldn't be allowed, however, because of her allergies. Fortunately, summer was the season when her illness seemed dormant, and she wanted to make the most of this time to put everything the doctor had told her into practice—to gradually open her lungs and strengthen them, and she imagined her bronchial tubes and all their branches as her own fleurs-de-lys, so with her hand on her heart she said, "I promise to do my best to breathe and run like the others. I promise to make progress, for myself and for my parents . . ." And because it thrilled her, she added, "And for France."

It was strange that the building where the summer camp was held, known as Les Marmottes, was so ugly, when all around the landscape was so beautiful: mountains of light, hills furrowed with rivers, houses with red tile roofs nestled together, a harmony between man and nature, the pride of the wilderness. The summer camp building was a mass of gray cement pierced with tiny windows. A cold gloom had settled in every room, like a semi-transparent mourning veil. Damp seeped from walls swollen with stains, as if the building itself had been sick. In fact, something unhealthy did ooze from it, something old and sour that would not let go.

No sooner had she arrived than Mariette went to sit on a rock facing the mountains. As she gazed at the panorama, she could feel how old it was, the birth of the world, and it frightened her. She could hear the long cry of a hawk passing overhead, and she looked as far into the distance as she could, but her gaze didn't land on anything, nothing stopped it, and she was surprised to find herself thinking about her parents' dead baby, its presence suddenly there in that boundless space, it was an eternal baby, and her older sibling, too, her secret. The brother her sisters didn't have. She breathed deeply, calmly, feeling an unavowed sadness, already wishing that she were elsewhere. Far away from all these people who'd shared the trip with her, shared the picnic, their arrival and settling in at Les Marmottes, all without seeing her. She was little, they must have thought she'd got her age group wrong, this was for girls who were eleven and twelve, and she looked two years younger. And here, even without a uniform, you were supposed to look alike, or else really stand out in some way, with some uninhibited, unusual characteristic. It made her angry, not to be unusual. And angry that she felt that way.

Once the priest got there, on the second day, everything changed. Father Lavière climbed off his motorcycle, scraping on the gravel, and Bénédicte, one of the counselors, said with a silly laugh, "He'll never change!" The counselors viewed him like an elder who is kind enough to treat you as a pal, and yet they respected the unspoken boundaries, and seemed to adapt to whatever the priest allowed—familiarity or respect, trust or discretion, subtle, constant variations. With the arrival of their chaplain, the atmosphere became more relaxed as the days went by, and there were moments Mariette looked forward to. She eventually made friends with two girls she didn't like very much but who made it possible for her not to look isolated. Their names were Fabienne and Blandine, and they smelled of citronella and green peas; there was something oafish about both of them, which hampered them and slowed them down.

As soon as she had gotten used to the group, Mariette tried to get away from them, but it was too late. Like two abandoned dogs, Fabienne and Blandine followed her, bound to her by an awkward attachment.

She liked to go hiking on the mountain, the cow mountain, as the counselors called it, where everyone fell silent amid the smell of pine trees, resin, and all the unfamiliar flowers you weren't allowed to pick, and which seemed all the rarer for their fragile beauty. She liked to climb slowly, deeply concentrated on her effort, the promise of the view that awaited, the joy of getting there, like the others. When they came back from these hikes, she was always disappointed to find that the people in the valley were still living in the afternoon hours. Had they left so early that the day was not over yet? She spoke to her lungs, thanked them, thank you for this progress, thank you for not letting me down. She couldn't wait until dinnertime, and then the campfire, a moment she particularly enjoyed. They would gather around the fire, and Father Lavière, with his friendly, lilting voice, would read a prayer or a passage from the Gospel, explaining that they had to learn to fear God and to love His Son, and the counselors sang with their guitars. Mariette gazed at the flames, dreaming of something else. She had tried to understand how, if God, His Son, and the Holy Ghost were only one single being, she could both fear Him and love Him. How was such a feeling possible? She had tried to find an equivalent in her life but hadn't. She didn't fear the people she loved. Even when their behavior was strange, she never felt threatened by them.

One evening after the campfire, as the sky was dark, made large with stars, Father Lavière suggested playing hide and seek in the dark. Right away, there were cries of joy, excitement among all the campers. The girls hopped up and down, some of them held hands, laughter in every direction, and the counselors drew straws for which two of them would count to a hundred. Girls immediately paired off, not really having time to choose, and disappeared at a run. Father Lavière told Fabienne she could hide with him, Blandine asked Mariette to be her partner, and off they went, cautiously. They were afraid of getting lost, and fearful of what they couldn't see, all the nocturnal animals they'd be disturbing. They crouched down behind the first bush they found, the others' voices reached them with the furtive sounds they made as they were hiding, little cries of pain mingled with nervous laughter, everyone speaking quietly, torn between the desire to win and that of being seen, to emerge from their hiding place and go and wait calmly against the wall with the losers.

The next day, which was also the last one, Mariette thought she'd better write a few postcards during their free time in the afternoon. She'd kept putting it off when she saw the other girls were writing and she was afraid of writing things as stupid as they had—the terrific weather, the super walks, the nice counselors . . . Those were lies, she thought. How could they lie to their parents? Yes, but how could you tell them the truth? How damp the dormitory was. The boredom. The silliness of friends like Blandine and Fabienne, above all how vulgar they were (immodest, her father would have said). Time was passing, she hadn't written a thing, and when a counselor blew the whistle for the camp to gather, she painstakingly tore up every postcard, one by one, into tiny pieces. "Are you crazy or what?" one of the girls asked her, and she was surprised to hear herself answer back, nastily, "Shut your face"—and, as soon as she'd said it, she wanted to apologize and weep.

Her lungs were tired. Their respiratory capacity seemed diminished, as if after the effort and awakening of the first few days, they had suddenly curled in on themselves, like two disappointed flowers, and anxiety mingled with fatigue. Pray God she wouldn't have an attack. Pray God no one would hear her wheezing and coughing, no one would see her turn purple, no one would send her to the infirmary or to stay all by herself in the dormitory . . . oh, pray God they wouldn't leave her on her own. The counselor had gathered the girls for a game of Octopus tag, he was motioning to her to join them, waving impatiently, demonstratively. The sky was turning a little above Mariette, above the earth with its weight of mountains and forests and hills; it turned a few times in one direction and then in the other, but the earth still wasn't moving, there was lead in the ground, and the more the sky turned, the more the earth was still, until there was a burst of anger way up there, the Lord they were supposed to fear and love was telling them He could see them, all of them, day and night, He had his eye on them, and she could hear the words of the Confiteor, *mea culpa, mea culpa, mea maxima culpa*. And she collapsed.

Long after she had come home from the summer camp at Saint-Martin-Vésubie, she would wake during the night and think she was back there, in the dormitory at Les Marmottes. It filled her with a sudden terror, a weight in her gut and on her chest which did not dissipate even when she realized she was at home. She would slowly sit up in her bed (a change of position could sometimes bring on an attack) and think about the girl. How unhappy she must be, in her bed or elsewhere, in every bed she would lie in, every dormitory, every room. She hadn't believed Fabienne when she told her what Father Lavière had asked of her, behind the tall oak tree. She had simply thought that this girl was really very vulgar, and so, not to hear any more of her disgusting fabrications, Mariette had fallen asleep with her back turned. But the next day, when the priest went up to her to ask her to go with him to pick blueberries, Mariette said no, and he didn't insist. She looked at his trousers, and the stain was still there, and that stain that was invisible in the night was something Fabienne could not have made up. She must have felt it, damp and sticky in her hand, when the priest ordered her to rub again and again, there, just below his belt, with his hand that he held against hers to make her go faster and harder. Everything she had told her, and that Mariette had taken for a horrible lie, the repulsive invention of a nasty little girl, it was all true. Because she had sworn to Fabienne that she would tell no one, because she was glad she wouldn't have to, because the silence made her feel ashamed, she opened the notebook her mother had bought for summer camp and where she hadn't written a thing, and on it she stuck a white label where she wrote, "Unhappiness Notebook," then started her story.

IV
Sincere Lies

It was raining in Hélène's dream, a heavy, relentless rain falling at the foot of a narrow stairway, with furtive figures passing by. Hélène couldn't identify anyone, but the mood in her dream was oppressive, as if each figure were conveying something sick and rancorous. The rain she could hear was the rain that was falling in the garden, something she understood when she awoke: she was in Arthur's bed, in his room, at his parents' place. The window was slightly open and the shutter was tapping gently, allowing the sound of the storm to enter the room, as if water were pouring straight in through a hole. It was a rotten summer. For a month, everyone had been saying so; it was raining all over France, except in the South, which was still a sort of free zone, the envy of all those who couldn't be there.

At his parents' place, Arthur lapsed into a sort of lethargy, he could stay for days on end inside the dark house doing nothing, speaking with whoever dropped by, close or distant family, Hélène mixed them all up—were they cousins, friends, brothers or sisters, what were their names? She observed them as if they belonged to some unfamiliar species; they were friendly-seeming dilettantes, at loose ends, they'd run into each other by chance, smoked heavily and drank coffee until late in the night; occasionally some would linger until dawn, unless they actually were newcomers, who sat and waited for someone to come by with whom they would get into a long, passionless discussion. When by good fortune the rain stopped, they took deck chairs out onto the terrace, sharing their chatter and boredom a few feet from the living room, to which they would hastily return at the first sign of rain. Arthur had invited friends who were medical students like himself; he was following the path mapped out by his father and above all his grandfather, a professor they never saw but spoke about constantly, everyone would inquire of his daughter-in-law Christine how he had slept, how he was feeling, when he would come down at last, a sort of god on Mount Olympus. The house belonged to him, and its unspeakable clutter revealed something of the man he must have been, a buyer of botany books and fine wine—unless those passions had been his late wife's, there was no way of knowing. The house seemed to be trammeled by the past, too weighted down to wake to the present, not living in the summer of 1978 but absorbing it and annihilating it. Georges, Arthur's father, was the sort of man who sometimes showed up for meals, but, the rest of the time, he was reading in his study, writing the odd article, or going off to the market to buy supplies for his many guests, from whom he expected no financial participation. His generosity seemed to stem from his absentmindedness, and this dazed kindness was something he shared with his wife. Christine had a chic allure and an astonished gaze; she had given up a career as a doctor to raise her four children and did not seem to regret it.

Hélène wondered why Arthur had wanted to take her along to his parents', when they showed no greater interest in her than if she'd been a mere friend or even a dog. And the worst of it was, they weren't making love—Hélène and Arthur, who ordinarily spent most of their time planning or improvising places for their lovemaking, here, they didn't even go off on their own for a nap.

"I can't, Hélène. My grandfather sleeps in the next room, I can't."

"But it's a celebration of life, a tribute to the life you owe him!"

"I'm afraid he'll hear."

"You told me he was deaf."

"Precisely. I'm afraid that in order to hear better, he'll put his ear against the wall, just there, just by the head of the bed."

"All this chastity is driving me crazy! I'm about to turn nineteen and I'm suffocating. I feel oppressed."

"No. Don't start."

"Don't start what?"

"You sound like your sister. All these demands. Please. My family is exhausting, I would've appreciated your support. Please, love . . ."

"I'll see you later. I'm going to masturbate."

"Hélène!"

"And you're not allowed to watch."

That night, awoken by her nightmare, Hélène listened to the falling rain, as if there were a mystery to be unraveled from its tenacity, but it was a monotonous rain, falling over the vastness of fields, extinct volcanoes, the moonless night, and all the nocturnal animals silenced by the deluge. There were sounds in the room next door, the professor's room. He wasn't alone. Next to him a child was crying, whimpering quietly, a timid, terrifying lament. Hélène placed her ear against the wall by the head of the bed, precisely in the way Arthur had feared his grandfather would. She could hear the echo of frantic movement, someone walking in the room, opening a wardrobe, slamming it closed. Then it all stopped. She went out in the corridor and gently, slowly, almost haphazardly, she pressed the handle of the professor's door. He was smaller than she'd imagined. Sitting on the side of the bed in striped pajamas, his legs spread, he was looking at himself in the wardrobe mirror: a poorly shaven old man, full of tears. It wasn't a child she'd heard crying. It was him. He turned to Hélène.

"Ah, Christine, Christine."

The room smelled of camphor and eucalyptus. Hélène slowly went up to him and took his hands in hers: they were dry and icy. She asked, "Did you have a bad dream?"

"Get me something to drink."

She handed him the glass of water that was on the night table.

"You have to lie down."

"Help me, would you."

She helped him lie down. His body was small but gnarly and stiff; she put her hands under his legs to swing them into the middle of the bed. He gave an abject laugh.

"What a fuss . . ."

She wondered what Christine did, did she kiss him on the forehead, tuck him in like a child, how should she take her leave? But he took her hand and kissed it gallantly.

"Oh, my dear . . ."

When she was by the door, about to go out, he said, "But you know that I didn't want to."

"Of course."

"That's what happens during war."

"Of course."

"That's it. Him or me, you know."

"I know."

"Poor lad."

She closed the door with the same care she'd shown in putting the old man back to bed, and, once she was in her own bed, she nestled against Arthur and unbuttoned his pajama top to place her head against his smooth chest. Now she understood why he couldn't make love here: on the other side of the wall an old soldier was reliving the war, the crime he had committed. *Make love not war*, she thought. *No war, nowhere. Make love.*

The next day, Christine forgot to make lunch, and no one pointed it out. The minutes passed, and, by early afternoon, everyone had gone to hunt around in the cupboards or help themselves from the fridge, and they gathered in the kitchen around the huge oak kitchen table. It had stopped raining and the window was open wide; the wisteria was dripping, shaken by a wind that had earned its name, *a wet wind.* Hélène thought about the professor. Was he going to eat all alone in his room again? Shouldn't she tell Christine what had happened during the night? She was roused from her thoughts when she realized that for a moment already, they'd been trying to get her attention.

"What does our biologist think?"

"Hélène? Hélène! Hey!"

"What?"

"The first test tube baby has been born. In England."

"Hey, she has a name: Patricia."

"It's not Patricia, it's Louise. Louise Brown."

"No, it's not, I read it in the paper, it's Patricia."

"Well, I read it in the paper, too, her name is Louise."

"Louise or Patricia, at least that's better than 'test tube baby,' don't you think?"

"Well Hélène, what do you think?"

"It's terrific," she said, out of politeness, and her answer was enough to get the discussion going again.

As they passed the pâté and the wine, some of them brought

up the Catholic church's opposition to artificial insemination, then, on a thick piece of paper, Arthur drew a rough sketch of fallopian tubes (there was some laughter when the name was invoked) and ovaries, and as he ran out of room on the paper he finished with a laconic "etc." which the others made do with. A girl whose name Hélène had forgotten (Marianne? Myriam?) began playing the cello, a Bach suite, and Hélène immediately felt sad. She had a sudden urge to call Éléonore, but Éléonore was in Italy, sailing in turquoise waters. Hélène would have liked to hear her authoritarian voice delivering a strong opinion; she was stifling in this house where everything was dealt with so calmly and unemotionally, she wanted to cry out that test tube babies were a discovery that would lead to a raft of questions about paternity that could not be unraveled, if the father wasn't the donor. The biological father is the father. No one else. The biological father is the father that's the law and that's that. And she stifled a sob. The little gathering gradually fell silent; the cello made the most of the silence to voice its furious nostalgia, embracing the air, the dripping wisteria, all living things, and because she could see everyone was expecting an explanation for her tears, Hélène simply said, "Arthur has stopped making love to me."

She herself was astonished by her confession, and her sadness receded. Marianne, or Myriam, stopped playing. The only thing they could hear was the stubborn chirping of birds and an echo of furious barking. Because sexual liberation had reached even this remote province, or perhaps, on the contrary, because no one was from there, a couple instantaneously volunteered to console Hélène, and this embarrassed her as much as it did Arthur, who sat staring down at his amputated drawing of the uterus, this terrible confession of his incompetence. Hélène placed her hand on his, it was seen as a sign of reconciliation, and coffee was served. The rain started up again, so hard they rushed to close the window, then stayed like that, in the long dark kitchen, to which the cigarette smoke gave the atmosphere of a back room or a billiard parlor in a back-country café. Arthur gently nibbled Hélène's ear, which meant, in a strange primary language, that he was asking for forgiveness. She thought that, in the end, this house would've made a good place to study, and she was sorry she'd left her books and photocopies in Neuilly. What was she going to do all alone in that huge duplex in her chic, deserted suburban Parisian neighborhood, whereas here she could have stayed on among a little group of idle but caring people? Suddenly Georges, Arthur's father, burst in like a shipwrecked sailor, in his yellow oilskins and wellingtons; he came into the kitchen, a tragic expression on his face, as if he had just heard some terrible news. They instantly made room for him on the bench.

"Godammit," he said, removing his sodden hat. "Godammit."

Then staring into the void, he said, "I've just seen the most horrible thing in my entire life."

They were all hanging on his words, somewhat apprehensively.

"I was on the road from Saint-Laure, and after a few kilometers, just before the junction with the secondary road, I saw a truck stopped on the shoulder with its hazard lights blinking. I slowed down, parked a little bit lower down, it was raining, I saw the driver was trying to change a tire, he was there with the jack, the chocks, this enormous tire, and I . . . I got out of the car and asked him if he needed anything, and the guy gave me a dirty look, then muttered that everything was fine, but I could see that everything wasn't fine, no, things were not fine at all. I could hear this unbelievable noise coming from the trailer, banging around inside so much that the truck was rocking from side to side, and the guy was getting nervous, and he said, 'Get out of here, can't you see it's raining, I know how to change a tire, I'm going to change my tire.'"

Christine had come in and was looking at him, and so he went on with his story for her alone, his voice crushed with disbelief.

"It smelled bad near the truck, a stench . . . worse than a dump in hot sunlight. And there was something dripping, a liquid constantly streaming out of there. It was blood. I told myself that, if I asked too many questions, the guy was going to bash me on the skull with the jack, so I pretended I hadn't noticed, and then I realized it was horses he was transporting, I could hear them neighing, and kicking. When I saw that his truck was registered in Morocco, I figured out he was taking them to the slaughterhouse. But there was a real ruckus going on in there, those horses were fighting, for sure, that's why he was taking the back roads, he was trying to go unnoticed because there was something weird going on. He was still struggling with the bolts, he couldn't get them loose, his hands were slipping on the jack, he was so nervous he was trembling. I didn't know what to do, how to intervene, and, anyway, this seems crazy, but I saw this cop car coming, I stood in the middle of the road to flag it down, the guy began insulting me, and, in spite of the rain, the cops saw me in time to slow down and pull up next to us."

He lowered his gaze. Let a long silence go by before continuing.

"I saw the cops open the truck. And I saw the horses. They'd been in there for more than two weeks without coming out; they were all mixed together, mares and stallions. The stallions had been fighting and they were covered in blood but the worst . . . Fuck! When the cops questioned the guy, he said . . . he said that a few days earlier, he'd lost his temper with one of the stallions and wanted to get it out of the truck. So, the horse panicked and resisted, and the guy cut its tongue. The horse bled to death. Yes. There was a dead horse in there. And it had been there for a while."

The countryside looked renewed, rain-polished, the contours of the fields dug deeper by the light, and there was humility and strength in the new sunshine. Before his father even finished his story, Arthur took Hélène's hand and made her get up, and they went out just as the rain was stopping, but even if it had gone on raining, Arthur would have taken Hélène's hand to get out of the house. As they walked, he held her close, accidentally tripping her up, and together they stumbled through pebbles and mud. Hélène wished they were near the sea, that they could go to a cliff and look out at the ocean, the huge, wild, ravaged ocean. But beyond the fields, there was nothing, only the birth of more fields, and, here and there, enclosures with electric wire, behind which dehorned cows rolled their great regal eyes. Then they heard thunder rumbling beyond the hills. Resonating in the distance, as if life were elsewhere.

"We're getting out of here," said Arthur, "we're going to leave, I promise."

"When?"

"Now."

"But where will we go?"

"I don't know, we're going to . . . We'll go to see Sabine, would you like that?"

"Yes, I want to see my sister!"

Her words brought a childish sob from her throat. And indeed, her sorrow was like a little girl's, full of rebelliousness and revulsion. She said, "So we'll leave right away, then?"

He put his arms around her and held her so tight it hurt. The storm was coming, and they had to get back, he was afraid of lightning and he didn't have time to tell her what he wanted to tell her, how much he loved her, how sorry he was that he couldn't stop things, couldn't put himself between her and the world, to slay dragons with a huge sword and right injustice, everything that was expected of a man, like he'd always been told, princes in fairytales and dick measuring contests in locker rooms, this boy who couldn't even make love if his grandfather was sleeping in the next room. He pulled her along behind him shouting, "I'm afraid of the storm! We're leaving right away! We'll get out of this dump! I'm afraid of the storm!"

They ran, the approaching thunder seemed to be chasing them, the sky had turned black all of a sudden, and it was raining again, sharp cold drops, and the cows with their shivering coats watched as they went by, a clumsy, hunched pair.

They hastily packed their suitcases, and from the way Arthur said goodbye to everyone one after the other, Hélène finally managed to place them, brothers, sisters, simple friends. When Christine handed her a basket of cold meat "for the road" she understood they had been thoughtless in equal measure, because, while Christine hadn't realized that Hélène was a vegetarian, she herself had never asked this woman anything about Arthur, when she might have told her what sort of child he'd been. When she went to put back a book by Konrad Lorenz, borrowed from Georges's library, she ran into the professor for the second time. He told her how delighted he was to meet her. He was wearing a slightly rumpled three-piece suit with a lavaliere, its delicate elegance appropriate for his fragile body. Georges had just finished introducing them when the old man complimented Hélène:

"You have eyes like Danielle Darrieux, the same sublime, unparalleled color."

"Thank you . . ."

"Have you seen *Beating Heart*?"

"No."

"You must."

"But Papa," said Georges, "*Beating Heart* is an old black-and-white film, you can't see the color of Darrieux's eyes."

"My son is an imbecile, Mademoiselle. In black and white, Darrieux's eyes are even more green. Don't let me keep you . . ."

He kissed Hélène's hand, and she was no longer quite sure whether he'd actually forgotten the night before or that Darrieux's eyes were indeed green, but she would leave this uncertain house consoled by the fact that something had happened: she had met Arthur's grandfather the way she might have traveled back up a stream, one that joined the river flowing into the same sea where she imagined her grandfathers. 1914. 1915. 1916. 1917. 1918. The global slaughter that had gone before them, its violence resonating inside them without their realizing. That was what was truly, stunningly thoughtless, the casual manner with which they viewed the past as being well and truly behind them, these baby boomers now enjoying the final years of those three decades they called the *Trente Glorieuses*, and whose glory could only be measured in the amount they consumed. For a few years now, starting with the first oil crisis and the rise in unemployment, the image of happy prosperity and never-ending repletion had slowly been losing its shine. But day and night, on the walls of buildings, in the metro, in airports and train stations, in newspapers, in movies, on the radio, on television: words, voices, images showed them everything they had been missing. And so, they bought things they had never needed. They thought they were happy. They were simply obedient.

In the Renault 4L, with its bright yellow paint and flimsy body, on a road full of potholes and streaked with rain, Arthur and Hélène spent the most beautiful hours of their summer. They had dared to leave on the spur of the moment, to free themselves from family and friends, and this gave them a new status: they were now a couple. While the car was buffeted by the flow of air and the trucks overtaking them, at last they could speak freely. Arthur tried to calm and console Hélène regarding slaughterhouses, whether in the provinces or in Paris:

"It's over, you know, in a few days the Vaugirard abattoirs will be history."

"But what does that change? They're merely shifting the problem elsewhere. Slaughterhouses will still exist. And in ever greater number. Bigger and more productive."

"They're going to build a park there instead, that's better than killing horses right in the middle of Paris, isn't it?"

"Sure, you leave the park and head straight for the butcher's where they sell horsemeat. At least there at Vaugirard it was staring you in the face, the slaughter, you could hear the trains, the trucks, the horses' hooves in the morning, it would wake people up, give them nightmares."

"Hélène, it's not as if everyone is obliged to live the way you do, with your convictions and your causes."

"But people should be aware, at least, shouldn't they? Someone must be telling them a dead horse brings in more money than a living one—why do you think your father even came upon that bastard this morning? Why don't they kill them back in their own country—in Morocco, Russia, Poland, or Greece, in your opinion? Because it creates jobs in France, that's why. A lot of jobs. For every animal you kill, you are providing a living for a worker so he can kill, and bleed, and cut off tails and legs and cut up thighs, and bone flanks, and skin them, and finish off their heads, and empty out their guts, and chop them up, and get rid of the unwanted flesh, and—"

"Whoa, whoa! I get it, you made your point."

"The point, Arthur, is that they stun the horses to immobilize them and that's it, and then they start cutting them up and they're still conscious! Have you seen the Franju film?"

"No, but since you've told me about it three times in detail, it's worse than if I'd seen it—they stabbed the horse in the mouth with a dagger, he falls to his knees, the blood steaming—I've seen it all, Hélène, thank you."

"Bled alive . . . shit!"

"There's just one thing I'm afraid of . . ."

"And what's that?"

"That they'll show the film again at the Cinémathèque and you'll make me go."

"Well for sure you won't get out of it!"

"To film inside a slaughterhouse without permission, that really took some guts. In 1949, Danielle Darrieux still had black-and-white eyes. And green ones, too!"

"I adore your grandfather."

"And your eyes? Do you like your eyes?"

"Are you imitating Bardot? It's stupid."

"I agree it's stupid, but what I like—"

"If you say one more stupid thing—"

"No. I'm serious. What I like is that maybe—I say maybe—you will at last start to appreciate the color of your eyes."

"Yes. Maybe. It will remind me of the professor . . ."

And they sang the song by Rezvani: *"My memory fails me, I can't recall too well / What color were her eyes, I don't think they were blue / Were they green, were they gray, were they verdigris . . ."*

Their voices rose and fell with the bouncing of the road, adding accidental hiccups to the song, which made them laugh and took the edge off their emotion.

That week, Sabine was performing in housing projects in the Mirail neighborhood of Toulouse, where forty thousand people lived in buildings that soared skyward with flagging prosperity and fading modernity. They'd been living there since the 1960s—peasants from the Ariège, repatriated former residents of North Africa, Jews, Christians, Muslims, all of whom had hoped to find in the southern sunshine some echo of a lost life they never spoke of. The first new city in France had no memory; the flagstones, walkways, bypasses, and underground passages had covered over the earth, and when the inhabitants went for walks in the eighteenth-century Parc de la Reynerie, which belonged to their neighborhood and France's cultural inheritance, they knew that they didn't belong—not there, only to those countries they'd left behind. The fathers were silent. The mothers stifled their sorrow beneath the white mask of neurasthenia. Their children adopted the accent of Toulouse and kept a low profile. In this concrete conglomeration that was the pride of people who didn't live there, a poverty reigned that was not shared, and already, people no longer referred to *inhabitants* but to *communities*. People no longer mixed, either socially or demographically, and yet it was when they were mixed together that you could hear them come alive. The first time Sabine came to the neighborhood, together with Éric and guided by Bastian, the director, she was surprised by the echo. The place *resonated*. Between the endless rows of towers reaching for the sky, voices and steps vibrated as if they were throbbing, a diffraction of bodies, their deepest vital rhythm. Unable to make out the words, she could hear *something* speaking, *something* calling, but words were lost in this vastness. She asked Bastian, "How do you know they're going to come?"

"Who?"

"People."

"What people?"

"You know . . . spectators!"

"Because they signed up . . . I showed you the list."

Éric suffered less from stage fright than Sabine; every evening when she was about to go on stage, she convinced herself that it wouldn't happen. The show would be canceled because nobody showed up. Or, if the spectators came, she'd lose her voice. Or she'd die before the performance. He was always surprised that there was nothing between her losing her voice and actual death, but he understood her fear that this thing that was so exceptional might not happen. He was always on the lookout for that something, and every evening he thought, "You never know who might be in the audience," and he gave his all, not so much for those who were there as for those he dreamed of seeing there—a producer, a theater manager, who would notice him and hire him on the spot. They weren't performing *A Life* in a ruined chapel or a disaffected factory, as Sabine had sometimes dreamed of doing; she was paid to deliver apartment theater and that was where the poetry was to be found, in an urban milieu and the new ways of the world.

After they'd performed and met with the audience, Sabine went to her hotel in the center of town. Before going on tour, she'd given Hélène the dates and cities for the show, and the telephone numbers of the hotels where she'd be staying. When she got back in the evening, the night watchman gave her slips of paper where he'd noted the calls she'd received in her absence. She kept these papers, the way she kept the notes Mathieu scribbled when he came to see her at the old surgeon's—little words on the pillow or the night table that unintentionally spoke of their intimacy. Mathieu had never written *I love you.* Or, *See you this evening, my love*, declarations that could change the course of events. He wrote down cinema schedules, the address of a bar, or of a friend's place where they were to meet, the title of a book. That was their life together, her life with this man she referred to in secret as *the love of my life*, and in public, as *my man.* He did not call her *my woman*, which would have meant *my wife*, and so *my man* did not imply marriage but sex. Sometimes in the morning, when he was about to leave and Sabine was pretending to be asleep, Mathieu would write directly on her skin. She could feel the pen on her arm, inscribing the place for a rendezvous, and she shivered with desire. Before leaving he kissed the inside of her wrist, gently; it was deliciously frustrating.

In Toulouse, when she came back to her hotel, she found a note Hélène had dictated to the night watchman: *Sis, I'll be here tomorrow with Arthur. There was one room left at your hotel. We'll wait for you there after your performance. I have a million things to tell you. Kisses full of rain. Hélène.*

It was hard to imagine Hélène here, with Arthur, the well-behaved young man, both of them used to discreet comfort. The hotel was run-down and dreary, its great age conferred no cachet. This, too, was being on tour, their austere everyday life, the rusty smell of trains, the clockwork of logistics with no chance of getting away. She missed Mathieu, she couldn't reach him, he was spending his vacation in America with a friend she didn't like, a guy who snorted, displaying a sort of tired irony, his boredom with others, and an unsurpassable love of self. She had no one to talk to besides Éric, but they were already getting tired of each other. Off stage he seemed absent, always lost in a book that he kept in the back pocket of his jeans, the same book for a month now, yellowed and dog-eared. She had gotten used to calling Paul and telling him about her tour, this man she nicknamed *the invisible ear*, so at least what she was experiencing was being recorded somewhere, the ephemeral nature of the theater was leaving its mark. It cost a fortune to call from a hotel, an exorbitant surcharge for every minute, so when Sabine wanted to talk to Paul, she let the phone ring three times and he called her back. For the last ten days, he hadn't responded. She wasn't worried, she thought nothing could threaten this man who was so unreal, who lived in telephone wires and airwaves, and she went on speaking to him in her head; through his silences, sometimes, he still replied.

Hélène and Arthur arrived in Toulouse as if it were a new country: the weather was fine, there were people in the streets, tourists hunting around with cameras on their bellies, disappointed when they didn't find what they were looking for, the exact place they had dreamed of. Hélène and Arthur took refuge in their hotel room, and on the lumpy, sagging mattress they made love with the deep relief of those who have missed each other. They did not notice the acrid smells from the plumbing, or the voices in the corridor; they pulled the sheets up over their heads, and, in the shelter of a dim light, their bodies knew each other. They slept in deep oblivion, woke up and made love again with a certain laziness, their bodies acting as if of their own accord, like animals that cannot be restrained, and their pleasure came again, obvious and familiar.

By the time Sabine and Hélène were finally together, it was late, and their desire to see each other had already changed. Hélène was sore and slow, Sabine was high on energy, the nervous jubilation of having been on stage. She was in the bar with Éric and Bastian, endlessly debriefing what they had just experienced. As if they had returned from battle. Finally, Sabine asked Hélène what it was she had to tell her, but how could she speak about the dead horse now? the professor and his nightmares? How, in this noisy, smoky café could she tell her how when she was walking in the rain, she had wept at the thought of seeing her again? Arthur came to the rescue.

"My father reported a bastard who killed a horse."

"What d'you mean, he killed a horse?" asked Bastian.

"He was transporting horses from Morocco to the slaughterhouse, and he killed one of them, a stallion."

"Oh, no! Don't tell us these horrible stories," said Sabine, "I'm performing, I have to protect myself."

"Your father did the right thing to report the guy," said Bastian, "and he'll pay for it, believe me, he'll pay a very heavy price."

Sabine abandoned her delicate diva posture to announce with unexpected pride, "Bastian is from the Larzac!"

Arthur and Hélène were puzzled. For over seven years, people had been talking about the Larzac, but they didn't really know what was going on there. They recalled there had been sheep let loose near the Eiffel Tower, and some cars had bumper stickers that declared *Gardarem lo Larzac* (often paired with *Nuclear Nein Danke*). And that was about it. Arthur asked, "Are you an activist?"

"No. I'm a peasant."

"But you . . . you're defending your land, so it won't be expropriated . . . isn't that what's going on?"

"Yes, I'm defending my land, but I'm telling you I'm a peasant, the son and grandson of peasants. And a Catholic, not a leftist. A native of the Larzac, born and bred, in other words."

"But you, I mean you peasants, you get a lot of support from the activists. Isn't that it . . . ?"

"That's true. Yes, it's true . . . if we didn't have the support of the leftists, and the unions, and the workers, then for sure our voices, I mean, the voices of hundreds of peasants, confronted with Debré,[8] and Pompidou, and Giscard, and all of them—what could we do . . ."

[8] Minister of Defense under Pompidou, until 1973.

It was hard to talk about it. He didn't feel like talking about it. How to explain to these people who were his own age that, for him and his family, expropriation would mean that their lives, their lands, were worthless? His people had fought in every war, and now the army was driving them out in order to enlarge its base, and it was the same story all over again, the peasants were the Republic's country bumpkins and its cannon fodder, and Bastian knew it would take more than a discussion in a café to explain why he belonged to another country, another culture, another struggle; not theirs. He felt as if he were from a time that had no part in those great years of progress; the Minister of Defense looked upon them—on him and his kind—as "medieval peasants vaguely raising a few sheep." When he thought of this, his anger returned, intact and scathing.

He said, "You know, Arthur, it's not some sort of folklore, our life on the plateau. It's a harsh life, winter lasts six months, do you understand? Last summer these girls from the MLAC came with their trailers and their bare breasts . . . It embarrassed me, for my grandmother's sake. She's been keeping ewes since she was nine years old, and she only speaks Occitan. She's afraid they're going to blow up her house, she's afraid when she sees the tanks and the guns, to her it's as if the war had started all over again. In summer, people come to us from Chile, Ireland, Greece, all over Europe, but I get out when I can, for a week or two . . . I lend a hand here, at the Maison de la Culture. I'll go home for haymaking season. And anyway, after summer, they'll all be gone."

"I have some friends who have friends who never left," said Arthur.

Now Hélène wished he'd be quiet. His eagerness to please made him seem pathetically soft. Bastian ordered another beer, his wave to the waitress meant the discussion was over. She thought again of the workers at the Lip factory, that evening in

Villers watching the news. It was to make as much money as they could, said Michelle. And now she remembered, the mention of solidarity between the peasants from the Larzac and the workers in Besançon, the two names together. "It will be like the Larzac everywhere!" She remembered it all, in a muddled sort of way, but did not try to take it any further.

The following evening, Hélène and Arthur went to the performance of *A Life* in an apartment on the ninth floor of a building in Mirail. Hélène was always amazed to see her sister perform: it was as if Jeanne's torments were Sabine's own, but she couldn't understand the satisfaction Sabine derived from being unhappy on stage. She suffered, and congratulated herself all the while on her suffering. *She'd done it*. That evening she recounted with unbearable precision how the priest killed the dog that was giving birth. She had decided to include this barbaric scene in the monologue, and injected it with fiery emotion. And yet, she viewed Hélène's struggle for animal rights as a superfluous thing, almost comical. Unless, thought Hélène, her denial was just a game, the kind played by two sisters who from earliest childhood have been hoarding their necessary differences to set themselves apart from each other. We have to go through it, to figure out who we are . . . After the performance, Sabine took her in her arms and squeezed her very tight, an actor's embrace. And she whispered in her ear, "I performed for you this evening, could you tell?" Hélène said yes, knowing that Sabine would say the same thing to Arthur or Bastian, too: sincere lies.

Mariette was now in the habit of hurrying through the streets of Aix, with her weighty burden of schoolbooks on her back. Her tiny body wove its way through the crowd of pedestrians, overtaking them without touching them, then suddenly she would sit on a bench or on the edge of a fountain, attentive and watchful. After class, she went often into the Church of the Madeleine and sat on a prie-dieu, her eyes closed but her face upheld, obstinate, the same here as outside. At the bus stop, she sometimes forgot to get on her bus and went on sitting under the shelter, lost in thought. The Mouse resembled a strange sparrow, an urban bird that survives with a fragile grace. Sometimes she came home with scraped knees, or a bruise on her forehead, and she said she had fallen in the street, or had missed a step on the grand stairway at Les Prêcheurs. In the beginning, her parents showed their compassion: Agnès applied some arnica, gave her a Band-Aid like when she was little, but one evening when Mariette came back from the collège with her ankle bandaged by the school nurse, she became worried.

"I don't believe it," she said to Bruno.

"Believe what?"

"That she falls in the stairs, down steps she says she missed, any of that—I don't believe it."

They imagined the worst: their daughter was getting beaten up in the schoolyard, or bullied here, in their changing apartment building: once a place for families, it was becoming divided; they could no longer recognize in these sneering adolescents the little boys who had been so endearing and polite. Boys full of cocky pride and disrespect: it made the grown-ups sad, and some of them even said it was time they were sent off to fight a good war.

"I'll make an appointment with Dr. Jeanvry."

"She's twelve years old, Agnès, she may be fragile but she's no idiot, you can't take her to the doctor when she hasn't had an attack since summer camp. It's probably growing pains."

"Or leukemia."

"Are you out of your mind?"

"I've been talking about it with Françoise . . ."

"Your yogurt jar lady? The same Françoise you invited to your birthday?"

"Yes, I mentioned it to her, her daughters are the same age as Mariette. She says that bruises can be a sign of leukemia."

"The woman is stark raving mad! A mail carrier delivering diagnoses sight unseen—I can't believe it! No, I think it's growing pains, she's tired so she bumps into things, she needs to get more sleep."

"She misses her sisters, she's bored with us, our conversation bores her."

"You think so?"

"I'm sure of it. She's bored with us."

And maybe this terrifying conjecture was true. Without Sabine and Hélène, their family seemed disjointed; it had lost its balance and its shine. Everything seemed ordinary, and they felt as if they were just like everyone else. So, they made plans to invite their cousins, and neighbors, and Mariette's friends; maybe they should buy her a slot-in record player so she could listen to music in her room, they had to find a way to restore some joy, to liven things up. The very next day, Agnès asked the neighbor on the landing what the music was her son liked to play so loud, and from among the records the neighbor showed her—John Travolta, Boney M., the Bee Gees—she chose the record by Bonnie Tyler, a girl with big blue eyes and a song entitled *It's a Heartache.* She thought the English meant, *it's a heart attack*, but the neighbor explained to her that it meant *unhappy in love* and swore that in spite of the title, it was a cheerful song.

"It's kind of rock, you know . . . or pop. Well disco, mostly."

"All of that?"

"Well, yeah, it's very modern."

"Are you sure it's catchy?"

"Yeah, sure. There are electric guitars."

That same evening, before dinner, Bruno put the record on loud enough for it to be heard from the living room. They had always expressly told their daughters never to make any noise, and the diktat that marked their life was, "Think about the neighbors," which over time was abbreviated to, "The neighbors," two words that meant, Turn the volume down, Take off your shoes, Don't flush at night—never-ending, useless precautions, because their apartments let the sound through as surely as light filtered under the doors. But that evening, Bruno put the music on loud, without warning. Mariette was sitting in her usual spot between her sisters' empty chairs, and when the guitar first resounded through the room she glanced at her mother warily, but Agnès only responded with an encouraging smile, and so she listened. A broken voice was singing, huskily, a tumble of unrecognizable words, but this girl who was singing in English was coming for her, there, in the kitchen in La Petite Chartreuse, as surely as if she had always known her. Her song was a fractured, shattering lament, the beat, strangely, was that of Mariette's life, the way she walked through the streets, the pauses she took, the stubborn rhythm that drove her on in spite of herself. But suddenly it all vanished. The phone was ringing, Bruno got up to answer, and he stopped the record.

"But that's incredible!" he shouted from the living room. "Agnès, come quick, it's Sabine on the phone! Turn on the TV. Put on channel 2."

Agnès hurried over to him. Mariette could vaguely hear the voice of the presenter on Antenne 2, a solemn, rather sad voice, but she also heard cries of joy coming from the television and could sense her parents' happiness. Outside, night had fallen, the hour when it got cold, when lamps were lit and smells of soup rose from the stairwell. She continued sitting in the deserted kitchen and her parents seemed as far away as if they were living in another apartment. It was a strange moment, teetering precariously; the silence of the room contrasted with the hubbub of the newscast, the jumble of sound. Bruno shouted for her to come, because it was a historic moment, a world event!

In the living room, the television screen cast its flickering light. All around everything seemed dark, almost erased. The screen showed a square at nighttime; a buoyant crowd was waving white handkerchiefs, jumping and screaming for joy. Bruno and Agnès were listening respectfully to an old man in a red alb who was reading at a microphone from a balcony, words from a book held by a man in a white alb: "His most eminent and reverend Karol Charles Cardinal Wojtyla." When he heard the name, Bruno tossed his head back and laughed, like a child confronted with a surprise that was both too great and unhoped-for. He leaned to Mariette and whispered confidentially, "How would you spell that then?"

"What?"

"Voytiva? How would you write it? That's the name of our new pope, Mariette! We have a pope, at last! And he's not Italian, you don't write his name the way you pronounce it . . . He comes from far away, from the other side of the Iron Curtain—"

"Like at the theater."

"What?"

"Sabine says that at the theater there's an iron curtain."

Bruno and Agnès looked at her despairingly then, more conciliatory, Agnès said, "You don't know how right you are, he is a man of the theater."

"The pope?"

"Yes. That's what Sabine said on the telephone. He used to practice sports, and acted on stage back there, in Kraków."

"There he is!" said Bruno.

And the pope appeared on the screen, to the applause of the cheering crowd. He was short. Smiling. Moved. Surrounded by a cluster of men. The presenter said he was young. To Mariette he looked like an old man. "John Paul II," Bruno repeated his name, in one breath. Then he said, "We're not orphans anymore," and he suddenly seemed younger, like a man who has found a father. Paul VI had died on August 6. His successor, John Paul I, died on September 28, thirty-three days after his election; there were rumors of poisonings and plots, but now it was over, on October 16, 1978, the third pope of the year had arrived. Holy Father. Bishop of Rome. Head of the Catholic Church. King of the Vatican State.

"Is he the representative of God, then? and of Jesus, too?" asked Mariette.

"Yes," said Agnès, "and he is infallible."

"Infallible?"

"It means it's impossible for him to make a mistake, when it comes to either faith or morals," said Bruno. "You don't believe me?"

"Yes, I believe you."

"Then why are you smiling?"

"I'm not smiling. I'm thinking about Jesus. He went barefoot, didn't he?"

"What does that have to do with it? What are you talking about?" asked Agnès.

"You would know about the pope's infallibility if you went to catechism more regularly," said Bruno.

"Look, leave her alone. She's a believer, that's the most important thing. You're a believer, right, Mariette?"

"I'm glad you're not an orphan anymore, Papa."

He looked at her, unsure how to interpret these condescending words, uttered with so much tenderness. He had found a father again, and now he felt as if he had lost a daughter, the last one. His own paternity was not infallible. He said, "Thank you, sweetheart," and was as sad as if his house had suddenly been emptied, the children's room abandoned. Fleetingly, he remembered the songs he used to sing to his daughters. What was he going to do with his songs? What would become of him, now that they no longer needed him? He felt Agnès's hand on his own, a strong pressure, a call. He squeezed her hand in return, saying yes. They needed a project. Needed to decide new things. They held hands in silence, still watching the universal outpouring of joy on television, feeling at last they could be a part of it.

A few days later, during an appointment with the principal at the collège, Agnès at last found out what was going on with Mariette. She wasn't being bullied, and obviously didn't have any blood disease. But she hadn't been lying: she did miss steps and bump into things. And it wasn't because she was distracted.

"Apparently you don't open your eyes in class, Mariette. Or even during recess or on the stairs. That is completely crazy!"

"Will I be expelled, do you think?"

"You're a year ahead, and you're top in your class in all your subjects, why would you be expelled? Tell me why you're doing this, huh, why are you closing your eyes?"

"So I can hear better."

"Do you have trouble keeping up in class if you don't close your eyes?"

"Oh, not in class, no! I'm listening to the world."

"The what?"

"The world."

"Are you completely crazy?"

Mariette realized it was pointless to explain to her mother the logic behind her experiment. Yes, she was listening to the world. Infinitesimal sounds that were superimposed, everything that lived together, and she thought it was strange that sounds were allowed to mix, to become muddled and disappear. This would never happen with images, they would never be placed one on top of the other, sight ordered everything, but sounds—you had to pay very close attention to them, because they came haphazardly, and there were not many words to describe them. She loved going into this invisible world, and she had understood that even when you're silent, when you're sleeping, silence doesn't exist. So, you had to be vigilant. All the time. To understand what was happening, when nothing was happening.

They'd all gone home. Each according to the rhythm of the seasons: departures in summer, returns at the beginnings of autumn. Sabine lived the other way around, and she liked it that way: performing at night, when others were finishing their day; going on tour in the summer and taking some vacation time afterwards. Her contract with the Maison de la Culture in Bobigny had run its course. She had performed *A Life* over a hundred and fifty times, now she had to come up with a new show for the producers.

She went back to Robert, her old surgeon, the tenderness she felt mixed with a little weariness, as she forced herself to listen to how he'd spent August in La Baule with his son Gérald, how they'd argued and played chess. In honor of Sabine's return, they shared a meal that Robert bought at the delicatessen—enormous vols-au-vent that were lukewarm and collapsed on their side. The kitchen was dark, pigeons were cooing on the windowsill, the wine was warm, it was unrelentingly dreary, nineteenth-century provincial life at the heart of Paris. Later, in the bathroom, when she saw the jar of shaving cream that hadn't been closed, and little white hairs in the sink, Sabine went straight back out.

Half an hour later, she was ringing at Mathieu's door on the rue du Père-Corentin, praying he'd be alone and wouldn't be mad at her for daring to show up without warning. But when he opened the door, he looked at her with no more pleasure than if he were taking delivery of a meal.

"What a surprise! Have you just come from Toulouse?"

"No. Robert's place."

"Has something happened?"

"No, why? Do I need an emergency to show up at your door?"

"Uh-oh . . . are you in a bad mood?"

He said it as if he were enjoying her aggressive behavior. But she wasn't in a bad mood. She was afraid she'd done the wrong thing, had infringed on their code by just showing up.

"I lost my keys and I didn't dare wake Robert up, and I couldn't find a phone to call you. I thought maybe I could spend the night here?"

He began to slowly unbutton her shirt, tilting his head to one side, evaluating the situation, and he smiled at her, that smile she loved, sure of himself, slightly raffish.

"I was expecting you tomorrow, but this is great. Really great, even. Hey, did you put on weight, on tour? All those apple pies?"

She instantly stepped back.

"But you look gorgeous! You're like Gina Lollobrigida! I love it!"

She felt like crying. From irritation and fatigue. She had wished he would join her during the tour, at least once, that he would have curtailed his trip to America in search of Jack Kerouac—where, in keeping with the writer's philosophy, he had surely not refrained from cheating on her, even if that word was not in their vocabulary, even if jealousy did not figure in their emotional range. She wished he'd been waiting for her at the station, that they could have run into each other's arms, like in a Lelouch film. And now she didn't even feel like kissing him. She felt ugly, depressed, and so tired. But he really wanted her, he was glad to see her again, and confronted with Mathieu's sweet attitude, his eyes full of desire, she was sorry she'd been aggressive, and she yielded to the easy way out, the thing he loved and which gave her an easy way out of everything. She lay on the bed, arms and legs spread, and said, "Do whatever you want." He gave a joyful laugh, pulled down his jeans, stumbling over them, and told her that she was fantastic.

Later, in the dim apartment, with its smell of coffee and stale cigarettes, and Mathieu asleep at her side, holding his hair the way he always did after lovemaking, she thought about Paul. He had vanished the way he had appeared, out of the blue, and she realized she knew nothing about his life, had never shown any interest in him, and maybe he'd eventually gotten fed up with her monologues, her egocentric behavior. She could smell Mathieu's familiar odor, could feel his soft, almost feminine skin, the apparent frailty of his shoulders, his long, slender, solid body . . . She had missed him so much. It came to her almost painfully, now that she was lying next to him in his bed, and on her own side of the bed, a habit that reflected true intimacy. She thought she was the only one who could occupy this place, the other girls surely did not have their own side in Mathieu's bed. She was the one he liked best, wasn't she? The favorite. The light filtering through the burlap curtains from outside gave the room a hesitant brightness. The last buses made the window panes vibrate as they went by, a dull, ordinary sound, like an animal breathing. It reassured her, to acknowledge the light and the sounds, their repetitive nature. Sabine stroked Mathieu's back over and over, the way he liked it, but he was asleep and she didn't know whether her caresses found their way into his dreams. She thought about how he would start teaching again soon, he knew exactly what he would be doing, as well as how much money he'd make that year, his salary down to the last centime. Maybe that was why he was always calm and sure of himself. A steady job. His own apartment. He left it in the morning and came back in the evening, free in every way, with what he did, with his time, mindless of what other people might think. How lucky he was. And yet, his studio (he had never once suggested she come and live with him there) was poorly designed—the hall was bigger than the main room, the kitchen was no better than a "nook," the bathroom looked out onto the buildings across the way, and, when the windows were open, you could hear the neighbors on the phone and the sound of corks popping when they opened a bottle. Above the mattress that lay right on the floor, Mathieu had pinned the poster of a chubby baby touching his penis: "The aim is to seek to be fully oneself, to encourage and protect the natural manifestations of life in the infant, the child, the adolescent, the woman, and the man, in such a way as to rule out forever any social trickery," said Wilhelm Reich. It replaced what Sabine had always known above the bed at home: a crucifix.

Living at Robert's during the week and at Mathieu's on the weekend, feeling at home nowhere, Sabine couldn't find a play to put on or a text to adapt. She had come back to Paris hoping to spend her time researching, to immerse herself in the thrill of a new project, but the more she wanted it, the emptier she felt; not a single subject called to her, nothing seemed relevant, it could all wait. And so, she decided to go to casting calls. She dipped into her savings to put together a portfolio. She didn't have enough to pay for a professional photographer, so she posed for Gérard, a friend of a friend who photographed her for five hours—at Mathieu's place, in the street, in the Parc Montsouris. She had to smile all the time, sitting on the sofa, leaning against a table, halfway lying down in the grass, pressed against a wall, a tree, the entrance door to a courtyard, her hands on her hips, her head thrown back, one finger on her cheek, a hand on her neck, turning this way, then that way, in profile, full-face, lids lowered, eyes open wide, she had to keep smiling, while Gérard encouraged her, "Come on!

You're in the groove! You're in the groove! Don't lose the groove!" At the end of the day, her body was sore, her jaws were aching, and she'd caught cold posing outside in lightweight clothes—she looked cramped in her coat, said Gérard. An actor is a body, right? She had to be seen as sensual and available. An actor lives in the director's desire, right? She was fed up hearing his inept words, and didn't even contradict him.

She didn't recognize herself in the photographs—all that makeup, as if she were going to a wedding, all dressed up and clumsy, the heels of her shoes sinking into the earth, and that horrible smile devouring her face, that winning look that was supposed to give her a personality—it was pathetic. She realized she didn't have what it took. She was provincial, she didn't come from *here*, she didn't belong to the huge filmmaking family, and you could tell. She wasn't the type a director would stop in the street, "Mademoiselle, you ought to be in the movies." She wasn't the type who'd go with a girlfriend to a casting call to feed her her lines and then be picked, *totally by chance*.

She took her portfolio nonetheless to do the rounds of the production houses. *Le Film Français* indicated the films in development; she read the long list of titles, with the director and main actors, and it was like reading a fascinating story that would never have anything to do with her. In the hopes of auditioning for a minor role, she tried the offices of Gaumont and UGC on the Champs-Élysées, and the premises of the SFP[9] at their studios in Buttes-Chaumont, the temple of television. In addition to the "Actors" file, there were listings for houses, cars, horses, even dogs and cats. But no one took down

[9] Société française de production, a major player in French filmmaking from 1975-2010.

her name and no one ever called her. Sometimes, when they were looking at her resume (padded with the three famous reviews from Le *Parisien, L'Officiel des Spectacles* and *Le Figaro*), they would ask her for her *latest update*. She didn't know what they meant. *Latest update*. A television word. Then she understood: her *latest update* was what she was doing, professionally. So, she made up a militant, iconoclastic project for the Parisian banlieue, and on seeing their indifferent expressions she adapted her lie: it was Feydeau revisited, the men would play women and vice versa, the great tradition of cross-dressing. But this wasn't the milieu of the theater, this was the movies. She decided to get an agent.

In a posh office in the seventh arrondissement, with an old friend from drama class, she performed a scene from Ionesco's *La Leçon* for an agent who had his back to them while he adjusted his curtains, and who concluded without ever turning around that with teeth like that she'd never get anywhere. She grimaced in the mirror and saw she had receding gums on some of her lower teeth. Another agent told her she was slightly cross-eyed. She didn't dare look people in the eye anymore because of this so-called strabismus, she began looking to one side; when she was seated at a table, she never spoke to the people directly across from her, but only to those who were on her right or her left. She even had her ID photos taken looking to one side of the booth. They criticized her accent from the south, and it was true that when she became anxious or emotional, it suddenly flared up, treacherously. There were so many things about her that people didn't like or found offensive, and now that she was aware of them, she thought about them all the time, and was ashamed she had never noticed; in a way she'd invented herself from scratch, but she'd been deluding herself all along, from start to finish.

A casting director told her he had something for her: she could do an internship to become a stuntwoman, they needed stuntwomen. Another one asked her to laugh. She laughed. To cry. She cried. He clapped his hands, Laugh! Cry! Laugh! Cry! And when she'd finished, he told her she was very ordinary. She sat patiently in the waiting room at prestigious agencies, where the photographs of famous actresses proved you could get there, if you had that little extra *something*, that striking presence, like Isabelle Adjani, Fanny Ardant, or Isabelle Huppert, that *something* you became aware of when they appeared on the screen, a sense that you'd been waiting for them alone. She realized she had never driven a man crazy, never aroused the slightest passion, never been irreplaceable, and she recalled one director who'd said to her, "Men will love you. But none of them will ever fall in love with you."

Through the grapevine, she heard that an old theater director, who'd had his glory days back in the time of decentralization,[10] had been granted a small space way out in La Villette and was looking for an actress for a Lithuanian play. She went for the audition at his place, an apartment of yellowed posters and dirty clothes, saturated with cat piss. He told her he'd feed her her lines, he'd play the father, but first of all she had to throw up in the toilet, or pretend to, she'd be playing an anorexic. So convincingly did she pretend to throw up (the toilet was at the end of the corridor and he must have been able to hear her from his room) that when she reached for a shelf she knocked the extra rolls of toilet paper into the bowl, stalled for time while she fished them out by vomiting all the louder, but then the director told her to come back. She confessed to

[10] A post-war government initiative to open more theaters in the provinces, largely successful.

her crime, he said it didn't matter, he took her hand and began nibbling her fingers. She got out of there with a feeling of nausea that was anything but feigned. He summoned her a week later, only to announce that she hadn't gotten the part, she was "too pretty to play an anorexic." But again, he took her fingers in his mouth and when, incensed, she asked him if he wanted to sleep with her, he replied with revulsion that she belonged to a brutal generation that had no idea what the word romantic meant. With a sigh he took off his sweater all the same, as if Sabine's question had been an invitation, as if she really did want to sleep with the old man. She left politely and cursed herself for being kind. A few months later, posters for the play went up all over Paris, and after her initial shock, she understood, when she saw the name of the actress, a graduate of the Conservatoire,[11] that the director had not taken *her* fingers in his mouth, that he had never revealed his pasty wrinkled chest to *her*, and the obvious fact of this was more than mere injustice, it pointed to a world beyond reach, barred to her, far removed from her own. Sometimes she thought about certain scenes in *Bérénice*, in *La Reine morte,* or the fables of La Fontaine that she used to rehearse at Jean-Laurent Cochet's, and then Kantor's *Dead Class,* or Peter Brook's *Cherry Orchard*, or Antoine Vitez's *The Misanthrope*, and those texts, those characters, that theater seemed to her to be the exclusive province of others, forever. She was between two shores: on one side there was poetry, on the other, the market, with its cynical, patriarchal laws, and the more she tried to please, the more she seemed to be draining away.

Éric had been taken on at Bobigny, he'd be working with

[11] Considered the most elite and selective drama school in the country. Graduates include Isabelle Huppert, Gérard Philipe, Vincent Perez, Louis Garrel, to name a few.

Peter Stein. He encouraged her to write something funny: "Not a monologue, either, a play with several characters, we could create a collective. Hurry up, Bobigny won't wait for you forever, there are loads of actors doing apartment theater now."

"That's disgusting."

"Why disgusting? You think you had a patent?"

"Ha, ha . . ."

"You see, now, if I were a director, I wouldn't want to hire you."

"Thank you for your support."

"And you know why?"

"No, and I don't care."

"Well, here's why: because you are gray, surly, and aloof."

She stood up slowly, and as she walked away, she let her hand run slowly over the table, knocking both cups of coffee onto Éric's trousers, a weary, facile gesture, hardly a revolt.

There was the checkbook he had taken from his inside jacket pocket, with an elegant, precise gesture, as if it were an extension of his hand, of his body. David was the owner of ten apartments in Paris and Neuilly, but they were all rented, and so the agency that managed his property had found a furnished studio for Hélène on the rue Jacques-Dulud in Neuilly, and David paid, not only the deposit, but also seven months' rent in advance, which meant she'd be all set for the rest of the school year. The studio would be free in one month once the redecorating work was completed. When he'd finished writing the checks and signing the papers, David chatted with the real estate agent about new areas to invest in, like Courbevoie or Levallois, and Hélène thought about Sabine, about the unsurprising disappointment she'd see in her gaze when she told her David was renting a studio for her. Her sister would be proud of her if she turned it all down, all she had to do was get up and walk out of the agency, nothing could be simpler, emancipation at the drop of a hat. Subsequently, she'd have to struggle, like everyone else, to earn her independence, to prove it and inscribe it on the roster of valiant deeds. But it was there, as inert as the checkbook, next to which was a key-ring: the possibility of having her own place and preparing her exams. The checkbook was paying for her future, her departure from the duplex where Joseph and Vincent often came with wives and children, babies who took their naps in her room and obliged her to go upstairs to be on her own to study. When David got the idea for the studio, he insisted she mustn't think of living there with her fellow, the virgin, what was his name again? Ah, yes, Arthur, he wasn't right for her, she needed a solid type, not a student. The studio was for her, and her alone. The contract made it clear, and she didn't think she would disobey David, because she did want to live alone to see what it was like. To have her own place for the very first time, like a womb she could retreat to, protection against everything that might distract her from studying for her exams and making it into third year. David had met Arthur two or three times, and she'd thought that Arthur's polite-boy courtesy had won him over, that upper-middle-class uncle of hers, but apparently Arthur "didn't make the cut," she didn't know why and didn't want to think about it. Now she had to study and pass her exams; proof of success was the only possible reimbursement.

When they left the agency on the Avenue Charles-de-Gaulle and David said to her, "Button up your coat, don't catch cold," she thanked him, far more for his words of tender concern than for the studio. He pointed to a house with a low roof squeezed between two buildings: "That's where I was born, over fifty years ago." The house was white, sober and solid, in opposition to the real estate madness of the multi-story buildings all around it. A clear image of a baby flashed through Hélène's mind and she said, "Don't you catch cold, either!" Then they each went their own way into their day, two trained little animals relentlessly aware of their stubborn determination to live.

That evening, Hélène went to see Éléonore at the home of the friends she'd be staying with on the rue Ordener while she was in Paris. She'd obtained her post-graduate degree that June and had come for an interview with the professor she hoped to have as her thesis adviser at the Institut Pasteur. Hélène hadn't expected there to be anyone else at Éléonore's friends' place, and she was disappointed to find herself in a confused mixture of other people. The indirect lighting made the rooms seem blurry and unclear, it took a moment to adjust, then Hélène prudently went looking for Éléonore. Were all these people math students? Were there any former students from the advanced placement classes in Aix, the ones who used to murmur among themselves in the covered courtyard at the lycée and never look around? A well-dressed young man was swaying back and forth to a David Bowie song, lips closed, hands white. Would her uncle like these boys better than Arthur? What about that one, sitting on the side of a deep armchair, talking while gazing into his glass of whiskey, adjusting the glasses on his nose from time to time; he had the concentrated air of someone setting forth a theory, and the girl in a miniskirt and boots who was sitting in the armchair stared at him, suppressing her desire to challenge him, on the verge of contradicting him. Hélène left her bag and coat on the bed in a room at the end of the corridor, following the instructions of the person who had opened the door to her without even asking her who she was, and now she made her way through the living room, trying to look relaxed, though she was anything but, and her awkwardness felt all too familiar. She was at the bottom of the class again, the awkward pupil she'd been in Aix. She felt a hand on her neck, precise and warm, inevitable. She stood still on feeling the warmth of that hand, and her heart began to throb, and her belly, too, she didn't know why. The hand moved slightly, taking a few stray hairs with it, gently pulling them, and Éléonore was there in front of her. She gave Hélène that huge, almost ironic smile of hers, with the ever-provocative joy that was so typical.

"Thank you for coming."

Éléonore removed her hand from Hélène's neck, and

Hélène felt as if she were about to fall over. She gave a silly smile, and scratched her elbow, the way embarrassed people do, people who have trouble speaking clearly.

"Did he like you?"

"Did who like me?"

"The . . . the professor!"

"It's tomorrow. I'll be seeing him tomorrow."

"Oh."

"Well, yes. I decided to get dead drunk the night before the most important interview of my life, that's all! So it goes, Mademoiselle Malivieri, you know!"

The alcohol gave her a Provençal accent again, and what a pleasure it was to hear it, and to be called Mademoiselle Malivieri. Éléonore suddenly left Hélène, turned up the volume, then came back to her. Bowie was singing *Heroes* so loudly that the music had become the only possible reality. Éléonore danced, facing Hélène; intoxication filled her gaze with raw release, her body moving with little jerks; there was such tense application to that freedom that Hélène understood she had no choice, she had to join in, to be with Léo, her magnetic energy, her sensuality. She felt as if she were immersed in icy water—her familiar terror, the public pool of her childhood in Aix, where the little girl had drowned. To move from the terrestrial world to the aquatic one, all you had to do was jump. She heard herself give a yell, suspended in a lofty space where bodies prepare their descent, their fall into the turbulence of water. Éléonore laughed, a laugh Hélène couldn't hear, then a girl slipped in between them, shouted something in Léo's ear, and they went off together. Hélène had no one left to share the intensity with, so she closed her eyes and plunged into the darkness; carried away by the music, she felt herself disappear, her thoughts, her body, everything falling apart and evaporating, except her mouth, which became a world. It was dreamlike and precise: with an unreal sharpness she knew

Éléonore's taste, the texture of her saliva, the softness of her lips, her tongue on hers, her teeth, her smell, her breath, the pressure of her damp fingers on her face, she'd never prolonged a kiss like this before, never explored what was usually only an introduction. The kiss projected her into a concentrated pleasure, generous and daring, existing outside everything, making a lifeless landscape of everything that was not the kiss. The song ended abruptly, the dancers scattered, chatting. Léo was on the balcony with friends, a beer bottle in her hand, deep in an animated conversation that made her bob up and down and wave her arms. Had she ever actually come back onto the dance floor? Hélène felt betrayed. She went to get her coat and her bag in the room at the back and left without anyone noticing.

The streets were strewn with figures on the ground, shadows that belonged to no one. The lights in the metro glared with raw intensity, everything seemed about to collapse in an unstable atmosphere. On leaving the metro at Sablons in the quiet of Neuilly, the danger of the night fell by several degrees.

Once she lay in bed, Hélène thought again of Éléonore's kiss, and, in remembering what may have happened, a warm, stinging shame washed over her in waves, her toes, thighs, belly, scalp, her entire body aching with a sensation of guilt and pleasure. She switched on the light, looked around the room, already it was no longer hers, toys filled the big, luminous closet, Caprice's old basket had become a bed for a doll, and all the framed photographs represented those who bore the name, the heirs. She realized this was her last childhood room, with its single bed, and the adults on the other side of the wall, and her schoolwork on the little desk. Sabine, do animals suffer? What? I'm asking you whether animals suffer. Go to sleep, Hélène, go to sleep . . .

There was, in the affection her dog had given her, something she had never found again since: the promise of infallibility. She understood that Caprice's last night had been here in this room, and his basket had not been moved since, he'd wanted to die where she used to hold him, where he could smell her trace, her atoms, her odor, the love that bound them like a rope. As a child, she thought, I already knew. Thanks to him, I knew. Animals suffer. Because they love.

Mariette eventually found out where silence went to hide. Astonishingly, it was while searching for the opposite that she found out. Her parents had bought her a record player, and, for the last few months, they'd been giving her some pocket money, which she spent entirely on music. She'd started with Bonnie Tyler's single, *It's a Heartache*, she knew the words by heart, poignant words that just sounded stupid the minute you translated them into French. So, the music was more powerful than the words, the music needed the words the way you need breath, and the English made this possible. But when she shared her theory with Joël, the employee at the record store on the Cours Mirabeau who gave her recommendations, he told her she should listen to Colette Magny or Jean-René Caumisson, then she would see how powerful poetry could be, even in French. It was as beautiful as Bob Dylan.

"Oh, I know Bob Dylan really well," she told him. "I grew up with his songs."

He smiled when she said this. He felt an almost brotherly tenderness for Mariette. He'd only been living in Aix for a few months, since he'd finished his service in the navy. He was an orphan, and he'd grown up in a foster family in the Lozère, and Mariette didn't know whether he was being serious when he said that the Langogne municipal brass band had been his initiation to music, but he seemed to live for nothing else and was constantly learning, with the dogged determination of the self-taught who always feel, one way or another, that they have a lot of catching up to do compared with others. He was twenty years old, with an adolescent's face—skin scarred by chickenpox—and he hid that face behind long brown hair. His narrow eyes, so black they were almost purple, always seemed to be on the lookout for something.

"Oh . . . you grew up with Bob Dylan songs, Mariette. Were you born into a hippy community?"

"Um . . . we listened to *The Times They Are A-changin'* a lot. And Cat Stevens too, and Joan Baez, all those guys."

"Yes, but nowadays Dylan's converted to Catholicism, his latest album isn't all that great, and Cat Stevens has become Yusuf Islam and he's stopped everything."

"What about Joan Baez?"

"Oh, her! Still playing Joan of Arc, as Dylan said!"

"Joan of Arc? I know all about her . . . Yes, my parents go from Dylan to Joan of Arc, just like that . . ."

He told her to go and sit in a booth, he had a surprise for her today. A poem, set to music.

She liked being in the booth. She felt safe there. From deep within the store Joël would play a record that only she could hear, as if it were dedicated to her personally. As she did every time, once she was sitting on the little bench, she took a tube of sweet condensed milk from her bag, in order to suck on it while she listened to the record. But a customer must have come in the shop, because Joël was taking his time starting the music. She waited a little longer in the smell of leather and cork, an electric smell like that of a small fire; she leaned back on the bench and started on her tube of milk, closed her eyes, blissful, and that was when she heard it for the first time. It filled the padded booth, almost humming, so alive that it filled the space, and her brain, too, her entire being. It was the silence. She thought that maybe Hélène might be able to explain to her what it consisted of, whatever it was that was floating in the atmosphere and mingling with the silence. Was it the same at the bottom of the ocean, at the bottom of a well, in her deepest sleep? Were there several kinds of silence, connected to water, to earth, or to death? In the silence of the booth, she tried to make a sound. She said simply, "Yes." And she heard how clear her voice was, how pleasant to her ear, more childish than she would have thought. She repeated it a little louder, "Yes." There was neither an echo, nor any interference, her yes sounded pure in the silence, and then she recognized the crackle in the loudspeakers, a few tiny seconds to prepare for a new atmosphere. First, there were violins, like in a tragic film, then the fragile strings of a guitar, and finally a man's voice, vibrating with a sad anger. What the man was singing, Mariette received it full on like a football to the gut, words that spoke of his despair, the color and texture of it, despair like a living animal there at your side, climbing over you, lying on top of you. There was a threatening, almost mystical, sweetness about the song, and it sent her the precise images of everything she had never dared to say, everything she felt so confusedly and violently, as if there were times when another Mariette lived inside her, older and wiser. At the end of the song, the man fell silent and the violins went on without him, but even without hearing him, she still felt his presence. And before it all stopped, he came back to sing a little more, with an accent from the south that added notes to the notes.

When Mariette left the booth, there were customers at the cash register, so she stood behind them, very straight, waiting her turn, mastering her emotion. When she got up to Joël, she tried to give him a slightly blasé smile.

"Did you know it already?" he said.

"What?"

"Léo Ferré?"

"Nah."

"And Baudelaire?"

"Well, yeah. Obviously."

"I'm sorry, you look upset. I should've warned you."

"Not at all."

"It wasn't a good idea, surprising you with *Spleen* . . ."

"No, it was great. I'm going to buy it."

"Are you sure?"

"Yes, I'm fed up with songs in English."

He hesitated to give her the usual discount, then in the end he gave her the record as a present. He'd charge it to his own account. He was so happy to introduce her to Léo Ferré. That man had saved him from loneliness and so many moments of despondency. Mariette asked him if he'd died a long time ago. He realized her family was not as liberated as she made out, so he told her about Tuscany, the vineyards, the olive trees, Pépée the chimpanzee, he couldn't wait to have her listen to Ferré's own songs, *Avec le temps, C'est extra* . . . Unless it was too soon for those songs. He promised to let her know the next time the singer was on tour; he never missed a single one of his concerts. She looked at him in silence and then she murmured, "Wow, that must be another world altogether . . ." And she left the shop, with the record pressed against her heart.

Baudelaire's opening lines were going around and around in her head—*When skies are low and heavy as a lid / over the mind tormented by disgust* . . . then she didn't remember the rest. So, it started over again, *When skies are low and heavy as a lid / over the mind tormented by disgust*, she thought she might be crying, but she didn't know whether it was from sorrow or pleasure, because there was pleasure in knowing that another voice besides your own could express your sorrow for you, more loudly. She closed her eyes the way she liked to do. She no longer heard the people around her, or the traffic, she thought about the poem, what it revealed, the dark feelings which, when others said them, gave her confusion some space to breathe, some truth. She didn't hear the motorcycle, or its horn, or its brakes when it skidded. She felt herself taking flight and falling. It lasted a long time, a fall that didn't end, and she was watching it without having any control over it, she was simply changing reality. In the shattering dance, she didn't let go of her record, she thought that Joël's present might break, she thought about Hélène, that she hadn't asked her what silence was made of, she thought about how worried her parents would be, all the inconvenience she would cause them, her parents who had lost one child already.

A white, unfamiliar world. Waiting. Lengthy patience. Time without limits. A body shot through with pain. The desire to live, too, in a way she has never known, like a truth that was hidden from her and has suddenly been laid bare. Her mother's voice by her ear saying words that are tireless in their tenderness, and her father singing in a low voice, *Here I am, the darling of Colorado / the king of the Browning and the knife.* Her father is nuts, she can hear her mother telling him, "You're nuts, don't sing that, it's an idiotic song," but he goes on, *Sittin' astride my trusty night-table / Never makin' a sound / In my boardin' house*, he's right, she wants to hear this song that makes her laugh, she likes the fact he has the nerve to sing it in a hospital room, and then she's tired, it's true, and she goes elsewhere, she passes out, it's infinitely sweet, she talks to the heavens, she asks, "Do I have a guardian angel?" she asks, "Was he watching over me?" because she's not dead, she knows she isn't, because she wants so badly to live. She can feel something cold in her veins, a new product, fighting pain and infection, a product that makes her like her father's song and talk to the heavens. She feels like throwing up, the dizziness is lifting her up, she is spinning in her bed without moving, she wishes she could sleep. She wants to live, but first, to sleep. She's so tired.

Recovering from the accident was a struggle, yet thrilling. Mariette was hurt and alive and every day she was building herself up again, as if she had to join and weld fragments of herself together, patiently.

"And *now*," said Sabine on the phone, "do you understand why you have to open your eyes?"

"Yes, I understand."

"Apparently you're completely covered in bruises, you're as blue as Smurfette."

"And I have two bandages on my leg. It hurts inside, too, I fractured a rib."

"I know, Maman told me. Don't go getting any asthma attacks!"

"Stop! Don't make me laugh, it hurts!"

"Did you get my cassette?"

"Your monologue is beautiful. It made me cry."

"Well, that's because I'm a good actress."

"Did you record it just for me?"

"Yes, *A Life*, just for you, my broken little sister."

"Maman wants to speak to you."

"Hugs and kisses, Mouse."

"Me too, and thanks again for Jeanne, I like her a lot."

"I like her a lot too, and I miss her."

She stayed eight days in the hospital. Every morning, she took pride in cooperating with the aides and the nurses, getting up, washing, checking how her wounds were healing, a ritual act where she showed her willingness to comply. The slightest gesture, the most elementary needs suddenly seemed heroic in the smallest ways and yet admirable. It was in the evening that she got discouraged, when a desolate silence drifted down the dim corridors, and the tiny safety lights made her think of the little red lamp in churches that hung near the tabernacle. She was eight years old when her father told her that the lamp was Christ, he was there, in that red light, his presence was real, he was right *before her eyes*. She'd been stunned. And to think she hadn't paid attention! To think she'd been standing next to Jesus without realizing! She'd been ashamed, she'd been frightened, and never taking her eyes off the little lamp, she walked backwards to leave the church, not out of respect but out of fear, she didn't want to take her eyes off the Son of God transformed into a light bulb, because if she turned around what would happen, wouldn't He seek revenge for her carelessness? She was afraid of that red color, forever connected with Him, the man who loves and who bleeds, the man who is killed and who comes back, the man who is both the Son of God *and* God, the man who becomes his own father, *God from God, light from light, true God from true God*, the prayers asked for total surrender, you had to learn them and recite them and put your whole heart into them, an innocent heart open to every enigma. In the hospital at night, she was in that mystery of the churches once again, where the atmosphere was threatening, but hope could be an option. Here, every presence seemed like an injustice, an evil twist of fate. She shared her room with two other girls. There was Lorena, who was her age and had been operated for appendicitis. She'd been born in Chile and had arrived in Aix four years earlier after the coup d'état. One evening, Lorena told her that her mother had lost her brother in Santiago, he'd disappeared, her grandmother spent all her time looking for him, she did nothing else. But she couldn't find him. Her father had been tortured by Pinochet's secret police. They'd immersed him in ice and in shit, too, they'd burned his stomach with cigarettes, they'd applied electric shock to his testicles. Mariette was afraid he would come and visit his daughter, she couldn't imagine he could possibly look like other fathers, with an attaché case and a pack of *Gauloises* in his pocket, she couldn't imagine him singing idiotic songs or dancing to Nat King Cole. Lorena left the hospital before she did, so her parents came to get her. To Mariette's great surprise, they looked perfectly normal. Her father was sturdy and smiling, her mother was a lively, brisk little woman. Mariette couldn't understand what they were saying, couldn't understand how, after what had happened to them, they could act so naturally while seeing to their daughter's bag and coat and shoes. Lorena's bed remained empty and its ghostly whiteness frightened Mariette at night, as if it were playing host to all the ghosts in Chile.

Then there was Fatia, who looked like she was seven but was actually twice that age. She had brittle bone disease, her bones broke one after the other, and her teeth were almost black. The physiotherapist came every morning and, using very gentle movements, rotated her ankles, bent her legs, massaged her back. Mariette liked talking with Fatia. They sat in the television room, and it felt like they were in a world of their own, important and serious. To them, the lives of boys and girls their age who lived outside seemed futile, so ignorant were they of the truest aspect of life, which was suffering. The first time they spoke of their ailments, Fatia said, with the relief of someone who has been spared the worst, "I'm at an intermediate stage, but if you could see the others . . ."

"What others?"

"The ones who are at an advanced stage. They're all deformed. It's as if they grew up in a vase, you know, like children in the Middle Ages, so they'd become fairground freaks."

"Oh, I see. Me too, I'm at an intermediate stage. For my asthma, I mean."

"You're here for your asthma, too?"

"No. I'm here because, you know, I like closing my eyes too much. Why are you laughing?"

"Well, because that's kind of rare, someone who likes closing their eyes, so that makes the two of us alike, since I've got a rare disease, too!"

Mariette left Fatia with the rather cowardly impression that she was abandoning her. She knew she'd be back here often, that it was the second most important place of her childhood. She was taking hours of recordings home with her. At night, secretly, she'd placed her microphone next to her sleeping roommates to record their breathing, the little noises in their throat, and the rustling of the stiff sheets. She'd also recorded the hostile silence of the corridors, the buzz of the safety lamps, and the alarm bells flashing a desperate red. She didn't want to forget any of it. Neither what she had learned, nor what had seemed obscure—that was life, after all, there were the things she understood, and the things that were elsewhere, in poems, prayers, silence. And never mind if it was complicated, the important thing, she thought, was to know it.

Now Sabine wanted to see him. What else did she have to do, anyway? Where was she supposed to be? Was anyone waiting for her? She was fed up with preparing for casting calls where, inevitably, she was found to be lacking—her height, her age, the color of her eyes, she was an appearance that changed with each passing gaze but never inspired anyone. Now she wanted to see Paul, to ask him why he didn't answer the phone anymore, she wanted to transfer her anger onto someone who was conciliatory enough to take it without flinching.

It was moving to be back in this quartier where she'd had her classes with Cochet, near the Batignolles. It was early one very cold afternoon, and the streets seemed to have lost their color. She realized it had been an entire year since she'd been . . . since she'd wanted to be thrown out of the course. It meant her friends would have finished their first year, they must be like her now, light-years away from the magnificent tirades in *Bérénice* or *Uncle Vanya*, making the rounds with their pathetic portfolio, their photographs done on the cheap by talentless people for pointless casting calls. But she had played Jeanne, after all. She'd done that. She repeated it to herself: It had worked, she'd done that. Others now, not as "gray and surly" as she was, had filled the gap, and, in the end, Éric had done the right thing, to get himself noticed and hired at the Maison de la Culture in Bobigny, that was also part of the job, to be there at the right time and seize the opportunity—unless that was what they called Fate, that thing that burst in out of nowhere and caused your life to take an unexpected turn, disastrous or magnificent, it was ineluctable and it left you no choice. She hadn't known how to make the most of her creation of *A Life*, and instead of going from one meeting to the next, she was going from one defeat to the next. If she'd kept that director's fingers in her mouth, if she'd slept with that yellowed old man, would things have taken a different turn? And Mathieu . . . Mathieu, too, was beginning to lose faith in her, to admire her less, and they hadn't become the inspired couple she'd dreamt they'd be. She wished he would translate an English play for her, it was stupid, the plays were already translated, and she didn't have the money to go and see any of them in London, not even to acquire the rights. Paul represented the final stage of her disappointment, the captivated man who'd suddenly turned away, and her anger rose to the rhythm of her steps, like a music accompanying her. She had no difficulty finding the agency where he worked, almost directly across from the infamous bar. In the window was a poster with a photograph of a bicycle in a ditch: *INSURANCE ONLY SEEMS EXPENSIVE BEFORE THE ACCIDENT.* She recalled her father, and Rose's bicycle in the trunk, the courage of a man who at the time had seemed heroic and was, in fact, only a young adult, already caught up in a process of duties and responsibilities, cast as head of household, playing his part over and over day after day with all his best intentions. From the sidewalk, she looked at Paul without him seeing her. He was alone in the agency. Sitting at a little metal desk with an enormous typewriter, meticulously placing a carbon paper between two neatly superimposed white sheets. When she went through the door, he looked up immediately, watched her walk toward him and sit down across from him, and now she felt that she had a presence. Why hadn't any casting calls, any agents or directors noticed this?

"Hey, where were you?"

"Sabine . . ."

"Huh? Where were you?"

"When?"

"When you decided not to answer the phone anymore, just like that, all of a sudden!"

He smiled.

"Can I buy you a drink? Shall we go to the café?"

"You've got a smudge of carbon, there, on your cheek. It's your fingers . . . they're stained."

He was looking at Sabine the way you look at a masterpiece, with timid admiration. Suddenly he said, astonished:

"It was raining hard at the funeral, there were ten of us at the most and it almost felt clandestine. It was very strange."

He was a halfwit, that's what he was, for months she'd been confiding in a total idiot, a nutcase.

"What funeral?"

"My father."

He reached in his pocket for a checked cloth handkerchief, of the sort only very elderly people still used, and dabbed haphazardly at the streaks of carbon on his cheeks.

"Oh, of course. Your father's funeral. Forgive me. I am truly sorry."

"Don't be sorry, Sabine, you couldn't have known."

"Oh! You didn't tell me?"

"Well, no."

"That's better! No, because . . . I'm not a good listener, but still . . ."

"Yes, still."

"Now I'd like to."

"To what?"

"Go for a coffee."

They sat at the same table as the first time, in the exact same seats. She immediately wanted to know what had happened, why he hadn't mentioned his father's death, why he'd stopped answering the phone, why he hadn't needed her anymore, why he'd dropped her, why she couldn't count on him, why she couldn't count on anyone in this city that was too big and where you never ran into anyone you knew, where you could never drop in on a friend unexpected, this city full of castes and unattainable worlds, and then she noticed she was talking only about herself, yet again, she burst into tears, and when he held out his checked handkerchief she immediately stopped crying and did like Hélène, blew her nose in her fingers, while looking him straight in the eye, to register his disgust. He smiled at her, then conscientiously wiped her snotty fingers with his handkerchief.

"That's gross!"

"No, it's not, Sabine, I change them every day, it's clean, I promise."

"Oh my God! He has a collection of cloth handkerchiefs. Like my grandfather! Did you fight in the war, too?"

That was when he stopped being so attentive, and drifted off silently into his own dark thoughts, and so, because Sabine realized that he wouldn't speak unless he were dazed, she ordered two glasses of cognac. He said, "I met my father at the Gare de Lyon. I was two years old. He had just come back from Algeria . . . the events, you know . . . In the photographs from that era, I look like a big doll with curls, on the lap of a sturdy, smiling man. I always saw my father smiling. I think his suicide was programmed, I think he held out for a long time, but, all the while, he wanted to do it. It takes time to accept pain. Your acting will get better and better, Sabine, it will be a beautiful sight to behold. You surely don't have to be Bérénice's age to play Bérénice. You need time to leave room for your pain."

He lowered his voice and looked outside, as if he were speaking to the street.

"My father was posted to the surveillance of the mined barrage on the border with Tunisia. He saw death up close and it never left him. It's hard to see, realistically, what's waiting for us. It's hard to get to know death, to . . . to provoke it, too . . . You know, Sabine, maybe I didn't answer you on the phone, but I liked the way it would ring three times, I knew it was you, it made me happy. After a while, you stopped calling and I didn't dare call you, I figured, it's too late, I thought you were disappointed, maybe angry . . . I wasn't wrong. Well! Here comes Brigitte!"

The secretary came up to them, a half-hearted ghost, and said the tax auditor had arrived. She spoke like someone with a toothache. Paul stopped her with a wave of his hand.

"Give him the ledgers, anything he wants, give him everything he wants. I'm with Sabine, can't you see? I'm talking with Sabine."

Brigitte shot Sabine an imploring gaze. In her imagination Sabine replied by giving her the finger, a clearly-drawn, insistent image. Brigitte went away again at once.

"You know, Paul, there were more deaths after the Vietnam war than during the actual fighting. Before Vietnam, people thought the end of a war meant you could forget about war. Now they talk about post-traumatic stress, a pretty nasty name for it, isn't it."

"You're interested in stuff like that?"

"Yes, I have kept a little room for other people, just a little room, yeah, a teeny tiny space."

It made them laugh. With two fingers Paul mimed how small the amount was, and repeated, "A teeny tiny space, yeah." And Sabine added, "Even smaller than that, Paul." They drank some more and felt like having fun. Paul suggested a game on the pinball machine. He didn't play well, he struggled against the machine instead of being one with it and returning the ball at the last moment, with a calculated impulse, moving the hips forward slightly together with a short, precise thrust of the shoulder. "The clumsiest guy I've ever seen," Sabine said to him, it made him laugh and it was strange, Paul's laugh mingled with the beeping of the machine, the electronic music and the sound of the score racking up in the flashing of the play field, the astonished laughter of a happy man. It was dark out when they parted, the cold early nightfall of November, and, on the sidewalk, their complicity instantly vanished, they no longer knew how to behave, and so again they said, Let's call each other yes of course we'll call each other, no really this time you'll pick up won't you, I promise get home safely, we'll call each other goodbye then goodbye take care. Sabine walked for a long time, her hands in her pockets, her body numb, her face lifted to the icy air, reinvigorating like a splash of water, night was settling in, the lights of the city, apartments twinkling behind curtains, infants in a parent's arms, people who'd bought their bread, people on their way into the wine store, people strolling aimlessly. Snatches of private life. She stopped at a phone booth to call Hélène, Michelle picked up, asked her what she was doing at the moment, so she made up a lie, she had just adapted a novel and would be staging it.

"Will it be funny this time?"

"Very."

"Ah, so much the better, because last time, your program, I thought it was some pamphlet from Amnesty International."

The next day she had dinner with Hélène in a little restaurant on the rue Campagne-Première that had withstood the passage of time—a place where, over fifty years earlier, Soutine and Modigliani and the others used to come, there was still a coal-burning stove, the tablecloths were checked, the two sisters loved the place even if the owner never recognized them, which made them a bit sad. It was a cozy, warm Paris, the inside of the beast, docile at last.

They had so much to tell each other that they kept interrupting, their words tumbling, bringing others with them, more urgent, more necessary, and they found the joy of being together again, an excited, slightly affected joy. Sabine laughed as she shared her professional troubles, turning humiliating episodes into funny stories, as if they'd happened to someone else. She was getting a little money from the state fund for unemployed artists, hardly enough to go knocking on the door of a real estate agency, but she could get by. Hélène was afraid she might bring up the topic of the studio Tavel had rented for her, but Sabine didn't mention it, and confessed with a slightly shamefaced enthusiasm that she'd been to see a fortune teller, just for a laugh, and the woman had told her she was going to meet a filmmaker and she'd be in a movie with a starring role.

"It's cheered you up no end, that's already something," said Hélène.

"Yes, I feel cheerful too, it'll work out, I believe in it, you have to believe in it, the energy feels right."

They talked about the letters they got from Mariette, short notes they didn't always understand, surely her teenage giddiness. They'd been worried when she was hospitalized and, now, they'd already forgotten their concern. They made plans to go together to see *Interiors*, the latest Woody Allen movie, the story of a man who leaves his wife with whom he's had three daughters. Woody Allen wasn't in the film, for the first time.

"Do you remember when Papa explained to us that marriage was in-dis-so-lu-ble?" asked Hélène.

"God that scared the shit out of me, it really gave me the willies!"

"Yeah, it was scary all right."

Their parents had believed that marriage was indissoluble, and the family, too, but nowadays they seemed happier without the two elder daughters; at the same time, they were hard to understand, and it felt to the girls as if they were separated by more than one generation. The fact that their parents had lived through the Second World War situated them in a remote place, that of history books and period films; their religion, too, distanced them. Nowadays love had headed in a different direction, it had cast off Christian morality, even while it invented another morality, that of a freedom that knew no limits, and that included children, whom many intellectuals agreed to view as consenting and sometimes even provocative. Françoise Dolto, Sartre, and Simone de Beauvoir had signed an open letter to the Commission for the Revision of the Penal Code: the law on the corruption of minors had to be changed or repealed, in order to "recognize the right of the child to have relations with persons of their choosing." The expression "indecent assault upon a minor" could not be invoked if the child was deemed to be consenting, if there had been no signs of violence; there was a steady stream of petitions to be signed. "If a thirteen-year-old girl has the right to take the pill, what do you think it's for?" Sabine and Hélène made their way with astonished good will into this emancipated world, where forbidding was forbidden.

"Our upbringing leaves a mark on us," said Sabine, "maybe we don't realize, but it's there, all the time, it weighs on us, it covers us like a skin, and look how sensibly we behave. It'll kill us."

"I like behaving sensibly. It suits me . . ."

"Why are you blushing, Hélène?"

"Who? Me?"

"Yes you, who else?"

"I don't know . . ."

"Do you behave sensibly or not?"

"I do."

"Ah . . . so you're practical, in other words."

"What's that supposed to mean?"

"It means it suits you, you're faithful to Arthur to keep things simple. And why is that?"

"Yes, why?"

"So you can pass your exams. That's all. Your behavior is calculated."

"That's cynical."

"No, you aren't aware that you're being calculating."

"And you, are you faithful to Mathieu?"

"Yes. But he leaves me free. Still, I don't take advantage of it. Oh, and besides, I just don't get it."

"You know, in the lab we studied the workings of the heart. It was awful!"

"Of course, the heart is awful!"

"Sabine! I mean we *really* studied the workings of the heart. How the heart muscle pumps blood through the circulatory system. We *saw* a heart."

"What d'you mean, *saw* a heart? They showed you a film?"

"The physiology teacher came in one morning with a jar full of live frogs . . ."

"Enough, I get it! Stop!"

Hélène looked outside at the white light from the streetlamps and the people passing by, always passing by, this city that never stopped. Where were they all going?

"Did you do it, too, Hélène? Did you dissect a live frog?"

"What do you think?"

"No. Of course you didn't. Forgive me."

"I was the only one who refused. The frogs were crucified. Then we had to watch their hearts beating and tear them out to put them in a physiological solution. And go on observing them."

"There's a price to pay for everything—our dreams, our plans, everything."

They felt a constant icy draft of air as the door opened and closed, so they would stiffen and shift in their wooden chairs, and the discomfort was like a slight malaise. In a hushed voice, Hélène said, "Last month, when I was still living at David's place, they had a party one afternoon, a little reception Michelle organized with people from her riding club. Michelle hired a catering assistant to come and help Maria."

"What's so special about that?"

"Just that she was extra help, from outside."

"So? What happened at their little party?"

"Nothing. Nothing happened. It's just that this woman was a mail carrier."

"What was she doing there?"

"What a lot of women do, odd jobs here and there after they've finished their rounds. Cash in hand."

"Did you see her?"

"Yes. She was at least fifty, she looked exhausted. Maria gave her the cold shoulder and Michelle said it was incredible that civil servants got paid to do nothing after two in the afternoon. I said she surely began her day at 6 A.M. and had put in her hours. Michelle didn't answer, I think she didn't even listen."

"They really are despicable, the ruling class, I don't know how you can put up with them."

"You know, David and I do disagree from time to time, about politics, about ecology."

"Wow."

Despite Sabine's irony, Hélène went on, more to feel she was on an equal footing than to convince her sister of anything:

"I told him that Giscard's second steel plan was a betrayal."

"And? What did he say?"

"He said it was time to close down the factories, because there were no more orders, and they were already I don't know how many billions in debt, and that the State couldn't go on helping the steel industry forever."

"Two years ago, Giscard said that the Lorraine should be the exemplary face of France in Europe, did you tell him that, at least? Did you even get your feet wet?"

"No. I didn't. Stop drinking, you're getting mean."

"Will you come with me to the demonstration on December 2?"

"What is it this time?"

"Honestly, Hélène! The march of the peasants from the Larzac! Bastian, remember? They've reached the outskirts now, the police prefect has forbidden them from entering Paris, but Sartre has said it's one of the worthiest struggles of the century, can you imagine?"

"It's just that I'm so busy with my studies, character divergences in natural selection, hereditary variations, and modifications of—"

"Ah! Hereditary variations! Now that's something I'd like to study!" said Sabine with a smile.

Hélène walked her back to Robert's place, the rue Raymond-Losserand wasn't far from there. They went past the squat at the end of the street, "We could live here," one of the sisters said, "Yeah, get high all day long and no rent to pay!" The place frightened them a little, but they didn't want to avoid it. They wanted to be free of their caution and fears, but their fears followed them, all the way from Aix, like the stubborn, drugged shadows who could sit for hours outside the squat and not feel the cold. A vicious wind was gusting, they walked arm in arm to keep warm, and, linked together, they formed a single powerful individual, as if poised on the same pedestal. When they parted outside number 121, with its elegant front door, they were once again simply two young women freezing in the cold night air.

"Christ it's cold. Hurry home safe to Neuilly."

"I'll call you so we can go and see the Woody Allen movie."

"It must be nice to have your own phone."

"It is. It really is."

Hélène walked to Châtelet to get the direct line, but, above all, to melt into the cold air of the street, the vulnerable nighttime world. She sometimes felt the need to be tiny, almost invisible, the way she'd been as a child. To be among others, however indifferent and mad, dangerous and lost. She couldn't get over how many people were sleeping rough in Paris—on the metro air vents, in tunnels, in phone booths. She had lived in the deep warmth of the duplex in Neuilly with all its opulence—the thick carpets, the enormous pillows, the plump comforters—a rounded universe made to soften you and slowly cut you off from the rest of the living, people who weren't likable, people who were battered—mail carriers, metalworkers, the unemployed, people who put in two days' work a day, or who didn't work anymore at all, simple folk, small investors, little ladies at post offices, little frogs with their hearts torn out. And yet, it was there in the luxurious living room in Neuilly that she had shared with David her embarrassment, surrounded by so much privilege. The night before her departure, they'd seen images on television of men and women crammed together with their children on the cargo ship *Hai Hing Panama*, like the inhabitants of a city detached from land, a cargo ship covered with tarps to protect them from the rain and sun and air, and maybe even from fear. Two thousand five hundred people, over a thousand children, and women giving birth, unable to breastfeed or protect their young ones. A ship filled with misery, motionless on the China

Sea. Driven back by the Indonesian and Malaysian coast guards, it had nowhere to go. On sheets stretched along the flanks of the ship the illegal migrants had written, *Please RESCUE us*, and they waited in the vast coffin of the sea. Their children were covered with eczema, their grandmothers had stopped talking, a few women still had the strength to sob. They were thirsty and hungry. They'd drifted a long way from Vietnam. Hélène had learned the expression *boat people*, and both she and David thought of Jersey, seasickness and whisky, the crack of dawn on the oily sea, and their laughter above the sound of the motor. Now neither one of them said anything, because what could they say, faced with this forbidden humanity, but both of them knew they had shared a sadness as heavy as shame. And yet, Hélène would not mention it to Sabine or to her parents, because it was so much easier for all of them to think of David as someone who was a stranger to compassion and sorrow, so much easier, too, to go on calling him *Tavel.*

It was a silence they were hearing in Paris for the first time, a silence struck by sticks beating the ground, the threat that was approaching with the Larzac "twenty-two," men and women and children who'd walked for twenty-four days, over four hundred miles. In silence. From his palace, the president Giscard d'Estaing said, "God be praised, in France there are institutions." The institutions would deal with them, and he would not have to receive them. Chirac, the mayor, had forbidden them entrance to his city, and the twenty-two marchers remained at the gates of Paris, on the boulevards just outside the most beautiful city in the world, and all they could see were the tall towers of apartment buildings, and red lights blinking for no reason, where thousands of demonstrators had come to join them. For over eight years, their resistance had been nonviolent, resisting an occupation that did not say its name, a colonization from within. And now, they felt the extreme fatigue of all those days marching, their nights away from home, they had crossed France, discovered it, they had walked past huge factories threatened with closure, towers of raw concrete, little suburban dwellings with their gravel gardens, they'd greeted the foreign workers from a Sonacotra hostel[12] who were on strike, and now they were eager to go home, back to the Causse, they were overwhelmed with nostalgia for their own land.

[12] Government-run residences for immigrant workers; residents went on strike in the 1970s to obtain better living conditions.

*

"Let the demonstration go by, and join the committee behind the procession, please!" shouted someone with a loud-speaker much farther along. Sabine wanted to get to the head of the procession, where the Larzac peasants were marching, she wanted to see whether Bastian was among them, but she couldn't get through, there were eighty thousand people demonstrating, and the crowd control was efficient, the Larzaciens were grouped together, in silence, far from the mass of demonstrators that followed like a fragmented body. Fathers held children on their shoulders, and the children held banners, a few lone brass bands accompanied the protest, leftist parties, ecologists, and unionists shouted slogans, *Land to the peasants, The land is for those who work the land*, and their words brought everyone back to a France that had been disfigured by war, reconstruction, industrialization, and the death of the rural world most of them had been born into.

Sabine elbowed her way forward. A girl was waving a sign, *Make Hay Not War!*, it was cold, and, when she laughed, a small cloud of vapor emerged from her mouth, she was walking hand in hand with her boyfriend, Sabine thought they couldn't be any older than sixteen, how had they found each other, they seemed so sure of themselves, so well-matched, she thought of Mathieu who was at his father's birthday party, she would have loved to share these moments of conviction and elation with him. He had simply asked her to have a good look to see whether Sartre was there, or Mitterrand, even if they would just end up buying *Libé* and read all about the protest. In the gray atmosphere of that Saturday with its pale sky, they were walking now past the fence surrounding the Parc Montsouris along the Boulevard Jourdan. Sabine kept moving forward toward the head of the parade, and it was strange to feel this connection with strangers, people who would have meant nothing to her on any other day. Nameless, yelling protesters, that's what the President in his palace must be thinking, but here, these thousands of people, who were standing up for sheep not cannons, wheat not weapons, were all the same age, the age to be alive, and they all came from the same place, planet earth, the earth of fields and of cities. Sabine could feel the energy each body released, the spontaneous alliance, the solidarity, thousands of Parisians, and people from the provinces, too, who'd alighted from their trains that very morning. One December weekend where they wouldn't be doing Christmas shopping, or going to family dinners, a December weekend like no other.

At first, she didn't understand what was happening. A shared tremor went through the crowd, a sharp fleeting charge, everyone scattered and began to run, hunched over, quick, fleeing an onslaught of teargas and Molotov cocktails. Sabine immediately thought of the Parc Montsouris, she knew she wasn't far from an entrance, she ran, protecting her face, while explosions shattered the cries of the crowd, someone screamed, "The children! Fuck, there are children here!" She began coughing and weeping, her scarf around her face, she couldn't see, she made her way toward the park, along the fence, felt a stone hit her back, she thought, "So this is war," and her throat felt ripped open, torn from her by fire, she couldn't see six feet ahead of her, but, turning around, she could make out riot police in the distance like giant scorpions, and, across from them, rioters were throwing stones, bottles, fire, the grates torn from the base of trees, "Bastards, bastards, bastards," the thought gave her the strength to keep going, even though she couldn't breathe, her lungs were burning, and she reached the side gate to the park, weeping acrid tears, vomiting onto her scarf, her feet, her trousers, it was an unreal moment, amplified by the violence, the screaming of the crowd mingled with the wailing of sirens, the rattle of helicopters, this new fear she felt was stretched above her, the precise and fleeting sensation of death.

*

She was ashamed. She was someone she never would have wanted to be, someone she had never revealed, stinking, pathetic, and stunned by fear. And so, how could this have happened? How did this boy dare to come up to her and not be disgusted, he talked to her, helped her to her feet, supported her, when she was so defeated she didn't even have the strength to tell him to leave her alone. She tried to push him away with clumsy, random little gestures, but he helped her over to a bench to sit her down, and he would wait, he said, until she felt better. She looked at her soiled shoes and felt the tangle of thorns in her throat, the oppression in her chest. The demonstration had started up again, they could hear snatches of music and slogans, the ambulance and police car sirens were moving into the distance, into an abstract Paris, if Bastian was there maybe he didn't know what had happened, the rioters were at the end of the procession, far behind the twenty-two, and Sabine knew it was over for her now, all she could do was go back to Robert's, take a shower, and wait until it was time for the news, a dispossessed spectator. The boy was still waiting, posted at her side like a stubborn dog, she couldn't see what he wanted and she thought of her parents' never-ending warnings to be wary of "strangers," in other words, everyone you didn't know, and who, if you spoke to them, would make you their prey. She could tell the boy was observing her, shooting quick glances at her. She forced herself to sit up straight, to breathe and confront the pain, and in a muffled voice she said, "I come from Aix-en-Provence."

He looked at her like someone whose patience has just been rewarded.

"And you came to Paris to support the people of the Larzac?"

"No, I came to be an actress."

The smile he gave her at that moment was something

Sabine would never forget, a smile filled with surprise and satisfaction, a perfect smile. He reached in his backpack and took out a little movie camera.

"I finished film school here three years ago. I came to film the demonstration."

Well then, thought Sabine, if fate exists, mine is surely not to be in the movies. In this park where she'd posed for her portfolio—made up, hair styled, smiling—now that she looked like a stinking dishrag, she had met a filmmaker! And when he told her his name was François, she immediately thought of Truffaut and lowered her head, humiliated and confused, even though she almost felt like laughing, and, anyway, she was sure she would laugh when she told Hélène the story, they could laugh about the scene for years, that much was sure.

"I've never seen anyone look so desperate," said François with surprising satisfaction.

She shot him a graciously ironic look, an Audrey Hepburn kind of look, she hoped, then she stood up and said she was heading home. From the way his movements followed hers, she understood that she hadn't gotten rid of him yet, but now she didn't care that much, it was all so ridiculous it had reached a point of no return. It was almost dark, and a strange tranquility hovered over their environs, as if a thin veil had drifted down with the night to stifle the din waiting to begin again. The atmosphere, as the Parc Montsouris emptied out, was desolate, the sadness that follows a failed party, where everyone leaves in silence. The Porte d'Orléans metro station was closed. On the Boulevard du Général-Leclerc, the traffic was gradually starting up again and the streets seemed lost, as if Paris were wearing clothing that was too loose. François went on observing Sabine, and, eventually, he told her that today he had filmed the demonstration, but he didn't only make documentaries; he was getting ready to shoot his first full-length feature. She heard the word as if it had pierced her physically, and she immediately thought of the fortune teller, this was it, she'd seen it all, the filmmaker, the encounter . . . In that moment, she felt as if she were waking up, she could feel again, those emotions she loved, impatience, stage fright. She asked him, trying to sound as casual as possible:

"What's it about?"

"I can't tell you just like that."

"I understand."

Bastard, she thought, he's got me, he's pleased with himself, playing the little master. She kept her questions to herself. They walked down the rue d'Alésia with its closed shops, its feeble streetlamps, as if after the virulence of the demonstration all conviction was lost. François eventually asked:

"Have you ever been in the movies?"

"Not yet, I've been too busy in the theater, I created a new concept, at Bobigny. But, well, I can't tell you just like that."

Spurred on by curiosity he quickened his step, dissociating himself from her for the first time.

"I'd been following you for a while already at the demonstration."

"Were you filming me?"

"I wanted to see how you moved."

"Do you have the right to do that?"

"Do you want me to tell you about my next film? Can we meet again?"

She raised her chin so she could look him right in the eye, and the movement also raised her body, and the sad, dimly lit street seemed as poetic as a film set by Marcel Carné; then, emerging from tragic black and white, the street regained its contemporary colors—the signs outside pharmacies, the bus shelters like luminous little cabins, the headlights of slowly moving cars and, above the leaning streetlamps, the sky splashed with stars.

It was a pregnancy Agnès was not yet about to share with the world, and the child was kept like a secret. She slept for a long time when she came home from her rounds, a sleep oblivious of everything that had been her life before—the hardship, the sorrow, the wrongs; all that remained was this pleasure of waiting, this gentle fatigue, and the distance of others. She slept in the middle of the afternoon, and she hardly heard any noise they made. Let them live without me, she thought, let them come and go I don't care, and she loved even the nausea that signaled the laborious workings of her body, everything infallibly falling in place. She moved with a slowness that was out of character, she was barely six weeks pregnant, but she inhabited an imaginary, multiplying body, she was unburdening herself of a warranted fatigue, a need for laziness. She was not surprised it had been so easy to become pregnant again at her age. The night John Paul II had been elected, she'd spoken of her desire to Bruno, and they'd delighted in it equally, with a forgotten emotion. Strangely, to be having another child liberated them from their three daughters—the way the girls, too adult now, looked at them, this family of theirs too ordinary in their eyes. This was surely what people meant by "a fresh start," this impression that life still owes you a few lovely things after all, it hasn't closed the door on you, you're free. The pregnancy had happened very quickly, as if the child had waited for permission with ethereal patience, the long patience of those who want to come into the world. In her eighth week, Agnès told Bruno. The joy of the father-to-be was immediate, and, once again, she became the seventh wonder of the world, the ideal mother, the magical woman. He placed his hand on her belly as if he saw light coming from it. He hadn't done this for his three daughters, he hadn't dared, not since the first child, the absent one. His hand was bigger than the child itself, warm and fatherly, twenty-three years on, it was the same attitude. Agnès began to have morning sickness, and headaches, then nightmares where the two children were connected, the eldest and the youngest. In some of the nightmares, they'd known each other for a long time, as if they were old babies, ancient souls; in others they merged, became Siamese, inseparable. Would not come unstuck. Fossilized. She never really awoke from these dreams, she carried them inside her like a burden. Bruno tried to reassure her, sometimes he read her a poem, a passage from the Gospel, the Song of Songs, she remained haunted, prey to premonitions, her body and her mind plagued by the same icy currents. Then she dared to say it with certainty: there was something wrong with the baby. They went to see a gynecologist, surely nowadays there must be a way to make certain everything was all right, medicine like everything else had made such progress, progress was the new air they breathed, the guardrail, the profane God. Agnès had an ultrasound exam. The black screen with its snowy images indicated the delivery date and the moving presence of an embryo. The room echoed with the sounds of Agnès's belly and her heart racing so fast she felt as if she were underwater, in some trafficked amplification of her heartbeat. The baby's heart seemed to be chasing after her own.

Bruno was reassured and thought she would be too. Far from it. She never felt the presence inside her of one child, but of several. Sick children whose ailments and defects were mingled. Night and day, she could feel her trouble growing inside her; she was oppressed, haunted by the threat of it. Bruno became impatient:

"All right! The baby is sick! Doctors are idiots. We didn't see a two-headed monster on the ultrasound, and yet, everything is going wrong. So now what?"

"What do you mean?"

"What do we do now?"

She knew very well what he meant. Even if the onslaught of hormones was changing her temperament, she had to be reasonable and admit that whatever happened, they would be responsible for this child and its soul. Bruno's new authority ridiculed her intuition and put her back on the straight and narrow; she stopped being the woman who wants a child then doesn't want it anymore, the capricious mother hopping from one foot to the other. She did ask him one thing, however: not to speak of her pregnancy to anyone, except Mariette, they couldn't exactly hide it from her, but if the older girls didn't come for a visit, they mustn't say anything to them, she would go on wearing loose clothes, and even at work no one would notice anything, so there would be no one to force them to act the happy parents, they would wait prudently for the delivery. He agreed to go along with this last whim of hers, a concession to her condition, and he resigned himself to patience. Agnès was no longer in the world of happy laziness of the first weeks, she was like a woman roused abruptly from sleep, aware she must come back but unable to, and an insurmountable space remained between her and everyone else. She was alone with herself and the sick child.

One morning, when she was waiting at the maternity clinic for her sixth-month check-up, she got the impression that all the women around her—in the waiting room, in the doctor's office, at work—all these women were carrying both promise and fear. They were pregnant and guilty. Guilty of wanting or not wanting. Guilty of their fear. Guilty of their distress. Guilty of their power. She waited and thought, "If the doctor doesn't call me now, I'm going to leave, I'm going to run away, I won't be part of the herd." But the waiting room was plunged in an immobility that seemed never-ending. No one spoke or looked at anyone else, it was a moment filled with solitude. At last, the door opened, the doctor's assistant called out a name, and a woman stood up, respect and timidity in her eyes. Why are we timid? wondered Agnès. She thought about unwed mothers, about their bastards, their ostracism, she thought about her mother-in-law's suspicious expectancy once she was married, "Well? Are you pregnant or not? You're certainly taking your time!" She thought about what they'd said to her after her little boy died, "You have to have another one right away. Have another go," her brother Thomas had said, and her sisters-in-law, so many of them and so pregnant, sitting there in front of her, knitting their pink and blue layettes, one of them had asked her if her baby had had a proper baptism by the priest and not just some emergency ritual with the midwife, otherwise he would wander forever in limbo at the gates of hell, and now, in the smell of ether and blood, the sharp smell of cold and iron, the nameless baby came back and demanded his share. Agnès stood up and left the hospital building, sat on a bench in the parking lot under a dry tree stalled by winter. She was like that tree. She had nothing more to give. This child could not be born, it was a disgrace to think like this, a crime, but shame, will, reason, love had nothing to do with the way she felt. *She simply could not do it.* This child, she knew, was swimming inside her like a toxic fish, he wasn't well, he was suffering, he was whimpering and calling for help, and yet he would never be hers. While he was suffering and growing inside her she was vanishing into a diffuse gray place where unhealthy drafts of air blew; this must be what was meant by limbo, and it wasn't that bad after all. A place with neither morality nor feelings.

V
A Singular Force

Hélène got off the bus, and they looked at each other with surprise: had so much time gone by? Mariette had grown, she was slender, her large eyes were softer; with her short hair and tanned skin, her shorts and sneakers, there was something agile and free about her, she had just turned thirteen and already looked like an adolescent, yet when she hugged Hélène, with her arms around her waist, Hélène could feel how young she still was. She was sorry she hadn't come sooner, that she'd devoted so much time to her year at university, to her exams and her articles, she had taken a different path to avoid her family and have her peace and quiet, but now that she was in Aix, she didn't think she'd be able to do without them for very long. She'd been missing her family without realizing it, like a once-loved smell or landscape that in your carelessness you have overlooked, unaware of the void their absence has left. Mariette suggested they stop for a while at the Parc Jourdan to relax a little before going back to the apartment. It was the time of day when children left their sandboxes behind, and teenagers came to sit on the backs of benches, opening their first beers, the tranquil hour of a late September afternoon. Mariette walked quickly, taking short little steps as if the ground were burning, and she smiled at Hélène when their eyes met.

"You don't look at all like a mouse anymore, you know."

"I don't? What do I look like, then?"

"You look like a squirrel, or a little wildcat."

The sweet, cruel smell of mown grass made them want to pause for a rest. They lay down under a linden tree, its pale leaves filtering a white sunlight. The park was a space where bodies came alive, searching for something. Toddlers learned to walk and to fall over, couples embraced, others sought out strangers. Alone, or frequently in a group, they got drunk, they took leave of their senses.

"Maman wouldn't allow us to come here," said Hélène. "Sabine and I believed everything she said: that every guy we saw here was going to open his raincoat to show us his dick, that they were all sex maniacs who wanted to kidnap us and take us to Marseille or Tangiers."

"Oh, right, the white slave trade . . . With me, it's Papa who won't let me use the dressing room in department stores. There are supposed to be trapdoors that lead straight to Africa."

"It's not too hard being on your own with them?"

"They've changed."

Mariette said this cautiously, somewhat solemnly. They looked, from their strange perspective, at the way the sky and the leaves mingled, both very near and very far away. Hélène sensed her sister's unrelenting presence, like when she was little.

"Did you recover all right, Mariette?"

"From what?"

"What do you mean, from what? From your accident."

"Oh, my accident! That was ages ago."

"Only eight months . . . Gosh, it smells like grass here."

"You mean weed. Yes, it's candy time."

"Wow, you're really up on things."

"I come here a lot."

"The parents don't worry?"

"They don't know."

"For sure it's easier to lie to them, when they ask you where you've been, who you were with, they're obsessed . . ."

"They don't ask."

"Wow! A revolution! I would've thought that since your accident they'd be even more worried than before."

"It was a long time ago, like I said. And I'm fine now, really."

Mariette sat up, ruffled her hair, and looked straight ahead, as if she were staring at a horizon that was vaster then the park.

"You know, I wanted to meet you at the Gare Saint-Charles, rather than the bus station, but I had to go shopping with Maman."

"You would have gone to Marseille all on your own?"

"I already have."

"I suppose the parents don't know about that, either?"

Mariette looked at her with sweet indulgence, and Hélène understood that something had changed in an unexpected way, that the rules weren't the same anymore. For a year she'd spoken to her parents only on the phone, and she'd sensed that something was being lost, was losing substance and truth. They'd exchanged their everyday news, but she hadn't really listened. Or else they'd told her important things that hadn't really interested her.

The smell in the stairwell was the same as a year ago, the same as twenty years ago, the cold smell of tiles, of gray stone steps where a hazy light was projected through the transom windows. The neighbors may have changed often, but the flimsiness of their front doors never did, vibrating slightly when you walked past, and the smell of garlic still had that familiar sour tang. To Hélène it was as if she had spent her life coming home, climbing these steps in this unchanging, insistent light.

On the threshold, Mariette was about to say something, then didn't, and the deep inhalation she had taken expired in a wordless sigh. Hélène walked in, fine needles pricking her right in her gut. Her parents were sitting on the sofa by the television, watching a quiz show. They looked at her as if they'd forgotten she was coming, the sight of her seemed to give them a shock. Bruno took her in his arms so awkwardly, it was as if he had forgotten how.

"Did you have a good trip?" her mother asked, then immediately told her what she had cooked, "Don't worry, no meat, just a few cold cuts, oh, no? Well . . ."

And they went straight into the kitchen. Hélène felt as if she had been thrust there like an inconvenient guest. Her suitcase stayed out by the door. She washed her hands at the kitchen sink and sat in her usual place. During the meal Agnès talked about the price of vegetables, about Simone Veil being President of the European Parliament, about what the neighbors' kids were studying, about Bernard Kouchner,[13] about the last time the Renault broke down, about the advantage of household soap over washing powder, about the incredible number of Dutch people buying up farms in Provence, and, finally, about how she simply could not drink instant coffee. Bruno did the serving, silently approving, earnestly trying to turn his wife's verbal deluge into a perfectly ordinary moment. From time to time, Mariette kicked Hélène under the table and flashed her a smile that was meant to be soothing. And then Agnès went completely silent. She looked at Hélène, rather awkwardly, as if she'd suddenly become aware of her endless monologue and it exhausted even her. Bruno went out of the kitchen and Mariette followed him, after running her hand over her sister's back.

"Well, here we are," said Agnès.

"Here we are."

"I missed you."

[13] Co-founder of *Médecins sans frontièes (Doctors Without Borders)*, who would later enter politics.

"I'm sorry."

Agnès shook her head, bit her lips, patted her daughter's hand.

"Don't worry about it."

Hélène was upset, perhaps because her mother had changed so much, and seemed lost, and Hélène didn't know why. Perhaps, too, because she had just heard, at the age of twenty, the words she had waited for all through her childhood, the essential words that had come now, a bit late. I missed you. Which also sounded to her like, You missed me, I was here all along but now I'm gone. And then Agnès left the kitchen, as if this confession, far from breaking the ice, had, on the contrary, cut short any possibility of discussion. So, Hélène worked out how long she had said she would stay, how many nights and how many meals, and she thought that her parents were so disoriented anyway that she could shorten her stay without them even noticing. She would have liked to call Sabine, to tell her to come, but Sabine was finishing a shoot and had asked her to get in touch only in a major emergency, which meant the funeral of someone very, very close, and in the Paris region if possible. The crickets were already chirring in the pine tree that hid the building across the way, and people were out on their balconies. Hélène could hear her snatches of conversation, peppered with casual swear words and expressions she never heard in Paris, and, for a moment, she wondered if she really had been born here, she felt like a spectator, and disappointed to be one.

She hadn't been here in over a year, but nothing had changed in her room except for the record player and Mariette's many LPs and recorded cassettes, and there was still the sour smell of Ventolin, like her personal perfume.

"Say . . . isn't Maman acting a little strange? She already sounded tired on the phone, but now—"

"Oh, she's very tired."

"But why?"

"She's constantly on sick leave, that's why. And I don't know when she'll start work again."

"But sick leave is the consequence, Mariette, not the cause."

Mariette looked at her, astonished at still being taken for the little sister, the one you had to explain the meaning of things to, and she wondered if it would always be like this, if, when she was the age her sisters were now, her life would still seem less well-informed than theirs and more uncertain.

They got ready for bed, and it was a good thing the day was over, that they no longer had to get through it together. The downstairs neighbor was taking a shower, they could hear the water running, and footsteps, and doors opening and closing, the lives of others at their most private and trivial. Hélène hoped the neighbors wouldn't make love; she'd be embarrassed to hear them with Mariette. Or maybe not. Maybe they'd have a laugh, the way she had with Sabine. She got up and went to lie down next to Mariette in her bed. Mariette was startled.

"You sleep with your socks on?"

"Winter and summer alike, when I'm not with Arthur, I love it. Move over a little, I'll fall off."

"I can't move over, I'm against the wall, it's a single bed, don't you remember?"

"All right. Now, tell me: what is going on here?"

Mariette got up and went to lie down in the other bed. She murmured, "Don't ask me."

"Ask who then?"

"Maman."

"But do you know?"

Mariette didn't answer.

"Fuck, I'm fed up with your secrecy! Has she killed someone or what?"

"Let me sleep."

"Okay, I didn't want to upset you, forgive me, Mouse. You can have your bed back now, and I'll have mine."

"I'm used to sleeping in both beds, I change nearly every night. Both of them are my bed."

"In that case . . ."

Mariette had missed Hélène so much. She had spoken to her every night for months in her head, had told her about Fabienne and Father Lavière, about Joël and Léo Ferré, Fatia and the red lights at the hospital. And then Agnès, of course. Agnès most of all. Now she asked her, "Hélène, is it true that you spent the month of August with pigs?"

"Not the entire month, no. I just went to do a report on industrial farming for the magazine. It will be out next month."

"But why pigs?"

"Because they're gentle, very intelligent animals, terrific companions. And also, because I wanted to have a better look at their living conditions . . . rather, the way they're locked up, all the torture they're subjected to. But I won't tell you about it tonight, you'd have nightmares."

"I don't think I'd have nightmares about pigs."

"I think you would. You know, for them, like for all animals raised industrially, it's less horrible to die than to live. I'll send you the article if you want."

"What name do you use?"

"What do you mean?"

"Do you write your articles under the name *Hélène Tavel*?"

"Of course not, why would I do that?"

"So they don't confuse you with Sabine. Now there are two famous Malivieris."

"I'm not famous!"

"But still . . . it's a start."

"Tell me, Mouse, how are you? Really, how do you feel?"

"You think my life is sad, don't you? I know that's what you think, but you're wrong."

"So much the better then. You have to get out, see friends, don't stay here too much, in this apartment, I mean."

Mariette didn't answer. She'd noticed that her sisters, when they came home, wished that everything were still in the same place, the place everything occupied in their memories. No doubt it reassured them to think that the past was waiting for them somewhere, like a pickle in a jar. But here they went on living, and she'd been through things that were so sad she'd told herself, "This can't be happening." And later she had simply thought, "Well, it happened."

Because it happened. And she would never forget that July afternoon at the hospital maternity ward a few months ago. It was one day that followed so many others with their burden of sorrow, and she had felt as if she were living in Mozart's *Miserere*, which she was sorry she'd ever heard in Joël's booth, and listened to so often.

When she'd asked for Agnès Malivieri's room, a male nurse had told her in a hushed voice where to find it, as if apologizing for having to direct her to that room. He could have said she wasn't allowed there, "Children under the age of fifteen are not admitted to that department, it says so at the entrance," but he gave her the room number, seeming somewhat confused. In the corridor where she passed young mothers with their duck-like gait and transparent cribs casually pushed along by pediatric nursing students, it wasn't the crying of newborn babies, filling the space like so many floating souls, that she heard, it was that damned *Miserere*, its chorus enfolding her in desolation and ethereal distress. She knocked gently on the door and went into her mother's room. A private room for a private event. She thought to herself, "She can hear Mozart, too," because on her face was that shattered astonishment, the massive incomprehension of those who live through a tragedy and are still sheltered just that little bit by their bewilderment. She kissed her on the forehead and was surprised she had done this, she had never kissed anyone on their forehead, and then she forced herself to look at her, at her and nothing else, not to be tempted to see the room. The huge void all around.

"Are you okay?" she asked. Her mother replied by transmitting, through her gaze, a little of that imploring music that rose toward an indifferent god. So, Mariette did a forbidden thing, she lay down in the bed. Agnès curled up against her then murmured in a thick voice, "Don't say anything to your father."

"I won't."

"He doesn't know you're here?"

"No."

"You'll never tell him, promise?"

"I promise."

"I was right . . . about the baby. I knew it. I knew it all along."

"Yes . . ."

"I could tell when it was coming, by the fifth pregnancy there's no mistaking it. And it goes quickly."

Mariette was struck by her words, as if by a blow. *It goes quickly*. Yes. And yet, it was far from over, she knew that, it would never end, and she thought no one should ever have the right to feel that much sorrow, to have to decide such a terrible thing. She slipped slowly out of the bed, like a fish down a rock.

"It was a girl."

Agnès stated it, factually, and, for the first time, Mariette would have liked to contradict her: she didn't need to talk about it in the past, she could have said, "It's a girl," and she thought how it depended on so little, because if it had been a boy, with an extra chromosome or not, maybe his mother would not have abandoned him. But it was a girl. And it had happened. A secret, all to herself. Mariette imagined this baby, given up at birth, and was crushed by the knowledge, and she, who for so long had sought to hear silence, now felt as if she had become that silence, because this misfortune could not be shared, it was a closed space, clearly delineated. To Bruno, Agnès would say once again that the child had not survived.

*

Mariette said nothing to Hélène, who fell asleep in the other bed with the unpleasant feeling there was something weird going on in the Malivieri family. The following morning, she showed Mariette her Walkman, put the headphones over her ears, Bruce Springsteen and *Born to Run*, the voice, the guitars, the bass flowing straight into her like liquid, and then she went off running with the music only she could hear. Mariette went out on the balcony to watch her, darting like a dancer without a partner, propelled and supported by the music. She envied her, but she knew that the Walkman, for her, would be too dangerous—all that fury and poetry, like a fix, maybe she'd never come back, or maybe she'd be less attentive to the world, and the world fascinated her, it beckoned to her and disgusted her at the same time. It was wild, it darted ahead of her so she would run after it. And she did run after it.

While she was out jogging that morning, Hélène came up with an idea that seemed as simple as it was obvious, but when she stood before for mother, she hesitated. Agnès had done the shopping and was already preparing the meal, it circled back relentlessly, the heart of the day, the ritual obsession, just like when they were little, "Maman what's for lunch when are we eating?" Hélène thought she'd say no, that she wouldn't want to leave Mariette on her own (Bruno had left for the day, they were getting ready for the new school year at Sainte-Catherine), but she said, "Yes, yes, your treat? That's nice." Mariette went out onto the balcony again to watch them leave, they were going to walk to the center of town in spite of the heat. Hélène was taller than her mother, but you would still think they were the same age, two girlfriends, their hands in their pockets, their silhouettes moving off beyond the trees, the parked cars, the red roofs of the entrenched villas, the brutal sunlight, and then nothing more. What would it be like if they didn't exist? wondered Mariette. Yes, that would be good. I wouldn't feel so sad eating all by myself while they're at the restaurant, I wouldn't be afraid of what they might say to each other, or what I have to hide. They don't exist. Ah! I feel good. I feel really good.

All the way there, in spite of the debilitating midday sun, Agnès talked the way she had the night before, jumping from one subject to the next, as if she were catching words and tossing them out at random, watching unsurprised how they fell into place to create a semblance of speech. Hélène realized that she must be taking medication, maybe antidepressants, something that was confirmed at the restaurant when she refused the rosé and asked for a pitcher of water. She couldn't stop fidgeting on her chair, as if every position was uncomfortable or slightly painful, then, suddenly, she seemed sincere.

"I'm always afraid the work inspector will come to the house when I'm not there. Of course, we're allowed to go out, but still, I feel . . . I always feel as if they're watching me, as if I didn't have the right."

"It depends on why the doctor gave you leave, doesn't it?"

"So! Mariette told me you have a thing about pigs now? But what does that have to do with those very complicated studies of yours?"

"You're right, it shouldn't have anything to do with them, except that it does, and it will, more and more. It's 1979 and we've been eating genetically modified meat for thirteen years, ever since the 1966 act,[14] it's all been extremely well organized and it's terrible, you know, all in the name of progress . . ."

[14] Law passed by the French government in December 1966 allowing genetic improvement of livestock, artificial insemination, and a raft of other measures favorable to industrial agriculture.

"No, stop! Don't you start, like all those people who criticize progress! Were you hungry during the war? Were you ever hungry even once in your life? No? So stop it!"

The couple at the next table turned and looked at them, astonished and indignant. Hélène thought she shouldn't have invited her mother to the restaurant, you have to be in good shape to go out in the world.

"When are you going back to work, Maman?"

"Not ever. I haven't told your father yet, but no, never."

"So, it doesn't really matter then, if the work inspector goes by the house and you're not there."

"Maybe not, but it doesn't stop me feeling this way, you know, as if someone were watching me. All the time. But I'm not, like they said in Parliament, 'a hypochondriac.' Apparently, people like me are adding to the social security deficit. Honestly."

"If you stop working, won't you miss your coworkers? Maman? You hear me? They were nice, those women who were at your birthday party."

"We have a new boss, he's from Paris, he doesn't get it. I don't know how his mind works; he doesn't understand a thing. He calculates time that doesn't exist."

"What do you mean?"

"Well, for example, he says we have to start distributing at 7 A.M., but the mail hasn't been completely sorted by then, and after that we have to load it, and by then it's already seven thirty, so by his reckoning we're already half an hour late, and then he says he's calculated how long the trips by bike take, he says he's done them by bike, and maybe he has, why not, but he didn't load his bike, so obviously going uphill he's going to be faster, and besides he's a guy, and he's young, so when there's the mistral, or it's pouring rain, what the hell does he care, he's sitting in the office, organizing things, well anyway, he knows diddly about it all, and he too, you know, he watches us, everything, all the time, and besides, it's silly I know, but now my shoes hurt, it's really weird, because they're good walking shoes—you remember my shoes? Well, now they hurt like hell. And then there are the dogs, ever since one bit me I've been afraid, oh you didn't know I got bitten, well I did, by this little dog on top of it, the kind you wouldn't suspect, but I had to have stitches, and, you know, it was worse than you'd think, sometimes I still feel the scar, it's sore, and my back really hurts, and then when I got my period . . . no . . . not my period . . . when I was . . . sorry. I don't know why I'm telling you all this."

"No, it's okay, it's interesting."

"Yeah, well."

They took the bus to go home. Hélène saw her mother, sitting at the back, looking out the window, her hands on her bag, on her lap. She looked like a woman who has no dreams or curiosity, a woman whose invisible fatigue has accumulated for over forty years and has suddenly broken out, like an attack, a stream of acid. She rested her forehead against the window and closed her eyes. The façades of the buildings were reflected on her face, which trembled when the bus shook. Hélène thought, "That's my mother." And suddenly in her inscrutable face she saw a singular force.

At the end of the day, she went to surprise her father, waiting for him by the gate at Sainte-Catherine. He was with a colleague and when he saw her, he introduced her, emphatically, "My daughter, who's studying biology in *Paris*! This year she'll get her degree!" The other man raised his eyebrows, as if he didn't understand, or was politely admiring, impossible to tell, but it was enough for Bruno, he now seemed like a man who was content with little. They went home by car, the synthetic heat in the Renault warmed by the sun, and the din of traffic when they rolled down the windows,

Hélène couldn't understand why her father loved the car so much, "My second home," he called it.

"I took Maman to lunch at La Rotonde today."

"And Mariette?"

"I wanted to be alone with Maman, she doesn't seem very well. I wanted to have a talk, try to find out what's bothering her."

"Well? Did you have a talk?"

"Yes."

"And what did she say?"

"Not much."

"Not much, and?"

"Well, nothing, she just said she was tired. But you know that. You look tired, too, actually."

"What is it you want to know?"

"Sorry?"

"You disappear for a year and then you're surprised to . . . to see . . . Well, we've changed, it's normal."

"I'm sorry I didn't come sooner. The time flew by."

"It's not good for your mother to stay home. Never mind the fact that school starts soon, and I don't know what she'll do all day without Mariette."

"Yes, but she needs to get some rest. Her job is really wearing her out."

"It always has. A mail carrier! I'll never understand what got into her."

"In the beginning she liked it."

"And so, you talked. About this and that, nothing special?"

"I suppose."

"That's good . . . that's good . . . that's good . . ."

"Papa?"

"That's good, good, it's good . . ."

"Papa, watch out, you're driving on the left . . . Papa?"

They were right next to the Casino supermarket, and he swerved abruptly into the parking lot. His hands were trembling, he had trouble holding the steering wheel. He switched off the ignition and looked straight ahead as if there were something fascinating in the parking lot, something he wanted to inhale.

"You want me to drive? Papa? I can drive."

He got out of the car. With his hands on his hips, he turned this way and that as if he were looking for help among the rows of cars and shopping carts. Hélène got out too, not daring to go up to him, she watched as he moved restlessly where he stood. He took out a cigarette, his hands were trembling, the matches broke before he could get them lit and he stood there with his unlit cigarette in his lips, then suddenly fell to his knees, sobbing.

"Papa . . . Don't, Papa . . . Get up, Papa, get up, there are people, please get up."

She got him to his feet very quickly, no one seemed to have noticed them and she didn't care, *she* was the one who didn't want to see it, she seated him in the car, on the passenger side, rolled up the window and closed the door. He immediately stopped weeping, as if he were stifled by the heat. Hélène got behind the wheel and drove in silence for five short minutes, which seemed so long. Now she was the one bringing her father home, it was the past in reverse, an anticipation of old age and the redistribution of roles. We are born, we change places two or three times, and we disappear. What is the point of taking so many things to heart, wondered Hélène, what is the point of all these worries since today everything has been forgotten? Everyone had tried to play the role assigned to them as best they could. Head of household. Housewife and mother. Older sister. Little sister. But with the passage of time, it was easy to see that it had all been nothing more than a vast, solitary prison.

But you don't seem to understand what I'm telling you, Sabine! He really got on his knees, there in the parking lot at the supermarket, and he was sobbing. And she's completely lost her bearings—sick leave, antidepressants, she talks nonstop, you have to go there, when you have some time off you have to go and see them. I'm really worried."

"Listen, I really don't have the strength to deal with their crisis and it's not up to us. I'm sorry, but I won't go."

"Try at least to call Maman when Papa's not there, she'll talk to you."

"But I don't want her to talk to me! There are marriage counselors for that, and there's that group of theirs, what was it called?"

"Les Foyers Notre-Dame?"

"That's it. Les Foyers Notre-Dame, well, let them go there. That's what it's for, isn't it? To help people put up with their marriage, their indissoluble marriage!"

They were sitting in the Luxembourg Garden by the edge of the Medici Fountain, an area of the garden that was sheltered from the sun and from tourists. Worried they might speak too loudly in this silent spot, they were growling softly, like two stubborn women. Around them people were reading, flirting, sleeping, regular visitors for whom the "Luco" on Sunday was a familiar place, where they could behave as they liked, but they kept their eyes peeled and as soon as an armchair was free, they'd quickly swap their less comfortable chair for it with petty satisfaction. They were at home.

"And what did you do, anyway? Other than cut your stay short and come home as quick as you could, right? When you have nearly four months of vacation!"

"I don't have four months of vacation. And they don't talk to me. I tried, they won't talk. Otherwise, I would have stayed."

"Really? I think you really came back to hide out in the university library. You have your draft dissertation and your revolutionary articles about the manipulation of porcine breeding."

"Industrialization."

"What?"

"It's not manipulation, it's the industrialization of porcine breeding. Are you finding fault with me now for writing articles for young people and earning some money?"

"Right, fine!"

Aware that they were about to break into a real argument, they fell silent, looking all around for something to distract them from their irritation, but the calmness of the people there merely reinforced their sense of defeat. The plane trees projected long shadowy shapes across the fountain that quivered in the water with a sad distorted grace. Hélène did not know how else to convey her fears to Sabine, her sense of urgency. She murmured, "The world is collapsing and you can't see it."

"But every time I see you the world is collapsing! And when it's not the parents, it's the planet!"

"What about the planet? What does that have to do with it?"

"You are constantly getting upset about something. You never stop . . . there you are, chasing shadows, voting for ecologists who never get even five percent of the vote at the European elections and who disappear the way they came."

"But Sabine, you cannot be against capitalism and not give a shit about ecology, you just can't! You can't march with the people of the Larzac and not see what's happening."

"I voted for Mitterrand and I'll remind you that the socialists got twenty-two seats in Brussels, so leave me alone! But let's not forget about you and your class consciousness!"

"Class consciousness isn't just for communists and socialists, who do you think you all are? At the G7 in Tokyo, the fact the seven even signed a declaration on the reduction of carbon emissions was thanks to warnings from scientists."

"Ah! We haven't heard from the scientists in a while! Hélène, I warn you, if you start talking about greenhouse gases, I'm out of here and you won't see me again!"

This time they really had spoken too loudly, and the looks their neighbors gave them clearly signified that they were spoiling the atmosphere.

"I'm going home to study," said Hélène.

"You do that, go study."

They knew they mustn't part like that, but what words, what gesture could have suddenly changed the course of things? They walked to the entrance to the garden, as if they were accompanying each other, and out on the sidewalk they kissed goodbye without a word and headed in opposite directions. Away from the Medici Fountain, the sun was shining generously, it opened perspectives, offered up such a beautiful late summer Sunday. But Hélène was going home to study, excluded yet again from sweet days of idle leisure. As she went back to Neuilly, she tried not to think about Sabine, or her parents, or Mariette; life, after all, *her* life, was elsewhere.

Sabine knew she had been unfair, but Hélène had no idea what she was going through, what her profession was all about. She could not be in the middle of filming *and* look after her parents. Who could understand this? She herself would never have believed it, because what was she doing, after all, apart from *acting*? Her profession was a game, nothing more—whereas her sister was a scientist involved in the most appalling discoveries, studying the life of animals as if she had created them herself! And yet, besides predicting catastrophes, what did she do? When it wasn't climate change, green algae, or nitrates, antibiotics, castration, confinement, and everything else, it was her parents who were suffering . . . But had her father really been on his knees, sobbing, in the parking lot at the Casino? The Catholic who taught at Sainte-Catherine? He did that? Suddenly, she saw the actual image before her eyes. Her father. On his knees. Her father . . . on his knees.

She refrained from calling Mathieu, because they had a pact: they wouldn't see each other until mid-September once the filming was over, and they wouldn't be in touch at all before then. They would meet up in Trouville and it would be like meeting up again after a long separation. They wouldn't take the train together, they would run into each other on the beach as if by chance, they would hesitate to kiss, they would flirt a little and then they'd get a hotel room, and everything would be forgotten, the separation, the exhausting weeks of filming, that Sabine had never imagined would be like that, but what had she imagined? She who had wanted to give her all had not known that the point was largely to hold it all back. And to wait, there among the throng of extras and crew—that busy world that paid less attention to her than to angles and lighting; to them, she was simply part of the décor, called on from time to time to come alive for a brief moment. When she had read the script, she had loved her character, Olga, passionately, and she was trying to preserve that feeling of admiration, but, as the days went by, it seemed to her that everything dissipated during the scattered moments of filming, and, to be honest, she was bored senseless.

Last December, the day after the demonstration for the Larzac, she met François in the bar at L'Entrepôt, a movie theater right near her house on the rue Pernety. It was the ideal place for an appointment with a filmmaker. Four years earlier, the film critic Frédéric Mitterrand had opened this art house cinema, with a restaurant among the bamboos, wooden tables, and a faithful parrot. Right away, from the first gaze, the director had been disappointed. He'd criticized her makeup, her neatly combed hair, her smooth look, and he'd handed her a Kleenex to wipe off her lipstick. She hesitated, remembering the girl at the collège des Prêcheurs who'd been forced by the sewing teacher to remove her makeup in front of the entire class. But she eventually obeyed, too, she wiped off her lipstick, and felt so drab she was afraid she would lose that fucking light she was supposed to schlep around with her as irrefutable proof that she was an actor the "camera will love." François was watching her, his gaze wary and impatient. Did Sabine deserve his trust? He seemed to hesitate, then he summed up his film for her, it was a militant film, he said, an *uppercut*, and he began to speak with an almost political enthusiasm, as if he were waging a moral combat. He asked her if she had read *La Dérobade*, Jeanne Cordelier's autobiography of her life as a whore—prostitute, that is? Daniel Duval had written the screenplay and was filming it with Miou-Miou and Maria Schneider. I think you're of the same caliber as Miou-Miou and Maria Schneider, when I saw you in the Parc Montsouris, looking so ravaged and disheveled, that was it, that was precisely it, that sort of animal femininity and decrepitude. What I suggest is that you take a few screen tests. For the lead. She thought he was bluffing, this was too much, the lead role, she was slipping through the looking glass, into the fairy tale. He explained that he wanted to make an anti-*Dérobade*, to show the other side, tell a different story about prostitution. His film was based on a real event, sixty-odd prostitutes who, for an entire week in 1975, had occupied the Saint-Nizier church in Lyon to denounce police harassment and repression. He had imagined their encounter with the priest who'd taken them in, and the people of Lyon who'd come to support them, it would all take place inside the church and on the square just outside, and he made it very clear, "There will be no sex scenes." She said, "It wouldn't have bothered me, I'm prepared to give my all," and in François's gaze she saw the shadow of a doubt, his eyelids half-closed, discreet irony and desire.

After several sleepless nights, trapped in an anxious, oppressive joy, Sabine arrived at the studio, looking "ravaged and disheveled" for all she was worth, to take her screen test. François wasn't there. If the tests were good, they'd show them to him. She was alone with the assistant, who was chain-smoking nervously and seemed to have no time to lose. She performed the text she'd learned for the little movie camera, a tirade delivered to the inhabitants of Lyon, "I am a prostitute and I'm a mother, just like you! I pay my taxes, just like you! And yet, the police harass me. The cops—" The assistant stopped her, that wasn't it at all, she started the scene several times over, with the impression that something sticky was clinging to her, some fundamental, inept error. A lipstick that wouldn't wipe off.

She didn't get the lead role, in the end she wasn't of the caliber of Miou-Miou and Maria Schneider, but they gave her a supporting role and the screenplay was terrific, yes, François hadn't been lying, it was an *uppercut*. And from that moment on, she lived solely for this project, a spotlight turned on her life.

And now, ten months later, there were only five days of filming left, and she could feel the weight of it. Five days not of this world, which would absorb not only her energy but also her ability to perceive any reality other than that of the film set. At every moment, even the ones she spent only waiting, there would be that hermetic break with everything that was not the film, and it seemed strange to her that people could be experiencing anything else and leading ordinary lives. During the filming, she sometimes spent entire days doing nothing—fully made up, dressed, her hair done, ready. The hours went by, there amid all these busy guys dashing around among the cables, projectors, rails, cranes, ladders, carts, a world that seemed disparate but was in fact united, it was like constantly moving house, quickly and incredibly efficiently. She would say her lines over and over, filmed from this angle or that, the same words relentlessly repeated with all the conviction and courage she could still muster, and as naturally as possible. She knew she would repeat most of them during post-sync, and Olga became a character who came and went, she didn't like her so much anymore, she had trouble telling how significant she was, and, in fact, it became clear to her early on that this wasn't even a supporting role, but actually a secondary role, like an accessory for the lead, who was Ulla, the part played by Gisèle Pirlès, a fragile-looking woman with a thin body, a lost gaze, and a rich, vibrato voice. It didn't take Sabine long to realize how well she acted, with a poignant determination to resist everything, every order and every constraint—François's stupidity, the slapdash nature of the script, the cold and fatigue. She was inhabited by a tension that gave her a unique presence that seemed destined for something beyond the film, a higher mission. A lot of the women on the set were, like Sabine, playing bit parts in little group scenes or private conversations meant to move the plot forward. Sabine learned by watching others—what they messed up, what they were good at, she liked watching Charlène, an actress her age who'd got her start very young making a commercial for soap, which led to minor parts in TV series and shows for young people, like *Children's Island* and *Recess Time.* She was fascinating, with her discreet beauty and sensuality, slender in a way Sabine would never be, with a deep, husky voice, and a freedom to her acting that gave her lines a unique and surprising tone. And just like Gisèle Pirlès, you could tell *she would be going places*. It was a disturbing intuition, which reflected the random nature of the profession, all the beauty and injustice of it.

That Sunday, after leaving Hélène outside the gates to the Luxembourg Garden, Sabine decided that since she couldn't go to see Mathieu, she would go to Paul. He lived in a yellow house in the Cité Debergue, most of his neighbors were artisans and the little street smelled of wood and lilac, of sewers too, whenever it rained a lot. Paul's house was squat, made up of little, poorly designed rooms, and he was often in the middle of repairing something—a shutter slot that had lost its plaster, a beam eroded by woodworms, patches of mildew at the base of a wall, and he talked about his house as if it were a mischievous little girl he constantly had to admonish. That was where he and Sabine would meet, because they could no longer possibly go on meeting at the agency or in that seedy bar where his secretary had come to fetch him as if he were a pupil playing hooky. When Sabine arrived that Sunday, she could hear strains of a tango by Astor Piazzolla in the courtyard, the long fugue of the bandoneon which, even when the other instruments caught up with it, spoke of solitude, the deep voice of that which cannot be shared. She opened the door a little, Paul never locked it, he was dancing with his eyes closed, and the least you could say was that he wasn't good at it, but in the way he let himself go, stumbling and off tempo, there was something infinitely sweet and infinitely free, maybe because he was unaware of how uncoordinated he was, or maybe because he didn't care. Sabine rapped on the door and said, "Knock knock!"

Paul was dancing with his arms around his imaginary partner, holding his torso very straight, bending his knees slightly, eight steps forward, eight steps back. He was counting out loud, and Piazzolla seemed to feel sorry for him, his bandoneon let out a dark, slow lament. Sabine said again, "Knock knock!"

He gave a clumsy little jump and turned toward her, his smile instantaneous. He switched off the music and he was sweating, so he reached into his pocket for a checked handkerchief to dab his forehead.

"What a pleasure to see you, Sabine! Have a seat, I'll make some tea."

She didn't sit, she lay down on the sofa. The cat reluctantly made some room for her, she curled up on her side and watched Paul rummaging about in the tiny kitchen. Either he hadn't put any gel in his hair, or else the gel had not withstood the tango, and he blew against a long strand that fell across his eyes. She shouted, "Why don't you let your hair grow, it's lovely!"

"What?"

"I said, I like it better when you don't put gel in your hair!"

He looked at himself in the windowpane, ran his fingers through his hair, astonished and talking to himself. There was something so unworldly about him that it made you want to grab him to test how real he was. What made him tick? How did he keep his feet on the ground—he seemed so immaterial, lost in some ancient poetry. Sabine got up and went over to him. He smiled, slightly embarrassed. She let him make the tea and stood behind him. His hair, too long, was curling against his neck and the collar of his impeccably ironed shirt; she gently placed her finger on his shoulder, then her palm, open, hesitant, he bent his neck, she liked not knowing what he was feeling, it was the first time there had ever been anything between them other than a cheerful camaraderie, but today she was in the mood to be selfish, to try something that might be good for her or at least surprise her. When was the last time she'd been surprised? Slowly, her hand caressed his back; the small of his back quivered, she could feel it move, he was no longer making the tea, the water in the kettle was whistling for nothing and steam was filling the tiny kitchen, she placed her cheek against his back, she didn't know whose blood she could hear beating and this was what she had always loved, mingling rhythms, sending them into a panic, like going off in a twosome. She thought something was about to happen, and that Mathieu had left her free, and she had never put that freedom to good use, she didn't even know if he was the jealous type, if she might make him unhappy. She put her arms around Paul's waist, he put his hands on hers and turned around, she met his gaze, astonished and frank, as it asked, "Why?" She put her lips on his, they were soft and slightly salty, she smiled with happiness, something new was about to happen, something unexpected. Paul responded to her kisses with a savoir-faire she would never have suspected, she would have preferred for it to remain playful, but he was taking this seriously, he led her into his bedroom, continuing to kiss her, and he made her lie down on the bed, before slowly lifting her skirt and placing his face between her thighs.

As she walked home to Robert's place the daylight was ebbing, and she felt blue. She wished things could have happened in a different way, but it was too late. How had Paul come to know so much about female sexuality? When she asked him, he replied that he'd been initiated when he was very young by a much older woman.

"You see, Sabine, it was sort of like private lessons. She showed me, physically, concretely, where your pleasure is born, what I have to do to make you come, it was very precise, and very sweet, too, as if I were opening a music box."

Now Sabine wondered how she would close it again, that box, because Paul had given her pleasure of an intensity she had never known, she didn't know an orgasm could last so long, she'd heard herself cry out, unable to stop or control herself, it was awfully embarrassing, especially when she realized that Paul's bedroom shared a wall with the house next door, but he simply said, "Well, now everyone knows that you've come."

Robert was on the telephone, absentmindedly stroking the areca palm that stood before the window in the living room and let in only a morbid half-light. Sabine stood in the doorway to listen, his eternal monologues to his wife, but there was a new emotion in his voice, it sounded as if this time he really expected her to answer.

" . . . dreams . . . we know that dreams, what happens in that world, it's the truth, we know that . . . Do you feel it, too? Dreams don't lie, don't you agree? We can meet in dreams, I've always known that . . ."

Then he sensed Sabine's presence.

"Talk to you tomorrow, my dear. Don't catch cold, will you, it's almost dark. Mademoiselle? You can hang up now . . . Cover her well, she gets cold, yes, even in summer."

To Sabine he said, as if still thinking about it, "At my bridge club, a fellow told me that people with dementia aren't that way completely. Well not always, I mean, not all the time. My wife is here after all . . . she is here, don't you agree? She's a spiritual being, isn't she?"

"I don't know, Robert. I don't know at all."

"Lately, I've been dreaming about her almost every night, it's as if she were coming home. There is a part of her that is . . . intact. Hidden, but intact, I swear, Sabine. I'm going down to buy some vol-au-vents, would you like to have dinner with me?"

"I have to leave at six in the morning tomorrow, I'm going to bed, I'm tired."

"It's the final week, isn't it? After that you'll get some rest."

"The producer has seen the rushes . . . and he said it's no good. Not what I'm doing, the film . . ."

"Don't you worry."

"We have to shoot a new scene tomorrow, a scene that isn't in the script, and I'll find out about it during the makeup session."

"Maybe that will be a good thing?"

"The producer thinks the film isn't raw enough."

"Ah . . ."

"And skin, too, he said there's not enough skin."

"Well, I'm going down. Are you sure you don't want a vol-au-vent?"

Mariette didn't know what music to listen to anymore, and, everywhere she went, she was bored. Nothing seemed authentic to her or really sincere. Life was made up of arrangements and little pacts. She'd started the school year at Les Prêcheurs and it was just as she'd expected, endless. The teachers were overwhelmed and didn't like their pupils, but what was there to like in these classrooms where thirty or more pupils were learning groupthink and life in a group? Whenever she opened her mouth, all the pupils would murmur in unison, *Little genius little genius little genius*, and sometimes she envied the dunces and came to dread being called on, because she always knew the right answer, it never failed, *Little genius little genius little genius*, what a bore. Sometimes she'd seek respite in the Church of the Madeleine, where she liked to light a candle and sit down. She liked empty churches, or Joël's booth before he put the music on, or white pages in her notebook, and she always loved the wind in the trees when she lay underneath. The sky absorbed everything, and weightlessness said clearly that all this would pass, a dissipation of breath and all vital organs, and, in the meantime, you were stuck on the ground and there wasn't much to understand other than confusion and fear. Fear was everywhere, it took surprising forms and strange detours. Before giving up her little girl, her mother had asked for her to be baptized. She was afraid she might go to hell. This never ceased to amaze Mariette. Original sin. Souls in purgatory that must be redeemed, their collection box was installed at the entrance to the church. Thus, the man who preached love had given birth to a threatening religion. She remembered a catechism class two years earlier, when the priest had explained to them that an unbaptized person went straight to hell, and if ever any of them were witness to an accident, and if the person in the car seemed mortally injured, they must baptize that person immediately, and to do this, it was enough to say, "I baptize you in the name of the Father and the Son and the Holy Spirit," to make the sign of the cross and, above all—this was more important than anything—splash them with a little water on their brow. The pupils had asked concrete questions—where would they find the water if they didn't have any with them, if there was none in the car, if there were no convenience stores or gas stations nearby? Well, replied the priest, all you have to do is open the hood of the car and take a little water from the engine. One boy had pointed out that the water would surely be boiling, and the priest had run out of patience. "You're afraid of burning your hands when you can save a soul from hell? I can't believe it!" Neither can I, thought Mariette, I can't believe it.

When she was in the street now, she kept her eyes open. Lying under the trees, she closed them. Listening to the sound of the wind and the leaves, this supple breathing where the light was dancing, she'd tidy things up a little. And that is how she came to give a name to her little sister: she called her Xmas, the X replaced *Christ* (who protected her anyway, that she knew), and the X had a certain significance, because it was the beginning of the story, the mark of her little abandoned sister's birth.[15] It was under the autumn trees, with their vulnerable

[15] In France, children who are given away at birth are known as "né(e) sous X," literally, "born under X," to signify the anonymity of their parentage.

branches, that Mariette decided she would go and see her. I will never abandon Xmas, I will always take care of her, when I come of age I'll adopt her, I'll introduce her to my sisters. All afternoon she was elated by her decision, but, by evening, the excitement had dissipated somewhat, and she left the Parc Jourdan to walk home through the autumn chill, which reminded her of previous autumns, a season that always seemed to be walking backwards toward her gloomiest memories. Instead of going home, she went to the Cours Mirabeau and waited for Joël to close his shop. When his day was over, he often found her like that, waiting for him outside the shop, as if she just happened to be going that way when he was closing. He liked it better when she came in to discover a composer, when he could do something for her in one way or another. But since her accident the previous year, he'd avoided playing artists who might upset her the way Léo Ferré had with Baudelaire's poems. That evening, without even greeting him, she said, "I have a secret to share with you."

For the first time, he invited her to his house. He lived on the rue Boulegon, and the smell of aniseed wafted over the street from a nearby bakery. The entrance to his old building oozed with moisture, there were cracks in walls that were covered with saltpeter, and a vile stench came from the toilets on the landing, enough to make you gag. Joël's apartment on the top floor looked out on the red tile roofs of the old town, and the sky as a backdrop to their ancient forms conferred an intimate poetry on the limited horizon. Through the open windows the fresh air smelled of the garden as well as of something faintly withered. The apartment had two little rooms, a very basic kitchen, and a windowless bathroom. The furniture all came from flea markets, and although nothing seemed to go together, the place had a unity and even a certain comfort about it. Mariette felt strange to be at Joël's place, she was as surprised as when, as a child, she would run into her teacher in the street—this incongruent displacement of a person to whom you've assigned a single place and function. On the wall, there was a black-and-white poster of Brel, Brassens and Ferré, and the framed photograph of a man in uniform, with stripes on his white cap and his blue tunic covered in medals, and a gaze full of a stern kindliness.

"Is that your adoptive father?" asked Mariette.

"It's my admiral. I owe him a lot."

"Ah . . ."

"I did my military service in the Navy, you know."

"I see."

She hadn't come to listen to Joël's story. She sat down and, without further ado, told him about Xmas. He listened with an emotion that seemed to come in little bursts, his head bent, as if he really did want to disappear behind his black hair. She couldn't get over the fact she was talking about this story with someone, it was easy, a simplicity in the telling.

"That's what happened. And now I'd like to find her. I want to know how she's doing."

He was troubled, and he felt as if he were looking for someone else's words—a singer's, a poet's—to speak for him, but nothing came. And since he was too fond of her to lie to her, he said, "You don't have the right to see her."

"But I won't say who I am. I have her date of birth, right, and the name of the hospital. And that's important, in order to find her, I know it is. And I won't ask for anything, I'll just look at her, that's all. I won't speak to her, I'll look at her."

"Mariette . . . In France abandoned babies are adopted very quickly. Your little sister has already found a family, believe me."

And he told her a story, the possible story. "They kept Xmas for ten days at the hospital maternity ward, in a secret room you had to have a code for, and where a pediatric nurse looked after her night and day, and then she was taken to a nursery in

Marseille for the duration of the withdrawal period. In case your maman wanted to keep her after all. And then when she was two months old, she was adopted."

"But Joël, what sort of family would want a little girl like her?"

He hesitated for a moment before replying, "A Catholic family."

She wept for the first time since Xmas was born, furtive tears that she wiped off with her sleeve. Joël explained to her that there were a lot of Catholic families who applied to . . . he almost said Save. He almost said Love. What he did say was Take. A baby with Down syndrome. So that dream, too, she would have to let go of, Xmas would never be her little sister, and she would never need her.

They parted almost immediately after that. What else was there to say? Mariette walked home through the city night with its streaks of artificial light and its nocturnal birds, and life seemed long to her, an enclosed territory bordered with prohibitions. For how long? And how far?

Little genius little genius little genius . . . Mariette began playing hooky, an expression she liked, the prospect of playing was much more attractive than sitting on the school benches where Sabine and Hélène had sat before her. "Oh! The third Malivieri sister!" some of the teachers would say, marveling at Hélène's career and deploring Sabine's, no one ever turned out the way they imagined. It was easy to skip class, all Mariette had to do, when she came back, was to stop off in the supervisors' office and show them her parental communication notebook where her absence letters were already written. Filling them out and imitating her parents' signature was child's play. The collège was an hourglass, where the years drained away one after the other, regular and boring, batches of pupils who then either went on to the lycée, or were sent to do an apprenticeship, leaving the teachers relieved to have gotten rid of pupils from whom they could expect nothing, and to whom, in any case, they had never promised a thing.

One day, Mariette thought it was time to gain some independence, and there was only one way to do that: she had to earn some money. Babysitting was out of the question, she avoided children. House cleaning was too boring. Joël's boss didn't need anyone in the shop and she wasn't old enough to work legally. And then she ran into Laurence one day on her way out of Chez Béchard, the fancy pâtisserie on the Cours Mirabeau. As usual, Laurence had loads of shopping and was badly dressed and joyful, she always seemed to be overflowing with energy, and running into her made you want to celebrate something. She asked for news of Agnès, and said that if she didn't come to see her, she herself would go and get her, and Mariette could tell her she'd said so. Then she informed her that Marius, her gardener, had died the previous month of Parkinson's disease. He hadn't been able to do much for several months already, but she hadn't wanted to let him go, so he stayed on at the *bastide* in his little cabin until the end. Mariette offered to replace him, and, even though she knew nothing about gardening, Laurence agreed and offered to pay her five francs an hour. They slapped hands on it then embraced, laughing. Mariette hurried home to write and tell Hélène her incredible news.

Sabine had said, "I'm ready to give my all," and thus far she hadn't given much other than her presence, her fatigue, and her hours of waiting. Today the makeup artist wiped the sponge over her neck, her shoulders, her breasts, her belly, her thighs, and her buttocks, slowly and meticulously, and, in the mirror, Sabine could see her robust body, left strangely bloodless by the foundation, but protected, too, as if the makeup created a second skin on top of her own. The makeup artist said, "You mustn't sit down, it'll leave marks."

"I know."

"If you need to go to the bathroom, now's the time."

"I'm fine."

"You're not cold?"

"I'm stifling."

"Do you want a fan?"

"No."

"Some water?"

"No thanks."

Now the makeup artist was at her feet, patting every toe with her sponge, she felt like saying something to reassure Sabine but didn't. She would have liked to tell her she was pretty, that everything would go well, that the crew would be reduced in number, that her partner was kind and that they'd come and get her soon, she wouldn't wait very long this time. But she knew that sometimes it was best to leave the actors to their solitude. She'd been in the profession for twenty years and she could tell when it was time to speak and when to stay silent. When it was time to be motherly, discreet, and efficient, before they went into the light and were swallowed up by it. Before it turned unforgiving. She could tell that Sabine was shivering, making an effort to breathe the way she had learned, in order to relax, through her belly, like babies.

"Do you have only water?"

She immediately took two little flasks from her overalls.

"Whisky or rum?"

Sabine chose the rum and said, "I was in the Cochet course."

The makeup artist knew what was happening, fear settling in, an uninvited partner.

"I have big thighs."

"You're lovely, your skin absorbs the light very well and the DP is one of the best, you'll see, the result will be beautiful."

The litany.

"There, I'm done. I'll leave you for a moment, I'll be back in five minutes."

She went out while Sabine stood there in the tiny room in the presbytery where they'd set up a makeup room for her alone, but very soon everyone would see her, and maybe it would have been better to be naked among the other actors, to laugh and act as if it were all completely natural. And absolutely vital for the role, François had said, scratching his neck.

"It's a story about the body, prostitution, the producer was right to say it's a story about the body."

"And . . . and am I the only one who has . . . this sort of scene? Does Charlène have one, too?"

He blushed suddenly.

"Charlène? Of course not! Only you. We're counting on you. The producer stretched the budget a little, but I had to cut two sequences from the script. With a scene like this you'll get noticed by the big boys, they'll talk about it, if we pull it off, they'll talk about it."

The reception given to *La Dérobade*, "a swamp of platitudes" according to *Le Monde*, plus the fact it was rated exclusively for audiences over sixteen, and the news that the actresses had suffered from ruptured eardrums, fractured tailbones, and bruises all over their bodies was making people talk; François was claiming to be an activist for women's rights to avoid criticism.

"You know, Sabine, this is a politically engaged film. For women, I mean."

"An uppercut."

"Exactly!"

She thought about Racine, a verse in *Iphigénie* coming suddenly to mind, *My glory less dear to you than my life?* This need of the absolute, this total gift of self and excessive sense of honor, elevating love to a sacrifice. Where were the extraordinary heroines, passionate about God, about vows, about immortality? The tragediennes and the amazons, the secluded women and the wild women, all those who dare and who resist? She recalled the images she'd seen on television of Iranian women demonstrating against the compulsory wearing of the veil. That's it, she thought, I'm going to tear off the veil, no more obedience to the veil, I'm going to do what I've been waiting to do for twenty-three years, give my all, and it will be like taking flight, like freeing myself from obedience. But suddenly she felt a cramp in her foot and the pain took her breath away, shit, she thought, holding her foot to stretch her leg, shit, and now on top of it I've got tears in my eyes, the makeup will be ruined, ruined . . .

The makeup artist put a bathrobe over her shoulders and went with her onto the set; there was a mattress on the floor covered with a white sheet, the lighting was already set up—projectors, screens, mirrors, frames, canvases, cloths, and panels—and the camera hovered close to the bed like a technological ogre: Sabine knew it would not miss a thing. Her partner was lying naked on the mattress, they greeted each other with a nod, François needed to speak to Sabine, his tone was protective and intransigent and she lay down next to the young man, who whispered to her that he'd eaten garlic to maintain some distance between them, and that he would like to apologize in advance in case he got a hard-on, and also in case he didn't. She would have liked to tell him that in either case she would not be offended, but she simply nodded, the smell of garlic gave his words a sickly ponderousness, and his penis, taped to his thigh, seemed a little pitiful to her. François sat down next to them to tell them what, exactly, he wanted, he was really concerned about what he called his "choreography," and Sabine wondered why he suddenly had an opinion when for over three weeks a certain vagueness had reigned over the set, interspersed with arguments between François and his DP, who bluntly put him in his place and set up the camera where he wanted it, "for the good of the film" and of his reputation.

"This is not a love scene," whispered François, "it's the scene of a struggle, the prostitute's body taken by a man who isn't going to pay her. He's a journalist, he's at the church doing his investigation, and he wants her, but doesn't want to pay her, which is the whole point, do you see how humiliating this is? But she . . . she—and this is what is interesting . . . the ambiguity—she goes along with the scene, I think she'll even come. I don't want us to know for sure. I want to keep it mysterious. But he takes her selfishly. She is there and he helps himself."

"Which means?" the actor asked, timidly.

"No tenderness."

"Why are they naked on the mattress if he's not showing her any consideration?"

"We'll shoot the . . . the, uh, tomorrow . . . the bit where he undresses her, the first penetration, the beginning of the sequence, we'll do that tomorrow. It will be more comfortable this way, for a first scene between the two of you. I would rather go easy on you, the better to take you further . . ."

Sabine felt like calling Paul: what would he have to say to this idiot?

"Get out of the way, then," she said.

"Sorry?"

"You're on our mattress, we've got to shoot this scene, move it!"

He looked at her with a vexed respect and left the bed.

"What a jerk," the actor murmured, looking Sabine in the eyes.

Their faces were right up close, and in spite of the pervasive wafts of garlic, they laughed like two children.

"The king of jerks, you mean," answered Sabine.

They agreed. And they already felt better.

François shouted, "Everyone who has no business on the set, out!"

And to them, "Okay guys, this is it now, for all you're worth, you play the situation, the whore and the journalist."

"The whore my ass," murmured Sabine.

"No, hey, you two, stop laughing! Gaspard—"

"Is your name Gaspard?"

"—on top of her, please, we're filming your skin close up, don't hide, be generous, kids, give yourselves, I want to see your face Sabine, okay let's go. Now . . . Gaspard, lie on top of her . . . No, hey, stop laughing! Lie down, stretch out all the way, she's well-padded, she can bear your weight. Come on, stop horsing around, okay? Perfect! We're with you. We're with you. Fantastic. Now, concentrate, kids."

That evening, when she left the studios at Bry-sur-Marne—the fake church, the fake streets, the artificial light, and the simulated sex scene—Sabine felt only a huge desire to sleep, but she knew that no sooner would she get to her room, no sooner would she lie down on her bed, than her mind would begin to dwell on things and try to understand what had just happened. She asked the assistant who was driving her back to Paris to drop her off at the Picpus metro station. She didn't want to give Paul's exact address, she wanted to mark a clear separation between the filming and her private life, if she could. She wanted to get away from that crew she lived with all the time and where they didn't really have any secrets from each other—their grumpy expressions in the morning, their fatigue at night, the cafeteria gossip, the affairs, their moments of hostility or mutual attraction, eventually they knew each other inside out without ever being truly close, because they'd be parting soon in any case, and they'd have to forget about each other, go home and go back to being the husband, the wife, the daughter, the parent, and there was no way they could communicate those moments of emotional upheaval they'd all gone through, as if they'd been constantly thrown against each other.

"His breath stank, his feet were icy, his cock was taped to his thigh, his skin was covered with red blotches from the stress—we had to interrupt the scene more than once for the makeup woman to hide them—he was moving on top of me and moaning, and all I could hear was his pain, so by the end of the eighth take I was fed up with his suffering so I closed my eyes, threw my head back, I had my hands on his lower back as he was moving and I kept saying to myself, over and over, I like it, I like it, I like it oh my god, I like it, I was moaning, I moved my head from side to side, I was imagining things, I called on all my fantasies, actually I was making my own film . . . Oh, it was so funny! And . . . and that's when it happened. Damn!"

"What?"

"Ah, don't tell me you can't guess, Paul. Not you!"

"No, Sabine . . . Sorry."

"Really?"

"Oh . . . oh, forgive me! I just got it."

She was torn between a nervous desire to weep and a sincere desire to hit him, how could she have climaxed while filming that scene, how could she have come, unwittingly, and in front of so many people, how could she have forgotten they were there, to the point of believing what she was telling herself inside in order to mime the fucking scene?

"I'm ashamed, I'm so ashamed, I didn't think it could happen."

"But Sabine . . . you're getting all worked up over nothing."

"What?"

"Is it really such a big deal?"

She looked at him as if he were the stupidest idiot on the planet, which might be true, but the previous Sunday, he had given her such an orgasm that she could not treat him as an innocent party.

"But you know this is all your fault!"

"My fault?"

"Oh, stop acting all sensitive! You made—you made—Ah!"

"Go on, Sabine, be vulgar, it'll do you good, and it's just between us."

"But what are you, anyway? Some giant pervert? A bastard?"

"Be vulgar, it'll be more sincere, and nothing can shock me, go ahead."

"You . . . you . . . you made my pussy explode, is what you did! With your 'expert's' cunnilingus!"

"There you go, isn't it easier now?"

"I was thinking about you during that fucking scene!"

"And, so, it went well, didn't it? I mean, the scene was a success?"

"A great success."
"And everyone thought you were faking it?"
"Obviously."
"Perfect. Shall I open some Brouilly?"
"I don't give a fuck about your shit wine!"
"Brouilly and spaghetti? There you go. Some music?"
"No, I hate the stuff you listen to, it's so . . . drippy."
"Drippy? Piazzolla? Well, then . . ."

He prepared the meal, aware that he had to make the most of this evening with her. She would go away that night and never come back, she would never forgive him for what had happened, in his room and on the set, and before long she would go back to Mathieu, the man who was elusive but with whom she could be part of what people called a handsome couple, a man she had to fight for, because she had an instinct for conquest and would never admit defeat. Shouldn't he tell her, before she left, that he was in love with her? I love you. I love you, Sabine, I love you . . . but if he did that she would leave before the first glass of wine, and that would be terribly selfish of him, she had to drink a little and above all have something to eat. He looked at her, she'd unceremoniously shoved the cat out of the way and was resting now, curled up on the sofa. Don't forget this, he thought, never forget how she lay down on that sofa, never forget that, once, that girl was in your arms, that once, that girl needed you. He looked at her for a long time and murmured, "Thank you Sabine, I will thank you my whole life long."

Agnès began hoping that the work inspector would find her and report her. That he would come and see she wasn't sick but was conscientiously adding to the social security deficit, and that, without even bothering with a reprimand, he would get her fired from her government job and it would be a relief. She'd had enough of feeling his meticulous, invisible presence, she was incapable of going back to work or of telling Bruno the truth, she was incapable of more or less everything. It was the end of November and chilly, the morning she decided not to wait for the inspector anymore; the milky purity of the sky was nauseating, she was all alone in the apartment and in the building, too, maybe, because everything was silent, she went from room to room and told herself she ought to do some housework. And shopping. And make a meal. She packed her suitcase, took the bus to Marseille, and then the Mistral Express to Paris, and the metro from the Gare de Lyon to the Gare Montparnasse, where she caught a train to Rennes. She slept for a few hours in a seedy hotel, took the first train to Laval the next morning, and from there a bus to Entrammes.

By late morning, she'd arrived at the abbey of Notre-Dame-du-Port-du-Salut, introduced herself to the innkeeper monk who ran the tiny shop that served as the reception. She'd made a reservation by telephone, they were expecting her. The monk asked her if she'd brought sheets and a towel, and she said no, so he provided them for her, indicating a ridiculously low charge, then he reached for a key and led her to her room. They went under a stone arch, and, even though it was very high, Agnès instinctively ducked her head, her feet on the gravel made a timid sound, drowned out by the solid flapping of the monk's sandals as he took his long strides.

The room was tiny, without a bathroom. (The toilet was at the end of the corridor and the showers in the basement.) It was dark and basic. A single bed against the wall. A sink with a mirror above it. A desk and a chair facing the window, which looked out on a little garden surrounded by a stone wall. She could hear the sound of water, the Mayenne flowing just behind them, breaking against the locks. Before leaving her, the monk told her the times for the liturgy—matins, lauds, terce, sext, nones, vespers, compline, and vigil, and on seeing her lost, concentrated expression, he told her that all the times were printed on a piece of paper on the desk, she could attend the services if she wanted to, she could take part in the meals with the other people on retreat, she could stay as long as she liked, and, without waiting for an answer, he left the room, his tall figure bent forward in his white tunic with a thick sweater underneath.

She turned on the little heater, made her bed, put her pajamas under her pillow like a child, removed her watch and put it away in her handbag, she was tired but too disoriented to rest, and so she went out of the room, "MY room," she thought, as well as, "My first room," because she had always shared all her rooms: as a child, with the two brothers born just before her, and who thought it was fun to go over to her bed at night and wake her with a start (she had never understood why it made them laugh so much), two boys who were kind and rather naïve, André and Benoît, driven half mad by the chastity imposed on their bodies flooding with hormones, two frustrated, likable boys. And they didn't leave home much before she did, so they lived together for a long time, the three of them, in that huge room with its strangely high window, a former storeroom that had been converted into a bedroom. Agnès would get changed behind a screen, and almost every night the two boys, after climbing into one or the other's bed, would silently masturbate one another into a towel that they quickly washed in the morning and put out to dry on the radiator, which was noisy and not very efficient. She never knew whether their goings-on were consensual, whether one boy had power over the other, she was simply happy to get away from it. After their successive departures for their military service, two little beds were set up for her older siblings' children, born one after the other without a pause, and they slept there next to their aunt. Before long she was faulted for taking them into her bed when they cried; they hardly knew her. Agnès married Bruno at the age of eighteen, a marriage of love and flight which enabled her to leave the shared childhood bedroom and move into the one which would remain, until death did them part, their conjugal bedroom.

Across from the building where the visitors stayed, she could see the wooden door of the church and the walls of the abbey, where she was not allowed. The Cistercians lived on prayer, work, and silence, and a very unusual tranquility emanated from the place, the intransigent tranquility of those whose repetitive, concrete gestures serve a radical humility. For a moment, she felt as if she were in a place she had once known in a dream—one of those sweet, misty dreams that take you nowhere but leave you with the impression of having known an elsewhere that might resemble death, were death a benign thing.

She found the towpath that went along the Mayenne, toward a horizon that opened onto snow-covered fields edged with trees; the naked branches of oaks and chestnut trees dissolved into the mist rising from the river, nature gorged with water, with the smell of humus and heather. The sky was dark with heavy-shadowed clouds, the lockkeeper's house looked like a model, small and trim, surrounded by rose bushes that had no blooms in this season, but it was easy to imagine them in the warm months, full of pride and color, well-suited to the nature of the people living there, who opened and closed the locks and shared beer and conversation with the passing boatmen. The abbey bell rang out, Agnès counted each chime to find out the time, but once the bell had fallen silent, she realized she hadn't counted to the end, she was absent-minded, vaguely dazed, she decided not to walk any further. She was bone-tired.

The room was already warm, she removed her trousers and kept her sweater on and lay down. How good it was to smell the clean sheets, her eyes were burning, she fell asleep at once, a passage without transition from one world to the next, she just had time to grasp how delicious it was before lapsing into a deep sleep that nothing disturbed, she slept until noon the next day, when hunger and a need to go to the bathroom woke her. She went out into the deserted corridor, hopping along the freezing tiles to the toilet, then returned to her bed and quickly fell asleep again, aware this time that she was entering an infinitely peaceful world where, she knew, she could let everything go.

Bruno found a short note on the bed, *Don't be angry with me*. It wasn't signed, but it didn't need to be. He put the paper back on the pillow, went out of the apartment, got into the car and drove for a long time, until nightfall, smoking one cigarette after the other and wondering what those words were supposed to mean. He understood that Agnès had had to go away, he even understood that she'd needed to be away from him. He knew that misfortune does not bring people closer but, on the contrary, drives them apart, because unless a person decides to exhibit their pain for all to see, most people will have an instinct for dignity, and it was better to disappear than to weep on one's knees in a supermarket parking lot. There was something elegant about that need for solitude. But it was the first time he didn't know where his wife was.

He had always liked driving at night, through the hours as they led one into another with none of the landmarks afforded by light. He liked this dark, full time, it gave him a feeling of freedom and even privilege. He also liked to drive barefoot, to feel the vibration of the pedals against his skin, he could relax and let himself go in spite of the speed, his feet, gently nettled by the pedals, kept him vigilant. He didn't understand why Agnès had left in secret, as if she'd been captive, but maybe she needed that, too, that feeling of escaping, he didn't know, he didn't know much to be honest, he got the impression he'd been lagging behind and hadn't seen it coming, he was still this man who was completely out of touch, but who was loved for all that, he didn't really know why. Agnès had refused to talk about the death of the little girl, and the death obsessed her like an unforgivable sin, her pain was physical. He didn't dare say that he missed the child and had loved her, too, even if he had never carried her. Pregnancy, something he would never know, was his failing, he was the spectator to a powerful, threatening mystery. He felt as if he had always lived with Agnès, and he rarely thought about his life from before. Over time, his childhood had become a fairly blurry zone, belonging to a little boy with a shaved head and a dreamy smile, as depicted in the photographs that showed him among boys in shorts and girls with dark braids, his brothers and sisters. It was so long ago, years without tenderness he wished he had never known. Agnès was not the second part of his life, she was all his life, a life now bracketed between two lost children, a terrible sorrow without memories.

After driving late into the night, he went home and found Mariette sitting by the telephone, worried sick. Obviously, she'd found her mother's note in the bedroom, and she figured that her father had gone looking for her, but how long it would take, she had no idea, and she was relieved to see him come home, even if he'd come without her mother. Those hours alone in the apartment had resembled what she thought her life might be after a disaster, or war—she'd find herself in the apartment as if in a huge crater, an all-forgetting land, blasted apart. Had the Malivieri family lived here once upon a time, had daughters been born here one after the other, each one ushering in a radical change that placed everything that had come before them in an irretrievable past?

That night, they didn't talk about Agnès's disappearance;

each of them had his or her reasons to understand or be sorry about it, that wasn't the issue. They had to live together without her now for the first time. Mariette offered her father a little curried rice she'd made, he accepted, and she stayed by his side while he was eating in what seemed an oddly empty kitchen, and, in that artificial peace and quiet, their new lifestyle settled in of its own accord, they would go on living while they waited for Agnès to come home, as the earnest songs say, and when she came home, well, life would simply resume, because that was its very principle, and the only hope they could place in it.

The morning after their first scene together on the mattress ("that violent fusion," said François, deadly earnest), Sabine and Gaspard met again on set. Once again "everyone who has no business on the set" was made to leave, and François whispered his artistic viewpoint to them, looking like an angry conspirator. What they were about to film was in fact the beginning of yesterday's sequence. There would be a cut between this scene, where they would stand in the corridor, and the one on the mattress. An abrupt cut. The image of the two of you together, he said. But part of a continuity all the same. This was a planned but free choreography, the point was to follow it but let themselves go, to be precise but surprising, to go far but stay within the boundaries.

Gaspard, standing in the narrow corridor, was supposed to undress Sabine, brutally, but without tearing her clothes or banging her head too hard against the wall; then he would mime an expeditious penetration, full of gasps, panting, and shudders. He was so afraid of hurting her that he couldn't do it. No matter how often they restarted the scene, he just couldn't do it. These were gestures he simply did not know, an aggressive behavior that paralyzed him. Sabine decided to help him: clinging to him, standing on a box that made her a little taller than him, she pulled him to her while pretending to be trying to get away, she found his lips while acting as if she were avoiding them, and before long her body was nothing more than a combination of elements to be controlled—help Gaspard, guide him, lift her thigh way up, lower her shoulder so she wouldn't hide her face, stay in the frame, be careful not to slip, she was at the controls of a robot-body, caught between a desire to laugh hysterically and extreme fatigue. It took all day, fifteen takes, of which fifteen seconds would remain if all went well.

François was elated, talked about *Going Places*, *Immoral Tales*, and even *Emmanuelle*; his films, he said, would be associated with the end of the great bourgeois hypocrisy of the years before May '68. Sabine's body was covered in bruises, her shoulders and buttocks grazed from rubbing against the wall, and she got a visual migraine, bright flashes appearing frenetically before her eyes, threads of light beating to the rhythm of her blood. She wished she could go and lie down in the dark, alone, for a long time. Herbert, the DP, came to see her in her dressing room. He was middle-aged, inventive, discreet, and efficient, he had knocked on the door but she didn't hear and when he came in, she was still naked. He immediately turned away and, without looking at her, he murmured that her skin absorbed the light very well, and she could rest assured that the scene would be beautiful. He went out again with a shy wave of his hand. He had not only reassured her about her work, he had just implied that he had never seen her naked, Olga had been there in her place. It was a very elegant compliment. The only one Sabine ever got. Her body was exhausted, aged, she didn't know whether she was angry with Gaspard for being so incompetent, or whether she thought he was touching. It didn't matter anymore in the least.

The filming was over, and the traditional wrap party restored them all to a sort of secular state, without costumes or makeup, without roles or any particular skill. Once again they all felt natural and slightly impoverished. The evening marked a break, meant that their life as a troupe would be split wide open, and suddenly all they would remember of these exhausting weeks would be the best moments. Some of them would go on at once to a new film, others were still uncertain about their plans; one way or another, they were all for sale.

And then it was no longer an abstract idea. Getting back together with Mathieu after a month of separation, spent in uncertainty and silence, the pain of missing him, his reassuring presence, and the apprehension of seeing one another again. Once the filming was over, Sabine stopped wearing makeup altogether. She realized that she preferred her naked face, it was more luminous that way, her gaze was more honest; her body still seemed heavy to her even if, since Paul, she knew that she had a prodigious organ between her legs, capable of extraordinary transports—but would it come again, that raw, almost nauseatingly powerful pleasure, could it become a familiar thing?

She really fancied him. She fancied him so much that she was overcome with a disturbing emotion that made her timid, as if everything was erased in his presence—words, the logical succession of sentences and gestures; she looked at Mathieu and she thought, "Fuck, that is my guy!" and the thought made her sick, he was her guy, that boy who didn't know she was watching him; she wasn't standing next to him to run along the beach in Trouville, but a few yards behind him on the boardwalk. The way he walked, sort of gangly and haughty at the same time, with his hands in his pockets, heading into the wind as it blew his hair, and he looked as if he were traveling, as if he had gone away a long time ago, was not merely passing by but a feature of the landscape, a fraction of its scattered light. Sabine was delaying the moment when she would go up to him, and then she said to herself she must be equal to what they had planned and imagined so often, so she ran along the beach to pass him then turn around and face him, she didn't really know who she was about to meet, Mathieu or her love for Mathieu, it didn't really matter, she was *living* one of her imaginary soap operas, and she could have taken flight or collapsed with happiness.

He gave a start when she stood there before him, breathless, overflowing with an elated joy, something imperative, he laughed at the surprise of it, she was so pretty, wearing no makeup, her hair tousled, she looked like she'd just got out of bed, got out of bed to come and find him. They decided to go to the hotel right away, and they found everything there conducive to love, they could hear the sea.

"What's this?"

Mathieu looked at Sabine's body, and there was the way he recoiled instinctively, there was suspicion mingled with disgust.

"What the fuck are all these bruises?"

He got out of bed and asked for an explanation, inexhaustibly, until evening, until deep in the night, and in the small hours they fell asleep, facing away from each other. He had said to her over and over that he wasn't jealous, and never had been, he had never asked anything of her, but this? This was, precisely, the limit. Her offended, abused body. How could he love a body that she herself had allowed to be mistreated? How could he respect a woman who cared so little for her integrity? She had told him the bruises were from the filming, but for him these marks were not "a game." She had misled him.

The telephone woke her at noon, callously, she had to

vacate the room, her husband had paid on his way out. It took her a minute to know where she was, what had happened here, what had been said, it was a muddled reality that seemed far away, Mathieu had already left . . . Mathieu had left her? The room was bright, the weather must be nice outside. She was stunned, the way people are when they hear news of a sudden death, something so hard to believe that they feel no sorrow, it is something new and distasteful they will have to get used to. She had to get dressed and go. Her clothes were on the chair, but the chair was far away, she could never reach it, and the air was cold, an unfair chill aimed against her. She picked up the phone and dialed Hélène's number, she prayed she would be there, that she would answer. She couldn't remember whether it was a weekday or the weekend, the phone rang in a void for a long time, she eventually put down the receiver. It wasn't Sunday, and Hélène was at the university. She was disappointed but relieved, too: she hadn't reached out to anyone for help. It took a great deal of will just to go to the chair and get dressed, and the attention she gave it distracted her from the stupefaction that was gradually numbing her, but she could sense very well that her mind was slowly taking in the fact that the news she had heard concerned her, and when she left the hotel and found herself among others, people making their way through the town just as they had the day before, just as they did every day, she knew that the sudden death was her own.

How could she possibly have slept so late? Twenty minutes past twelve was a time that did not exist away from the university, the library, or the lab. If the phone hadn't rung, Hélène would be still sleeping. The flu was starting to go around. If only this could be the flu, a virus that had been identified and that could be given a name, because everything had to have a name, had to be verified, classified, labeled, registered, put away, you had to cognize and recognize, but she no longer recognized herself and she hated it. Since the beginning of the year, her classes had seemed like huge monuments, and she stood at the foot of these monuments, terrified by them and obsessed, too. In the morning, she got up early to study before going to class, and, when she came home, she studied some more. She didn't sleep in order to rest, she slept in the hopes of integrating in her sleep what she had studied during the evening, and when she dreamed it was as if she were still studying, her mind still immersed in reactions, combinations, compounds, theories, theorems . . . It all swelled and vibrated inside her, the world devoured by the script of numbers and symbols, and faced with this invasion of formulas and enigmas, of discoveries, probabilities, and errors, she became afraid of mixing everything up, and wondered worriedly what she would retain: what she had learned or what she had dreamed. The border between those two worlds eventually blurred, day and night, science and dream, and today, if the telephone had not rung at twenty minutes past noon . . . she would still be sleeping. It was astounding. Worse than missing a flight or her own wedding. It was as if she had stepped outside her life, had slipped and fallen. Twenty minutes past twelve. All these hours that had gotten away from her: as if she had lost them and this loss had dug a hole in her entire existence, like a piece of burned cloth. She knew very well that, for some time now, she'd been having difficulty understanding any language other than that of her courses, but no one realized, no one tried to hold her back. She and Arthur met rarely, they called now and again in the evening to apologize, neither one of them had the time or the energy to come over, and beyond their disappointment they were reassured to know they were living at the same rhythm, absorbed by their studies. Was it Arthur who had just phoned? At this time of day, it couldn't be. She tried to remember what she'd done the night before, what could have compelled her to sleep so long, had she been drinking, did she get home late, had she smoked something toxic? No. Her desk was tidy, as it was every night after she finished studying, and she'd prepared her book bag in advance and her clothes as well, the ingrained habits of a careful schoolgirl. Next to her books and notebooks, there was some administrative mail she hadn't dealt with—the utility bills, the social security, a meeting with the other tenants—all these dreary obligations which seemed, bizarrely, to be so important. Nor had she sent her letter to Mariette. She hadn't even finished it yet:

Mouse,

A few days ago, I had a dream. It was nighttime, we were together and we were gazing at the sky, it was full of stars and a black that was almost blue, then it got darker and began to rain, the stars came loose and began falling to where we were, but when we bent down to pick them up, we saw that the ground was covered with fish and that the fish were dead. I don't remember what we felt at the time. I think I woke up.

In September Roger Heim died. You've probably never heard of him. He was an old gentleman, the former director of the Museum of Natural History and the president of the Academy of Sciences, and we were all so sad, as if one of our fathers had died and with him something sensitive and knowledgeable that sheltered us a little from a world obsessed with profit, a world of industrialists on the rampage. He tried to warn us about institutionalized dishonesty and the destruction of species, but who was listening?

Did she really write this to Mariette? This death announcement? She had simply wanted to warn her sister against the pesticides she would find in Marius's toolshed. And all she'd written was a requiem. Maybe Sabine was right, she was a sort of bird of ill omen, announcing one catastrophe after another, and she knew that everyone was fed up with all the scientists' warnings, it was easier to believe the authors paid by Monsanto to write articles for sales departments. Maybe you had to keep what you knew to yourself, and only see what was visible with the naked eye, stop thinking about what was inside things, at the heart of reality, maybe you had to go on behaving like the people who ruled the world. Shut your eyes. Shut your mouth. Keep all the proof secret. She tore up her letter; anyway, Mouse was used to writing to her without ever getting an answer.

She took a scorching hot shower, the water stimulated her muscles like a massage, she bent her neck forward to feel it on her nape, continuously, the heat hammering on her neck, the tension letting go, and she moved her head a little from right to left, her neck cracked gently, as it relaxed it became more supple in the vigorous, scalding spray. The bathroom was covered in steam, she slid down onto the tiles in the shower stall, curled up, her face against her bent knees in the intense downpour, she could hear the song, *Heroes*, far away, staccato, and above the sound of the water, Bowie crying, *We can be all us, just for one day!* She put her hands firmly on her neck, the way Éléonore had that evening to make her turn around, a hand that took and that knew what it wanted. She squeezed her fingers against her neck, her nails biting into her reddened skin, she felt a pain that brought relief, a pain like truth, and now she knew. She needed someone to put their hand on her, truly.

Agnès abandoned herself to the routine of the monastery, a slow and ordered time, the significance of every hour devoted to the entity some called *God*, and this crumbling, impoverished world, this waste, suddenly seemed worthy of respect. She didn't observe the liturgy of the hours, didn't attend the vigils, had never witnessed the awakening of the monastery, but later, when her day began and the cautious December morning appeared, wrapped in her blanket she looked outside. She knew that beneath its apparent lethargy, nature was preparing for rebirth. She knew that every animal, from the most harmless to the most powerful, was patiently and dangerously hunting for food until nightfall. The unchanging order of things brought relief.

Now she knew all the paths through the forest, their acid, decaying smell and, from the top of the hill, the view onto villages drowned in fog, the snow-covered fields deserted by cows now warm in their stable. Everything seemed to be on the verge of disappearing, and she liked this sunless sky, this barrenness, the restrained colors, the tarnished snow, the palette of faded grays—a life without brilliance, but it was rooted, unchanging in what it offered human beings: the possibility of disaster, of course, famine, war, epidemics, but, above all, a steadfast attachment to the country of her birth. There was something tenacious about it all that she found touching, as if she had known the lives here, as if she had played a part in them in a distant past, and she felt a tentative nostalgia for these places. She loved the sound of her footsteps on the dead wood, the spongy moss, the saturated leaves, the gravel in the courtyard. She liked the way the wooden door to the chapel creaked a little, and how austere it was inside, and almost completely dark. She loved sitting and listening to the monks' monodic chants. She loved this world where there was little talk. Her first meals in silence, shared with the other visitors, had left her ill at ease, and then she came to love them, too, with their absence of the usual codes, and she barely listened to what came from a loudspeaker in the monks' refectory, the scripture readings and universal prayer. She was losing the meaning of words. And yet, the day was approaching when she would be faced with them again, with their darkest significance. She thought of Bruno and Mariette. She had not taken the risk of writing to them or leaving a message on the answering machine, they might have been able to find out where she was, where she was calling from. In the shop, she bought a penknife with the inscription of the abbey, and every afternoon in her tiny room, dark so early, she sculpted the wood she'd gathered during her walks. She was clumsy, but she wanted to do something with her hands, and, in the beginning, when she saw her failed efforts she thought, "You really are useless. Oh this is pathetic," and then she told herself that to do what she had to do, it would take so much courage that, strange as it might seem, she would have to show some regard for herself, and she learned that kindness is a weapon. One morning, she realized she'd been there for over three weeks and she could not keep wondering whether she was ready. She had to be. She went on her ritual walk, and the landscape she was about to leave seemed paler than usual, there was a sour smell, and everything seemed wet, penetrated with drizzle. She knew that nothing here would remember her. She was in a hurry now, no time to lose. At two o'clock she went up to the porter, who led her to the priest. She went into the abbey for the first time. A quivering light filtered into the cloister where hooded figures walked, their steps elastic, the soles of their sandals sucking against the flagstones. She was breathless with apprehension. The porter opened a side door, pointed out the little step to her and disappeared. The room was cold and smelled of candles and fungus. The priest seemed enormous. He motioned to her to sit down, pointing to the chair that was closest to his. This was the first time Agnès had ever made confession outside the shelter of the confession box. He made a broad sign of the cross. She looked at the floor, the irregular stones with their floating film of dust. Then she said, "I gave birth to a little girl with Down syndrome and immediately abandoned her."

Mariette had spent the month of December paying renewed attention in class, no longer playing hooky but, on the contrary, showing herself to be serious and hard-working. As for the other pupils' caustic remarks, the nasty litany of *Little genius*, she stopped noticing. And her boredom in class, the teachers' discouraged manner, she couldn't care less. She needed order, both at school and at home. Every evening, she cooked for Bruno and reassured him, Agnès would come home soon, people don't just disappear, people don't go away never to come back, do they? Both of them knew this wasn't true. A love, a friend, a child, you can lose everything, from one day to the next. *It happened.* The brutal way in which ties could be broken, could snap like a neck breaking, a wall crumbling, this unexpected violence—Mariette and Bruno were experiencing that very thing, and the *never again* with its scandalous overtones of death was something they breathed in every evening, alone in the apartment.

Mariette waited for Joël more and more often at closing time, and, as Christmas drew near, the shop was constantly busy. One evening, she told him that her mother had gone away. It felt good to be able to tell someone, as if she'd made a successful pass with a ball. His turn to play now: did he think she might come back one day?

"Listen, she's alive. That's the main thing."

His remark, both fatalistic and full of hope, made her

realize that she'd never shown any interest in his life. She'd always gone to see him so that he would give her something in some manner or another. Now she looked at him differently, he could have been her older brother after all. She said, "You shouldn't hide behind your hair, it's a shame not to see your eyes."

She raised her hand slowly to push back the strand of hair hiding his gaze. He recoiled slightly. She asked, "What are you doing for Christmas?"

"I'm going to Langogne, to my parents' . . . well, my foster family."

"They became your parents, I mean, your real parents."

"No. Don't look at me like that, I like them very much, but no. They were paid to have me there, and there were a lot of us bringing in money for them, working in their fields, so even if they were good people, and I'm very fond of them, I've never looked on them as my parents."

She was going to tell him about Hélène, but she didn't know how to describe the situation. David Tavel paid to have her. Her parents got money not to have her. Oh, it was too complicated.

"Your mother will come back, Mariette, don't worry. She must miss you terribly."

"Thank you."

"Sometimes it just takes time to notice how much you miss someone."

In the same way she prepared meals for Bruno, Mariette prepared Christmas. She set up the nativity scene, the tree, she went shopping with her father, and when people asked where Agnès was, they said she'd gone to stay with her own mother, who wasn't well. It wasn't hard to lie to the people around them, it was like finding fake excuses for the absence slips in the parent communication notebook, but it was harder to hide the truth from Bruno about Xmas, and Mariette felt the urge more than once to confess to him that the baby was alive, that she was six months old now, but that was something else she had learned, how to keep a promise. Answering her sisters' questions over the phone, feeding them the same lie about Agnès being at Mamie's sickbed, it made her feel awkward, and she was disappointed when they believed her. Joël was the only person who carried the burden of the secret with her, which made him a silent accomplice. Bruno didn't open the administrative mail addressed to Agnès Malivieri—the work inspectorate, registered letters, sanctions, maybe she'd been struck off the payroll, and this world of threats, compared with his wife's terrible absence, seemed both ironic and incongruous. The administration, like some obsessive God, wanted supremacy, but nothing was stronger than sorrow. Every morning, he got up and went through his day, and every night in his bed he was dying of loneliness. He had never lived without her. He didn't know how to do it. The only thing he knew was that he hadn't been there. She'd given birth alone and then . . .

And then it was Christmas vacation, and Bruno and Mariette went to wait for Sabine and Hélène at the Gare Saint-Charles. This meant they would have to confess that Agnès had not come back and they would have to find an authentic reason—but what? Of course, they wouldn't mention her pregnancy, which she'd hidden from her older daughters, and Bruno realized that his wife had walked all alone along a cliff edge for months on end, until the most solitary blow of all, life and death in the same moment, birth and mourning for that birth, simultaneously, and Bruno understood that she would never forgive him.

Sabine and Hélène stood waving on the station platform and Mariette instantly knew the feeling she thought she had lost, the powerful emotion of seeing her sisters again. She ran toward them, panicked, as if she might lose them in the crowd, and she already felt she was using up her last ounces of strength, her last lies, her last courage. All three embraced and stood huddled together, their faces no longer visible, just their coats, and their caps tilted together. Bruno looked at them and found them so grown up, when had they grown like that? My daughters, he thought . . . And he laughed like an idiot, all by himself at the end of the platform.

Sabine and Hélène realized as soon as they arrived that Agnès had never been at their grandmother's bedside. One morning, she had simply packed a bag and left. The shame they felt at having been absent for so long meant they could voice no reproach, and only very few questions. They decided on the menu for Christmas Eve and prepared it days ahead of time, the seven meatless dishes for the traditional Provençal *Gros Souper* and the thirteen desserts were in the fridge, in every cupboard, and even out on the balcony—vegetables, fish, dried fruit and nuts, candies, bottles of wine, champagne—it was as if they were preparing a huge amount of food that would go to waste because their stomachs were knotted with anxiety. They peeled and sliced the fruit and vegetables; smells of baking bread, of cabbage and aniseed permeated the rooms and slowly suffocated them, yet the apartment, now filled to the brink, remained deserted, and Agnès reigned over the solitude. Who was this woman who had suddenly left everything that had once been her entire life? What was it inside her that had been lost or revealed? What was it inside her that was not who she was? The questions rose slowly to the surface, like the signs of a sickness, the premonition of a coming ailment, grave and unstoppable.

One evening when Bruno was not there, and they were sitting out on the little balcony facing the windows of the buildings all around, with the blurry light from television sets, Mariette asked Sabine for a cigarette. Sabine didn't object, she understood that something was happening, like a change of rhythm, a different melody. Mariette listened to the silence she was about to break, silence as familiar as a creature you've allowed to settle in your house, and who watches over your meals and lies in your bed. When had it all started? How could they have been so generous and negligent? She exhaled the smoke, watched it tremble then vanish in the night, and said, "Maman has had several lives, I mean, several lives without us. Away from us."

"Shocking," murmured Sabine.

Hélène put her hand on her arm to silence her.

"Before you were born, Sabine, she lost a baby, a little boy."

Sabine and Hélène felt like laughing. They didn't understand what Mariette was talking about. Some wild imagining, their sister was muddled, Mouse and her little-sister stories. Mariette knew this slightly creased and crackling silence that came before the onset of emotion. She was about to tell them some more, but some mopeds with holes in their exhaust pipes had just arrived on the parking lot, and the boys were shouting above the din, their crass words disturbing the night.

"Aren't those the Manard brothers?" Sabine asked, looking over the balcony.

Hélène leaned over with her.

"Fuck, haven't they gone to the dogs, the half-pints."

"I remember changing his diapers, the short one with the brown hair, what was his name again?"

They turned abruptly toward Mariette, as if what she had told them had only just reached them with a slight delay.

"What was it you just said? Huh?"

"What's this all about?"

And Mariette told them what she knew about the little brother who was their older brother and whom their mother had given birth to, without ever seeing him or touching him or naming him. There was nothing to say in response, and they said nothing. They stayed together on the balcony open onto the shared night, onto other people's noise, and everything became muddled: what did a baby that died twenty-five years ago have to do with their mother's absence today? To them, Agnès seemed both very old, burdened with a former life, and too young, a girl of eighteen in a blood-soaked bed. Their father, too, became someone else, the man who'd chosen to "save the mother and not the child," the man who'd had that power, when he was twenty. But their parents' ages were all wrong, and they figured that *back then*, in that time that had belonged to their parents, to be eighteen or twenty years old was something different from what eighteen and twenty really were. It might correspond, roughly, to twenty-eight or thirty, nowadays. You had to convert the numbers, the way you did with French francs, old francs to new ones, or multiply them the way you did with a dog's age.

"Papa doesn't know that I know . . . about the little brother," said Mariette.

And she crushed the stub of her cigarette underfoot, turning this way and that, as if she were trying to embed it in the stone. She could smell the slightly damp odor of Hélène's sweater, and the chill in her hair. Her sister had just pulled her close, holding her face against her and not letting go. Mariette was stifling a little in this protective embrace, and yet what was happening was very gentle, as if she had slipped into some lukewarm water, slowly, with her entire body; she could feel her sister's heart beating under her ear, and she liked it. She thought that being held like this would make it easier to tell them about Xmas: it was the time to do it. She heard the match, the crackling of the paper, Sabine's breath. She heard the short sob in Hélène's chest which, for a moment, upset the regular rhythm of her heart. She heard the key in the lock, the shudder of the door opening, the shoes rubbing on the mat, and she buried her head into Hélène's chest, clung to her sweater and closed her eyes even tighter. A burning air swept out from the open door, a distant force like wind from the sea, a phenomenon you could not avoid. That sound of feet being wiped, twice, before coming in, she knew it well. She heard the front door close and reverberate against the bare walls. She thought, "Here it is, it's happening." And she heard the sound of Agnès's bag dropping to the floor, her steps in the kitchen, the sound of the cupboard, of the glass banging against the sink, the water running too hard and splattering the dishes drying in the rack. So, she stepped back from Hélène to look at her mother. She could see only her back. She was drinking slowly, the way you do after a dangerous thirst, a long wilderness. She was coming back to the place that had been hers for so long, this yellow kitchen where, day after day, she had fed them, putting down her baskets, tidying her cupboards, adding things up on the back of the paper the meat came wrapped in, tying her apron, peeling and cutting more vegetables than they would ever peel and cut for a hundred Christmases. It seemed to them that their mother could not stop drinking, filling her glass again as soon as it was empty, and maybe she had only come now for no other reason than to drink and then leave again, they were simply somewhere along her way, and she was about to keep going, to walk straight ahead without ever looking back, to leave them forever with the memory of her sturdy back, her generous shoulders, and the water that could not quench her thirst.

VI
The Original Rhythm

Sabine and Hélène boarded the train again at the Gare Saint-Charles, impatient to get back to Paris, yet feeling blue nonetheless, as if their departure were merely a foretaste of what lay ahead—round trips between Paris and Marseille ever more frequent, ever more troubling, because being with their parents didn't mean simply seeing them again but also *seeing themselves* again, the way they used to be, and deep inside each one of them there was a patient little girl waiting for something, she didn't know what, but waiting, as if that something had been promised to her and she hadn't received it. They were returning to Paris with the unpleasant sensation that they were no longer Bruno and Agnès's entire life: to become father and mother their parents hadn't waited for the girls, they'd had a secret life without them, years that they'd kept to themselves, like war years. The girls did not dare admit that, beyond the sorrow this aroused for their parents' sake, they were slightly annoyed. It was not Sabine's coming into the world that had made them a family, her birth was not a victory but a replacement. It had all begun with a stumble.

Amid the stubborn huffing of the train, its smell of rain and hot dust, they gazed out at the landscape as it changed progressively, like an image being twisted, as they went through fields, past rivers, small towns and suburbs, until finally a black stone wall appeared suddenly, just before the Gare de Lyon, with its letters in red paint, *Paris*, and the girls' emotion was the same as when they had seen it for the first time, Sabine could recall her shock at the age of seven when she read the word in red on the decrepit wall, the ugliness heralding so much beauty. The train slowed. The lights on the platform threw a harsh glare on the faces of the passengers as they bustled about, already shoving one another, already turning into Parisians. The voice on the loudspeaker informed them that Paris was the final station. After Paris there was nothing.

Arthur was waiting for Hélène at the end of the platform, and Sabine noticed how cautiously—probably because she was there—they greeted one another, hardly kissing, then turning to her, would she like to have dinner with them? She declined and they were relieved. She saw them leave the station to go for dinner in the Bastille quartier, a working-class neighborhood where, apparently, they went regularly. Arthur carried Hélène's suitcase, and he made an attentive little gesture toward her, running his hand through her hair; does everyone in love behave the same way, wondered Sabine, do all the couples in the Gare de Lyon experience this moment in the same way, with the same fear, the same hope, and the profound joy of sensing that it is here and only here that life is waiting for them, in this loving hopefulness, and that nothing ever makes you feel worthier than a lover's gaze, the lover who has seen your face when you come, when you dream, who knows the skin on your shoulders, the curve at your lower back, the taste of your sex, your voice, your breath, the way you sleep, the way you eat, everything you don't know and will never know about yourself. And which you have given him, or her. Sabine stayed there amid the diffuse vibration of people walking toward each other and leaving together, and she missed Mathieu to an inadmissible degree, missed him as if without him she were no more than the soft part of herself, constantly compelled to forget him and also *to do things*—go alone to the cinema, spend an evening on her own, eat vols-au-vent with Robert then watch a film on TV followed by a debate about it, take a little stroll just to get some fresh air the way children do, survive a sunny afternoon that brings out all the lovers, learn not to weep on rainy afternoons, and of course go out—to friends' openings in inaccessible theaters, to film previews where she knew no one but the extras, always putting her best face forward because nothing is worse for an actress than to be anything less than bursting with vitality, and she must remain desirable, but not a cocktease, available but mysterious, free but not idle, unemployed but full of plans, accessible but not stupid, single but not frustrated. Not a danger to other women. But how she missed him, that man of hers! She missed him all the time, insidiously, in niches and details of her life she would never have suspected, she missed him when she read in *Le Monde* that Aragon had taken part in the demonstration against American missiles in Europe, when she read a want ad in *Libé* from a man looking for a stranger who'd smiled at him on Line A of the RER, she and Mathieu had been in the habit of leaving the newspaper on the table to read it together, and now the news wasn't important anymore, nothing made her want to fight or have fun. She missed Mathieu's lovemaking and the after-lovemaking, when they would stay in bed and whisper for hours while she caressed his back, tirelessly. She missed him at night when he would sleep, holding his hair. She missed him in the morning when she felt too lazy to get up and he would make tea, something he didn't know how to do, but she drank it with an indulgent happiness. She missed him when she was trying on clothes in a shop and he used to wait for her outside, forcing her to stand by the window, and with great waves of his arms he would signal to her whether it was fantastic or shabby. She missed the way he used to light his cigarette. The way he threw his head back after the first puff, the faint bulge of his Adam's apple, his fingers removing a speck of tobacco from the tip of his tongue. His butt in his worn jeans, which she would pat as she walked by, "How ya doin', cowboy?" The way he would murmur, "I love it . . ." when she was going up the stairs and he followed so close behind. The notes he left under the pillow or wrote directly on her skin, his voice when he would hum, timidly, always off key, the way it was impossible for him to say words of love, to confess to his sorrows, and she even missed his desire for other women, because sometimes when they were making love it aroused her to think about all the women who'd been pleasured by her guy's cock, it increased her own pleasure tenfold. She missed his skin, the imperfections, the moles, scars, rough patches, everything she knew better than he did. His warmth against hers, his blue eyes darkened with pleasure, and the damp hair with its smell of heather on his chest and groin, where she liked to lay her face, close her eyes and rest. She missed everything. Above all, the future. She had a tiny little life now, as if shriveled, left out on the landing, a life that was going nowhere and could envisage nothing. There would be tomorrow, and the day after, and beyond. She saw nothing besides what was there before her, concrete, proven, high walls of proof and exactitude. She no longer dreamed that Mathieu would be proud of her one day, that she would dazzle him, splash him and drown him in her light, she didn't dream about anything anymore. It surprised her that she managed to spend her time in Aix with so much determination—dancing, cooking, talking with her sisters, kissing her mother on Christmas Eve, Merry Christmas! raising her glass as if nothing had happened, and, even then, she had thought of Mathieu, thought about how this was one more thing she would not be telling him. The brutal, complete dissociation of her life from his, this lethal sealing-off, was not something she'd anticipated. When he had left her sleeping, there in the room where they could hear the sea, she knew nothing about disappearance, and now she was finding out.

The blackout of never again. She might be an orphan, or have had ten brothers born before her, he would not know. Marguerite Duras or Jean-Luc Godard might contact her, he would not know. She might only ever love him, devote her life to his memory, he would not know. And who would tell him if she died? And her? How would she know when he died? Who would tell her? She wondered what would remain in her life of that pain that is called a broken heart, the name of a song to describe a feeling that is raw and without poetry. When she was old, what part of her life would seem most important to her—the part of her life she'd cherished, the part of her life when she'd been totally herself? For the time being she was only a lost girl in the Gare de Lyon on December 29, 1979, and it was incredibly cold, a relentless cold that got under your clothes, under your skin, to burn your bones. She had enough change for a phone call to Charlène, whom she hadn't seen since filming ended, but she knew that she never went to bed before dawn.

Charlène was twenty-three, and she was what people called a girl who had no qualms, and Sabine envied her a little. She wasn't the type who got insomnia, who cried when she heard a certain pop song, who melted at the sight of an elderly couple walking hand-in-hand, or got upset when a child was crying because its mother had shouted at it, any more than when a handicapped person struggled to climb down from the high step on the bus, or a homeless tramp was told roughly to move on by a shopkeeper, or a timid dog had its hindquarters in a brace, or an ugly girl was being taunted by a group of schoolboys, or she saw a bird's nest on the ground with its little eggs crushed. No. She wasn't that type of girl. Charlène didn't get emotional or afraid, she intrigued women and attracted men, they instinctively saw that what some women took for nonchalance was actually a lively sensuality that ran under her skin and filtered into her gaze, her gestures, her tall slender body, so brown and free, and they were sure that she could "teach them something"—better still, that she'd know how to make them believe they knew everything.

That evening, Charlène was not surprised that Sabine had called her so late, and didn't think for a moment that she might have had a problem, and Sabine did not stoop to confessing it to her, she simply said, after the first sip of Bordeaux, "Fuck it, Mathieu's left me, the stupid jerk!" And put like that, it was almost true, because, after all, you really had to be a stupid jerk to leave a girl you got along with so well and "on every score." But Charlène took it very seriously, and, after a pause of attentive silence, she made an announcement: she was getting married. Sabine dared to say, "Getting married? Why don't you just have an abortion?"

"Abortion? What for?"

"Sorry . . . but aren't you . . . you're not pregnant?"

"You have to be stupid to get pregnant in this day and age, don't you? And I don't see what that has to do with getting married."

"But unless they're pregnant, nobody gets married anymore, Charlène."

"Nobody but me."

"But hey that's great, congratulations! You must be really happy, that's really—"

"Guess who it is."

"Do I know him?"

"Of course, I met him on the shoot."

"Oh."

Sabine didn't dare come out with a name, every combination seemed absurd, she pictured Charlène and François, Charlène and Gaspard, Charlène and Herbert, the perchman, the first assistant . . . no one seemed to fit, this hurried wedding was like a joke.

"But hey are you really getting married? You're not pulling my leg?"

Charlène lit a cigarette, Sabine saw her long bare fingers, her delicate wrists, her discreet smile above the gap in her front teeth, and her perfectly drawn cheekbones grazed by her rich black hair, and she understood that what people said must be true: physical love to her was a committed act into which she put a lot of know-how and a profound elegance. Charlène said, her voice strangely low:

"I'm getting married to Henri Montmartin, the producer. Don't look so flabbergasted, I know he's my father's age. Oh, of course I know I could sleep tactically with him and not get married, but that would be a fairly degrading waste of time. You don't sleep with an old guy of fifty-five. You have to belong to him. A man like that doesn't need yet another secret mistress, you see, he needs a public conquest. Otherwise, where would that leave his pride?"

"But do you love him?"

"That's a new one."

"What?"

"Since when has marriage been about love?"

"Sure, sure, you're right! No, I just wanted to know if you're happy, because . . ."

"Because what?"

"Because they say that old guys . . . I mean, apparently they have problems . . ."

"You mean problems with their erections? Sure, they do! And so what? Once you know, all you have to do is work around it. The first time, as a rule, they'll tell you their emotion kept them from getting hard, and that it had never happened until they met you, or else they'll tell you they're tired, and then, in the end, after a lot of stimulation, it works out, but that's not the most important thing, what's important is not what the guy gives you, the man with his floppy dick, his pot belly, his bald head, or the hairs in his ears, what matters is where you take him. And that, believe me, that can be really exciting, or at least it excites me. Before he met me, Henri had never made love with more than one person at a time, had never seen two women together, he didn't know that sex could be such an adventure, he was already over forty in 1968, can you imagine? The revolution didn't concern him in the least, he spent his time shouting at his son who was a student at the Sorbonne and friends with Cohn-Bendit!"[16]

Sabine couldn't understand Charlène's enthusiasm, she wished she could share it, draw something from it—support, hope. But making love with some old guy, flattering him, charming him, stimulating him (she could picture the interminable blow jobs—disappointing, exhausting) . . . so much effort . . .

"You're feeling down about Mathieu, aren't you? You're acting tough, but you're feeling down, I can tell."

"I miss him."

"If he asked you to marry him, what would you say?"

"He's against marriage."

"You'd say yes, I'm sure you would. Can you see yourself living with a teacher who'll never make enough money to live anywhere besides a tiny, cramped apartment? Can you see yourself spending your whole life afraid that you'll never get another role, or that the government support might dry up? Not to mention having to have kids, that would put you on the subs' bench right away."

"Don't you want children?"

"That's not the issue. I'm twenty-three, I don't know. But I promised Henri and it will probably happen sooner than

[16] Daniel Cohn-Bendit was one of the leaders of the student uprising in May 1968, also known as "Dany le Rouge" for his left-wing politics.

expected, except in my case it's different, Henri's goal in marrying me is to have a child, I know that, he wants to be able to do again at fifty what he used to do at twenty. Marriage and fatherhood are external signs of youth, don't you see?"

They finished the bottle of Bordeaux and opened another one, Sabine was so woozy that she went along with everything Charlène said, even wondered why this truth had never seemed so patently clear to her before, because, basically, what could she expect? Humiliation and nothing but humiliation. The humiliation of casting calls, bits of screen tests, degrading sex scenes, constantly having guys trying to pick her up, unemployment, compromises, mediocrity, career changes and regrets. And you could avoid all that if you had a producer husband to champion you during filming, to make the whole film industry respect you. They'd eventually look on you as a woman who'd made her man happy "like never before," the same man about whom everyone had assumed that, if he was with you, it was because he was a good lay. "In short, you take an old man and make him a new man." Sabine wanted to make her lifelong dream come true: to act. Without having to wonder how, by what roundabout means, she'd get there. She wanted to belong to the big family. To join the circle. And yet there was still something that bothered her, and, as if she had hit on a stumbling block, she asked Charlène, "And when this old husband of mine is sixty-five or seventy, what do I do then? Huh? Do I get a divorce and lose everything?"

"For a start, getting divorced would bring you a ton of money, particularly if you have a kid, but you won't want a divorce, you'll have grown used to that life, and believe me, all the Mathieus on the planet will be no more than distant memories, as distant as your first parties or your first period. And, for decades, your old husband will have been turning a blind eye to all your extramarital affairs, as long as you've kept them secret. As long as society goes on thinking he's a young man married to a young woman, the bargain is kept."

Sabine looked at her empty glass, focusing distractedly, then she set it gently on the carpet, rolled over on the sofa and fell asleep, snoring. Charlène took off her shoes, covered her with a throw, and went out of the room, leaving a light on, because Sabine was the kind of girl who couldn't sleep in the dark. Anyone could see that.

This isn't a good idea, no, not a good idea at all. I have my first exam session in two weeks!"

"Oh, hush, we'll be there in two hours."

"I should be studying right this minute."

"Unwinding, you mean, you're on the verge of exhaustion, I know you, right, I can see how pale you look."

"We won't get back too late tonight?"

"Shut up and listen to this. It's perfect road music."

David turned up the volume on the car cassette player.

"That's Harry Nilsson," she said, "it's at least ten years old! Where have you been?"

"I'm a grandfather now, don't forget, so I'm a little behind on things, especially music. Joseph gave me the cassette. I could drive all day and all night to this."

"The university library is open over Christmas vacation. I should be there now. What are you doing? Why are we stopping?"

David had pulled the van over to the side of the road. Before opening his door, he removed his cap and put it on Hélène's head and said, "Drive, if you're a man!"

She got out of the truck. She knew it was pointless to tell him that the road was icy, that she'd never driven a van, not to mention the fact she didn't have a license for driving vans. She looked at the horrible gear stick, the huge steering wheel, the sagging seat, the windshield splattered with slush and bird shit, and, because she didn't want to disappoint David, she took off her jacket, put it on the seat to make a cushion and took her place. David climbed into the passenger seat, not looking at her, and she understood that he wouldn't show her anything, neither the gears nor the ignition, nor the rearview mirrors, she'd have to figure it all out, he was drumming his fingers on the dashboard, acting impatient, so she tugged on the visor of the cap and started the engine. Behind them, the thoroughbred kicked and neighed, he was a three-year-old racehorse, stressed out, highly strung, magnificent, called Pablo Du Lac. They drove in silence, listening to the music that warmed them a little, and when the horse let out a sigh, they knew that he had calmed down at last. It was cold in the truck, and gusts of icy snow mingled with the rain. Hélène focused on the road, the long uphill stretches and sudden descents, but she did force herself to relax, to drive more flexibly, she thought about the horse, this responsibility equal to the trust David placed in her.

They arrived in Crèvecoeur-en-Auge in time for lunch, David had reserved a table at the Auberge du Cheval Blanc, where the owner, proud to know this distinguished guest, greeted him with effusive jollity. People respected David, but his simplicity still contained a trace of superiority; he was proud of his own spontaneity, he savored it with a childish joy, always a twinkle in his eye and a joke on the tip of his tongue. He knew who he was and what he was worth.

"This is straight out of a Chabrol film," said Hélène, looking around the restaurant—the starched white tablecloths, the napkins folded into fans, the Restoration-era chairs, and the slightly Sunday-best atmosphere you often found in country restaurants, with their lonely traveling salesmen and pensioners tying their napkins around their neck, the smell of meat fried in butter, and on the windows with their tiny panes, the warm steam collecting behind the potted plants.

"Oh, yes, straight out of Chabrol or Simenon," said David. "The atmosphere before a murder."

"Or after adultery."

"The same thing."

"If you say so!"

"It's a nice place, don't you think?"

"Yes, it is."

"The livery is ten miles from here, we'll be back soon, you'll have time to study tonight."

"What livery?"

"For Pablo Du Lac."

"The horse is going to a livery stable? Why don't you keep him at the club in the Bois de Boulogne?"

"He's too tired. He's been bleeding from the lungs and has micro-fractures in the bones of his legs. He needs to rest."

"He started racing too young, is that it?"

"All thoroughbreds start racing before they've finished growing, that's not the point."

"You didn't tell me we were going to leave him at a stable two hours from Paris."

"You didn't ask me where we were going, you were so caught up in your studies! He'll be fine here, he'll be out in the pasture twenty-four hours a day, he'll have friends, maybe even a fling or two, who knows?"

She laughed and he leaned back in his chair, relieved to have changed the subject. He asked her how her classes were going, what the atmosphere was like, the professors, he was fascinated by this unfamiliar world of scientists.

"I've heard that they're crazy."

"Who is?"

"The true scientists, the geniuses."

"I don't know, I'm a third-year student."

"Oh, don't go acting so modest. Is it true they're crazy?"

"The great mathematicians . . . sort of."

"Paranoid?"

"Mm. Paranoid, maniacal, absent-minded, anorexic . . ."

"And people criticize the financial world!"

"They maintain a very . . . child-like quality, sometimes."

"What do you mean?"

"Well, for example, their jokes are really awful. They love awful jokes."

"Such as?"

"Well . . . 'Sex is like equations, after three unknowns it becomes interesting.'"

He liked it so much that she went on, "Or this one, 'And God said, Let there be Darwin!'"

"Not as funny."

"No?"

"Nowhere near as funny."

David had gotten married in church, had his sons baptized, and attended Christmas and Easter mass. His faith was solid, like a folder carefully filed away, that won't cause any worries. The world had a creator, and that creator was called God. David was what people referred to as a "non-practicing Catholic." To start the conversation up again on a lighter topic, he said, with a touch of humor, "You'll have to get your truck driver's license, you know, some day you might get us in trouble."

She burst out laughing, and he laughed too, and the owner called out, "Ah! I see everything is going well, Monsieur Tavel!"

David leaned over to Hélène.

"He must think you are a young conquest."

She shrugged her shoulders and looked at him with delighted indulgence.

David was driving. Hélène wished the livery were much farther away, they would have stayed together in the van, with the horse at the back and Nilsson singing *Without You.* She played the song three times over, David complained, "I can't take it anymore!" But she saw his happy smile. Who else could either of them feel so good around, so natural, on such an equal footing? All things considered, Hélène was glad she wasn't his biological daughter. She'd always wondered how long this would last, if she would be replaced, he had so many other nephews and nieces, and grandchildren, too, but suddenly, while the truck was bouncing along a rutted dirt road, and the music kept to the rhythm of the shaking, she understood that he never had chosen her. She was the one who'd wanted it. She was the one, as a little girl, who had sought out that uncle, who'd done everything so that he would open his door to her, and he hadn't had the heart to refuse, he'd come up with that excuse, after the fact, of sending the monthly check to her parents, her paternal grandfather's bankruptcy and his folding trailers that had never opened.

When they got to the livery, David stopped the truck, and, when the music and the engine had fallen silent, the countryside suddenly seemed offered to them. Fields as far as the eye could see, horses in the distance, bent over what little grass there was, or standing in pairs, occasionally heading off at a trot, not for long, it was like a painting come to life, old-fashioned and gentle. Hélène went over to the paddocks, David followed her quickly and before she had time to understand, he said, "The livery functions as a sanctuary, too."

She didn't answer. She walked farther away, toward the pastures.

"Hélène!"

She motioned to him to be silent. She walked through the mud, slowly, and the farther she went, the more real it became, and yet impossible. That someone had done this to them. They were so thin that their skin was no longer their skin but a threadbare blanket placed over their perfectly visible rib cage, and their eyes closed with abscesses, and their festering kneecaps, their bloody flanks, their scorched necks, their scarred mouths, and farther away, on his knees forever, the horse walking on his ankles, both forelegs bent, on the verge of collapsing but not collapsing, and that pony with its curved hooves eight inches long, trying to walk but stuck in the mud. Stunned, aged little donkeys. Hélène looked at them, their resignation under the hanging clouds, wild animals tamed by man, his finest conquest and his greatest shame. It had stopped raining and a few birds were singing, but the horses, in their gentle distance, heard nothing now because nothing more could surprise them.

When she came back to the stable, David was waiting for her to set off again. She avoided his worried gaze and greeted the owner, Madame Jouvin, and went to say goodbye to Pablo Du Lac. She felt no particular affection for the horse, she'd just seen him two or three times when he was about to start his dawn workout, a very emotional thoroughbred that broke out in a rash during races and had to have a long massage afterwards to calm down. She stroked his nose and felt the warmth of his nostrils on her fingers; she spoke to him quietly, as if she were speaking to him but also to all the others: the most prestigious that were sold at auction in Deauville, the pride of the emirs, the racehorses and warhorses, the steeplechasers and farm horses, those that worked in the mines, and those that worked in the circus, wild horses, lab horses, the mounts of the Republican Guard, trotters, racers, stud animals, champions, cavalry steeds. All of them, however, had fallen one day. And been earmarked for another purpose. Sold. Horses ready for the blade. Horses that someone, well aware of what he was doing, had butchered. Regardless of age, or sex, or whether they were about to foal, horses that were twenty years old, foals of eighteen months, all sold to be eaten just the same.

"He's an emotional one, isn't he?"

Madame Jouvin, a large-bosomed woman with a stocky figure and determined face, was standing behind Hélène.

"Your father is waiting for you."

Hélène held out her hand and thanked her; she seemed surprised.

"You know, without David the sanctuary would have . . . a long time ago . . . because it's tough, you know, and he's generous. That he is."

They drove through the fine drizzle with no music other than the labored scraping of the wipers against the windshield; behind them the warm odor of the horse was slowly evaporating, while the straw kept a damp, unpleasant acidity. From time to time, Hélène looked at David, his sharp profile under his gentlemen farmer's cap, his thin eyeglasses, his pursed lips, and she wondered, outside of his family circle, or work, or the places where he carried out his duties as son and husband, where he ran his teams and signed his contracts, she wondered what his life consisted of. He turned to her.

"What's wrong?"

She was so embarrassed that she mumbled hastily, "I think I'm not in love with Arthur."

He didn't understand who she was talking about, then he suddenly exclaimed, "Ah! Arthur!"

Then, dismayed, he added, "Oh my god . . . Arthur."

Now she was staring at the rainy road beyond the ballet of windshield wipers. She couldn't believe she'd said that, someone else had spoken in her place, and now it was too late. She was angry with herself, but she was crying, her pathetic existence, her helplessness, that sanctuary full of tortured animals, but what had she thought? That by learning theorems and chemical formulas she would be fighting against barbarity? She'd do better to go and change the straw in the sanctuaries, and never mind if they were overwhelmed by the endless, ever-increasing number of crippled creatures at the end of their road. David pulled over onto the shoulder and clumsily took her in his arms murmuring, "Oh dear, there, there," and Hélène moaned, "But what can we do, what can we do?" "About Arthur?" he asked, "Not much." The effect was immediate, she burst out laughing, splattering her parka and her silk scarf with snot, "Forgive me," she said, "You're most welcome," he replied, elegantly. Then he stared at the motionless route ahead of them, and that was when she knew he hadn't taken her to the sanctuary by chance, he'd wanted this day on his own with her. He was breathing in and out like a man trying to give himself courage, a man about to dive into cold water. His breath left little puffs of vapor in the icy truck. Finally, he said, "It's no big deal but I think I've got a little cancer I started chemo gone three times it's nothing just a little daytime chemo, outpatient chemo they call it, but one day if I'm too tired well if I die so to speak, which happens to the best of us, well you can go on supporting the sanctuary in my place I've drawn up all the papers Madame Jouvin has been informed don't worry about a thing."

Then he pulled back out onto the secondary road, the 613, with green fields on either side as pale as the sky and the clouds. When they got to Paris, it was completely dark, the early nightfall of winter, the afternoon night-time. They felt as if they'd been gone for more than just a day, that they'd gone on such a long trip that they could never tell anyone else about it. And anyway, no one else would ever understand.

Mariette was sitting at the edge of the empty swimming pool, her legs dangling down. She was swinging them rhythmically, keeping time with the abrupt, regular, almost plain sound of the piano coming from the open living room. She looked at the March sunshine on the lavender plants she had to repot, on the yellowed stone of the pool, the rusty iron table, its ultramarine color that no longer shone, the linden tree swelling with buds she wouldn't see in bloom, the tree whose shadow and smell she would no longer know. Laurence's husband had asked for a divorce, he was getting married again, the property had been entrusted to a real estate agency and the poetry of the place had become a sales pitch, this "Provençal farmhouse with its lush vegetation," which would surely be divided up into offices for lawyers and doctors. The end of the Bohemian life.

Mariette listened to Laurence playing the obsessive notes of Arvo Pärt; they mingled with the sounds from outdoors, the muffled, constant roar of cars on the new stretch of highway, the scattered songs of birds, dogs barking in the distance, and furtive silences like rescued breathing. She closed her eyes and tried to determine which was dominant, the piano or the world. She pictured Laurence bent over the keyboard, the mature woman she had become, suddenly looking her age, another skin under her skin which, after absorbing years of hassles, laughter, and sunshine, was suddenly emerging and covering everything. Her sadness went into her playing, as if she were digging deeper into it, but she insisted on reassuring Mariette: she was sad, and she wanted to be sad, profoundly sad, and then it would pass and she'd be used to it, you get used to everything. She'd asked her to freshen up the area around the swimming pool, "Plant some agapanthus and lavender, something blue in pretty earthenware pots, then you can trim the clumps of flowers and bushes that are most visible." Mariette needed the money, she had to give her things to do, and the *bastide*, even if it were sold to a new owner, had to preserve its beauty. But Mariette didn't feel like making a garden just for show, she wanted to let it take over again, let the lawn embrace the weeds, let the leaves from the linden tree decay at the bottom of the pool, let the moss grow between the stones, and the bougainvillea climb up the closed shutters, and the ivy spread along the gutters, let the dormice live in the closet under the stairs. Since they had to give back the keys to the realm, they might as well give it its freedom, too.

Now Laurence was playing something different, an oppressed sorrow, borne with indulgence, subdued. Mariette thought about Joël. A few days earlier, a girl had come to see him, a petite brunette, who looked docile, he'd said, "almost colorless." She was ten years older than him and she asked him if he remembered her, her name was Corinne and she was his sister. He thought about all the children he'd lived with at Geneviève and Maurice's place in Langogne, and while he was looking at the colorless young woman, trying to remember her, she clarified, "Your biological sister." When Joël told her about this, Mariette immediately pictured Xmas doing the same thing one day. The same miracle. But the story was different. Through Corinne, Joël learned that, at the time of their parents' death in a car crash, he had been two years old, and the family lawyer reckoned that the child wasn't conscious of what had happened, so while his sister had been sent to live with an aunt, Joël had been placed in a foster home. Family is a carved-up body, thought Mariette.

There must have been a traffic jam now on the new stretch of highway, they could hear horns blowing discordantly, aggressive and invasive. Mariette went to join Laurence inside. She looked like a woman overwhelmed by her fatigue. Laurence asked, "Would you like to try?"

"I've never played. I can't read music."

"You could start with a few chords. To accompany you."

"Accompany me for what?"

"For singing, for example. The left hand is for harmony and rhythm, and the right hand for melody. You'll pick it up quickly, you'll see."

She rummaged in a pile of sheet music on the piano, and put a score in front of her and began to play.

"Do you recognize it?"

"Véronique Sanson, *Vancouver*."

"*Going from town to town / That's something I know well / All my life I've been living / Adrift on this lost raft* . . . Want to try?"

"No."

"Well then go back to repotting the lavender."

And she played some more Pärt, from memory, her eyes closed. Mariette felt a new, living desire welling inside, virulent. Joël had told her that after the brass band in Langogne, it was his admiral in the navy who'd introduced him to the great composers. They'd met through music, music was a matchmaker. She asked Laurence, "Can you play Bob Dylan?"

"I'm not a jukebox, Mariette."

"What I mean is . . . I'd like to learn, provided it exists, the sheet music for singing Bob Dylan."

Following Laurence's advice, Mariette went back over her

music theory, Mademoiselle Chef's music classes would finally be of some use; she learned chords, practiced scales, and, before long, she felt that beneath her awkwardness something important was pulsating, something she found hard to define. It was the possibility of a life devoted to something other than constraint and ordinary discipline, a life that had a purpose, aspiring toward beauty. Laurence wisely stayed away, packing her boxes while Mariette practiced—scales rising and falling, her first arpeggios, chord progressions Mariette began to hum to, not even realizing, then music, clumsy and bold, carrying her on, in spite of herself; she didn't sing Dylan, she sang her own words. Initially she experienced the proud, carefree headiness of the novice, then she asserted herself, really took off, and the musical phrases burst forth, quickly, imperatively. She fell silent when she realized that what she had been singing was so violent she did not recognize herself. Mariette, tender Mouse, silent confidant, little sister and good pupil: when she opened her mouth it was to spew toads and snakes. She looked at the keyboard as if the ivory keys were traitors, they let you approach gently, in order to read your fingertips like an open book, and then blood as black as pitch poured forth from your little heart. She closed the piano lid, tried not to think any more about what she had been singing, and went to work in the part of the garden that needed it most, slaughtering a few clumps of boxwood, crying "À la française!" ruthlessly razing them, trimming the bushes crookedly and leaving flowerbeds full of holes. She made a bonfire with the last dead leaves and a few worn rattan chairs; she mowed the lawn so thoroughly that Laurence could not walk barefoot on it without shrieking, the garden was hostile to perfection, in keeping with her mood, and she had the courage not to weep when she went through the high gate for the last time, and it creaked as always. It was springtime, a springtime launching bouquets of generous, carnal scents into the open sky, and when she was out in the street, she felt the time from before slide over her and disappear, fourteen years or more, her time and the time she carried for others without realizing it, the myth of perfection, the united, indestructible family. She had left it there, that myth, in the garden and the house of childhood. She had loved believing in it, but it was all made up, she knew that now, and with poignant pride she understood that she had grown up. She crossed the road and didn't look back, unaware that behind her the garden, proud and rooted, preserved the memory of her passage.

So, this will never end, thought Sabine, we will always be subservient to men in one way or another, we will always be like merchandise waiting to be bought, marriage or poverty, a barter we still go along with even to this day, we want to get married as quickly as possible before our expiration date—and when is that, anyway? Twenty? Twenty-five? Thirty? Would Sabine actually turn thirty one day? The age of mothers . . . She didn't ever want to be that old. She wanted to love a man and be loved in return. To give herself and nothing else in exchange. No marriage or procreation, no social climbing. She wanted to devote herself to love the way you do to the noblest of causes, because without love, what was the point of living? She needed to love because loving made any other social, material, or family concerns seem ridiculous, and reality was not marrying someone like Henri Montmartin then waiting around for the blood work on his prostate, reality was taking flight, *being transported by love.* She adored that expression. Loving was the only place to go, the only place where you could be strong, unreasonable, selfish and even superficial, because when you loved, your life was sacred, but also full of futile concerns and ridiculous details, life was transfigured, life flowed amid the exchange of fluids, of smells and promises, it was lived with the other person as well as without them because you carried them inside you, and you loved until you wore it out, that double existence. You had to be capable of endurance and suffering in order to love. Sabine knew how, and she would never give up on the insanity of love just so that, thanks to some producer husband, she could have, not the starring role in the cinema, but that of the wife or mistress of the starring role. A foil. She resented girls like Charlène who perpetuated the cycle of domination, congratulating themselves all the while for having made a good deal. But for all that, Charlène's upcoming marriage would prove very convenient to Sabine: she would be leaving her her apartment, and Sabine felt so relieved that it was as if, until that moment, she hadn't had enough air to breathe. She said her goodbyes to Robert, promising to come and visit, but she knew she wouldn't, she would think about it and then not think about it anymore, and she'd feel the barest remorse when she learned of the old surgeon's death, this man who spoke of love to a woman whose mind was gone, a madwoman who didn't even know that she was loved. In the end they were alike, Robert and Sabine, each one was alone, but in their minds their love was shared. Had Mathieu loved her? He'd been terror-stricken when he left her, her bruised body with its spots of decay like on the skin of a fruit. He had not so much loved her as tasted her.

As time went by, she missed him less, but the girl she had been with him, the girl in love, was someone she missed terribly, and not being anyone's woman made her feel restless and bored. When she moved into Charlène's old apartment, she was once again sleepless with happiness and elation for a brief period. She was proud to have her own address, as if she were enrolled in the city; it seemed as if she had touched on something both ideal and concrete, the realization of a childhood dream that had never erred. She was meant to live in Paris and always had been. She loved everything about her street—eating breakfast at the bar the way people did here, on the phone she would say, "I've got to go, I'm going down for breakfast . . ." Because she had a telephone, and she loved coming home to hear it ringing, she would hurry to open the door and grab the receiver, breathless, "No you're not disturbing me, I just got in," and pulling the phone cord behind her, the way they did in the movies, the receiver wedged against her lowered face, she would walk back to the front door and kick it closed. She wanted to live like a native Parisian, to be used to the rhythm of the city, to its open-ended hours. She did her shopping late, bought her beers at midnight at the Arab's, and at night when she lay in bed, the never-ending flow of traffic in her street delighted her, and she would think, "That is the sound, the murmur of Paris," and the shadows from headlights on her wall drifted past like clouds on an open sky, everything was vast, enlarged, night and day alike. She had new ID papers made, where her address was printed: Sabine Malivieri, 88, rue Blanche, Paris IXe. Her address was her lover, every evening she loved coming home to it, rediscovering the musty old smell of her apartment, the sun setting on the wall in the living room, the traces of recent movements—the cup in the sink, the unmade bed, the book lying open. And yet at first, in spite of her joy, or next to her joy, she had shed many tears in this place over the death of love. She had reached a very advanced age, made of dissolution and attrition, her sorrow had burrowed into her features and she could see what her face would look like later; there were mornings that face appeared in the mirror like a patient double. She had spent evenings in total solitude, and her life felt arid, sterile. She was bored, and it seemed to her that it would always be like this, other people would be working, having fun, loving, while she would always be this woman with two faces, alone in her beloved, noisy apartment. She drank a bit too much. Smoked a bit too much and got used to it. She still read the newspapers to feel the way she used to, concerned by the outside world, but the world was too vast and she knew that her indifference would not hurt anyone. She'd promised a friend she'd go with him to Plogoff one Sunday in March to lend her support to the inhabitants of that little village who were protesting against the construction of a nuclear power plant at the Pointe du Raz, and if she ended up not going that Sunday, it wasn't out of a feeling of sudden indifference to the danger of the all-nuclear solution, but because something strange happened during the night. On a piece of paper, she wrote: *I wanted to die for love and I blew it.* And the images mingled with the words, the words with the emotions, she began writing and could not stop, a great stream until dawn, everything had poured out in a mass—her parents whispering in the kitchen about the Gabrielle Russier scandal, Hélène's suitcases, Mariette's cough, the tiny, bare, extravagant room of her childhood. She relived the chaos of her feelings as they were then, her desire for novelty, her fear of betrayal, the apprehension of failure, but, stronger than anything, the urge to go away. By getting married to an old man, Charlène had not only given Sabine the keys to her first apartment, she had also restored her love of rebellion. Sabine was the loving woman a man had abandoned in a hotel room because her body suddenly disappointed him. She was a girl from the provinces who'd allowed a film director to grope her before he gave the role to another woman. She was the actress who'd been required to play a bad sex scene in order to entice the spectator. And not once had she voiced her opinion. She was too accustomed to obeying, too eager to please, digging ever deeper the female furrow of submission and gratitude.

When she reread what she had written, she didn't know what to do with it. It was too personal to be performed the way she had performed *A Life*, and she was not Maupassant. She put the sheets of paper in a pretty cardboard sleeve, and put the cardboard sleeve in a box, and the box under her bed along with a suitcase and a few shoeboxes.

It was just before the Great War. In 1912. Safaris were being organized along the coast of Brittany by the Western Railway, and hunters showed up every Sunday to shoot the puffins that came to nest in France. They would go away again in the evening, leaving behind birds full of lead, starving chicks, and crushed eggs. One man, Lieutenant Hémery, decided to put a stop to the massacre. He created the Ligue pour la Protection des Oiseaux, and hunting in the seven islands off of Perros-Guirec was outlawed. Nowadays, the league for the protection of birds has more than 2500 members, and I thank you all for coming here this evening to listen to my presentation. I would also like to thank Seb for making the bar available to us."

Hélène had just seen Éléonore come into the café; Arthur waved to her and, threading her way through the tables, she went to sit next to him, toward the back. Hélène saw no one else she knew in the small crowd of students she'd managed to assemble with such difficulty, sticking little posters on the bulletin boards in the cafeteria and distributing fliers outside the university building, the way Léo used to do at the Lycée Cézanne, five years earlier.

"For four years now, the seven islands have been designated nature reserves, and the birds have been coming from all over—razorbills, common guillemots, northern gannets, gray seals, and many other species. This is their only nesting place in France, and it's the largest marine bird sanctuary in the country."

She turned slightly and pressed the projector button. The slide showed a pair of puffins, their little clown-like heads on the alert, their long made-up eyes, their colored beaks highlighted with two golden spots. She let the audience admire the birds and said with a hint of regret, "I would have liked to make it possible for you to hear the song of the puffin. I wish I knew how to imitate it, when it mingles with the sound of the wind it's sort of like . . . let's see . . . you know what a door sounds like when it needs oiling?"

The audience laughed. Éléonore must be relieved, she'd said to Hélène, "Don't be like me with vivisection, above all, don't turn them off, make them laugh if you can!"

"In the month of March, these ocean birds return to the islands, take possession of their burrows and find their partners again. They are faithful, and yet they live for a long time (a few chuckles among the listeners). Sometimes as long as thirty years. When you see them flying, they look sort of like penguins in the sky, don't you think? Speaking of penguins, let me show you a picture of a razorbill, which looks like a little penguin, this is the rarest and most endangered bird in France."

Éléonore had to put her elbows on her knees and her chin in her hands. She was staring at Hélène with encouraging concentration and, sustained by her gaze, Hélène began to enjoy talking to the students, *captivating them*, as Sabine might have said. Despite the gravity of her presentation, she could feel that sensation of control, even seduction.

Once she stopped speaking, she could have almost touched the silence. The vibrations that went through the listeners had weight and energy. She clicked for the next slide: a little island covered with white spots.

"Since 1930, northern gannets have been drawn to the island, because it is protected. These thousands of white spots are gannets in their colony on the island of Rouzic, often called the bird island. They chose it because it's a safe place, but also because the conditions all around are optimal when it comes to wind, mobility, and food."

In the audience someone shouted, "And how do gannets sing?" There was some awkward laughter, a pause that felt out of place. Hélène threw her head back and let out a rhythmic, staccato trill, a sort of succession of husky, repetitive, laughs. She couldn't believe she had dared to do this, to make a sensual display of something that could have been so comical. And maybe it was.

"That is more or less what a gannet sounds like."

There was some brief applause. Hélène let a moment go by. She looked sternly at the gathering to prepare her epilogue, and her anger returned, her disgust and sorrow. She pressed the button and an entirely black photograph appeared.

"This is a wave that can no longer break."

And the photos came one after the other.

"This is a bird that cannot fly. This is a white bird that has turned black. This is what it looks like now, the coast known as the Côte de Granit Rose. 1967. 1978. 1980. *Torrey Canyon. Amoco Cadiz. Tanio.* We may forget the names of the ships and the dates of the oil slicks. We may forget the names of the oil-covered birds—the fuel from the *Tanio* killed roughly forty thousand of them, more than twice as many as the *Amoco Cadiz.* We won't be able to save the puffins, and their eggs are covered with hydrocarbons and cannot possibly hatch."

Now she had come to the end. And this was not the easiest bit, far from it.

"But what I fear we will forget, above all, is our own sins. I don't think we are any better than those broken oil tankers, because we often dump oil illegally, we throw our plastic bags and bottles wherever we like, we don't question our agriculture or our industry, or the products we put in our washing powder or our paint; no, we are no better than Shell or Total!"

In the room indignation gave way to astonishment; some students were already getting up and leaving noisily, one man shouted, "Down with the multinationals!" Others protested feebly against their leaving, but they were disoriented and wary. Hélène raised her voice to drive home her point, what was closest to her heart:

"Fifty percent of our untreated, polluted water ends up in the ocean! We are our own worst enemies, and the worst enemies of fauna and flora! We are the worst enemies of life!"

Then lowering her voice, as if to herself, "Thank you for coming."

She kept her eyes down on her index cards, pretending to be sorting them, she didn't see Arthur, who had stood up and was applauding, which made others join in, timidly. No one asked Hélène if they could join the League for the Protection of Birds, as the little sign on the table next to her invited them to do.

"Mademoiselle Malivieri, you are incredibly brave," said Éléonore, hugging her.

"Your conclusion was very professional, well done," whispered Arthur, stroking her cheek with his hand.

They were like two parents at a party for the end of the school year, two parents whose pride is unconditional. Hélène knew that she wouldn't have dared to do anything without Éléonore and Arthur, and maybe she had, in fact, been speaking only to them. They left the neighborhood to finish the evening at a tiny bar on the rue Francoeur behind the Butte Montmartre. The tables were sticky, the lights glaring, and the clients looked lonely, most of them men who seemed to be roughly the same age, the age of men old enough to have slaved away at hard jobs and drunk a lot every night and even sometimes early in the morning before work. Arthur, in this place that was nothing like him, was joyful. At Éléonore's urging, he imitated Hélène imitating the gannet, he lost his inhibitions and it made him funny and sexy, laughter made him a little bit coarse and bold. Exhausted from the emotion and the failure of her presentation, numbed by the alcohol, Hélène felt good sitting there across from Éléonore and Arthur. Their tipsy kindliness, the mutual challenges they set one another (perhaps in the hope of impressing her?): it was all delightful, even Arthur's questions didn't bother her, whereas, under normal circumstances, they would have made her feel terribly ashamed. Looking Éléonore in the eyes, and speaking rapidly like someone who is embarking on a rather salacious interrogation, he dared to ask her if she had ever been to jail, if she wanted to be a civil servant one day, and if all lesbians were members of the women's lib movement. As a medical student he said he knew that homosexuality was a psychiatric pathology, but he had difficulty classifying it, and he had to confess that he found it easier to grasp the notion of female homosexuality than male. He spared her the question of what constituted the age of sexual maturity for homosexuals, or the issue of police records, but Hélène could see that Éléonore was relishing these naïve questions, as if Arthur were getting in way over his head and, every time, she had an advantage over him. While he was ordering his umpteenth vodka, she gave Hélène a long smile, which confessed to such deep desire that Hélène felt as if she were falling into the wind.

They said goodbye out on the sidewalk, Éléonore to head down to the rue Ordener, Arthur to spend the night at Hélène's, the way they always did after an evening together. They walked down the rue Francoeur, and the cherry trees in blossom, in the light of the street lamps, created dazzling apparitions, the stairs that climbed up to Montmartre tunneled a clandestine pathway through the night, everything seemed to be enfolded by an inexhaustible beauty. But when they crossed the Caulaincourt bridge, it all changed, they were walking above the cemetery and leaving behind the heights of the city sleeping in its poetry. They took a taxi from the rank on the Place Clichy and went back to Neuilly with the sense of relief of a bourgeois couple who, after an evening slumming it, is about to return to the comfort of their domestic feelings. Hélène put her head on Arthur's shoulder. She wasn't sure she didn't love him anymore. She wasn't sure whether she could do without him. She was terribly sleepy.

Agnès had started work again. She had received an official reprimand, virulent reproaches on the part of her superiors, she saw the company doctor again, and after a brief, mumbling interrogation, he had signed a paper saying she was fit for work. Then she saw her colleagues again. It was like waking from a long coma and finding forgotten faces at the foot of her bed; they look at you, she thought, as if you were someone they've missed, someone you no longer are. Did she have to be that person for life to start up again, for all to see? In the cold darkness of early morning, this meant putting the heavy satchels on her bike, pedaling against the mistral, stopping outside gates, opening doors to buildings, businesses, offices, delivering good news and bad, holding the inexorable power of words in her hands . . . *I gave birth to a little girl with Down syndrome and immediately abandoned her.* Her words. Confessed and forgiven. But it hadn't gone the way she'd expected. In the secrecy of confession, she had admitted to her sin and received God's forgiveness, and that had been the purpose of her stay at the abbey: to confess and receive absolution. But after forgiveness came penance. She waited for it ardently, had hoped it would be severe. She wanted to feel spiritually cleansed. But instead of telling her to say the usual prayers, the priest had to told her to simply go home and tell her husband the truth. Agnès's heart had stopped beating for a moment, as if protesting against the injunction; she wanted to cry out, "Never! I'll never do that!" What was the point of confessing if it meant going away feeling even more overwhelmed than before? She had hesitated to ask for something else, to speak of the mortification of the flesh, she would agree to mistreating her body, to subjecting it to cold, heat, hunger, thirst, she would do anything she was told, but she would not tell her husband the truth, ever. But because she had received the sacrament of the confession, she simply bent her head and said, "Amen." And now she felt poisoned by that order. She regretted her confession. Her religion. Her beliefs. But she did not regret giving up the child. She had feared her own incompetence, and she had feared the child, its need for affection, its lifelong dependency. That little girl with her moonlike face: she had nothing to give her, and she would be better off without her. Bruno wanted to share in mourning the child, and sometimes he disgusted her with his ineffable kindness, his love for her that blinded him. "I'll be sorry all my life that I wasn't there, it makes me sick to think that yet again you were all alone, I keep seeing you, I can't help it, I keep seeing you all the time." He had whispered this to her one night, in the half-light of the room, and Agnès wondered if he didn't know everything already. Let's not talk about it anymore, let's not talk about it ever again, it's the only way for me to get over it, she had said, and he had believed in her mercy. Since then, she had started work again and resumed her family life like before. She had simply erased a part of her life, nothing that belongs to the past exists, and soon this misfortune would be nothing but an old sorrow, nothing but a moment of silence.

Before leaving the *bastide*, Laurence had called her. She wanted to see her, and they decided to have a drink together in Aix. The weather was warm, they met on the terrace of the Deux Garçons. When Agnès arrived, Laurence was already there, she stood up to kiss and hug her. Agnès could feel the closeness of her entire being with a surprising precision—the shape of her body, her breathing, her quivering, loyal life. Agnès had gotten out of the habit of hugging, and she stood with her arms at her sides, as if restrained by a poorly cut garment.

"I'm so happy to see you! I've missed you."

Agnès smiled, as if her words were mere politeness.

"I've missed you too."

"Have you been back at work long?"

"For two months, since February."

"The coldest month."

"Yes. The coldest month."

"You're not too tired?"

"But that's why I started work again. So that it would tire me."

There was a group of students from the lycée at the next table: they were speaking loudly, using filthy language as if it were completely normal, the girls brandishing swear words usually only heard coming from boys. Laurence said, "Looks like Aix has changed, or is it just me?"

"A bit of both, I think."

"I feel really out of it!"

"I think we are."

And they were. They wished they weren't. Laurence wished she could still be that woman who was in step with the times, but a tiny lag had already come between her and the present day. She was astonished by a movement that had just been founded and which she referred to as "the oxymoron": the young Giscard supporters. Did young people ever stop demanding the impossible?

"Time passes so quickly, look at us, I feel as if it was only yesterday that we met at the market. Mariette was knee-high to a grasshopper."

"And now she's waist-high . . ."

"No, she's lovely, she's really got something, incredible charm. You can be proud of your girls."

"How is Rose doing?"

"She didn't respond when I told her I was moving out of the house. I was hoping she'd come just before I had to move. She didn't."

"That's the younger generation for you. I never see my eldest girls."

"No, I think it's just Rose's character. My daughter's a snob. She's very pleased with her rich husband. How is this possible? What did I do wrong?"

"We did everything wrong, I think. When you think about our dreams. But in the end, our daughters are doing what they wanted to do, and that's the main thing. Even if we don't understand any of it."

"Well . . . you've changed too, my dear Agnès. And I didn't see it coming."

"No."

Her assertion was so sharp that Laurence recoiled slightly.

"I can't remember the last time you came to the house . . . It was with Mariette, but when, exactly?"

"It wasn't with Mariette. It was over a year ago, in February, I just dropped by, without warning, but there'd been some gangland skirmishes in the north of Marseille and you had to leave to report on it."

Suddenly, it became all too disastrously clear. Laurence saw the scene again, exactly, how she had lied to Agnès. She wasn't on her way to report on anything that afternoon. She had a rendezvous with a man she liked, and who had just phoned to ask her to come and see him. She wasn't about to let anything stop her. Now she remembered Agnès's face, a face she had seen on so many women, as if they were up against a wall, at the end of a road. She'd noticed it and thought to herself, "Never mind, so what if I'm going to be a little selfish, she'll tell me later whatever it is she has to say." But later never came. It was after fleeing her appointment at the hospital maternity ward that

Agnès had gone to Laurence's place, to the aptly named Embassy. That day she would have agreed to anything Laurence suggested, would have taken any advice, any words. By the next day, it was too late. The next day it was already impossible. And besides, Laurence hadn't asked her a thing.

And so Agnès had gone on with her secret pregnancy, slowly slipping into a protective world of lies and distress, effacing herself to make room for duty.

They finished their drinks and paid the bill. As they were about to part, Laurence said, "I'd just like one thing, I hope you'll agree, that you won't think I'm sticking my nose into something that doesn't concern me."

"Tell me."

"I'd like to have my upright piano delivered to your place. I don't have room for it in my apartment and I'd like to give it to Mariette."

"To Mariette?"

"Yes, she's talented."

"On the piano?"

"Yes, I think she should take lessons. I owe her some money for the gardening. I'll give it to her, along with the address of the teacher Rose used to have. You don't mind?"

"No. That's fine."

"I'll have it delivered on Saturday, but I'd like it to be a surprise, so don't say anything."

"I won't say anything."

These were the final words of a friendship that had united them for ten years, right to the deepest place in their hearts.

Sabine had sat down on the edge of the sidewalk on the boulevard Raspail, because she was ashamed. She was crying so hard, choking with sobs, it was too much, she knew it, too expansive, too intense, too immodest. How could other people go on like that, walking, silent and dignified, their sadness buried deep within like a stake twisted into their guts? Paris was numb with sorrow, the city had slowed, almost two hours had passed since the procession left the nearby Hôpital Broussais, the funeral procession like a huge, clumsy animal, surrounded by hundreds and thousands of men and women, children and old people, all stunned with grief by the passing of Jean-Paul Sartre. The black hearse, covered with long red sprays of flowers, was being escorted by policemen, their gestures so gentle you could hardly recognize them as the same people who had arrested the intellectual so often during his lifetime. There were no police barriers, no crowd control, not even any detours, the usual Parisian frenzy had simply come to a halt to make room for the mournful numbness of a crowd of strangers all sharing this same grief. Rumor had it that Yves Montand, Simone Signoret, Françoise Sagan, and the socialist politician Michel Rocard were among the crowd, but it didn't matter, no one was famous, everyone was devastated and somewhat dazed. The moment did not seem real. Sitting on the sidewalk, Sabine saw the feet of all these strangers who had gathered without being summoned, without any rallying cries; they had waited for hours outside the hospital for the coffin of the defeated man. Now they were joined by people pouring out of the metro, the streets, the buildings, as if the magnet of a compass were attracting them, people for whom the loss of Sartre was the loss of an eminently meaningful figure. Paris was honoring a philosopher the way kings are honored. In the windows of newsstands, beneath a portrait of the writer, the giant headline of *L'Express* said: *Sartre Confronted With His Era*, and Sabine thought that the editorialists of the weekly magazine could not have imagined what was happening now, because the crowd surpassed the obituary: on this nineteenth day of April, 1980, Sartre was *confronted with his era* more than ever, confronted with all those who had read him, as well as those who had never read him, who had heard him, seen him, outside factories or in the street, in cafés, forums, at demonstrations, all those who loved him for this or that stand he had taken, this or that era, a book, a play, mistakes, reversals, all the sincere moments of wonder of a noble conscience. Sabine saw the pedestrians of Paris and no longer knew where the procession had gone, but it hardly mattered, because Sartre was more than the dead man lying in a bare coffin with Simone de Beauvoir sitting next to it, it was as if he were everywhere, all over the city, and all the other cities, in France and in the world. The little man who thought he was so ugly, the thinker who was almost blind, was mourned the world over, and Sabine wondered if there really was nothing left of him, or whether he could receive some of this universal tribute: do the dead do us the honor of greeting our tears, or are they all already in that great glacial state of nothingness? Where was he, that man who had lived through an era of wars, colonization, and revolution, and who had questioned it all? What would carry him, now that everyone would want to speak for him, interpret him, analyze, contest, argue over him, this clique or the next one, this current or the next one, for naturally there would be schisms, insults, and efforts to monopolize? Sabine had stopped crying, she felt simply the confused fatigue brought on by sorrow. She made her way slowly with the silent crowd and arrived at the cemetery without even realizing it, long after the funeral procession. The crowd suddenly seemed less anonymous, as if everyone had been overcome with fear when confronted with the unthinkable, concrete wall of never again, and the titles of his works echoed strangely, *The Wall*, *Nausea*, *Being and Nothingness*, it was as if everyone were thinking about them, and they became a hymn, a secular prayer. Sabine understood that the people had not, in fact, been accompanying Sartre's coffin; it was he who, once again, had led them to the foot of what must be strikingly obvious. As she entered the lanes leading through the cemetery, constricted by the crowd, Sabine again pictured the photograph on the front page of *Libération* that she had framed and hung on the wall at home, a black and white photograph of Sartre walking into the wind, his shadow not following but preceding him, because that was the direction he was headed, into the realm of shadows.

She heard the disorganized, teeming multitude. People were climbing on the graves, knocking over headstones, some fell and were hurt, a baby was screaming, television reporters held out their microphones, young men took photographs. Terrified by death, people returned to their tangible concerns to evade it, and the place of mourning was taken by curiosity and feverishness. Sabine left the huge, unquiet cemetery behind.

She walked aimlessly through the city, past the Luxembourg Garden, until she reached the Place Saint-Sulpice, a landscape that always emerged from behind the trees, surprising. Drawn to the colors and the high shop windows with their gilded lights, she came to a stop outside the

Yves Saint Laurent boutique. She could just make out the depths of the shop, which must smell of polished wood, leather and flowers, something powdery and spicy, too, like a lemon sliced open, and it was troubling to think that, in all likelihood, she would never open the door and go into this place. Standing outside at the window all at once she saw, trapped in the haze of clothing hanging on lacquered mannequins, the blur of her own face—with so little about it that was pleasing, her body squeezed into a poorly cut coat . . . and she recognized her mother. That tired face, that ordinary figure outside the great couturier's shop window: this was Agnès, a young woman of twenty-three, silent and cautious. Then, as if she had taken her by surprise and their meeting was somehow indiscreet, Sabine turned away. She hunted in her bag for change and went to the phone booth next to the newspaper kiosk. She was agitated while dialing the number; she didn't know how it would go, if she would have the courage to speak, but she needed to say that, in spite of the distance of these recent months, and despite everything she had found out, her love was intact. Perhaps even stronger than before.

The phone rang for a long time before Agnès picked up. She had the sleepy voice of someone who has been taking a quick nap and no longer knows, in the middle of the day, what she is really emerging from.

"Hello? Hello?"

"Maman, it's me, it's Sabine; listen, I only have three francs, can you write the pay phone number down and call me back? Yes, yes, everything's fine, don't worry, it's just that, you know, I've just been to Sartre's funeral. Sartre! Yes . . . the philosopher. Okay, call me back please."

She gave her the number and hung up, tense, feverish, as if she could only speak to her mother from this pay phone and they would have to hurry. Children were playing around the fountain, she saw them without hearing them; they were scattered here and there, radiant as they splattered one another, stamping their feet, the sprays of light forming strange halos around them. The phone rang.

"Sabine? You went to Sartre's funeral? What did you do that for?"

"To be there."

"You know that the Church has condemned his writing."

"One point in his favor."

Agnès hesitated and said, "Funerals are sad."

"Maman, what I wanted to say . . ."

She had to tell her now, that she knew, about the death of her first baby, long ago when she was young.

"It's just that . . . I'm the same age as you. In fact."

"What do you mean?"

"The age you were."

"But why are you calling to tell me that?"

A group of Asians were taking pictures on the steps of the church, between the massive columns. What country were they from? Why did people here think they all looked alike?

"Maman, I wanted you to know . . . Mariette, she told us, at Christmas, on the balcony, well never mind where, before you came back, she told us about the baby—"

"I can hear your father coming in."

Agnès's hostility traveled down the phone line like a long throbbing nerve.

"Your father's here."

Sabine made a huge effort to continue the conversation, "I'm standing next to a fountain. With children. There's a church, too, for the funerals of famous people . . ."

Agnès was speaking to Bruno, "It's Sabine on the line. Yes, she's fine."

It was unlike Sabine to call in the middle of the afternoon, but her father, apparently, hadn't taken the receiver, Agnès was speaking to him as if he were in another room, coming and going, possibly, putting down his briefcase, his jacket, taking off his shoes. His voice came to her from the background, a metallic reverberation.

"Kiss Papa for me."

A man knocked on the door of the phone booth then tapped his watch. Sabine gave a start, and, in the time of that start, her mother had hung up. The guy was shouting now, as if he'd missed a train and it was Sabine's fault, he felt well within his rights, he was immortal and powerful.

Sabine sat on a bench, pictured her mother at her side. Aren't you cold? Paris is like this in April. But the children don't care, look at them, they're already soaked, they'll get told off when they get home. Or maybe they won't, it's probably their usual after-school game. Proper little Parisians. I know why I was so sad today. It scares me, that freedom Sartre talks about, I'd like to be able to make the most of it and I can't. I cried a lot. I'm cold, I'm going to walk some more. Don't stay on this bench. Go inside the church of famous people, there are some Delacroix, blackened by time, *Jacob Wrestling with the Angel*, you'll see, he's a sturdy angel, an athlete, but he doesn't look like he's struggling, he looks like he understands.

She left the bench and thought, "and there wrestled a man with him until the breaking of the day." And she was astonished that she knew this biblical phrase she didn't think she'd ever read or heard.

Mariette didn't want Laurence's piano. "I don't want it!" That was what she said, spontaneously, when Agnès, breaking her promise to keep it a surprise, informed her that it would be delivered Saturday and that one of the beds would have to come out to make space for it in her room.

"It's out of the question! It's my sisters' bedroom. Where will they sleep when they come? In one month, it will be summer!"

"But they don't come. Or hardly ever."

"That doesn't matter. What matters is that they *can* come. I'm not taking any beds out."

"If I'd been this lucky when I was young, to have someone give me a piano . . . ! You get everything handed to you on a platter and you can't even appreciate it. It's sad and . . . disheartening and . . . disappointing, too. Yes, you're a real disappointment!"

"You take the piano, then, since it's so wonderful!"

"Are you really going to turn down such a precious gift? A piano on your fourteenth birthday?"

"But I don't know how to play, what would I do with a piano?"

"I saw you going over your notes from music class again, what was that for? And Laurence told me you have talent. That means she heard you, it means you played for her."

How could Mariette tell her mother that music came easily to her fingers, but with it came a flow of threatening words that chilled her to the bone with fear, like those nightmares when you stumble, and feel the earth splitting open under your feet?

"I don't like music," she said emphatically. "I like silence."

Her mother laughed and turned away, and she was still laughing when she went into the living room, where she turned on the television, and laughed some more at the commercials for the little ready-made meals by Bolino (*Bo-li-no! Bo-li-no!*), which she must have thought were every bit as stupid as her daughter. Mariette slammed the door so hard when she went out that the keys hanging on the wall rack fell to the floor with a sorry clatter.

"What an idiot! Bitch! Stupid bitch!" Mariette mumbled insults that brought no relief. She couldn't stand her mother anymore, that pathetic new laughter of hers, the laughter of a liar, of a woman who runs away and leaves you, laughter to camouflage her morbid memories and her remorse. She saw her standing motionless in the kitchen, or coming out of the bathroom not even washed, coming home from shopping with the net bag half empty, and smoking out on the balcony, her obstinate gaze, waiting for who knows what. She got lost in the apartment as if the six hundred square feet were a maze and she didn't know which way to go. Mariette felt like rolling up her sleeves to challenge her openly, "Go on then, go ahead! Go ahead and hit me if you're a woman!" And she would have covered her with blows, right where it hurt, she would have split her open like a taut, juicy fruit, splat! "Bitch! Stupid bitch! I hate you! My god, I didn't know I could hate you so much."

She'd been walking for a long time, and so quickly, and now she was taking tense little steps through the damp, narrow streets of the old town in Aix, her breathing hot and painful. All of this, she thought, is because of those chords that come all on their own, because of Laurence, because of Joël, too, and poets, because of my sisters, all my sisters, Sabine, Hélène, and above all Xmas, I hate them all, everyone I love, I hate, I hate them, I love them I hate them I love them I hate them . . .

With the passing weeks, walls had cracked open deep inside her, releasing a sadness that was unbearably sincere. She was discovering an unfair world, and her pain was so great that there were times she had to cherish it not to die from it. She was trying to find her weapons, her defenses, her talents, and she couldn't. She sat on the steps of an old building where pigeons were cooing, and she took her face in her hands, "Help me please, I can't stand her anymore, help me . . ." She prayed to her lifelong friend and struggled to regain that lost feeling: love. She leaned back against the peeling wooden door. The pigeons, with their tired eyes, clucked at her, offended, she knew she shouldn't stay near them, she didn't have her Ventolin with her, she'd been forgetting it more and more often, forgetfulness like an emancipation: that was *another* medicine she would really rather do without. She stood up, feeling nauseous . . . and she thought she could hear the Bonnie Tyler song. She'd forgotten about it, that magnificent song that made no sense. She remembered the dreary kitchen, the meal interrupted by the news, *Habemus papam*, and the song and the Pope were forever associated, as if, in the end, both were ordering to do the same thing, "Love one another! Go on then, and love each other!" knowing all the while full well that it was impossible, a real debacle, a planned massacre, and far from helping you to live, the advice would only discourage you and leave you helpless. On the Cours Mirabeau she went over to a little fountain covered in streaming moss. She splashed her face with icy water, then her hair, her neck, her shoulders, she was soaking, her T-shirt was clinging to her skin, she was almost cold now, Bonnie

Tyler was still singing, so she kept pace and, relaxed the way you can be after you've been running or dancing, with her hands in her pockets, she walked to Joël's place. Since music was to blame, for everything.

She'd never gone there without prior notice. She'd never gone there without him, without going first to get him at the shop. She rang the bell for a long time, and now she was looking at him from the threshold with the delighted expression of someone thinking, "Here I am, I had to come I had no choice, isn't that funny?" He didn't think it was funny. She was disturbing him. He was tired and feeling a bit low that evening. He gave her a towel so she could dry off, and one of his shirts, which hung down to her knees, and she drifted in it like a lost sparrow. The shirt was white and she began slowly flapping her arms.

"When I was little, I had a picture of Joan of Arc, one of those religious pictures obviously, Joan of Arc was burning at the stake and the smoke gave her these magnificent angel wings. Like this, see? Do you see my angel wings?"

"Do your parents know you're here?"

"Forget about my parents, they haven't cared about where I am for a long time now, and I just had an argument with my mother."

He glanced at the telephone.

"All the more reason to let her know where you are."

"Hey! I know what I'm doing, okay? I don't need to call them. Why don't you get me something to drink?"

"Tea? Fruit juice?"

"Are you messing with me?"

"No, you're messing with me. Do you really think I'm going to give you alcohol?"

She flopped down into an armchair with a sigh.

"I had enough water at the fountain, thanks!"

He let it go, that slightly false moment where she hid her sincerity behind an awkward insolence, a forced casual attitude. She would eventually tell him what was troubling her and then she'd go. So, he waited, sitting opposite her, his arms on his knees, his gaze still a little veiled by his long hair that was supposed to hide the face he didn't like. Time went by and gradually he saw she was breathing differently, relaxing her shoulders, slowly closing her eyes, and then pressing her lips when the emotion welled up and caused the skin to vibrate on her cheeks and her forehead, where her damp hair left tiny little beads. When at last she spoke, her voice was so low he had to strain to hear her.

"She taught me some chords and then I began singing and playing the piano, and that's when it happened, you see, the words, they were horrible. Mean. I'm not a mean person, I swear. And I don't really like music, I told my mother, I like silence, so what would I do with her piano? And what about my sisters? They can't go sleep somewhere else! It's hard to sleep alone and not hear them breathing, I miss it, not hearing them breathing. So, I can't accept that piano. I don't have room."

Since he didn't entirely understand, he simply said, "Don't worry, you're not mean."

But that must not be what was bothering her, because she kept looking at him, waiting for more, for words of support. He said, "And music . . . well, music . . . it *is* silence."

There, he'd got it right. She sat up, and her tiny body, in the shirt that was too big, suddenly grew larger. He lowered his eyes, looked at his hands and twisted them a little, as if playing with them.

"What do you mean, music *is* silence?" she asked.

"For a start, if you're listening to music this much, it means you like it, and then—and this is very rare—it means you know how to hear the silences that make up the score. When it's part of the rhythm, silence is very active."

"Really?"

She stood up to walk around the room. She was thinking about what he had just said, shooting suspicious glances at him, as if to check how serious it was: could she believe him? She came to a sudden halt.

"Actually, I knew that! Music and silence, I've always known it was the same thing, but I didn't know how to say it."

He didn't dare ask her to leave, but he knew her, she was going to pick over her thoughts, then ask him some more questions, and he could feel a deep fatigue overwhelming him like a weakness. She was elated.

"So, this means—correct me if I'm wrong—that I can play music, well . . . say things with music without needing words?"

"Exactly . . ."

She rushed so quickly into his arms that he held her, not understanding what was going on. In her forward rush she had bashed his forehead.

"Oh, I'm sorry, I hurt you!"

"I'm okay, really, I promise."

He pushed her away gently and went over to rummage through his record collection, there was something he had to do.

"What are you going to play for me?"

"Schubert. The first movement of the *Sonata D 960* performed by Brendel."

She sat on the sofa. He put on the record and joined her, murmuring, "With Schubert, silence is fundamental. Listen . . . the piece lasts fifteen minutes. Listen carefully."

And they listened. The struggle between elation and fury, anger and joy, while the silences held something threatening. They weren't ready for any of it and the music poured out like a furious torrent, a splendid waterfall. Then the silence became frustration. They felt like shouting in it. And the game continued, giving them barely a moment of calm before the most lucid turmoil. They listened, tense and excited. Beneath the pianist's fingers, his seemingly endless number of hands—how many hands were there?—seethed the energy of the struggle. They were two travelers caught in a storm, and Schubert was telling them, "You have to live, but I am warning you of the danger." When it was over, they weren't quite the same anymore. Their fingers were entwined, Mariette's head was on Joël's shoulder, the music had thrown them together. They didn't want it to stop, this interlude in their life, because it seemed to them that, in this shared moment of calm, despite the turmoil of the sonata, they could rest, at last, they could detect one another's smell, rising faintly, strangely familiar. The water from the fountain on Mariette's hair, and Joël's slightly peppery smell, subtle and thrilling. Mariette slipped down to place her ear on his chest. It was the rhythm of a march or a rather slow dance, the original rhythm. She listened to the relentless, miraculous workings of his heart as it took the blood and cleansed it, took the blood and propelled it back into the body so the promise would live. "I love you." She said it to Joël, trembling with joy. She loved. The feeling had come back at last with surprising, almost troubling ease. He placed his open hand on her hair, it covered almost her entire skull. He could feel Mariette's veins throbbing, her eyelashes fluttering against his chest, the sound of her throat when she swallowed her saliva, he could feel it all as if she fit in his palm. She was strong and tiny. Determined and instinctive. Life itself. He wanted to pull her closer and kiss her, lift the shirt that was too big and inhale her skin. Love her for a long time, tenderly, for hours on end, days and nights. She was barely fourteen years old. He said to her, "Time to go. Get your clothes and go home to your parents."

She stood up slowly, not speaking, not disturbing anything, and when she went out, he heard the sharp little click of the lock, not to close a door, but to seal a pact.

VII
The Promise

Hélène thought spending the weekend in Villers would be a good idea, it would keep her from obsessing over the wait for her exam results from the May session. And how could she not be there for David's fifty-fifth birthday? He'd never liked celebrating his birthday, but this time he gave in to Michelle's wishes, and, in his concession, there was a new docility. He never spoke about his cancer, he went on leading the same life as before, at the same pace. He had told Hélène that the days he had his outpatient chemo, in a room with other patients, were precious moments for him. He admired those people. Their courage, their life stories, so different from his own. She felt he would have liked to open up a bit more, but as she remained silent, so did he. She was embarrassed when he allowed her a glimpse into the fallible part of his life. To Hélène, he had always been the man at the helm, impressing others. She remembered when she'd been ten years old or so, going to visit the headquarters of his company at La Défense. He was very imposing in his suit and tie, tall and slim, striding briskly down the corridor, his secretary talking to him while trotting along behind, then holding out a paper for him to sign and he had signed it *while walking.* Hélène had been stunned. He'd shot her an amused glance: he'd wowed her, hadn't he? And so, she understood he'd done this for her benefit, not the fact of signing *while walking*, something he must do every day, but the way he'd acted so utterly casual and relaxed about it. Almost a state of grace. She could not have admired him more if he'd walked on water.

She got to Villers the day before the birthday, and everyone showed up the following morning. She hadn't seen them in a long time—her cousins, their spouses, their children, and their friends, boys and girls she'd known when they were the age she was today, and whom she'd admired so much. Back then they'd lived their gilded youth with a potent, indisputable joy, as children of the rich. They were twenty years old and she thought they were splendid. The girls were full of a joyful, open sensuality, they sat leafing through magazines and picked out the clothing they intended to buy for the next season. At the time, Hélène didn't know you could do that, pick out your clothing in a magazine, and go to a shop to find the things the models were wearing in the pictures. The girls who flirted with Vincent and Joseph used her as a go-between with their notes and errands, calling her "the little messenger" and laughing, while waiting apprehensively for the answers she brought back. Sometimes she lied. But it was so easy to sow confusion in those nascent couples that she didn't do it often. It was a terrifying power for such a little girl to have, and she wondered how lovers could change their minds so suddenly. For her, love was not a game. For her, either you were very old, or you were little. But young, never.

Now she was watching them arrive, and not all the erstwhile lovers had become the married couples of the present day, but they were all happy to see each other again and to celebrate David. He had to force himself a little, welcoming them with open arms, but he seemed to be counting them mentally, like an actor on stage checking how many people are in the audience, "Well? How many have shown up, in the end? Oh, so we'll have to make do with what we've got . . ." Invariably they told Hélène she'd grown, and she'd changed, and they asked, "How are things in Marseille?", they checked whether she was wearing an engagement ring, they hesitated to ask her straight out whether she was single, because she was no longer their little messenger girl, and they no longer fell in love, or in any case didn't talk about it. They either loved their spouse or kept their secrets. Past the age of thirty you didn't live with a cohort of friends but in a relationship, you no longer hung around together on the beach or at the club stables, you invited each other to dinner. That didn't prevent a return of complicity, the complicity they'd known in their youth, those last moments of freedom before they had to fall into line (they called it "assuming their responsibilities"). Get married. Have children. Make a living to raise the children. And by then, it would feel as if the important things had been taken care of. You'd followed in your father's footsteps, or your mother's, and you'd kept to the straight and narrow. The falls would come a little later, deliverances and destruction, and perhaps by then their twenties would seem like they'd been their best years.

Now those girls were young married women, well-groomed and wealthy, and growing older had conferred a different sensuality on them, more assertive, like a musky perfume: they knew what they were worth. In a way, they had taken charge. They'd obtained their degrees from the finest schools, degrees that served no purpose; they ran their households, saw to renovations and redecorations; interior design and furnishing took up all their time, and when it was finished, they would move house. And begin again elsewhere. One time Vincent's wife, on opening the door to Hélène, had said, "Sorry about the noise, I've got the workmen in, I don't know what they're doing." It was the height of wealth and the leisurely approach. Nowadays these girls couldn't get over the children who were *their* children, drowning them in love and anxiety, above all, showing them daily how quickly time was passing. "When he was two, he was already wearing a four-year-old's clothes."

"But darling, he *was* four years old!" "She used to fall down all the time, do you remember? I was so ashamed when we went into Jacadi! She'd skipped three whole shoe sizes! Feet are what grows the fastest." And then there were the mutual compliments, the wondering where they'd found that absolutely incredible dress or handbag. Tips were swapped, "The best manicures are in Manhattan, don't you think?" and without a transition they moved on to more serious topics—whispered, sincere dismay, they needed to confide in each other, women confide so easily, it's almost a courtesy, thought Hélène, observing them just the way she used to do when she was four.

Smoke from the barbecue was invading the cliffside garden, and fragrant clouds wafted down to the beach, spreading a pungent smell into the sky. David and Michelle had literally gone the whole hog, and there were cries of admiration when the guests saw the pig roasting on the spit, turning slowly above the flames. Everyone contributed advice regarding the embers and the cooking time, the air all around grew warm, like their faces when they stood too near the barbecue.

David said, "You'll have some anyway, won't you, Hélène? You all know that Hélène is a vegetarian."

Hélène smiled, apologizing. One girl gave her a pitying look. Joseph said with a laugh, "Oh, these green types! What a bunch of wet blankets." Michelle said, "No, I'm sure she'll have a bite." She had the authoritarian manner of someone holding all the cards, and she spoke about Hélène as if she were a little girl being asked to taste before refusing, and not to say, "It's not good," but rather, "I don't like it." Hélène didn't obey her anymore, but she knew that by showing up alone, without a partner—"unaccompanied," like a child on an airplane—she was leaving herself open to this sort of remark. She wouldn't expose Arthur to the judgment of the Tavel family, to David's hostility, and on her own she lacked legitimacy. On occasion, Michelle still asked her to play the young lady of the household. This was how she indicated who she was: neither a servant, nor immediate family. Vincent called for an aperitif, and that changed the drift of the conversation: they spoke indifferently about the benefits of the Liberty and Security Act, the upcoming races at Deauville, the latest Action Directe shooting, the Audi Quattro four-wheel drive. The pig was taking ages to roast, the children were hungry. They went up to the creature shouting, "Eeew, yuck!" Some stuck their tongue out, one little girl asked, sobbing, whether it was dead. They explained to her that of course it was dead, otherwise the poor thing would be in terrible pain. "But then why can we see his head?" "Don't you see his eyes are closed, you can see he's dead, don't be silly." The little girl cried all the harder and then her cousin started up, too, the effect was contagious. The adults looked spitefully at the impaled pig, it's true it wasn't a pleasant sight, its head and body pierced through with the spit, its legs curved back and trussed up. They decided to settle the children in a spot under the trees with a packet of chips and some Coke, never mind, they'd eat better that evening.

After the meal, everyone went off for a nap, while Michelle helped Marylin, the domestic employee, a young student from Lisieux, to clear up and put away the silver and the crystal glasses properly. This was the sweetest moment, when everyone had gone off and was being lazy, after this meal that had gone wonderfully, and at the end the children had come back carrying David's cake and singing Happy Birthday. At around five o'clock, they decided to go for a walk. The tide was low, the beach was vast and deserted. The landscape belonged to them and held so many memories that they were surprised to see their children running around and blurring their images of the past. Some couples held hands, in the grip of a nostalgic tenderness. Others avoided each other and overplayed their role as parents, noisily goofing around with the children, who were gleefully surprised. They eventually settled on the sand. The tide was coming in. They couldn't see it yet, but that silvery, hazy glitter on the horizon could only be the sea. Hélène lay down in the sand, the June sunshine was as light as a veil, tossing in the wind, she could hear the cry of the seagulls, not so harmonious when there were so many birds. Everything seemed a little bloated, scattered. She began to speak out loud, to herself, to the others, keeping her eyes closed and still feeling the breath of the wind, full of sunlight.

"Zola didn't know why he got so upset when he saw animals suffering. It's difficult to formulate such suffering and even rather shameful. I've studied pigs at length. The one you've just eaten, a product of different crossbreeds, is known as a Large White, and I know its story."

She thought she could hear laughter. Adults? Children? She didn't know. Her own voice went on resounding between her ribs, and, as she spoke, she felt as if she were banging on a drum. She liked it. She went on:

"For the pig to be born, the pig-keeper had to masturbate his father, and a woman had to sit astride his mother—don't laugh, when you're in a hurry you have to accelerate the onset of the heat, and this entire story is nothing more than a story about time, what I mean is, profitability. *Time is money*, right? Besides, with these new pigs the male cannot possibly service the female, his heart would fail. Genetic selection has made them extremely frail, their muscles are weak, they are more flesh than bone, their vital organs have been sacrificed and the gene of sensitivity to stress has been removed, because it acidifies the meat . . ."

She could tell people around her were moving, the sand was crunching slightly. Were they still listening? The breeze was blowing harder, the air felt a bit wilder, with the smell of kelp, dry and salty, stronger in the heat, as if marinated.

"To get back to our Large White. To his genitors. Following

insemination, the sow is fettered for a few days, not to lose any of the seed. She's been in the dark since she was born, but she's not alone. Thanks to hormones, all the sows, several hundred of them, get pregnant at the same time and they'll give birth at the same time, receiving the same injections to accelerate their contractions, and they'll drop litters of more than fifteen piglets. Sows were not programmed for such a number, so they get help, if the piglets are not taken out quickly enough, the last ones will die, so the breeder puts his hand in, searches around inside the uterus, takes out the piglets, some of them will have malformations, others are asphyxiated, but even then, these losses have been figured in. If the sow is really too weak, she'll be entitled to a cesarean. They knock her out, split her open, and they take out what's left. If she can't feed her litter, they'll send her to the slaughterhouse. Often her nipples get infected, they give her more antibiotics and anti-inflammatories, and after twenty days the piglets are weaned and the sow is inseminated again. The hormone injections have reduced her cycles and so she is hyperprolific. At this pace, she won't live longer than two or three years. Like all the males, she'll get an astounding number of hormones, injections, and medication, including quite a lot of antidepressants, all of which end up on our plate. Due to all the antibiotics they've been fed, pigs have also developed resistant bacteria, and they pass them on to us, too. Bon appétit! In fact, there's not a single animal that gets as much medication as pigs do. I don't know what Zola would have made of all this . . ."

Hélène could hear the undertow. The sea, our sick blood, was coming back in. She thought about the fettered pigs in tons of shit and urine, slipping on the grating; she thought about everything being dumped daily into the ocean. She thought about oil slicks. About green tides. She heard the children singing a nursery rhyme: *Ring-a-round the rosie / A pocket full of posies / Ashes! Ashes! / We all fall down.* The same one she used to sing as a little girl. She didn't need to open her eyes to know she was alone. And as often happened in such moments, he came back to her. Silent. Fanatically tender, whimpering, attentive. The dog that had loved her and guided her toward the animal world, toward the suffering that human beings thought only they had the right to own. As she dug her fingers into the sand she felt as if she were touching Caprice's soft fur, his fine coat, slightly bristly on his trembling hide. I have to do more, she thought, I have to speak to the children. Not just in magazines for subscribers who are already aware. I have to go and see the children. In schools. Summer camps. Libraries. Wherever they are, speak to them. And take them to nature reserves, parks, teach them about nature and animals. I have to inform the adults of tomorrow. *Ring-a-round the rosie / A pocket full of posies . . .* She sat up. The sea had come very near, now, it was spreading across the beach, and the sun was setting, soon everything would be orange and gray, dark. She watched the children dancing, the dazzling light that distorted them slightly. She thought it was incredible how they could circle for so long without feeling sick.

Sabine was walking so quickly down the rue Boissière that it sometimes felt as if both her feet left the ground at the same time, like when you're running. She was practically leaping, propelled by the energy of her anger, but now she was about to twist the dagger of insult and plunge it into other bellies besides her own, with all the smiling and nervy confidence and artistic hysteria necessary. She was going to get her way, occupy the territory, land another part. She was an actress and she was afraid of nothing, neither scorn nor barriers, she knew how to withstand vexation, disdain, salacious gazes and disinterest, too. She could do anything. That was what she kept telling herself, on her way now to a screen test at a production company who were looking for an actress her age to play the daughter of Marlène Jobert's neighbor. She had two scenes, one next to an elevator, the other next to a mailbox. And she knew her lines by heart.

It was getting close to half past six in the evening, the street was slowly turning gray, peaceful after the agitation of the day. It was Friday evening, and here in the sixteenth arrondissement with its old-world beauty, women walked out of boulangeries with ribbon-bound boxes that must contain treasures. Everything seemed more imposing, more massive here, and perfectly organized. The Eiffel Tower had not yet made its entrance into the night; it was waiting for complete darkness to turn on its projectors. Sabine always felt moved when she was near it, and near the Théâtre de Chaillot, forever associated with the time she first met Mathieu. It had been in October, exactly three years ago. She could already, in Paris, count off her memories from several years ago, reference points from six years ago . . . Six years she'd been living here. There was what she had dreamt of, and what had happened . . . She held her portfolio to her chest, with its photographs of the filming of *Girls of Words*—on one of them, her intense gaze, her edgy sensuality, then more provocative on others, the girl who's afraid of nothing, the actress who can *give her all*. Photographs from the set! She would show them to the casting director she was doing the test for, she was proud of them, despite her dubious attitude toward the film itself, which was due to be released in a few weeks. The press screening had been held ten days ago. There were no innocents in the theater. They were all journalists who knew the tricks of the trade and were on the lookout for the kind of film that would be identifiable but surprising, with discreet nods to the masters but its own freedom of tone, a creative élan backed up by a flawless film crew, and original, good-looking actors. But the movie seemed like a distortion of what Sabine remembered filming, a penniless parody. She'd waited for her own scenes, but didn't see them. They'd all been left on the cutting room floor, except the ones with Gaspard, and Sabine had become a wall of a woman on screen, a stockade, skin and nothing but, the skin of an outsized doll, with a thick voice, splayed breasts, a massive back. She'd never seen herself from behind, she had the back of a woman warrior, tough and awkward. She'd sensed the expectancy and annoyance all around her, the critics had seen worse, sex scenes were now as inevitable as credits, they should have taken things further. Or not as far. Anything but this half-hearted sensationalism, with this carnival actress . . . !

She tried not to think about it anymore, to save her energy and let go of her anger, she had to hurry, because she was going to be late for her screen test. It was almost dark now, she liked the way the décor was changing, this sudden nocturnal plunge leading to an entrenched landscape. *Good morning, No, I haven't seen him, Oh, it's out of order again, Goodbye, Madame Martin, It's stuck on the seventh floor I think, Yes, a good day to you, Good morning. Oh, it's raining.* She rehearsed her dialogue, it accompanied her like a little song, and she turned into the rue Yvon-Villarceau to the rhythm of the words she was repeating, *No, I haven't seen him, Oh, it's out of order again* . . . Memories mingled with recitation. Chaillot. *Dead Class*. Mathieu sitting next to her. Unacquainted. Unseen. *Goodbye, Madame Martin, It's stuck on the seventh floor I think*, two bodies as yet unknown to each other, *Yes, a good day to you, Good morning. Oh, it's raining*, the theater and the stage breathing together, *Good morning, No, I haven't seen him* . . . The noise was so loud it was unreal, unfamiliar, paralyzing. It was as if the air was sucked away then blasted back again, as if the earth trembled and shifted on its axis, buildings exploded, glass burst from the sky to fall in fine blades, piercing clothing, lodging in skin, covering the ground and mingling with fire and blood and a strange charred snow that filled the sky and transformed it into an apocalypse, a snow of ash and metal. Sabine didn't understand what was happening. She was imprisoned in her fear, unable to breathe, her gaze frozen, incapable of decision. Tall, thick black flames barred the horizon, and the fumes from the smoke were stifling. Cries and shouts were mingled with stupor, the street was stunned, disfigured. Shop windows, cars, motorbikes, windows: all gutted, nothing left, calcified carcasses, collapsed ceilings, floors flattened, shutters blown off, they were already walking on ruins. Pedestrians screamed as they ran, dust covering their terrified forms. The sirens of fire trucks, ambulances, and police cars, of the gas and electricity companies, soon mingled with the clatter of invisible helicopters. There was a constant crunching underfoot, like that of a creaking jaw: the shards of glass all over the ground, trampled by the crowd. It was completely dark out now, a darkness of nightmares, a prison. Sabine could go no further. She stood motionless in the middle of the road, jostled by everyone trying to get away from the trap without knowing how. Still more terrible cries came from the rue Copernic a few yards away, lamentations, orders, whistles and sobs. On the sidewalk, a woman was holding a baby close and imploring Sabine, "It's my baby! My baby!" Sabine couldn't move or answer her, her body had stopped, and it seemed nothing could revive it. A man took the woman by her shoulders and led her away to find help; firefighters and doctors were offering medical assistance here and there along the devastated street. Sabine, still holding her portfolio tight against her chest, saw this disfigured life; the street lamps cast fragments of unbearable reality onto the ground. She was waiting for everything to be back to where it should be so she could continue on her way, but the chaos seemed to feed on chaos, the tragedy kept unfolding relentlessly. She wondered if the people at the production company had gone to their windows, if any of them were hurt, if she could still take her screen test, someday. Would she remember her lines? Would people still make movies? Were they going to live? There were more and more people in the street in spite of the barriers the police were putting up; people looking for each other, people trying to get home, to telephone, an old man was asking if anyone had seen his dog, a very handsome labrador, very friendly, with a collar, he called out to him, staggering, "Énarque! Énarque!" What a funny name for a dog, thought Sabine, and the man came up to her. She didn't want him to speak to her, she shook her head, Don't speak to me I haven't seen your dog I didn't see anything I don't know what is going on. She wasn't part of that chaos. She was absolutely not concerned by any of it. The man put his hand on her forehead, "Mademoiselle, you need to see a doctor," and he showed her his bloody fingers. And then, as if by putting his hand on her he had woken her up, she felt the pain, a cramp all through her body, it seemed as if she had just opened her eyes. And that she would never close them again. When she faltered, the old man caught her by the arm, and that was when she saw it, while her own body was slowly bending and falling to the pavement of crushed glass: it was lying full length on the sidewalk, under a long red sheet. How was this possible, since Sabine was alive, that death could be so near? Who was under that sheet? Who had taken on that appearance? How could anyone die so suddenly? In the street. Among the crowd. Where were the bombs and the rifles, where were the soldiers? She didn't see them. She wondered whether they had switched on the projectors under the Eiffel Tower, was it burning there, too? Where was Hélène? Was this a war? Was Paris burning? And still looking at death where it lay on the sidewalk, she passed out.

It was just the two of them now in the pew at church on Sundays. Bruno and her. Agnès recalled the family they used to be, and how she'd been so proud, two young parents and their three good little girls. She didn't know whether her daughters were believers, yet it was in this church that she missed them the most, this place of family representation, of prayer and rest. Before, Sunday used to be the day of the Lord and of their picnic, waiting in the car. As soon as mass was over, they spent the day in the country, all five of them, and came back in the evening, glad of their "healthy breath of fresh air." No sooner did they get to the apartment than Agnès ran a bath in the tub for her three girls, and she didn't start making anything in the kitchen. She nicknamed the Sunday evening meal "Bread butter milk hot cho-co-late!," and, in lieu of dinner, she simply took the milk and butter out of the fridge, and the girls dunked their bread and butter in the hot drink. Naturally she got something else ready for Bruno, cold cuts, camembert, and rosé wine, not unlike the lunchtime picnic. He made do with that. He felt good, because she did, too, because she relaxed and forgot her role of nurturing wife and mother, a role imposed on her, a role they'd all ended up thinking she'd taken on by choice. And now it was just the two of them. A couple on their own. Standing at her side, Bruno sang the hymns with the fervor of a young boy scout. When he knelt and took his face in his hands, she wondered what he was thinking about, and there were times she envied him his hopefulness. She would have liked to pray, too, to address someone. The way she used to. Now she attended mass as if it were a show she'd seen hundreds of times, in which the only novelty was to be found not on stage but in the audience, the worshipers changing over time as they relocated, had children, died. Agnès looked at her husband's bent neck, she had held it so often when they made love in silence, eventually laughing from the effort of not making any noise. It was still a beautiful neck, solid and square, with some gray hair already that seemed to have landed there by chance, on the wind. When they were engaged, he used to take her on his motorcycle, and she would hold him around the waist and look at his neck, he had a crew cut back then, and when she ran her hand over his hair the wrong way it was prickly, and she liked it. But she didn't overdo it. They mustn't get carried away by sensuality, mustn't let it go too far. One day, at a bend in the road, the motorcycle had skidded. She still had a scar on her knee, and the regret that he hadn't known how to protect her. Like all adolescents, he tried dangerous things, he told her that, one night with a cousin, they'd made their way along the outside of a moving train from one car to the next, clinging to the door handles, finding footholds on the steps. Maybe he was boasting a little to make the presumed good boy a little more attractive, make him the boy who had imagination and nerve. The summer he was sixteen he went all along the beaches on the Côte d'Azur astride a camel, vaunting the merits of Ricard pastis, with advertising in the form of a cloth hanging down the camel's side. In the black and white photographs with their deckle edges, she saw a boy in a suit and tie, handsome and smiling, nonchalantly leaning against the camel curled up at his feet. Yes, he was handsome. An American actor, Cary Grant, or Gary Cooper in *High Noon*. When they were newlyweds, he used to sing the song from the film to her, *Do not forsake me, oh my darlin' / You made that promise as a bride / Although you're grievin', don't think of leavin' / Now that I need you by my side . . .* Later, he had sung for his daughters. And now, only for the priests. Or to himself, on his own. He sang in the apartment, going from one room to another, pouring wine into bottles, trying unhappily to repair things. She was thinking about all this, that Sunday, when there was the little commotion among the worshipers that was always brought on by the sign of peace after the priest's injunction, "The peace of the Lord be with you always." Agnès had never liked this bit—turning to the others, shaking their hands and murmuring, *Peace be with you.* Members of the same family, of course, would kiss each other, "the kiss of peace." On Sunday when Bruno kissed her, *Peace be with you*, she felt awkward, as if he might suddenly change the formula and murmur, *Tell me the truth.* But why would he ask her for the truth, since he thought he already knew it?

Unless truth was indeed to be found in that church, on that Sunday. She knew very well that she was alive, that little girl she'd given up for adoption exactly seventeen months and eleven days ago, and she had the right to live where she wanted. That day, when the time came for the sign of peace, as she turned toward the parishioners in the pew behind her, Agnès saw her, in the arms of a strange man. He and his wife were in their forties. Five other children were at their side, between the ages of eight and fifteen. And then her. In her father's arms. Adopted? Biological? *Peace be with you.* The man held out his hand to Agnès, and as she could not take her eyes off the child, the little girl, after smiling at her, suddenly buried her face in her father's neck. It was a game, she looked at her, then took refuge again, close to him, hiding her face for a few seconds, then showing it again—more surprising, more moon-like, more smiling, too.

Agnès left the church without shaking the man's hand. Bruno caught up with her outside, jostling past the worshipers who were going up for the Eucharist, the body and blood of Christ. She was walking, taking short, stunned steps, breathing so hard it almost sounded as if she were humming. He followed her, like a man who has come late, and suddenly he put his arms around her. She stiffened, her mouth closed, her fists clenched. And he was the one who wept, the tears of a man who is not used to crying, with moans and spasms as if he were imploding. She pulled away from his embrace and walked through the streets of this town you could go around so quickly, and which from wall to wall, from square to square, reflected all her memories to her, all her ghosts, every age she had ever been, and it seemed to her that as she walked through the city, she was walking on herself.

Later, they were together again at the apartment as if nothing had happened. Agnès was in her room reading, Bruno was in the living room marking papers and preparing classes, Mariette had come to have dinner with them. She answered their questions distractedly, they listened just as distractedly, yes, she'd practiced all day long and no, she said again, it didn't bother the record dealer to have her piano at his place, most of his neighbors were old and deaf. She now had an irritating habit of drumming her fingers on anything she found—a table, a stool, a cardboard box—she was working, she said, practicing rhythm and the independence of her hands, and she maintained she was still working when, not long after, she left the kitchen to shut herself in her room, lying on her bed with her Walkman on full blast in her ears, she even had the nerve to say, "Don't disturb me for any reason, I'm doing like Alfred Brendel, I'm learning by listening to the great pianists."

But that evening, they did disturb her. Bruno told her he

was leaving for Paris the next day on the first train. Agnès sat on her bed and held her, a gesture she hadn't made in a long time.

"Sabine just called," said Bruno.

"How is Hélène?"

"Sabine has been . . . slightly injured. In the attack on the rue Copernic on Friday."

They sat together looking at each other, as if they had just noticed they were there. Something had taken hold of them, ruthlessly reuniting them. Even if they had been trying to avoid each other, they still kept the memory of the others inside—father, mother, sister, daughter, it was written, and it was enough for the telephone to ring and for there to be news for each one of them to be unwittingly projected back into a family they had thought they were free of.

"When I think," said Bruno, "of all the things we've worried about since the girls were born, never, never once would we have thought—a synagogue? Seriously? Who could have imagined . . . a synagogue?"

Mariette could not help but burst out laughing.

"Oh, Papa! Is life playing tricks on you?"

He nodded, lost between his anguish as a father and his failure to understand.

In light of her reprimand and her recent reintegration into the civil service, Agnès could not afford to miss work. Bruno had never been absent from the collège, not once in more than twenty years. So, it was logical that he should be the one to go and see their daughter. But Agnès wished she could stop him. She suddenly remembered what Sabine had said on the telephone the day of Sartre's funeral. How much did she know, exactly? She would talk to Bruno. It was a source of such anxiety that Agnès eventually concluded that maybe it would be better this way after all. For everything to be revealed, in the end. She was still incapable of doing the penance the priest had ordered, and if she started seeing the little girl there across from her, like that morning in church, where would it lead? Bruno felt a bit dazed to be packing his suitcase and leaving alone. He'd written down the address of the friend's place where Sabine was recovering, 8 Cité Debergue, near the Picpus metro. The next morning, he left La Petite Chartreuse with the sensation that, at last, someone would be expecting something from him. And he felt guilty: given the circumstances, was it normal to be happy?

It was very odd to see him show up in Paris, this father of hers who came from the unchanging city of her childhood. His presence disrupted the order of time, like a little mistake, like stubbing one's toe on a familiar obstacle. Hélène had surprised him by waiting for him at the Gare de Lyon, and she saw him walking toward her, this dazed man, with his old suitcase and poorly cut raincoat, far too light for the season. He sat down in the metro car, vigorously saying, "Bonjour!" to the other passengers, then he spoke loudly, calling Hélène "my little Parisienne!" She spoke quietly, hoping he'd adjust to her level, but he went on at the same volume, "Your mother isn't getting any better, I don't know how to help her anymore." She was about to ask him to be more discreet, and then she figured that all these people around them existed only if she decided that they did. It was easy to make them disappear. She found it moving to be there with her father, Bruno Malivieri, who, twenty years ago, had waited for her at Marignane airport with his ID card, and even his card for the large family discount, just in case. One thing was for sure, he wouldn't have come so quickly if she'd been the one who'd got a piece of glass in her forehead, he would have thought she didn't need him, she had another father to take care of her. Maybe it was time for her to explain to him how wrong he was.

Hélène went with him to Paul's place, where Sabine was waiting. Bruno felt better once he'd seen her. He'd expected something else, his daughter in bed, her head in bandages, something more dramatic. She had a huge bruise on her forehead and a few stitches, but she seemed fine and glad to see him. He hesitated to ask her the question that had been troubling him ever since she'd called: this Paul she was staying with, who was he to her? Were they living together? Did they practice what was referred to nowadays as "free love"? But he didn't dare, and he dreaded the coming night, when he would go to bed and know the two of them were in the same room. Before heading back to the university, Hélène had advised her father not to speak about the attack if Sabine didn't bring it up herself, and he didn't know what to talk about.

"I love Paris."

"What do you mean you love Paris, Papa?"

"When I was in the army, I was a driver here for my colonel. I took him everywhere. Military service lasted a year and a half back then."

"But did you know your way around the city?"

"Not at all."

"Then you must have gotten lost."

"I found my way around thanks to the landmarks and the Seine, and whenever I headed in the wrong direction, my colonel told me where to go. He never fired me. I think he really liked me. And I really love driving."

"But Papa, you never told me you loved Paris."

"I was afraid it might make you want to live here. That was stupid of me. You wanted to live here anyway. I thought it was too dangerous for a girl on her own . . . anyway . . . Well. Let's change the subject."

"Did Hélène tell you not to talk about the attack? We can, if you want to."

"What were you doing in that neighborhood?"

"I was on my way to a screen test for a film."

"Did you take it?"

"No, it happened just before, and, anyway, I don't care about the movies, I don't want to do any more movies."

"Don't say that."

"I thought you'd be glad."

"You know, whatever you do, I'll worry. In any case, the worst things happen just when you least expect it. Who'd have thought you'd be one of the innocent victims of the rue Copernic?"

"Innocent?"

"Not Jewish, I mean."

"Oh . . . you sound like Raymond Barre[17] . . . it's awful, awful to hear the stuff those men say."

"The bomb wasn't meant for you. Is that true or not?"

"It's true. It was meant for hundreds of children who were celebrating their bar mitzvah."

He knew what she thought. But they weren't about to get into an argument now. They had to agree about everything, they had no choice.

"I'm glad I came, I feel better, you seem to be doing . . . not too bad. Right?"

She smiled at him. And it was as if she were smiling from a great distance, as if she were on a ship pulling out of harbor.

"In a little while, if I can borrow the telephone, I'll call your mother to reassure her. She was so worried! I'll call when she's back from her rounds."

"Of course. And since you love Paris, go out for a while. Would you mind getting me some cigarettes? I've run out and I'm going crazy."

"Yes, it will do me good to walk. To see what your neighborhood is like."

[17] Prime Minister at the time. He was criticized for making a similar remark in a public statement after the attack.

"It's not my neighborhood. I live in the ninth. There's a bar-tabac just over the way, rue du Rendez-Vous."

"What an incredible name."

"Didn't your colonel ever ask you to drive him to the rue du Rendez-Vous?"

"Most of the time we were somewhere around the École Militaire and Les Invalides. I always looked forward to the evening, to the moment when they lit up the Eiffel Tower."

"I understand."

Half an hour later, Sabine called Paul, he had to come home right away. In the time it took him to close the agency and take the metro, he was there. He found her curled up on the sofa, holding the cat, stroking it vigorously, which the animal didn't seem to mind.

"I don't know what he's doing, I just asked him to go and get me some cigarettes!"

Paul handed her his own pack, and she lit one immediately.

"What the fuck is he doing? He's been gone for an hour!"

"He's exploring. He's wandering around. If he gets lost, he'll ask someone the way."

"My father never 'wanders around,' I can tell you don't know him."

"Maybe he's having a coffee . . ."

"And he was supposed to call my mother to reassure her!"

"Perfect. He probably found a phone booth."

"Please, Paul, go and look for him."

"But how will I know it's him?"

"Listen, he's my father, you'll know him."

"Do you have a picture? Can you tell me what he looks like?"

"I don't know, I suppose like me, he looks like me."

"Like you?"

"Listen, Paul, use your imagination! He's my father, he's

wearing an old, unfashionable raincoat, he has graying temples, and he looks Catholic, that's it. Don't tell me you've never seen a Catholic?"

"So, he stopped off in the Church of the Immaculate Conception . . . he, uh, he's praying . . ."

"Never mind where he went, go find him!"

"I'd be glad to, Sabine, but it could take forever. I'll go off and look for him, he'll come back, you'll worry about me, and ask him to come looking for me, he'll go out, I'll come back, he'll be gone . . ."

"And you think that's funny? I really don't see what's funny about it."

"No, Sabine, I'm smiling because . . . I just realized I'm saying *tu* to you. And it seems perfectly natural."

"I want my father to come back!"

And she burst into tears. He took the cigarette from her fingers and held her close, gently rocking her, as if he were dancing. He always seemed to have a little tune in his head, to be following a melody only he could hear.

Bruno came in not long after that, with the cigarettes. Sabine didn't tell him how worried she'd been, nor how afraid she was of the street, of absence, of dusk. She didn't recognize herself anymore. This lack of courage, this cowardice. And she was someone who'd so loved Racine's heroines, the force of their sorrows, their passionate foolishness . . . She felt as if she'd never dare to set foot outside, ever again, that the Paris she had loved so deeply was no longer waiting for her, but lay in ambush, like an enemy.

That evening, Paul made one of those very basic meals he had a knack for: pasta and wine. He put on a record by Carlos Gardel, and to this slow, wrenching, crackling music, Sabine watched him talk with her father, and could not decide which one of the two of them seemed further behind the times. She saw how Bruno was trying not to interrupt Paul to ask the only question he really cared about: When are you going to marry my daughter? If she had told him that Paul wasn't her fiancé but a friend, he wouldn't have understood. Since they got along well, and the man had a good position, and a place to live, and obviously cared for her, Sabine would have a good life with him. She wished she could view life that way, with honest simplicity and clear convictions.

"Did you like the quartier, Bruno? The twelfth arrondissement is one of the nicest in Paris, full of little dead-end streets, pretty houses, and the Bois de Vincennes is only fifteen minutes from here. On foot!"

"I didn't know this neighborhood at all, I wandered around a little, it was nice."

"Papa?"

"Yes, my girl?"

"What have you got there on your arm? That bruise inside your elbow?"

Embarrassed, he hastily pulled down the sleeve of his sweater.

"Papa? Do you really think that was reasonable after such a tiring trip?"

"You see, Paul, how my daughter scolds me?"

Paul didn't know what was going on, he simply sensed between the two of them a current of complicity and tenderness, something he had never known. His own father, despite his constant smile, had been the saddest man on earth. And Paul would never have dared scold him in any way.

"I wandered around, like I said, and there was this little van . . . just there in front of me. And so up I went."

"And you gave your blood?"

"Listen, Sabine, I had just gone past that children's hospital, behind your place here—"

"This isn't my place, Papa, I told you. The Trousseau hospital?"

"Yes, maybe. And an ambulance from the pediatric emergency services pulled in and, oh, it broke my heart and I thought about what you told me . . ."

"What did I tell you?"

"About those children, those young Jewish children who were about to have their—what did you call it? Bar something or other?"

"Bar mitzvah."

"Let's not talk about the attack anymore, I'm sorry, Sabine. Who is this singing, Paul? He must have had a very unhappy life."

"Gardel? He had above all a lot of success, even if he came to a tragic end, I'll grant you that. I can put something else on."

"No that's very kind of you, I'll get used to it."

When they were lying together in the same bed, in their pajamas and far enough apart not to touch, Paul dared to ask Sabine if her father regularly donated his blood like that. She told him that he was a universal donor, that he'd even received a medal, and on the windshield of his car he'd put a sticker, "Be a sport, give your blood," in the French tricolor. When she was little, she sometimes went with him, there was a place in Aix specifically for donating blood, an old building with broken floor tiles and peeling walls. She remembered her father lying among the other adults giving their blood, he always had a kind word for the nurses, and they all adored him. They knew he didn't always respect the eight-week gap between donations, but there was so much demand that after lecturing him a little they drew his blood all the same. And I suppose, said Sabine, that that was one of his rare moments of disobedience.

Then very soon, like every night, she pretended to fall

asleep. This reassured Paul, and meant he didn't have to be constantly looking out for her, practically suffocating her with care. She had tried sleeping on her own, it was impossible. Hélène had offered to take her in, but she knew her well enough to realize that she really didn't want to. Nor did Sabine want to go back to the way it used to be, the two of them in the same room, and now she was the older sister who'd become fragile, afraid of the dark like a child . . . ! Once Paul was asleep, she sometimes got up and went to sit on the sofa. The cat would come to her. She'd stopped chasing it away, she would hold it and not let go. She wouldn't do that tonight; her father was sleeping on the sofa bed. She'd always thought that the day he came to see her in Paris, he'd be with her mother and Mariette, the entire family there for her. She would have left their names at the box office and asked for the best seats, and they would have been like royalty, applauding her with the pride of people who've switched off the television to enjoy a live performance at the theater like real Parisians. A live performance and their daughter's victory.

Testing, testing, can you hear me? It's Mariette. Hi, Sabine! Since I don't have the money to come and see you, and since you don't have a piano at your place—at least I don't think so—I'm making you a cassette. When I was in the hospital, you know, after my accident, you sent me the recording of your play, *A Life.* I listened to it a lot, it really helped me pass the time—well, I mean, it helped me. A lot, even. Anyway. Enough talking. I wrote some music for you. I'll put the microphone on the piano and play it for you. It's not much, all right, I'm just starting . . . okay I'll stop talking. It's called, *For Sabine.*"

Mariette closed her eyes. She'd practiced the piece she'd composed for her sister so often that she knew it by heart. It was inspired, in part, by her Czerny exercises, and more markedly by her stunned disbelief at the murder of John Lennon. But she wanted there to be some hope and strength and also, obviously, moments of silence. She knew that one day she would really compose, and that she'd be able to express herself. For the time being, she had to learn, and she wondered how far she could get with her knowledge, her discoveries and progress, could she accomplish something in the end, was there a point beyond which you stopped learning? If that turned out to be the case, then it would be like dying. For the time being, she applied endurance and ambition to her exercises. Her music teacher, during her piano lessons, was also showing her how to use her body, not only to build the muscles on her hands and make her fingers supple, but also how to move around, to walk, to come back to the keyboard and play standing on her feet, touching the keys with a glissando, familiarizing herself with the sensuality of playing, how to caress, find roundness, fullness, learn how to hammer and strike and wrench, how to grate, too. The exercise that seemed hardest to her was the one where she had to become aware of the weight of her arm, to imagine it being held by a thread, and then this thread suddenly breaking, her arm "in free fall," as her teacher put it. And she thought, "I'm learning how to free-fall, if my parents only knew . . ."

That was all she wanted, to fall, indefinitely, and for everything to be new, possible, dangerous, unknown, and even this delightful waiting, Joël's promise, it was like breathing when the sun is too strong, she looked at him when he wasn't aware of it, she listened to him as he came and went in the apartment, she spoke to him when he wasn't there. He was in her life. *Her life.* Until now, she'd always felt as if she'd been tied up and forgotten somewhere, in a bedroom, a classroom, a family. And her sisters: for fourteen years she'd tried so hard to grow and catch up with them . . . her thoughts made her lose her concentration and now she was improvising, moving away from the piece she'd composed for Sabine, she was playing, or rather the music was playing *itself*, another melody, freer, less effortful. She had wanted to grow up tall to be closer to Hélène and Sabine, and she'd stayed so little, barely five foot tall, the irony of it . . . A mouse, a little sister, with their shared secrets, Xmas Xmas Xmas, the music went faster than she wanted it to, carrying her along like a rushing current, alone with her father in the kitchen, waiting, the lies, Xmas Xmas Xmas, now the music went with some chords that were awkward and others that were instantly beautiful, but without pauses, or half notes, or silence, with neither control nor mastery, Xmas Xmas Xmas, she was being carried away, drawn by something more powerful than she was. Then suddenly it was over. She stopped playing. Switched off the tape recorder. She remained at the keyboard, her hands on her knees, staring straight ahead. It was almost dark out, the coming storm had changed the color of the sky, it felt like evening even though it wasn't even two in the afternoon.

"You have to keep that piece."

Joël had come in, how long had he been listening?

"You have to transcribe it and keep it, Mariette."

"It's not for me, it's for Sabine."

The sky was rumbling but the rain didn't come. The wind blew along the roofs of the close-knit streets, you could see the dust it raised, the dance of Christmas decorations hanging from the trees. In the sky, there were vibrant streaks of lightning they couldn't hear, and then, suddenly, a dull sound like stones collapsing, mountains cracking, far away.

"I don't like it," said Mariette. "I'm going to wait a little until I leave."

"Don't you have a class at two o'clock?"

"Gym. I have a dispensation. Really. You don't believe me?"

"You don't have asthma anymore."

"And that's why. I don't want to have a relapse."

"I see."

"Are you all right?"

"Mm."

Christmas was not a good time of year for Joël and never had been. The shop was crowded, there was the Christmas Eve party at Langogne, and now that his sister Corinne had found him, he wished he could forget them all, his foster family and his biological family, kiss them all goodbye. Corinne had sent him a photograph of their parents' wedding, and he had felt crushed for weeks. Since then, he'd been buying notebooks where he jotted down ideas and excerpts from songs. He hoped that this flow of words would drown the past, but his cramped, nervous handwriting was proof that it wasn't working.

"Hey! Can you believe someone posted this at school?"

Mariette held out a paper, which he didn't take. And so, she read it out loud.

"'I call on all slackers, sleazeballs, druggies, alcoholics, fags, women, parasites, young people, old people, artists, jailbirds, dykes, apprentices, Blacks, pedestrians, Arabs, French, long-haired vermin, crazies, transvestites, former communists, and convinced abstainers—everyone the politicians overlook—to vote for me, to sign up at their town hall and to spread the news!' And he finishes with, 'Everyone unite, let's shove it up their ass!' Isn't it great? It's Coluche.[18] You could almost set it to music, don't you think?"

He laughed. She gently pushed back the lock of hair hiding his face. He let her do it now and no longer shrank away from her. She said, "I'm taming a feral cat." He replied, "I'm taming the penal code," and took her in his arms. Holding each other close, they breathed better and relaxed as desire rose, a desire as sweet as laziness, and which they allowed to pass over them before they parted without breaking the law. This was good, too, this desire and their perception of what they would experience soon. Belonging. Pleasure. Mariette would be fifteen in just six months.[19] When Joël thought about it his heart felt ready to burst. Would he know what to do with her? Mariette

[18] Coluche (real name Michel Colucci) was a much-loved, irreverent, at times controversial French actor and comedian active in the 1970s and early 80s. He ran briefly for president in 1981 against François Mitterrand. He died in a motorcycle accident in 1985 at the age of 41. He is also remembered for founding the charity, still active, Les Restaurants du Coeur, which provides meals for the needy.

[19] The age of consent in France is fifteen, set in 1945.

might say over and over, "Juliet wasn't even fourteen when she loved Romeo," but he could tell she was acting a little brazen. He desired her the way he desired a woman. But he wasn't very sure of himself. What if he hurt her? What if he ruined her adolescence? He desired her the way he would desire a woman he would never leave, with whom he could start a family, and if she didn't want to, if she only wanted him and the piano, well that was all right, too. That song by Ferré often went through his head, and he understood it better than ever now. *Ah! Little one Ah! Little one / I'll teach you the verb to love / Which is conjugated gently / Far from jealousy or torment / Like the sunlight slowly fading . . .*

"My father read in the paper that Coluche got sixteen percent in the polls, just behind Giscard, Mitterrand, and Marchais.[20] My parents are obsessed with the elections, they say if the Communists win, there will be Russian tanks on the Place de la Concorde and they'll close the churches. Do you think it's possible?"

"No. And anyway the left will never win. Let me walk you to the lycée before it starts raining, I know you're afraid of the storm."

"You're the one I'm afraid of! You should see your expression . . ."

"What do you mean . . ."

"I swear! You're grouchy, you know, when it's holiday season. It doesn't seem to make you very happy, the birth of Jesus Christ!"

"On the contrary, for shopkeepers it's a godsend!"

"If Jesus saw all this he'd be disgusted, I'm absolutely sure of it."

[20] The Communist candidate.

"Well then that's something he and I have in common. Let's go, before the storm comes."

"Will you kiss me?"

"On one condition."

"Try me."

"Promise me you'll transcribe your improvisation before you send it to your sister."

"But it'll take me forever!"

"Promise!"

"Okay. I will. So, are you going to kiss me?"

He didn't know whether she was being provocative or innocent, whether there were times when she was playing with him, or whether she wanted to belong to him, if she understood what it meant. Was she asking for a kiss because she loved him or not to go to class? He was both attracted to and puzzled by her youth.

Hélène couldn't get over all the colors—clothing, skin, the range of countries, horizons, this variegated life she had never seen until now. And now she was taking in the incredible energy of this quartier with its codes, barriers, complicities, transgressions, much more obvious than anywhere else. People sold everything, everywhere: on pieces of cardboard under the elevated railway, on bits of sidewalk, quickly and illegally, in narrow shops, in dark premises, in multi-story buildings. They sold fruit, miniature Eiffel Towers, magical herbs, bags of fake leather, textiles. They sold girls, too. Whether it was on the Boulevard de Clichy or the Avenue du Roule, Hélène wasn't fooled by what this cut-rate exoticism or opulence might be hiding in the way of trafficking and oppression. But now she lived here. And she breathed better than in Neuilly. She felt as if she were in a different country, and it amazed her that she could travel between the two addresses just by taking the metro. Éléonore had told her about a friend, Raphaël, who was a dancer in Joseph Russillo's company, and was rarely in Paris. In his apartment on the rue Germain-Pilon there was a room free . . . and an impressive number of plants that needed watering. In exchange, Hélène would pay only a modest amount for the rent. The five-story building at the back of a tree-filled courtyard dated from the early nineteenth century and was divided into twenty or more apartments. The minute you opened the entrance gate you consigned the noise and commotion of the boulevard to oblivion, like finding shade after the midday sun.

Hélène had obtained a scholarship, and, in addition to her articles for the youth magazine, she gave private lessons in physics and chemistry to students just starting the lycée. So, for the first time in her life, she was completely self-sufficient. David had insisted on depositing some more money in her account; she had refused. He had asked her if she still loved him, and when she rolled her eyes and gave an exaggeratedly weary sigh, he told her that he thought it was all very good indeed. He wasn't used to people not asking him for things—work or a loan or a gift, or could he pull some strings, or find them a house here or there for vacation, or an apartment. He was the man who helped others. And whom they always begrudged slightly in return. But Hélène didn't want anything. And because this bothered him all the same, he said, with a mocking air as if he were joking, "Please don't tell me you're getting like your older sister Sabine, are you?"

"What do you mean?"

"That you sing the *Internationale* and raise your fist whenever you walk by a bank?"

"My sister never does that!"

She laughed. Her emancipation had nothing to do with any ideology; up until now she'd felt no remorse in taking advantage of David's money. Life was sweeter with money, and she knew how cruel and demeaning it could be when you didn't have enough. Money freed you from doubt, it solved problems before they even arose. But now she simply didn't want to be indebted to anyone, to ever need someone else's money, be it from a father, uncle, friend, or husband. This financial emancipation meant she could allow herself another one: pecuniary independence meant she was gaining sexual freedom. Never again would David be allowed to give his opinion about

Arthur. Or anyone else. Never again would anyone try to find her "someone suitable." She didn't love Arthur the way most people imagined love should be, he didn't fill a void, he wasn't her other half, because she didn't feel she was missing a part of herself. She didn't look on him as her destiny, or as a kindred spirit, he wasn't "the one," as the English called it, she wasn't looking for a "special soul." She wanted "the two of them." Him and her. Éléonore was her first guest at the rue Germain-Pilon, the first to whom she opened her door and her bed, in that apartment her friend already knew, which wasn't really Hélène's but which signified her entrance into an "exclusive" life—one that excluded other people's curious gazes.

To experience something she had so often imagined was as life-changing as finding herself in a different era. She was astonished by what she dared, it seemed to her that, for the first time, she was deciding something personal, allowing herself to live her life. She was exactly where she ought to be. It was a simple as that. She had never wept after an orgasm, she didn't know how it could be wild, irrepressible, violent. It often happened when making love with Éléonore, and she couldn't understand where this sorrow came from, these sobs waiting like pearls of water to be hurled against a wall and explode. After lovemaking, Léo would light a cigarette and open a bottle of champagne—"I know of nothing more beautiful than two champagne glasses on a night table." Hélène had filled her fridge with bottles of cheaper vintages, and, before long, this penchant came to represent that winter of 1981, cold and snowy, giving Paris the look of a city dressed in white and nocturnal darkness, a milky sky, an early night washed down with a pale wine that left in their mouth a taste of fruit, skin, and leisure.

It now took Hélène barely ten minutes to get to Sabine's place, and probably that proximity had something to do with her decision to live on the rue Germain-Pilon. She needed to know that her sister was nearby, and she dropped in regularly; sometimes she got the impression she was disturbing her, as if Sabine, since her return from Paul's place, enjoyed her solitary withdrawal. It was outdoors that she suffered. A shout, the sound of a motorcycle, someone bumping into her still startled her; the onset of night made her jumpy. To Hélène she said, "I'll never look at old women the way I used to. I know what it means to feel vulnerable when you're surrounded by people in a hurry, or sick among so many healthy people. I don't like them anymore, those vigorous, ambitious people who always win, I like people for whom just crossing the street is a victory." She'd always been astonished by the way everyone woke up at the same time in Paris—artists, naturally, with their fictional world, narcissistic and flamboyant; and scientists like the ones Hélène met, researchers, geniuses, scholars; but also ordinary people in offices, factories and schools, people who'd been at work since dawn or who were finishing their night on duty—invisible cleaners in office buildings, foreigners behind bars at the Préfecture, patients in hospitals on their way into the operating room, prisoners at la Santé, the young blind people from the Institute, bellboys at luxury hotels, prostitutes at the Porte Dauphine, Carmelite monks in Montmartre, girls from the Lido . . . thousands of lives in fragments. Sabine could sense them when the sun was rising over Paris, and their combined energy had often given her strength. Now it filled her with a restrained, shameful melancholy. She knew they were all ready for death. But did they know it? Did they ever think about it, now and again?

That Sunday, she entrusted Hélène with reading the notebook she'd started to write in again. She hovered nearby, pretending to be busy with other things, but waiting expectantly for her reactions, the slightest gesture, her silence, and when she laughed it was like approval.

"May I ask why you're laughing like that?"

"But Sabine . . . don't you realize?"

"Realize what?"

"How funny it is!"

"It isn't funny! It's political."

"Listen, just listen:"

And Hélène read out loud, "'They were in the kitchen like two burglars caught in the act, and, looking at them, I realized that their baptism had served no purpose. My parents bore the weight of original sin like the old man carrying his bundle of sticks, an unavoidable and constant burden. Eve was the eternal poisoner, as well as the Good Mother, and her virginity doomed every woman, because what were my parents discussing that day in their kitchen in La Petite Chartreuse? They were stunned to learn that in the city where they lived, people fell in love without asking permission from the Pope, and women pulled up their skirts without the authorization of a lawyer.'"

"It's the Gabrielle Russier affair, Hélène, not a skit! You're reading it ironically on purpose, but if you read it seriously—"

"Well, it would still sound funny."

"Precisely the mood I'm in right now."

"It's like a sad clown. And stop squeezing the cat like that, you're going to suffocate him."

"He's used to it, he doesn't mind."

"Honestly, you will never understand a thing about animals."

"He understands me, that's the main thing."

"And what does Paul have to say? Doesn't he want him back? Doesn't he miss his cat?"

"Paul is Paul."

"Which means?"

"I'll introduce the two of you someday."

"Oh! So, it's serious . . . What? Did I say something stupid?"

"Paul is a savior. He has an armband with *SOS Sabine* on it. That's all. Right. I'm going to make some madeleines."

"Again?"

"Again."

"Can I stay for a while?"

"Are you that curious to read what comes next? I thought you were working on your thesis and your master's and all the rest, and that you had no time for yourself, for a change."

"I'll stay, I really like watching you bustling around in your kitchen, you're like a commercial for Moulinex, I didn't think it would suit you but it does."

"I'm glad you can at last see some of my qualities."

It was a Sunday evening in February, insular and quiet, Paris was deserted, each quartier felt like the provinces, emptied of those who worked there during the week, only residents remained, people together, taking their time. Hélène lay down on the sofa, she would have gladly taken a nap, a little siesta for ten minutes, restorative and dreamless, but she was gripped with curiosity, a desire to know and a slight apprehension about what might come next, an unhealthy curiosity, Arthur would have called it.

"Vacation at the campsite in Ramatuelle was the only carefree time in this worried life we lived the rest of the year. You wouldn't have recognized my parents. They seemed so young that more than once it was all I could do not to enroll them in the Mickey Mouse club. My father invented a new way of swimming, halfway between sidestroke and napping: 'Corsican swimming,' he called it, and I loved going in the water with him—even if he always, once we'd gone past the buoys, far out from shore, said, 'Can you feel the sharks brushing against our legs? Can you feel their fins, their enormous mouth?' I was frightened and I liked being frightened with him, I loved it when he was joyful and carefree. Once vacation was over, he seemed as drab as his teacher's smock, and he would hurry to Marignane airport to pick up Héloïse, as tense as if he'd been summoned there by the border police.

"My sister, whenever she came back from *there*, always seemed a little suspicious of us, as if we were somehow substandard, and I fully expected the health inspectors to show up at any moment to check the expiration dates in the fridge or the size of the tub where we took our bath—the same water for the three of us, and it's true that whoever came last was out of luck, that's why every Sunday in the car on our way home from our picnic one of us would suddenly shout triumphantly, 'First dibs on the bath!' She'd won the clean water. The other two would shout, 'Seconds!' often simultaneously, so our father, like any good head of household, would arbitrate. I think I can safely say that none of us ever held it against the winner. We were always free to try our luck the following Sunday.

"I often had to bite my tongue not to tell Héloïse what I'd seen in the stables that day, it would have given me no end of pleasure to knock down her pretty house of cards. I didn't envy her the buzzer for calling for service at the dinner table, or the bed with its gazillion pillows, not to mention the endless farting of her horrible short-haired dog, no, what I envied was the unconditional love she got, our uncle's regard for her. He saw someone in her that we didn't know. But our cousin was fucking the groom and I had witnessed it. Maybe I never told Héloïse about it simply to keep something to myself that she didn't know and, for once, to have something over the Tavels."

Hélène put the notebook down and went to join Sabine in the kitchen. The madeleines were already in the oven, they smelled delicious, almost nauseating. Sabine was wiping the table with the sponge, with the concentrated air of someone who is miles away from what she is doing. Without looking up she said, "Did you read it? Did you like it?"

"A lot."

"Do you think I should keep going?"

"Of course."

"Where are you? How far did you get?"

"I've read the beginning."

"You still think it's funny?"

"Yes, there's humor, but it's . . . it's political, too."

"I don't know what I should do with it . . . a book, a play, or . . . since it's so funny—"

"I didn't say it was funny, I said there was humor."

"Well, since 'there is humor' maybe I could work it into some sort of . . . stand-up."

"Why did you make a face when you said that? 'Stand-up?'"

"Look, Hélène, maybe it makes you laugh, because you recognize our parents, but I really doubt it will make other people laugh . . ."

"Well, so much the better."

"Why?"

"Why? Because apparently you don't really want to make people laugh, that's all."

"The madeleines are almost ready, don't you want some?"

"I have to get going, Arthur's waiting for me."

"Is it new, this Sunday evening ritual?"

"Going to a restaurant? Yes, Arthur thought we weren't seeing enough of each other so . . . I suggested it."

"And the rest of the week, you're on your own?"

"Yes. Well, you'll go on writing, won't you? Promise?"

"But you're sure it's not too—"

"No."

"You don't know what I was going to say."

"Write, Sabine, and don't question it."

"Ah . . ."

Just as she was leaving, Hélène hesitated to add that she hadn't known about Vincent's bisexuality, or homosexuality, and that it had given her a bit of a shock to find out, but also that she felt close to him, even closer now. She also hesitated to tell her that the girl Sabine had portrayed, this "Héloïse," was nothing like her, Hélène. But she hadn't needed to read those lines to know that no one can say precisely, with simple words, who you are. When have we truly opened our hearts? When have we dared express our torment and distress and our darkest thoughts, our moments of wonder, our solitude? These successive layers of protection had woven a long cloak over time, and by keeping us safe and warm, it turned each of us into someone others hardly knew.

It happened just when they were least expecting it. For some time already, the upcoming election had been a primary source of anxiety to them and a constant topic of discussion. Glad that they finally agreed about something, Bruno and Agnès could talk about it forever, and their shared nightmare became a pause in their demoralized marital life. While others were not worried (the break between socialists and communists four years earlier had weakened the left), Agnès and Bruno had immediately sensed the danger. And now Mitterrand's victory seemed plausible, even if some people were still counting on the "the voting booth reflex," where common sense would prevail. Bruno and Agnès felt as if the carpet on which they'd always stood, upright and loyal, was being pulled from underneath them, and their fall seemed as inevitable as that of the French franc. Obviously, they did not belong to that wealthy sector of the population who were envisaging exile in Switzerland should the worst come to pass, but, when they pictured communist ministers in government, their impulse was to flee. They didn't know where. They had never traveled.

It was in this atmosphere full of both apprehension and understanding that the truth emerged. A simple, administrative task. The sort of chore one always puts off until later. Bruno's *carte d'identité* had expired, and this was not the time to have invalid identity documents. So, he went looking for the *livret de famille*,[21] the little official booklet the mayor of Aix had given him twenty-eight years earlier, and even though both he and Agnès believed it was the church that made their marriage official rather than the town hall, this document was proof of the trust placed in them, proof that they were adults, and their life would be recorded in it. It started with the names of their respective parents, and they had laughed at the string of Christian names all of them had, "Lucien Léopold Pierre Marius," "Marie Blandine Marthe Aimée," then their own names, suddenly joined by their family name, Malivieri, and, finally, the blank pages for the children they would have.

That day, Bruno took the booklet from the drawer in his desk, where it was kept next to the checkbook and the receipts for the rent and the ID photos he had just had made, and he went off to the town hall. He didn't know that he held in his hands all the misfortune of the world. There were three people before him in the waiting room at the office of vital records, and he sat patiently on a cheap plastic chair. After smoking a cigarette, he leafed absentmindedly through the municipal newsletter on the coffee table, and then he opened his family booklet, not really thinking about it, worried as he was about how long it might take to get his new ID card, even if his driver's license was up-to-date, and in order to vote it would be—He opened the booklet wider, bending back the spine . . . his hands were trembling . . . he couldn't turn the pages . . . he felt a fear and sorrow welling up inside him as violent as a beating . . . He could hear them calling his number . . . He turned the pages, again and again, maybe they'd got it wrong at the hospital, had inscribed it in the wrong place . . . He heard a

[21] See above, footnote 5 page 130.

number and couldn't figure out if it was still his . . . He couldn't find it . . . Where was it for God's sake where was it? Now he was moaning as he turned the pages, whimpering like a sick kid . . . It was blank . . . the page was blank . . . He was having trouble breathing . . . Someone was speaking to him, "Monsieur? Are you all right, Monsieur?" But where was the child? Where was the child? Good God, where was his daughter? He looked up, showed his family booklet to the woman leaning over him who was saying something about getting him a glass of water, or calling a doctor, and he was still waving the booklet where his little girl's name had not been entered, the girl who died at birth over a year ago, she wasn't there, he looked on every page and every which way, the booklet was soiled now, the pages were creased, the little girl wasn't there, the woman could take a look if she wanted, no he wasn't thirsty . . . he wanted to say . . . he couldn't speak anymore . . . he wanted to say . . . He wanted to say that this was good news, a wonderful piece of news, and the most horrible thing imaginable.

That evening when Agnès got home, she gave a start when she switched on the light and found him sitting on a stool in the entrance, like a man with a rifle in his hands on the lookout for a burglar. The burglar was Agnès. And so, she looked at that man she had loved so deeply. He was pale, and for the first time almost ugly, disfigured by anguish. She saw her life go slowly past her and disappear, she could almost feel the faint draft left by its passage, it was precise, fatal, it left no going back.

"You said, 'It has a soul, the embryo has a soul,'" said Agnès. "You said, 'It's possible to recover from a birth, but not an abortion,' you said it was your baby, they weren't sure about anything, and you'd love it no matter what, even if there was a—a problem, and you already loved it . . ."

"It was true."

"Yes, it was true. But I knew there was something wrong. And I was right."

"You were wrong. About everything."

"You . . . when I told you that I was pregnant, you were, you were—"

"I was happy, like you. We had both wanted it."

"Yes. And when I told you I was pregnant, you put your hand on my belly for a long time, a very long time, do you remember? You didn't speak, you were happy and confident, and it was like before. With the little boy."

"It was a blessing."

"No. It was the opposite."

"Are you crazy!"

"That baby, when I saw it—because I saw it—that baby hadn't lied. It was just what I had feared for nine months. I looked at it and . . . oh, my God, I couldn't. No, I couldn't. I don't know why, but it was . . . impossible. Believe me."

"Impossible? But what can be more impossible than giving up your own child?"

"Keeping it."

She was this woman he would never love again. This woman he had never known. Whom he could never understand again, or trust, or look at. She had stolen his daughter. The flesh of his flesh. That tender, living child, who carried his genes just as much as the others did, his genealogy, his plans, a Malivieri who'd been left on the roadside, on the scrap heap, rejected like a bastard. In a low voice, almost coarse with disgust, he said, "Where is she?"

Her laugh was caught in a sob. What a question! How should she know? In someone's arms, surely. Someone the infant called Papa, or Maman, and who, maybe someday, would break her heart when they explained to her that there were two hidden people in her story, two shirkers.

"She . . . promise me that . . . please . . . tell me—"

"She was baptized."

He took his head in his hands and wept for so long that she thought he was going to die from it, and perhaps in the end that would be for the best, his life was stopping at the same time as hers, that was all. Could they leave it at that? Not live out the rest of their lives? Yes, the best thing would be for it all to end there at that very second. To make that happen, she would have to deal the fatal blow:

"Mariette knows. She's always known. She came to see me at the maternity ward."

She shocked him into silence, and he stopped weeping. He raised his stunned face to her, his mouth agape, eyes wide as he stared at this monster of a woman who was his wife. He was as tired as a boxer who has been pummeled to death, he felt himself drifting into a world of gray light without any horizons, a box. He stood up. He walked slowly into his room, arms dangling, like a man sleepwalking. Agnès heard a chair creak, some noise, some things being moved around. She decided to go and have a look, to remember. And that is what she did, from the threshold of their conjugal bedroom. He had taken a suitcase from the top of the wardrobe. So, he was leaving her. He was right. She was relieved. She thought he was ugly and brave, and she hoped he would leave without asking any more questions, without a reproach or another word of any kind, she hoped he felt nothing for her anymore, neither hatred, nor disgust, nor even a little pity. She wanted him to be as old and empty and contemptible as she was.

It was an unstable time. Nothing will change, asserted most of the adults from the height of their experience, their knowledge of life. Everything can change, declared most of the young. The voting age had been lowered to eighteen, so there were a lot of them, and they no longer had time to turn reasonable before voting. And, bit by bit, they were scaring everyone else. A right-wing government had been in power for twenty-three years, and so what? Would the world collapse from one day to the next? Would France turn red with blood in the space of an evening? The posters of presidential candidate Mitterrand might well show a placid face standing outside a church, illustrating his "Quiet Strength," there would always be some who saw a knife clenched in his teeth. Abolition of the death penalty, free contraception, wealth tax, thirty-five-hour work week, equal salaries for men and women, increase in the minimum wage, old age benefits, family allowances, a fifth week of paid leave: it was all bound to end in moral and financial bankruptcy, according to some. It's only fair, said others. It led to confrontations between determined voters failing mutually to persuade, and acrimonious rifts in the sincerest friendships, never to be mended.

For the Malivieri family, the times had already changed in La Petite Chartreuse, solitude had comfortably settled in, as if reclaiming its original place. All the rest, the family years, had been nothing but an interlude, as fleeting as a handful of seconds. Now that Bruno had gone to live with friends, Agnès had the three-room-plus-kitchen apartment to herself, a perfect place for a family of five, or six, or seven . . . Good Lord, how many of them had there been, how many should there have been? When Mariette came home in the evening, she wolfed her dinner down in a few minutes, her eyes on her plate; it was obvious she had a melody going through her head and it seemed to infringe on the law of the household, and she couldn't seem to wipe the smile off her face . . . Did she think her mother was so naïve? That she couldn't tell when a girl was in love? Agnès looked at her and wondered what would become of her, that mouse she had held close above the sink for nights on end. When the steam fogged up the mirror, she had loved that impression of disappearing with her ghostly child in her arms. She'd felt legitimate back then, almost light-hearted, despite her concern. Now she would have to take Mariette to the gynecologist's, get her on the pill, but she doubted her daughter needed her for anything. She belonged to a rescued generation for whom making love was not reduced to "being careful." Her daughter was born free.

"If you were old enough to vote, Mariette, who would you vote for?"

She'd asked her one morning, passing her in the narrow corridor. Mariette had paused, then said, "I'm going to drink my hot chocolate out on the balcony, are you coming?" Agnès thought it was strange, they never had breakfast on the balcony, they mostly stood out there, one behind the other, when posing for a photo on a day of communion or a birthday or when the grandparents were visiting.

Mariette was holding her bowl in both hands, sitting on a stool, squinting in the promising sunshine of the first of May.

"I wouldn't vote in the second round. Not for Giscard or Mitterrand, oh no . . ."

Agnès refrained from telling her that she was careless and irresponsible, let her go try and live in a dictatorship, let her go to the Soviet Union or Czechoslovakia.

"And if voting were compulsory, in the first round I would have voted for Arlette Laguiller,[22] because she's right when she says all the politicians are lying when they talk about women, they feel nothing but disdain, but, without women and their salaried work and the work they do for free, society would collapse. You, for example, you could manage the state budget much better than they do."

"Me?"

"Yes, you'd know not to invest money in weapons but in life—in hospitals, child care centers, schools."

"Nurseries for children waiting to be adopted."

Mariette wasn't afraid of pauses without words; often they were justified. This pause was like a thread snapping sharply. She looked at her mother, her blue nightgown, slightly transparent against the light, her long legs, her sex, her belly. Her face, aghast. Mariette said, "Yes, Maman, nurseries."

Agnès's eyelashes were fluttering rapidly, Mariette could see her struggling, like a bird you hold in your hands that doesn't know whether it is being protected or trapped. Good. Evil. But maybe there was something between the two? Maybe we had the right to be monsters sometimes and exemplary at other times. Maybe we even had the right to hate people now and again, while still loving them. Maybe it was possible to accept such contradictions. Agnès sat on the floor in a tiny spot of sunlight and said very quietly, "If I were president, or minister, I would do something for abandoned children. A little letter from their maman, a few words to say . . . I don't know . . . Yes, I've got it! To say that we don't know. But that we suspect it's better not to live together. And maybe it's the child we have to ask for forgiveness from, not God."

Mariette stood up, she was on her way to see Joël, she was

[22] Far-left Trotskyist candidate.

late. Before leaving the balcony, she ran her hand over her mother's hair; Agnès let her face fall against her arms clasped around her knees. Mariette hoped she would relax a little. And then go out. Make the most of this day off, one of the last ones before the second round.

It's a countdown, like a rocket launch. A few seconds counted by millions of men and women, their hearts have stopped, they are holding their hands to their lips, preparing for the shock, there in front of the television. Five. Four. Three. Two. One. A bright, garish drawing slowly appears on the screen. The top of a man's head. Thinning hair. Then his forehead, his eyes, the eyes of François Mitterrand, and then the cries and tears of an entire country. Happiness and terror from deep in their guts, from their truest selves.

Eight o'clock in the evening on Sunday, May 10, 1981. Agnès is alone in front of the television. The building is shaking. The building is screaming. Like when the Olympique de Marseille scores a goal. No need to look at the screen to know. She reaches for the telephone, she's going to call Bruno, what will become of their daughters, what will become of them? But she hangs up before dialing the number, she goes outside, and already everything has changed, people are outside, like after a bombing raid, the stunned faces of people emerging from cellars, they need to be together to believe it has really happened. Young people are dancing in the parking lot, the music on full volume, beers in their hands, splattering their T-shirts, their arms, and their faces, girls and boys kissing on the lips. Agnès is having trouble breathing, she walks through them and they don't see her, she's used to this. For a while now, no one has noticed her. It's as hot as in the middle of the day, and very light out, there are firecrackers, this is the sign of things to come now, a noisy, messy, immodest country. Agnès has almost reached the end of the housing complex and she turns around. Will they set cars on fire, the way they do in Marseille, in the neighborhoods to the north? She thinks about Laurence. She must be happy this evening. She's never afraid of anything. There are a lot of adults outside the buildings now, what are they hoping for? She thinks about her boss, the one from Paris, who makes life miserable for the rest of them, comfortably ensconced at his desk. She thinks about the pitiful retirement pay she'll be entitled to. She thinks about the price of books and notebooks, of compasses and calculators. She thinks about the price of meat, gas, vacation. She thinks about her family allowance which is always so measly that she has to supplement it with money from the Tavels. She thinks about Tavel. How astonished he must be this evening. Only yesterday, Michelle didn't believe it would happen, she'd called her, the stock market was still going up, there was nothing to be afraid of, "The markets are confident." And Agnès had laughed to herself, imagining the greengrocers in Aix, shouting "confident," like Parisian bankers. Now she's not laughing anymore, she pictures the tanks. Camps. Churches closed. No more subsidies for the Sainte-Catherine School. She is walking quickly, she feels as if she is late for something, and the sensation goes through her like a blast of cold water, she *is feeling* something and despite the pain of it, it's good. It's good to be in a hurry and to have something she must do.

She goes through her town and doesn't recognize it. People bathing in the fountains. There are traffic jams everywhere and horns blowing non-stop. She's always been afraid of crowds. She was born three years before the war. She remembers the turmoil, the incoherence and hunger. Tonight, Aix is jubilant. But all crowds are alike, they join in the same forward rush and their power has no limits, no conscience. Agnès, however, makes the most of the shared emotion, this turmoil born of joy, to allow herself her own portion of folly.

"I promise to be true to you in good times and in bad, in sickness and in health. I will love you and honor you all the days of my life." Their marriage vows, which they exchanged and have always remembered. And now she likes the fact that it is hard to reach her husband. A way of the cross. She is overcoming her fear of crowds and is going toward him as if moving back in time, and she remembers what she was like as his fiancée. It was the first time anyone had ever been tender with her, and the way people used to look at them! The joy and hopefulness they shared, so strong. Then they got married, and then they were accused of having given the dead baby only an emergency baptism. Being a parent, she thinks, walking through the transfigured town, means constantly being accused of something. A man in the street hands her a rose. This evening, she is visible. This evening, she is going to keep her promise. She will love her husband all her life. What else does she have to give?

She is outside his door. He's not alone and she knows it. But there could be a hundred people around him and still he would be alone, since he is waiting for her. She rings the bell. Tonight, everything is allowed. It's like carnival, you can dare to do anything. She rings again. She realizes she is still holding the rose she was given. What will he think? She can hear a lot of noise inside the apartment. Neighbors rushing down the stairs. She rings again. He'll hear it eventually. She has all the time in the world. She has come for him.

Hélène has hope, she tells herself that maybe things will improve, maybe they'll start to take them seriously, the people who for decades have been crying in the wilderness. No, that's not right. Not decades. The physicist John Tyndall and the chemist Svante Arrhenius had warned them: prolonged combustion of fossil fuels would cause the Earth to overheat dangerously. That was in the nineteenth century. Will people finally start acting like adults? Will this man, François Mitterrand, do what he promised, implement his environmental charter, which is to guarantee the protection of natural sites, green spaces, shorelines, forests, bodies of water? He doesn't mention animals, no one mentions animals, not even Brice Lalonde, the ecological candidate, not a word, it's as if animals didn't exist, or that they've simply been put here for us, to be entirely at our disposal. As for Mitterrand, they say he likes birds and that he eats them, ortolans above all, and she can picture him with his big white napkin on his head, his little eyes blinking with pleasure, will he invite David to join him on his presidential hunting parties? She pictures David and Michelle by their television this evening. She remembers the Lip strike, *I'll be back in Paris tomorrow*, and the telephone call to Franz Tavel in Geneva. She wishes she could see David, the more she knows it's impossible, the greater her urge, she cannot imagine spending this gloomy evening with him, his scorn for everyone who voted on the left, as if they were spitting on his years of toil, his ambition, the jobs he created. Neuilly must be very quiet this evening, they'll be sharing the indignation of civilians facing the invader, the thieves, the bandits. Tomorrow, suitcases will be filled with other things besides linen suits and silk gowns. People will depart, their inheritance held in their hands. She wants to see David. She'd taken him by surprise the other night, opening the door to his study without knocking first, she'd come unannounced, a bad idea. He'd given a start, and the face he showed her was not the face she knew. It wore the tense, yellow mask of pain. And next to him, a spilled bottle of medication. She went away at once, gasping for breath, not saying anything, not going to him. She's always known it: everything can come to an end from one day to the next. She's known it ever since David saved her from drowning, and, deep inside, she has preserved these little fragments of death and fear. But what about him, who will save him?

Arthur screamed with joy when he saw the top of Mitterrand's head on the screen. He recognized it before anyone, he'd studied it, he said, impervious to ridicule. Hélène didn't know he had such leftist sympathies. She rarely spoke about politics with him, she rarely spoke about politics in general. The diamonds Bokassa gave Giscard; the Soviet invasion of Afghanistan, which Marchais supported; Mitterrand in Vichy; ambition and pride, secret deals, canny betrayals, and that thirst for power . . . PSU, LO, MRG, UDF, PS, PCF, RPR, LCR, FN, MEP, all these abbreviations for political parties, what did they all mean? She thinks about the scientist Théodore Monod, an anarchist and a Christian, walking through the desert, demonstrating in Paris for every life form. His voice is too human, they don't listen to him. This evening she and Arthur are drinking one of the bottles of champagne meant for Éléonore. They raise a toast and kiss and then Arthur says, "I worry about all these bottles in your fridge. You're not turning into an alcoholic, are you?"

"Of course not."

"But you know what an alcoholic really is? It's not, like people think, the neighborhood wino. An alcoholic is someone who's become dependent, who can't do without."

"I'm not dependent."

"Two little glasses every evening coming home from work, *that's* alcoholism."

"Oh look! It's Annie Girardot!"

"What?"

"Rue de Solférino, that's Annie Girardot! The Gabrielle

Russier affair! You wouldn't understand. I'm going to call Sabine."

Annie Girardot, by appearing on screen at the headquarters of the Socialist Party, has just saved her. Hélène had forgotten to call Sabine, who must be so happy tonight. All of a sudden, she notices Arthur's expression. The conciliatory good pupil has been acting rather fussy of late. But just as she is going over to the telephone, that fussiness seems to have acquired something new as well, a trace of suspicion. A nasty little flame, something pinched and sharp. Sabine's line is busy. She hopes her sister is talking to her leftist friends, that she hasn't just left the phone off the hook, not to be disturbed; she hopes the noise from the teeming streets is not scaring her too much.

"We have to go to Sabine's place, I'm worried."

He smiles at her, says it's a good idea, and she feels guilty about her hidden relationship with Éléonore. Every day she tells herself she will confess to him, and every day she grants herself a reprieve.

In the street, he's fidgeting like a teenager, talking with strangers, you'd think he was about to offer the entire neighborhood a round, his voice alone is enough to tilt the scales to the left, as if they owed this victory to him, he's as happy as a champion. Four years ago, these mannerisms of his, the naïve boy so easy to please, were touching. Now Hélène finds something a bit off-putting about them; she has never liked one-night winners. She's in a hurry to get to Sabine's place, but Arthur is taking his time, now he's on the median strip on the Boulevard de Clichy, singing, the air stinks of merguez, Arthur's got his arms around the shoulders of young men braying like he is, dancing an endless round dance. Hélène waves to him and screams, "Come and get me at Sabine's!" He doesn't hear her. He isn't looking at her. She's furious and walks off. She makes her way, head down, butting through the crowd like a little ram, trampling roses underfoot, there's a smell of grilled meat and of the powder from firecrackers, their crackling sound lost amid the commotion of car horns, why have people taken their cars? They are leaning out the windows flashing the victory sign, others are climbing onto the hoods, there are children on their father's shoulders, teenagers hanging from streetlamps and even restaurant canopies, as if everyone wanted to gaze out at the throngs of people. Suddenly a hand grabs her arm so hard she cries out as she spins around.

"Couldn't you have waited?"

Arthur is holding her as if he is about to shake her or knock her over. She looks at him as disdainfully as she can, and he apologizes, tells her that it's terrifying to lose someone in a crowd. She takes his hand and once again he becomes the docile obedient child. He was scared. He gave the cohort of strangers everything he had in the way of energy and togetherness, and now he's had enough. They head down the rue Blanche, and Hélène can still feel a slight pain in her arm.

There's a crowd at Sabine's place, a dozen people or more, old friends from the Cochet classes, movie people, neighbors, and Paul. Hélène is surprised, but what did she expect? That just because her sister was the victim of an attack seven months ago, she had no more friends? That she lived alone with the cat and never went out? She is loved. The thought surprises her. She is loved by people I don't even know. And it's like at a funeral, when people go up to the microphone one after the other to speak about the dead person, and you thought you knew all about their life and you find out you knew only a tiny portion. Sabine introduces her sister with pride, the way she used to at the Lycée Cézanne seven years ago, and Hélène realizes that, until now, no one, apart from Paul, had even known she existed.

*

Her mother doesn't answer. Mariette has called her father and sisters, too. No one answered. Where are they all? Joël's apartment seems to be suspended in the sky, the party echoes against all the walls of the town, and they're like people who don't celebrate New Year's then suddenly, when they hear the bells tolling midnight, they feel a bit left out. They've been overtaken by an elation they don't share. Something has changed, so abruptly. The left is in power, like back in the days of Léon Blum, in the history books; is tonight a night for the history books? They lean out the window and look down at the huge spontaneous dance—strangers hugging and shouting, flags waving in the falling darkness, while the streetlights create squares and streets and arcades full of expectancy, as if a play were about to begin. But nothing more can happen.

Now they're in the street, hand in hand not to lose one another, they are walking slowly, people shove them, hurry past them, Joël puts his arm around Mariette's shoulders and holds her close. They're in the middle of the crowd, no one can see them, they can see everyone. Mitterand obtained not even fifty-two percent of the votes, but you'd think everyone had voted for him. Where is everyone else? Where are Giscard's supporters hiding?

They walk down the rue Matheron, the rue Montigny, and, this evening, the streets seem longer, and it takes them so much time to get where they're going. Once they are on the Place des Prêcheurs, Mariette asks Joël to lift her up on his shoulders, she wants to see everything from up in the sky. The marketplace, the square outside the collège, the church, and the courthouse. The Place de Verdun is small and is a world unto itself. If someday someone asks her where she's from, she won't say the name of her town, she'll say, I come from the

Place. And she can hear it, like before, the anthem of the struggle, they're singing the *Internationale*, fists raised, heads in the stars. She is enveloped by the song as it carries from one country to the next, one century to the next, the voice and fervor of people who have nothing left to lose. She places her lips on Joël's hair, it smells of the cool night, she puts her hands on his face, those scars he doesn't like, and caresses them as if she were blind, and it hurts, this desire she feels for him, he's afraid of breaking her, she knows that, tonight she'll take the first step, she's made up her mind, it's the perfect evening for it, and she'll coax him into seeing nothing else in her besides herself. She is swaying a little on his shoulders, too many people are bumping into them, and just when she is about to ask to go back to his place, to turn around, she sees them. So different from the others, how could you not see them. They project the clear image of who they will become later on, a tired man and a tired woman, marked with their undying, inevitable love. Her father is on the other side of the street, but he sees her, his daughter perched on top of a man, caught in the light of the streets. Agnès sees Mariette, too, and she sees the man.

Has everyone been so starved for hugs and kisses? To Hélène it seems it will never end, at the drop of a hat, they squeal and rush over and throw their arms around each other. She is drinking now (like an alcoholic, who knows?). She is drinking to find the courage to tell them all how much she envies them. Mitterrand is appearing in public for the first time since his victory, and whenever he speaks they cry out in unison, "This victory is due to the strength of our youth," and they are the youth, "The strength of creativity and the strength of renewal," that's who they are, "It is up to history now to judge every one of our acts," they are literally transported by these last words, they are chanting *Mi-tter-rand-Mi-tter-rand-*

Mi-tter-rand, as if this were the new rhythm of their life. Hélène recalls, at La Petite Chartreuse, how Sabine told her it was time for her to choose sides, Tavel or Malivieri. She hadn't known how to reply to something that hurt so much, she was fifteen years old, so she simply walked out of the apartment. Now she knows the answer, and she's going to give it. To Sabine and the others. But, at the moment, her sister is busy. She is talking with Charlène, who says the apartment is much nicer than when she lived there herself, Sabine has done such a good job fixing it up, she, Charlène, was just passing through, already working so much. And she smiles with a knowing air, thrusts her chin in the direction of her lover, Adam, a "completely crazy" young filmmaker. After moving in with Henri Montmartin, she left him virtually the day before their wedding, "I got along really well with his ex-wife, but his kids! Help! And every night he fell asleep reading a screenplay, his half-moon glasses sliding down his nose . . . Oh the boredom! The boredom!" Sabine relishes the news in silence, this is juicy, she thinks, I'll use it all, write it all down, I won't leave out a word. This girl who constantly positions herself with this man or the next one is no better than a tart. She thinks she's liberated, but she's dependent, she needs constant male protection. Charlène reads what she thinks is envious admiration in Sabine's smile, and it fills her with sensual delight. She murmurs, "I'm glad Adam got to meet you, you may not realize but he's watching you, he watches everything, all the time, he has a movie camera in his head. Right, now that he's met you, we'll be on our way, okay? There's a little party over at Gérard Depardieu's place, I don't know if he'll be there but we absolutely have to be there. I'll call you tomorrow and let you know whether you made an impression on my sweetheart, don't worry, in *Women of Words*, beyond how ridiculous your scene was, he could immediately tell that you have something that might come in handy . . . so to speak!"

And she bursts out laughing, she's had too much to drink, or else she is too happy, too much in love, something is making her head spin and she's overflowing with emotion. Hélène is waiting for this girl to leave to make her announcement, to say that she refuses, she totally refuses to take sides, to justify her life. They have asked her to choose between two families, they have asked her to choose between the suffering of human beings and the suffering of animals, they have asked her to choose between loving men and loving women. She has a big heart. She has room for everything. How can she make herself heard in this tipsy little gathering? Should she stand on a chair? On a table? Sabine, holding the phone receiver, waves to her and shouts, "Hélène! Telephone!" She knows who it is. The only person who knows her sister's number. The only person whose thoughts she can read. She doesn't need to stand on furniture for everyone to understand. She looks at Arthur, walks past him, banging into his shoulder, "Oh sorry I have to get the phone." She takes the receiver, smiles the way only people in love smile, a smile you can't suppress, bold and shy, full of innuendo. She turns away, runs her hand over her scalp again and again, an impatient, electric gesture, because now she'd like to rush out, to go to her where she's waiting, on the Place de la Bastille, by the hairdresser's at the old Vincennes line station! Léo has to shout to make herself heard, she says the atmosphere there is incredible and Hélène asks, "So you're not mad at me anymore?" "What?" shouts Éléonore. Laughing with emotion, Hélène shouts louder, "I said, you're not mad at me for not going with you to the march for homosexuals?" Éléonore shouts, "With Mitterrand it's all going to change for us, don't you see? Get over here! Get over here right now!"

Sabine watches it unfold in slow-motion, the trajectory of the gesture, the precision of it, but she cannot move. She is on the rue Copernic, frozen in the disaster. Arthur springs over to Hélène, tears the receiver from her hands so abruptly that she falters, tries to hold onto him, but when he leaps to one side, Hélène's face hits the forward thrust of his arm. She falls to the floor without a cry.

Joël puts his hands under Mariette's shoulders, lifts her up, then forward, and deposits her on the ground at her parents' feet, as if he were bowing down before them. Were it not for the boy's blushing face, his embarrassment, Agnès and Bruno might have thought he was merely their daughter's friend, but everything about him indicates . . . Bruno cannot even think of the word. He looks at Mariette and tries to associate her with his child, he struggles with his words and the pain of it, and as Mariette is looking straight at him, with a gaze he's never seen, of anger and emancipation, yes, because of that emancipation, he slaps her, and instantly regrets it, and instantly it is too late. This guy might be her . . . lover . . . fourteen years old, for God's sake, a baby, fourteen years . . . this guy might be her lover, and he looks completely inadequate! He stands there, arms dangling at his side, after the slap, it's incredible, the coward, the pervert, the bastard. The *Internationale* vibrates against the walls of the courthouse, the stairs, the columns, the immense sky. Mariette is screaming at her father, something he can't hear, Agnès is holding her close, leading her away from the crowd, and soon all four of them are in the passage Agard, which echoes like a well and stinks of piss and crushed flowers. This is not a place for a discussion. It's not here that they can explain things. Bruno demands to see Joël's ID card, Agnès puts her hand on his arm, but Bruno wants to protect his daughter, to save her from the predator, and no one can take that courage from him. Mariette, like the others, has duped him, she has always lied to him, dispossessed him of his rights as a father, but tonight he is reclaiming his place. Joël hands him his ID card, Bruno memorizes the last name first name address—and date of birth, which makes him want to puke and lash out some more, what are they doing to him, what will he become, this loving father, this caring, nurturing father, and he wonders, Do all children turn us into monsters? Joël puts his ID card back in his jacket and looks at Mariette, he would like to tell her that it will all work out, they've done nothing wrong, can she read that in his gaze, his trust? She turns away to follow her parents.

The apartment is calm again. The cat sits and watches them solemnly with his tranquil eyes. Then he slowly moves away, avoiding the bottles on the floor without a glance, and the cigarette butts and crushed potato chips; with a light bound he jumps up on the sofa where Hélène is lying, and he spreads out on top of her, calm and disdainful, immediately purring. Hélène strokes him, his mossy, thick softness, secret vibrations and constant warmth. Sabine is sitting by her side with a book in her hand, and she says, "I think she goes too far, but hey, I thought about you while I was reading it. And the first woman to be elected to the Académie Française, if you please! Paul! Close the windows, I can't stand this racket anymore, I'm going to read my sister a story."

And with a laugh she adds, "Hélène has always liked reading about horrible stuff."

She opens *The Abyss* at a page where the corner has been turned down.

"Meat, blood, entrails, everything that has throbbed and lived, was repulsive to him at that time in his life, because beasts die in pain, as do men, and he did not like digesting moments of dying."

"I've already heard this," says Hélène. "But you read it well."

"Oh, damn! I've got nothing left to teach you, then!"

"Yourcenar thinks that slaughterhouses ought to be filmed and shown on television so that people will understand. She also thinks that since we've allowed the worst possible things to happen, since we allowed humans to be deported in cattle cars, it was because we'd already grown used to it. With animals. If men killed fewer animals, they wouldn't go killing each other so much, violence leads to—"

"Stop! Stop! I just wanted to show you that writers can be just as hard-hitting as your famous scientists. And now let's do something else, you get up and let's go out."

"But where do you want to go?"

"To find your friend, at the Bastille."

"But it's too late now, I'll never find her."

"Hélène's right," says Paul, "you can see it on television, there are thousands of people at the Bastille. And anyway, it's started raining."

They look at him, dismayed. He's come up with this argument about the rain because he knows that Sabine will be afraid of the crowd, the noise, and the dark. And naturally they laugh. He pretends to laugh, too. He says he's going to go home now, and he kisses Sabine, who is quivering with a joyfulness he breathes in like perfume. He kisses Hélène, careful to avoid the bruise on her cheek. Outside, the crowd coming down the rue Blanche restores him to his solitude. It's a good companion, the ally of his freedom. He's not in the mood to go home. He's in the mood for the night, the rain, the city aroused by hope. He takes a few tango steps, joins his imaginary partner, and hums quietly for both of them.

They walk home slowly, fearful that their "little girl" will have an asthma attack, they don't know where the twenty-four-hour pharmacy is and they feel this threat for which they are to blame, once again. Bruno would like to ask her to forgive him for the slap, he has never struck his children, his parents think it is weak of him not to, womanish. From time to time, he looks at Mariette, she is livid, he can see her face in the headlights, he'd never imagined going home like this one day, with defeat and so little pity. He doesn't know, with the left in power, what will become of his private school. It all seems so fragile, what he has constructed, what he has believed in. What can he hope for now? He walks slowly, not to tire Mariette, in spite of his haste to get home so she'll have her Ventolin within reach; the miracle of chemistry. They have reached the Avenue De-Lattre-de-Tassigny, the Casino supermarket, the X-ray center, everything is closed, as if forever. The sound of police sirens reassures him. They are not completely alone. Agnès walks without looking at him, without touching him, but the familiar waves of those who have loved flow between them, although they do not know whether that love is their curse.

In the apartment, the television is still on; Mitterrand, cheered by the crowd, is together with his wife on the terrace of a restaurant. She is at his side, slightly behind him, in the shadow. Bruno switches off the television. He hears the door to Mariette's bedroom slam angrily. He locks the front door and puts the key in his pocket. You never know. "We'll talk to her tomorrow," says Agnès, "she needs to be alone, come to bed." Banal words, words from yesterday, when no doubt they had been in pain, but they'd been together, with neither wariness nor hostility.

It's as if nothing had happened. Nothing has ever happened. Aix is asleep and maybe it was all in their imagination, one of those collective hallucinations that purge people who are used to too much servitude. Mariette is out on the balcony, *Anne, ma soeur Anne, ne vois-tu rien venir?*[23] There is no sister,

[23] Often-quoted line from Charles Perrault's *La Barbe Bleue*, (1697) where Bluebeard's young wife implores, "Anne, sister Anne, do you see anyone coming?"

no horizon. She is alone with the night. "For me the basic rhythm is the rhythm of the heart," her piano teacher said to her at her first lesson. Her heart is a functioning muscle, nothing more. She listens to the undefined silence. Last night she and Joël played a game, describing the silence of each great composer, she imitated a much-loved radio quiz show host and proclaimed, "Dear friends, good morning!" then asked Joël what was the function of silence in Schubert. He didn't hesitate, "Dramatic. To mark an unexpected turn of events!" "And silence in Chopin?" "A very full silence, I would say . . . accompanied, yes, a transitional silence." Going for broke, she asked about the silence she found hardest to fathom: Schumann's. Joël thought for a moment, he was playing in earnest, she was counting on him, "I wouldn't call it silence, in Schumann's case. I'd call it breathing." Now she places her hand in front of her mouth, the way people do with the dead: is she still breathing? She can't hear the night anymore; space is simply a hole. She takes the iron railing in both hands, she wants to get out of here, this imposed life that doesn't suit her. She leans forward a little, five floors, yards of impenetrability, to be so close to the treetops, and then lie underneath them. There's an animal out on the neighbors' balcony, something moving in the dark, Mariette gives a start. There's a rustling of cloth, breathless grunts . . . A figure is standing. It's an old woman, probably the grandmother. Maybe she sleeps out there, it's too hot inside. Her face is ugly, reflected in moonlight that catches her pockmarked skin, exaggeratedly aged. She is staring at Mariette with owlish eyes, unsmiling, immobile and watchful. Mariette looks away, but the grandmother's eyes won't leave her, two motionless lightning bugs. Mind your own business, thinks Mariette. I can never get any peace. She suspects the old lady doesn't smell too good, a mixture of stale tobacco and citronella. Again, she grips the railing, sways forward and back, the old woman is watching her without budging, Mariette is swaying faster and faster, like a child on a swing. Is God silence? And then she releases her hold on everything, and goes back inside. The railing vibrates slightly, like a tuning fork.

She sits down in the deserted living room. She doesn't know what life has in store for her, now that her father has found her out. There is always a stain when others set their gaze on what is dearest to you, and how can it be erased? She listens to the apartment—the creaky wicker armchair, the boiler, the fridge, the wood of the buffet, the life of objects without us. She can just make out the mute ugliness of the television with its enormous hunched back. The long table in the living room where they used to say grace, until Sabine and Hélène made fun of it, and they stopped. She liked giving thanks for the bread. She liked seeing her sisters winking, amused, at each other, and their father's solemn diligence, their mother's sigh, because she knew it would only take them a few minutes to gobble down what had taken her hours to prepare. She remembers her father writing on the wall with the peeling wallpaper, "People lived here," and then covering the words over with glue and the new wallpaper he always applied so badly that he had to go around puncturing the bubbles with a needle. Her fingers are playing on her thighs as if it were a keyboard, she can hear the melody, it always frightens her when it comes, the fear she has of failing, of not being good enough, she listens and repeats it in an echo, she hums, tries to commit it to memory, and the ringing of the telephone makes her jump. She answers quickly, the phone at nighttime means danger, but maybe it's Joël. She says very quietly, like an entreaty, "Hello?"

Something screaming on the other end of the line, she can hear drums, chanting, she walks farther away with the phone and sits on the floor with her back against the wall.

"Hello?"

Hélène shouts, "Hey, Mouse! How are you? What's it like in Aix? Everyone's going crazy here!"

It's like a voice from another world, her sisters caught in Paris's tentacular embrace.

"Did I wake you up?"

Hélène didn't find Éléonore on the Place de la Bastille, but she knows she's not far away, in this crowd in the rain, and that is enough. Sabine wanted to come. Sabine has left the house for her, so that she could meet her friend. They took the metro, they went through tunnels, through the multitude, the night, the turmoil, and now Hélène does not take her eyes off her, from this phone booth she had to wait ages for. Sabine is dancing rock 'n roll with a tall boy who has to lean forward, a quick happy boy, and Hélène can hear Mariette's stifled voice speaking softly, the way she used to at night in their bedroom:

"There was an old woman out on the neighbors' balcony, so I came back in, she wanted me to come in, I think. A real cop."

It's never easy to understand what the Mouse is saying, Hélène thinks it's a good thing she's writing music, she'll get better and better at composing, and surely someday they'll understand her.

"Listen! Listen to them!"

She opens the door to the phone booth and the cries seem to rush in, "Mi-tter-rand! Sun-shine! Mi-tter-rand! Sun-shine!"

"I told you they were crazy! I hope the parents aren't too devastated! How are they taking it?"

"Badly. They take everything badly. That way they're happy."

"You have to come and see us, that's what Sabine and I were thinking, we have it all planned, when are you on vacation?"

Mariette can hear her heart in her throat, her guts, her ears, she is overwhelmed by the rhythm, flooded with blood, she's lost, and she wants to be, she wants to drift, to let herself be guided. To explode with life.

"Have you got your exams for the end of collège this year? Oh, I've run out of change, here's the number, call me at—"

Shit, thinks Hélène. She goes out of the phone booth. She feels like begging, Spare a coin please, so I can call my sister. Suddenly a spear of lightning rips through the darkness, lights up the square like a giant camera flash popping, and Hélène can see the whole colorful, teeming, exultant crowd. And then the thunder rumbles, a sovereign growl. The ground trembles. The rain comes down even harder, as if dumped all of a sudden, transforming the crowd into tiny blades of grass, besieged. Sabine stops dancing. The leaning boy rummages in his pocket, finds a pen, rummages some more, Sabine holds out her hand, he hesitates, throws his head back and seems even taller when he laughs. His face bent over Sabine's hand he writes, then walking backwards takes his leave, vanishing. Sabine comes over to Hélène, brandishing a closed fist.

"You got his number? Great! What's his name?"

"Shit, I forgot to ask!"

"That's fine. You have all night to make up a name for him. And a job. And a destiny."

"I don't always make things up."

"No. You just alter reality a little, you're the best embellisher I know."

The rain eases up, it's two o'clock in the morning, they are made of water and blood, of cold air and life. They walk home, with the *Internationale* and the *Marseillaise* stuck in their heads, they hum from time to time, then forget. The city is resting but not sleeping—the power of past rebellions, the blind courage of those who confronted death to rescue hope, have all been aroused tonight. Open wounds flow like the river, and the trace of them is everywhere, if you only know where to look.

"Can you tell, Hélène, even in the dark, even in the rain, it feels like fine weather. Everything is going to change, for everyone—women, the unemployed, the farmers . . . Bastian will get his land back!"

"Ah, yes, I'm sure of that . . ."

"I'd like to go and see where he lives, see their victory."

"I've been there."

"To the Larzac? And you didn't tell me?"

"Would you have wanted to camp out on the Causse to observe the vultures?"

"Absolutely not, I think vultures are repulsive!"

"Some people think they're repulsive. Others say they're holy."

Weariness suddenly catches up with them, as if a spell has been cast. If it weren't raining, they would lie down on a bench and sleep under the stars, to be woken by the first rays of the sun. They walk in silence, arm in arm. They don't know how long it will take to get home. How long they will sleep. And, above all, how they will feel when they wake up, how any of them will feel when they wake up, tomorrow.

Acknowledgments

Thanks to my editor Véronique Ovaldé.

Thanks to Ariane Ascaride, Dana Ciocarlie, Antoine Gessain, Marina Moroli Zingraff, Vesna Pacail, and Marion Vaqué-Marti.